# September Moon

## By the same author

*Brensham*

*The Fair Field*

*The Blue Field*

*Dance and Skylark*

# September Moon



*by*
*John Moore*

J. B. Lippincott Company
*Philadelphia* · 1958 · *New York*

Printed in the United States of America

Library of Congress Catalog Card Number 58-6902

*For Lucile, once again,*
*for the same good reasons*

# Author's Note

*I have used in this book real Herefordshire place-names; and my delight in these has led me to re-draw the map to suit my book. Since it is a work of fiction, its ordnance sheet is a work of fiction too, upon which Weston Beggard, Edvin Loach, Stretton Sugwas and Much Birch appear in positions quite unrelated to topographical fact.*

J. M.

# Table of Contents

# Part One

## *The Crescent over the Hill*

# 1

Only the sun was slug-a-bed. There was one of those late summer mists which make the mushrooms grow; so dawn came late and slowly over Malvern. But Sollarshill village was astir before the owls had gone to bed. The kennel huntsman on his way to cubbing, clopping down the street with his hounds that looked like ghost-hounds in the half-light, saw the lamps lit in bedroom windows, cracked his whip outside the Royal Victoria, and had a startling brief glimpse of old Mrs. Agnew, in a strange chemise, standing before a looking-glass as she fixed a black velvet band round her scraggy neck. Doors banged, figures to which the day had not yet given their proper shapes stumbled out, a sleepy man on a bicycle wobbled among the hounds. Then they suddenly rioted in pursuit of Mrs. Agnew's ginger cat, the first whip cantered after them, the man on the bicycle woke up and let out a holloa, Mrs. Agnew leaned out of her window yelling: "Save my poor Moggie!"—and if there had been until then one late sleeper in Sollarshill he slept no more.

The huntsman trotted on along the road that went between two small hills as round as haycocks. Through the mist that clung to them he could just make out, like patches of dark jungle, the hopyards hanging on the slopes of the hills. Here and there were wayside cottages, waking up one by one; they had a blear-eyed look as their lamplight gleamed fuzzy in the fog. Its wet whiteness furred the horses' ears with tiny drops. The huntsman came to the crossroads where a crooked signpost pointed to SOLLARSHILL, STOKE EDITH, WESTON BEGGARD AND THE HOPE. It was crooked because Tommy Tomkins, the owner of the Hope Farm, sometimes collided with it as he turned the corner on his way home from the pub. But there were lights in the farmhouse at the top of the hill; even the little drunkard was up early this morning. So was his daughter, the girl they all said was no better than she should be; she came suddenly over the stile by the crossroads and flitted across the road. She stood there to watch the hounds go by, and the huntsman wondered what she was doing so early. Going home? he thought ungallantly, as he took off his cap; but she climbed a gate and went into the river meadows, in the opposite direction from the Hope Farm. The huntsman called: "Cup, cup!" and turned into the main road. Here he encountered a policeman pushing a bicycle, who called out:

"Where are you meeting?"

"Tedstone Wager, to draw Fenton's Furze. He says he's got a leash of cubs there."

"Wish I could come," said the policeman, "but you know what it is with these pests of gipsies arriving."

Round the next corner came the first of the pests, in three yellow caravans with lurchers running beneath their wheels. The longdogs snarled and snapped as the inquisitive hounds sniffed round them. The huntsman stood up in his stirrups and flicked Blazer neatly on the nose; then because he hated lurchers he sent the lash curling between the spokes, and the lean, brindled beast went back on its haunches and bared its teeth so that it looked just like a caricature of a dog in a Rowlandson print. Meanwhile Blazer ran howling down the road and was nearly run over by an old saloon car which had MISSION TO HOP-PICKERS inscribed on it. The huntsman rated

Blazer in terms which might have suggested to the occupants of the car that a Mission to Hunt Servants was needed. He had just collected his hounds once more into a tidy little pack when a red bus swept round the bend. It was full of Welsh girls singing "*Sospan Fach.*" The first whip, holding out his crop, careened in front of it like a highwayman who cries: "Stand and Deliver," and the brakes came on with a squeal. The girls stopped singing at the sight of the red coat and blew kisses through the bus windows. The huntsman's leathery face crinkled as he doffed his cap three times very quickly, just as he would do at the meet when he said: "Mornin', me Lady, Mornin', me Lady, Mornin', me Lord." The bus edged by, and then came more caravans. "Gets more like Piccadilly Circus every day," said the huntsman.

And so it went, all along the road, although by Summer Time it was barely six o'clock: the gipsies were gathering, farmers were driving their tractors, labourers were going to work before their time, even old Dave Huggett who was nearly eighty trudged along backbent on his way to Sollarshill Manor Farm. For this was the day when everybody in all the little villages that lay among the haycock hills got up earlier than usual and set about their diverse preparations: it was September the first, the day when the hop-pickers arrived.

## 2

Tim Sollars, sipping his cocoa at the back door of the Manor Farm, watched his father stride away through the mist with a gun over his shoulder, looking huge as a hero of some old tale. He was going to look for a covey of partridges because it was his custom always to bag a brace before breakfast on September the first. He had never failed. They would be hung for a week in the cool cellar so that they would be ready for Mrs. Sollars's birthday on the seventh. Such customs had sanctity at Sollarshill Manor Farm. Life went by the calendar there, and John Sollars would no sooner omit the little ceremony of the partridges than his wife would forget to make the dripping cakes which went with the morning cocoa at hop-picking time.

For this was a custom too, instituted when Tim and Carol were children and continued now because it had become traditional. Tim's father and mother shared the view, which they'd never put into words, that if you broke with an established tradition, however trivial, you were sticking your neck out for some unspecified sort of trouble: it was like walking under a ladder. So every morning during September, when everybody went to work early and came back late for breakfast, Mrs. Sollars hotted up the dripping cakes, and they were there at the back door with the cocoa for anyone who came along between half past six and seven.

Tim as he stepped into his gumboots caught a ghostly glimpse of his mother now, as she went in her white coat towards the dairy. It was a world of wraiths. Doves like the spirits of doves fluttered round the buildings. Some grimalkin of a farm cat was silhouetted on a roof. Dave Huggett, who'd remembered the dripping cakes, came like a hobgoblin through the mist.

"Up with the lark," Tim said.

Dave answered alliteratively. His sentences often sounded like lines from *Piers Plowman*. He said:

"Bellyful of beer be a bloody good 'larum."

Tim handed him a dripping cake and a cup of cocoa.

"Were you drunk last night, Dave?"

"I had a *rage* of beer."

Dave always got drunk on the eve of hop-picking; but now he faced a whole month of abstinence, for he would be on continuous duty in the kiln. He would eat there and sleep there and never see the sun: a high priest of the hops, the kiln his temple and the drying-chamber its ultimate sanctuary. Now and then as a priest preparing incense he would arrange some lumps of sulphur on a tray. It had to be just the right quantity, it had to be offered up to the Hop-god at the precise moment. Ceremonially he would burn this sulphur and the fumes would go up the chimney with the hot air from the furnace, into the drying-chamber above. The purpose was to "cure" the hops and give them the colour and smell which the brewers favoured. Since Dave spent much of his time with his head inside the drying-chamber he became more or less cured himself by the end of the month: his eyes went red, his throat grew sore, and he achieved a remarkable thirst which he saved up lovingly and satisfied only when hop-picking was done. Then like a camel that has crossed the Sahara and scents the sweet well-water in the oasis ahead, he would hurry down to the Royal Victoria. He would drink, in four crowded hours between six and ten, some eighteen pints of beer. This quantity constituted what he called a *rage;* and as it seethed and rioted within him he would stagger home and fall into bed. He would sleep for the better part of three days; and then he would return to his normal life and his work of hedge-laying on Sollarshill Manor Farm.

"I wants some withy poles," said Dave, "to knock together some frigging frames for the picking-bins"; and he stumped away. Tim went through the white-shrouded farmyard over which the oast-houses loomed dimly, dove-grey in this light although they were built of old red brick that had baked to a kind of pinkish orange. Monkishly cowled, with their vanes motionless, they brooded like monks in meditation. The mist clung close about the buildings, distorting, magnifying, making the familiar strange. Tim going about his jobs was treated now and then to a poet's-eye view. The combine they'd been using yesterday loomed up like some fearful chariot of a future war; the broken wagon with its shafts upended towards the sky might have been the débris of an earlier one. A cockerel on top of a smoking midden crowed there with wings outspread; it was a crested bird of fable, the Phœnix risen from the fire. Samson became the Minotaur; twin jets of steaming breath spurted threateningly out of his nostrils, condensed and hung on the still air. Bold as Theseus, Tim gave him a soccer barge, shoulder to shoulder, as he pushed by him to pitchfork the hay into his rack. Samson snuffled wetly into Tim's face, and Tim pulled his white woolly forelock. The bull weighed three quarters of a ton, and if he'd had a mind to he could have pinned Tim against the side of the pen, pounded him with forehead and forefeet, and squashed him flat as the tigerskin rug on the hearth in the farmhouse sitting-room. But Samson was too good-mannered; he had waddled with dignity round a score of show-rings and worn the blue rosette between his horns. He was worth one thousand seven hundred and seventy-five pounds; that was the sum which had been offered for him by the Artificial Insemination Centre. Thence, if Tim's father had sold him to the Ministry, his diluted seed confined in bottles would have been dispatched by air to three or four continents, that it might fertilise the ovaries of Herefords on Kenya uplands, Uruguayan pampas, Australian stations, Canadian ranges—cows that knew nothing of the power of Samson's loins. John Sollars, however, had refused to sell Samson; he preferred to breed his own beasts from his own bull, as Samson himself had been bred. In any case he didn't hold with A.I. and thought it contrary to nature, curiously immoral. He delighted to quote a rude rhyme about it, composed by some wag during the war, in which a cow complained sadly:

*These Land Army tarts*
*That play with my parts*
*Still have it the old-fashioned way!*

Tim filled the hayrack, found his way out blocked by Samson's great bulk, so ducked under his belly and left him happily munching. He went to fetch the tractor out of the open shed. Carol in blue dungarees was perched half-way up a ladder against the shed. She said:

"Take your old tractor away—and you can't bring it back here after this morning. I want to rig up my counter."

She was fixing a noticeboard to the side of the shed. It was done in Gothic lettering: YE OLDE FARME SHOPPE. The hop-pickers could buy necessities there to save themselves the two-mile walk to the village. Last year Carol had bought a camera out of her profits. This year she was more ambitious and wanted a new dress for the dance they always gave at the end of hop-picking. "Off the shoulders," she said. "Low. The kind Mummy won't buy me." Tim started the tractor and drove out. He shouted to Carol:

"There's cocoa at the back door."

"Hate it," she said. " 'Cocoa is a cad and coward, Cocoa is a vulgar beast.' "

"Dripping cakes too."

"I know. I've had four. Mustn't have any more, I'm slimming."

She was in the stage of puppy-fat. "You'll bulge out of that new dress like a suet pudding," Tim said. He stood up on the tractor and gave her a slap on her round bottom as he went by. The farmyard gate was open for the cows to come in. He went through it and drove fast up the hill, crossing the misted fields by guesswork or some compass in his head. When he throttled back to look for a gateway, he heard the cowman coop-cooping in the Home Ground just below; but he couldn't see the cows, nor the covey of partridges which just at that moment went whirring off into the mist and then glided, with a light flick-flick-flick of wings, down into the valley; with luck, a covey for his father. He found the gateway, roared through it, and suddenly the mist vanished, it parted before him like a curtain, and he was looking into the sunrise that came in shining splendour over the black Malverns. Before him lay the field called Abbots, from which yesterday they'd carried a crop of barley. Tim's father, with his squirrel's anxiety to store his harvest and his miser's ambition to hoard it in his barns, had hurried up the combining in order to be finished before the hop-picking started. Yesterday afternoon, as the combine shaved off the last whiskery tuft in the middle, he'd said sharply: "Now, lad, get in there with the plough." First thing this morning he'd said: "Now finish it before the varmints arrive and we're all at sixes and sevens." He called the hop-pickers varmints, and he hated them all, but in these degrees: the Black Country folk least, because they were fairly orderly, the Welsh next, and the gipsies most, because the anarchy of their lives was an affront to order.

Abbots lay now like a silver lake on the hilltop; a myriad little spiders had busied themselves all night weaving cobwebs among the stubble, and a heavy dew had fallen on top of their close webs. Tim felt as if he were launching a ship when he drove the tractor into it. He hitched on the plough, he began to tear up the stubble and with it the cobwebs and the spiders and the shell-pink bindweed and the creeping scarlet pimpernel. Looking back over his shoulder, he saw the new-turned earth glowing rose-pink in the sun. Later on, when the winter rains came, it would darken, until it was a very deep red-brown exactly matching the coats of the Hereford cattle. But this almost incandescent pink, the same shade as the brick walls of the oast-houses, was the summer colour of Sollarshill. Tim loved it, and delighted to see the bright furrows unwinding themselves behind him. A hare rose leisurely from her form and lolloped off. Nut-brown pipits flew away from him like chaff on a wind. Larks got up, and though it was September trickled down out of the brightness some small cascades of song. Tim was happy and curiously excited because hop-picking was about to begin. The parting of the mist had made him think of the curtain going up on a play; and the hop-picking was indeed a kind of play acted for a month in this amphitheatre that lay between the Malverns and the Welsh hills. The hop-pickers provided the chorus: miners on holiday from Wales, factory-workers from the Midlands, gipsies and half-gipsy "travellers," all thrown together against the green frieze of the hops under the hot sun. They worked and played, sang, drank, stole, quarrelled, fought, loved, and praised Bacchus according to their fashion. They were a pretty lively chorus. But the simple plot of the play was the race against the weather, rain and frost and the oncoming autumn. If John

Sollars won that race by the first of October, there would be seven thousand pounds' worth of hops in the big white sacks called pockets stored in his barn. It would have cost nearly five thousand to grow and to pick them. The stakes were high, therefore, for in some years rain held up the picking and part of the crop was spoiled; there were blights and moulds to reckon with; and always during the last week you had a sense of winter standing in the wings, ready to rush onto the stage, scatter the characters, smash up the scenery and spoil the happy ending. There was no let-up in the drama until the last load had been carried to the kilns; and then Dave swept the hop-floor clean, the circular wall was draped with hop-bins, and Tim and Carol invited their friends to dance there. In such a setting even the most respectable farmers' daughters became as nymphs, and a score of young farmers looked (and sometimes behaved) as if they concealed hairy goats' hoofs under their dancing-pumps. It was a fitting finish to the play.

So Tim loved the hop-picking. He loved the bustle and urgency and the busy commotion of it; the hopyards suddenly populous that until now had lain so quiet, the banter of the women, the giggling girls, the rough jests, the brewing of tea, the smell of the hops on sticky hands, the ubiquitous children, the evenings in the Royal Victoria, the brief loves and fleeting conflicts, the quarrels of the gipsies blowing up suddenly and as suddenly subsiding, like dust-devils out of hot sand.

Thinking of the gipsies, he remembered Sue; and he found it strange that the thing he remembered best was not her sun-bleached hair, nor the surprising eagerness of her lips, not any bodily thing, but the swift silent way she had left him on that night last September. It was just after the pay-off, the hops were finished, and the pickers were drinking away their money in the Royal Victoria. Tim had gone down there to have a last beer with them. Sue's father, Black Bartholomew—Black Barty as they called him—was drunk with his cronies and her mother, Betsy, was in a mood for fighting. While both were preoccupied Tim had seized the chance of a whispered word with Sue; she'd nodded, and when the pub shut she had slipped away from her own people and met him at the stile into the Old Wood. She'd come suddenly out of the dark, making him jump because he hadn't heard a sound. Afterwards, without a good night, she'd vanished. More than anything else, it had made him aware of a difference, not of degree but of kind, between him and her. Standing there, listening for the twig to crackle that never did crackle beneath her feet, he'd had a sense of adventure and even, most unexpectedly, a whiff of danger. When he'd got home it was well past midnight, but his father, who slept very little when the hops were drying, was still prowling about by the kilns. He said sharply: "Where have you been?" and he didn't wait for an answer. It was extraordinary that he'd guessed about the girl. "Make a young fool of yourself," he'd growled, "in any way you like. Hottentots, I shouldn't care. But gipsies, that's the end."

Tim wondered whether Sue would come back this year. If so he must be careful; the old man had sharp eyes.

## 3

John Sollars had heard the partridges as they whickered along the hedge, and because he knew every inch of his farm he could guess exactly where they had gone down. There was a small patch of kale in the field called Twelvetrees; but they wouldn't like the kale, it would be too wet for them this morning after the heavy dew, so they'd be at the edge of the fodder-beet just beyond it. He whistled his bitch to heel and breasted the steep hill towards Twelvetrees.

He was still in the mist as he walked up the streamside, but even if it had been a pea-soup fog instead of what he called a mushroom mist he would have known to a yard where he was. He recognised every clump of fern along the stream, and the patch of tall pink flowers which had some outlandish name—Tim with his booklearning knew it but to John Sollars they were just pink flowers, a landmark as the fern clumps were landmarks, and the sandstone outcrops, each of a different shape, where the stream had worn away the soil. This soft red rock lay everywhere underneath the earth of Sollarshill: here and there it had fossil fishes in it, and the prints of ancient crawling things. Tim said it was hundreds of millions of years old: more booklearning, which John half-despised, half-respected. He'd been afraid it might spoil Tim for a farmer, when he sent him to the expensive school where they filled his head with Latin, Greek, Shakespeare and tommy-rot, but it hadn't done that, and as he listened now to the rhythm of the tractor's purr up on the top of the hill he knew that Tim was ploughing as straight a furrow as he could do himself. Even with a headful of airy-fairy poetry the boy could plough! And John comfortably assured himself that the poetry was just a folly of youth, like girls and reckless driving and Tim's young wildness in general. It would be forgotten, as the silly young wenches would be forgotten, when Tim settled down. But John thought it was about time he did settle down, at twenty-four.

He got to the plank bridge over the stream, crossed it, and climbed the stile into the kale. He came out into the sun suddenly, and the wet kale heads were shiny all round him. They came up nearly to his shoulders. Looking over them, he saw something moving against the hedge at the far side of the field. He thought at first it might be one of his men, and wondered what he was doing there. Then he thought it was a poacher and he angrily began to push his way through the kale. But now he saw it was a girl, a girl in trousers, walking by no means as a poacher walks but bold as brass, with her hands in her pockets and her shoulders thrown back. She whistled as she went along; and now with astonishment he recognised her as that good-for-nothing daughter of

Tommy Tomkins next door. "Hey!" he shouted, and he knew she had heard him, for she quickened her pace without looking round. Well, thought John, neighbour or no neighbour I'm damned if I see why she wants to walk across my farm at seven o'clock in the morning. She was heading for home too; where the devil had she come from? John thought he'd intercept her and ask her what she thought she was up to. The partridges were forgotten as he hurried through the kale. She went out of sight behind the bend of the hedge, and he knew he'd have a job to catch her. It was heavy going, for the kale field, well mucked, had grown plants like little trees. As he brushed through, the dewdrops showered off them, and he was aware of the wetness soaking through his trousers. He was aware of something else, odd and disturbing. His breath was coming short, he had a pain in his chest, and he was sweating. Pain was unfamiliar to him; he'd hardly ever been ill in his life, and he couldn't remember pain. He was trying as it were to analyse and identify the feeling, and he was hearing his breath heaving in his chest as it had certainly never done before, when suddenly at the edge of the kale, exactly where he'd expected them to be, the covey got up just in front of him. They were big black blobs right in the sun. He fired at one and heard the shot hit it with a *slap;* saw it somersault and fall; swung his gun to follow another which was crossing him from left to right, the angle he liked best, and then even as he pulled the trigger the pain clawed at him fiercely, it seemed to jerk his gun at the moment of firing and the bird flew on. John lowered his gun and bent almost double, pulled down by the pain. It let up for a moment, returned, but less sharply, and then it was gone. He felt the sweat very cold on his face. Shaggy, the red setter, stood before him wagging her tail. In her soft mouth she held the partridge upside down, its head hanging limp, its claws opening and shutting with some reflex action, for it was stone dead. The action of the claws reminded him of the pain.

He took the bird and saw it was a red-legged one. There weren't many on his farm, and he didn't like them; he fancied they did harm to his stock of English partridges. He called them Froggies and was prejudiced against them because they were foreigners. Likewise he hated Spanish owls, grey squirrels, all parvenu and alien creatures which damned fools had let loose in the English countryside—as if we hadn't got enough pests of our own. Damned fools, he thought, like Tommy Tomkins. He was capable of any such silliness. He had gone in at various times for Chinese geese, white turkeys, Muscovy ducks and pedigree goats. His latest act of lunacy, committed two years ago when he still had a little money left, was to buy a so-called hornless Hereford bull. He intended to start a herd of these unnatural creatures. In due course he put the bull to a hornless cow and it begat a calf which to John Sollars's delight sprouted as straight a pair of horns as he'd ever seen on a beast. Serve Tommy right. The very idea of a hornless Hereford offended John Sollars in the same way as a sailor would hate to see a ship without a funnel, or a horseman would be shocked by an Arab with a docked tail. He looked upon the whole business as a sort of genetical blasphemy. God meant 'em to have horns, he told himself, just as He gave horns to the devil; and *he'd* look a pretty queer customer without 'em.

## 4

John could see the eastern slope of Tommy's farm from where he stood. The sunlight showed up the darker feggy tufts in a field not properly drained; blackberry bushes growing up in corners between the hedges; a patch of furze. A kind of dull after-ache of the pain persuaded John that he ought to stand still for a few minutes before he went after the covey to get another bird and make up his traditional brace. He told himself the pain was simply indigestion; he was reluctant to put it to the test and perhaps discover that it was something else. So he leaned on his gun at the edge of the fodder-beet and contemplated the Hope Farm, brackeny, furzy, feggy, a farm in ruins. He knew that it was mortgaged up to the hilt; every season somebody at an N.F.U. meeting took him aside and told him confidentially: "Tomkins is filing his petition," or "Tomkins is being sold up." Yet somehow the queer fellow hung on precariously, borrowing from the bank, borrowing from his friends, perpetually robbing Peter to pay Paul. He had once borrowed two hundred pounds from John Sollars, which he'd paid back in driblets, with five per cent interest, over a period of four years. John had been tolerant about the delay but perversely he nursed a vague resentment against Tommy for paying up in the end and so confounding his prediction that the loan had been "money chucked down the drain." If Tommy had proved to be a crook John would have known where he stood with him. But he turned out to be merely feckless; and John often said that he liked crooks better than fools. Tommy was a great fool, because he'd had a good deal of money once and he'd frittered it away on wild and woolly enterprises, damnsilliness, moonshine. Two calamitous passions possessed him: for mechanical invention and agricultural experiment. He had spent ten years, and a few thousand pounds, inventing a hop-picking machine which wouldn't work. As for his farming, one crazy project after another went whirling through his giddy pate; the Chinese geese and the Muscovy ducks, the Tamworth pigs and the pedigree goats turned what had once been a good farm into a menagerie, while in the neglected fields the thistles multiplied and the ragwort, which John could see clearly from where he stood, poured out from the woodland edge and seeped in golden trickles down the slope of the hill.

Custom, tidiness and good order were very dear to John Sollars. Tommy Tomkins's mania for strange beasts (he'd have bred pedigree unicorns if there had been such things) was a sin against custom. So was the fact that he had married a foreigner, a Frenchwoman, though John charitably forgave him for that, since the woman was now dead. He couldn't forgive his preoccupation with Heath Robinson contraptions like that hop-picking machine which incorporated, among other extraordinary components, ten thousand hairpins. The man offended in other respects too. Ever since his wife died, nearly three years ago, he had been drinking a good deal; and that would doubtless complete his ruin, which was his own affair. What annoyed John Sollars was Tommy's habit of drinking night after night with his own labourers in the Royal Victoria. This, he felt, let everybody down. You could go into your local for a pint, buy one for your carter, pass the time of day with him while he drank it with a "Best respects, sir," and still preserve the proper, ordained, relationship of master and man. To get drunk with your carter was a raffish thing. If the gentry chose to do it, so much the worse for the gentry. Tommy came into that category, John supposed. He himself was a yeoman, something more rooted, stable, and indigenous.

Then there was that girl of Tommy's. Tim used to take her out, on the back of his first motor-bike, when she was about seventeen. She'd been a fairish handful even then—which was due to the French blood in her, John ingenuously supposed. Nobody had been surprised when she got herself into trouble and ran away to London, though the gossips had speculated unkindly about how she earned her living there. But only a week ago she had come back, out of the blue it was said, and within an hour or two she and Tommy were celebrating her return in the Royal Victoria! John Sollars had a curious attitude about all this. If Tim had run off to sow a crop of wild oats (which incidentally the young limb was quite liable to do) his father would have received him back with love and forgiveness and killed a fatted calf for him. But he believed most illogically that it was "different with a girl." Take Carol. She was only a kid, of course, eighteen, so the question didn't arise. . . . Hey, wait a minute, Tommy's girl was only eighteen when—but then she was half French, wasn't she? John supposed they matured earlier. Anyhow,

Carol hadn't woken up yet, thank goodness, to what used to be called love and was now so nastily called sex. She wasn't the kind that would lose her head; but suppose she had been that kind, and she had got herself into a mess, John Sollars knew that he would have said with absolute finality: "She has made her bed; let her lie on it." After all, there were no Prodigal Daughters in the Book.

Therefore, that Tommy should have welcomed his girl back—indeed he went about telling everybody, "Marianne's home!" as if he were actually proud of her—was just another example of his weakness, foolishness, and lack of principle. Lastly his farm was untidy, and that offended John Sollars most of all: he even kept his fences badly, and nobody could be called a good neighbour who did that. Looking across at the Hope Farm now, John let his glance travel down the ragwort-gilded slope to the meadows that lay in the bend of the river, where a boundary hedge and a small stream divided his land from Tommy's. On the near side of it there were some of his own cattle—he could recognise Sollarshill Sally, heavy in calf to Samson; she was due in a fortnight's time. Beyond the hedge, which was Tommy's hedge and therefore straggly and unlaid, he could see some beasts which Tommy had bought in to fatten—he certainly hadn't bred them—and even at this distance they looked a scruffy lot. John, who had the best eye for a beast in three counties, couldn't have told you why he didn't like the look of them. Perhaps it was the colour of their coats—the slightest hint of mousiness mixed with the red—or the way they moved, or simply the way they held their heads. He knew that if he'd gone close to those cattle he'd have found them what he called "tucked-up," stary-coated, rather as if their skins were too tight for them: dealers' cattle, bought at market.

It disquieted him to see them there, in the field next to his own beasts, with only that bad hedge and the shallow brook in between.

John looked at his watch. It was nearly half past seven. He had been standing there for a quarter of an hour, putting off the moment when he must climb the hill again after the covey of red-legs. He called Shaggy, who was ranging twenty yards away; she wasn't accustomed to so long a wait. Then he strode off through the fodder-beet. Soon the slope became steeper, and he was conscious, not of the pain, but of a kind of tightness in his chest which might be a premonition of the pain. He discovered that he was frightened of it; and he was angry with himself, because he knew that there were people who lived with pain, who had grown used to it as to a companion disliked but inescapable. To him it came as a stranger, barging into his life roughly and rudely. What was it *doing* here? What did it mean? His feet were stumbling among the hard knobbles of the fodder-beet. He was sweating again. He went on a little farther, and then his uphill strides suddenly petered out and almost without making a conscious decision he turned gradually away from the slope and back towards the farmhouse. He told himself it was breakfast-time; Molly would be sitting at the table already tap-tapping so delicately at the top of the boiled egg which she pecked at in her birdlike way every morning of her life at breakfast. At half past eight he had an appointment with that hated sanitary inspector who always turned up before the hop-picking. ("Where you get a lot of people crowded together there's always a risk of epidemics, you see.") But John Sollars recognised that he was making excuses. He was afraid of the pain; and for the first time in his life he was afraid of a hill. So there would be only one partridge this morning, when he gave Molly the usual kiss and she smiled: "Where's my present for September the first?" A custom had been broken; and that was a bad thing, somehow ominous.

He pulled the partridge out of his poacher's pocket and turned it over in his hand. To make matters worse it wasn't even a young one. It was the old cock. John held it up by the neck and disliked its beaky Gallic expression. A damned Frenchman. And that set him thinking about Tommy again, and the boundary hedge which probably had weak places in it because it had been so long unlaid, and Sollarshill Sally grazing close to it, too close for his liking to those scruffy-looking cattle of Tommy's.

## 5

Tommy Tomkins had meant to see to the boundary hedge, and he had actually recorded this intention on the back of an income tax envelope under the heading T.D.T., which meant "Things to Do To-morrow." Almost every night before he went to bed he made out a list like that; it was in the nature of a good resolution, an affirmation of his belief that to-morrow would be a different kind of day, that he himself would be miraculously reborn, metamorphosed, would make a new start, a purposeful, sober, sensible beginning-again. But he hardly ever looked at the list in the morning; he usually found it in his breast-pocket days later, and read through it, and was discouraged because it was still valid as a list of "Things to Do To-morrow." None of them had been done.

This morning, however, because it was the first of September and the sun shone so bright and he remembered as soon as he woke up that Marianne was home—this morning he could almost persuade himself that the miracle had happened; that it was a new kind of day and that he was a new kind of man. He read through the list as he waited for the kettle to boil; it contained some extraordinary items such as *Do Money* and *Bat off bank till pigs are sold* but they did not daunt him to-day. Whistling, he took a cup of tea up to Marianne's room, knocked at her door, opened it, and had a moment of sheer horror when he saw she wasn't there. The bed was made, everything was ominously tidy as it had been on that morning when she went away. So he thought, for a second, that she had gone away again. Then he saw her nightdress neatly folded on the bed, the suitcase in the corner, the things on the dressing-table. Reassured, he went downstairs, and in the dining-room the table was laid and there was a note in Marianne's out-of-character handwriting, so unexpectedly prim: *Gone mushrooming. Cold ham in larder. Love.*

This pleased him so much that his sense of purpose was restored and reinforced. With a giant-killer's resolution he put on his mucking-out mac; for he had decided to tackle the beastliest job first. As he went through the hall he paused to look at the picture by John Martin which hung there. John Martin was a Victorian painter, rather out of fashion now, but Tommy loved this picture, which was called "Adam Sees Eve for the First Time." The artist had a Brock's Benefit style; he used every colour he could lay his hands on, and matched the streaky pink sunrise clouds of the background with rosy flamingoes in the foreground. But somehow or other he had contrived to imbue and inspire the whole painting with a glow and a glory, a light that never was on sea or land, surely the light of paradisial morning. The sun was rising upon a brand-new world, new flowers and flamingoes, new trees, new beasts, new wonder and new love. Tommy, most painfully aware of the wonder that had left him long ago, often felt very wicked when he looked at his picture, especially as a looking-glass hung close to it, in which he could see the reflection of his puffy cheeks, his red-rimmed eyelids, and cigarette-stained moustache. This morning, however, he faced the picture squarely; he even felt, for a moment, that he had a share in the innocence. He strode forth to muck out his pigs.

This took him half an hour. Then he fed the turkeys, and the hens which lived in a run he called the Place of Skulls because the household scraps during many years had turned it into a kind of Golgotha, where your feet crunched on old sheeps' heads and rabbits' vertebræ, the legbones of chickens and the last Christmas turkey's breastbone like the keel of a child's boat turned upside down. Such was his mood this morning that he added: *Make new run for fowls,* to his list of "Things to Do To-morrow." He actually cleaned out the fowl-houses. He also swept clean the hop-floor in readiness for the first load of hops. The ground floor of the kiln presented a more complicated problem, because it was cluttered up with the parts of a homemade still which he had invented for the purpose of turning cider into applejack. He had thought there might be a market for applejack, and he had dreamed of making a little fortune by turning all the surplus cider, and indeed all the cider he could buy, into applejack as the French made Calvados in Normandy. Then he had learned that he would have to pay spirit duty on the applejack and the project had been shelved, though he had made a few experimental bottles before the still went wrong. He now moved the still, piece by piece, into an adjacent outhouse. By the time he had finished all these jobs he was exhausted, and he went in to have breakfast. He got tired very quickly nowadays. Too much drink, too many cigarettes; but he told himself it was only twelve years ago that he'd walked a hundred miles in three days. True, he'd had the Huns after him then, but he thought that if he really set about it he could get fit again easily; and everything was going to be different, now that Marianne was home.

She wasn't back yet from her mushrooming. He cut himself a slice of ham, which was another step towards rehabilitation; he hadn't often been able to face breakfast lately. Then, while he ate, he Did His Money. This was giant-killing indeed, for *Do Money* was the most alarming of all the imperatives on his list. He generally funked it; but not to-day. Seizing a sheet of writing paper, he put a heading, "Assets," on the left-hand side, and another, "Liabilities," on the right. In an access of righteousness he crossed out "Liabilities" and substituted with brutal honesty the word "Debts." Then he began his calculations. "Assets" first: ?£650 for that bunch of cattle down in the meadows when he sold them; ?£75 for his apples; ?£200 for his barley; ?£2500 for his hops, but it would be two or three months before this came in; ?£6 apiece for ten little pigs when they were weaned assuming the sow farrowed successfully, assuming she had ten pigs, assuming she reared them all; and so on. Upon the opposite side: Arrears of Income Tax £600; Arrears of Mortgage Repayments due to Brother George £1750; various bills ?£375 *et cetera.* Most of the figures, in all Tommy's calculations, were preceded by question marks, which were his private acknowledgement of his fallibility. Zealously he pored over the sheet, and Doing His Money became, as it always did in the end, a kind of grim game which he played alone, as he sometimes played Patience alone in the evening. Card games bored him unless he played for high stakes, so to make his solitary Patience interesting he would play it against God or the Devil or whatever represented Fate. He would say to himself: If I get it out this time it means my luck will change and things will get better; if it doesn't come out things will get worse. But the stakes were so high, if you played with Fate like this and kidded yourself into believing in the game, that sooner or later you were driven to cheat. Tommy always started with a vow that he would be strictly honest; but when the cards ran against him he slipped very gradually into a kind of compromise—he would look at the card underneath just to see if the game *would* have come out, and from that it was quite a short step to fiddling with the cards to make sure that it did come out. It was the same when he Did His Money. Somehow he must make the Assets equal or outweigh the Debts. But alas, those poor platoons on the credit side were no match for the battalions ranged against them, so, like a despairing general planning a hopeless battle, he was fain to reinforce them with paper soldiers, phantom artillery, imaginary supply, more question marks than ever before, which stood for unknown quantities, remote possibilities, pious hopes. This morning he even wrote a "?Applejack" in the left-hand column; but subsequently a twinge of conscience caused him to cross it out. He was less scrupulous about the item "Bank." His bank manager reluctantly and in perpetual trepidation allowed him an overdraft of £250; by means of various agonising calculations Tommy decided that he was overdrawn at the moment to the tune of £215. This left a margin of £35. So Tommy entered £35 on the credit side: Cash at Bank.

He had just done so when the post came. It always came late at the Hope Farm, because the postman had such a long walk up the hill. Tommy went out into the hall just as the letters came fluttering through the flap in the door. There were only two, and he recognised the disastrous import of them both even as they were tumbling into the wire box. The blue envelope was addressed in the crabbed, meticulous handwriting of his brother, George. The white one was from the bank, and it had the word "Private" stamped smudgily upon the left-hand top corner in that ominous shade of purple affected by Lloyds. This could mean only one thing: he was overdrawn beyond the £250 limit. Something had gone wrong with his calculations as usual. He hadn't got £35, or even the use of £35, to tide him over until some more money came in. He had nothing at all.

Now Tommy, whenever he received any very bad letters, such as those from the income tax or the bank, had an immediate instinct to hide. He picked up the letters and stuffed them into his pocket, and fled to the only place where he oddly supposed that the slings and arrows of outrageous fortune could not reach and assail him. He did so now. He seized the horrible envelopes, gave a despairing glance at the John Martin picture as he passed it, and rushed upstairs: he went into the lavatory and shut the door; and sitting there he opened first the letter from the bank, which was as he expected, and then the letter from George. It began:

> *My dear Tommy:*
> *I have been meaning for a very long time to tell you what is in my mind. Believe me this letter distresses me as much to write as it will distress you to read. It is about the mortgage. Unless . . .*

Tommy read it to the end, and folded it, and put it back in his pocket. Finish, he said to himself; *kaputt,* as the Huns with their hands above their heads whined in 1945. He heard Marianne come in; he heard her calling him from the hall. He would not answer. Briefly, oh so briefly secure behind the locked door, he sat and stared at the auctioneer's calendar which was hung up on the back of it. The first of September. It was to have been a different day, a new start, a beginning-again, a day when all the "Things to Do Tomorrow" were done. But as he sat there, hope and resolution both faded. It would be the same as all the other days; only the footsteps of disaster, which he fled from all day long, would come just a little closer and would pad just a little louder, because of what George had written in the letter which ended: "Your still affectionate brother, George."

## 6

The tractor bucked like a horse across the ridge and furrow, and Tim, who enjoyed the sensation, let it rip. They said this twenty-acre piece between the hopyards had once been the common field of Sollarshill village; it was queer to think that those "lands" which the tractor bounced over had been moulded up by peasants five or six hundred years ago, to divide their strips of cultivation, each man's from his neighbour's. The monks had owned Sollarshill then: the monks who always knew rich land when they saw it, and who shrewdly believed that they could serve God best where the grass grew tall, with plenty of flowers for their bees, and where the slopes were towards the sun, so that they could grow vines even in England. There wasn't much left of their abbey now; it was a grey ruin, five miles away across the next hill; but all over the six-inch ordnance sheet the place names kept alive their memory: Friary Lane, Priory Wood,

Sollarshill Saint Benedict, and Abbots, which Tim had just finished ploughing.

He gave a thought now to the people who had ploughed it before him, sweating serfs with their laborious breast-ploughs, men with cruel goads to drive forward the heaving oxen, old labourers who plodded like their heavy-hoofed horses, monks' men, lords' men, Frenchmen from Normandy, Saxons, perhaps even Celts before there were any monks or lords. Everything was old here; the landscape had an assurance, an air of custom and continuity, that came from long cultivation. The spinney that had been planted in 1815 to commemorate the victory of Waterloo was called the New Spinney; the Old Wood, full of great oaks, was mentioned in Domesday. The church with the square tower, down in the village, had stood there for eight centuries. Its parish register went back to 1550: Tim's father was the seventh John Sollars whose name was written in it. Six Timothys came between them—always a Timothy succeeding a John and vice versa. Presumably all those Timothys, except the one who had died of smallpox when he was eleven, had at some time or another ploughed the field called Abbots. But they'd probably never ploughed it on the first of September within twenty-four hours of carting off it a fine crop of barley. It was only when you had a very dry hot summer you could do that.

Tim had missed breakfast and he felt as if he could eat three breakfasts; but first he must meet his father in the lower hopyard, where he'd promised to be at half past eleven. To-morrow Tim would be in charge of the pickers, and his father always liked to have everything planned beforehand: where they should start picking, where the gipsies should be allowed to park their caravans, and so on. The gipsies would turn up any time now. Tim thought of Sue, and his excitement about the hop-picking in general became particular to her; his whole body shared it as the tractor bucked and reared. He opened the throttle fully, and the engine, racing during the downward plunges, gave a series of loud yelps. Thus he came to the gate of the hopyard and swung into it; and there was his father leaning on the blackthorn thumbstick which he always carried now: feet planted well apart, absolutely motionless, with the air of an oak tree or a rocky outcrop, part of the landscape. He said:

"I gave you the M.G. so that you could break your neck in that, rather than smash up the farm machinery."

John Sollars was in a bad temper. The sanitary inspector had turned out to be a new one, even more fussy than the last. He had demanded to see the hop-pickers' accommodation.

"We house 'em in the pigsties," John had said.

"Mr. Sollars! We must have *some* respect for human beings."

"*I* have some respect for my pigs. I'll show you."

He'd taken the man round. The pens where the sows farrowed were brick-built and airy. Always before hop-picking they were whitewashed afresh and boarded up into separate cubicles. Each cubicle would be provided with a couple of bales of straw on which the pickers could lay their mattresses and bedding. There was electric light, which removed the risk that the Saturday-night drunks might set the place on fire with oil-lamps; and it came in useful outside the hop-season, when the sows were farrowing. The Black Country people occupied these pigsties, which were therefore called Dudley Mansions. The Welsh had a big barn, Abertillery Hall, and the gipsies, of course, lived in their own caravans.

The sanitary inspector had said doubtfully:

"I suppose you disinfect the sties thoroughly before the people go in?"

"Yes. I also disinfect them thoroughly before I put my pigs back."

John Sollars hated all officials. Thoroughly ruffled, and troubled still by a faint inkling of the pain, he had walked down to the hopyards to get himself calm again. He always walked among them on the last day before the picking. The bines, fifteen feet tall, swung like a green arras in the gentle wind. Between them there was a cool green shade. He loved to see the hopyards like this, inviolate, still. To-morrow the pickers would begin to pull down the bines. The picking-bins would be set up between the rows. Cigarette packets and ice-cream cartons would litter the red earth which made such a lovely contrast with the hops' bright green. The cool shade would gradually disappear as the torn curtains let in the hard, bright sunlight.

But to-day, for John Sollars, the hopyards represented as it were his private poetry; beauty was a concept which had narrowed down as he grew older, until it was simply hops and Herefords—Samson in his lustful strength, Sollarshill Sally barrel-sided as her belly swelled, the red herd standing knee-deep in the grass beside the Wye; and those green soft-swinging curtains strung between the poles. He stretched up his hand and pulled down towards him a handful of the pale green bobbles, forbearing to snap off the branch, as if he were reluctant to do even the smallest violence to the unravished hops. To-morrow the deflowering!

He said:

"It's a good crop everywhere: easy picking. It won't hurt 'em to pick for one and two."

"One and tuppence?" Tim was surprised; last year the hops had been much thinner, certainly, but they'd paid the pickers one and sixpence a bushel. One and two seemed very little, especially as everything was more expensive than last year. A penny on a pint of beer at the Royal Victoria! There'd be some lively arguments, and perhaps even a strike.

"I'd have thought," Tim ventured, "we could make it one and three at least."

"You would, would you, Master Know-all? Well, fertiliser's gone up, labour's gone up, even string's gone up, and they tell me the sale of beer is going down. So it's got to be one and two. We fixed it last night, after the N.F.U. meeting."

By "we," of course, he meant half a dozen of the biggest growers: Revel of Stretton Grandison, Barker of Edvin Loach, the Johnson brothers, Remington, Ferrers. The little men didn't count.

"Tomkins wasn't at the meeting. I tried to get him on

the phone but I couldn't. Cut off again I suppose."

Tommy was only in a small way, and his agreement to the price which the pickers were to be offered wouldn't ordinarily matter. His farm being adjacent, however, it would cause discontent among the Sollarshill pickers if he were so foolish as to pay a penny or two more.

Tim glanced at the teeming hops. From his high seat on the tractor he could see what a good crop it was, each bine going up like a Roman candle with the sprays falling in green fountains about it. Easy picking; but he still thought one and two a bushel was miserable pay. It was never any use arguing with his father, though. He changed the subject.

"I put up a big covey. It flew your way."

"And I only got one of 'em." John didn't mention the pain. He wasn't going to tell anybody about that. "They were blasted Froggies," he said. At once his thoughts went back to the farm across the valley.

"Have you seen Tommy's girl since she came back?"

Tim shook his head.

"Well, I have. Seven o'clock this morning, walking over Twelvetrees without so much as a by your leave! Just as the partridges got up, too; I might have peppered her." The thought that he might indeed have done so made John all the more angry with her. He had the good old-fashioned attitude to his gun: that it was a lethal weapon to be treated as a lethal weapon, and that he must always make sure there was no one in the line when he fired it. Another person's folly would be no excuse. His father, old Tim Sollars, had put a couple of shots into the hat of a trespassing blackberry-picker who rose up unexpectedly from behind a hedge. Although it wasn't his fault, and although shooting was his dearest hobby, he had locked up his gun and had never gone shooting again. So even as John said: "It would have served her right if I'd stung up her arse with a pellet or two," he caught himself sweating at the very possibility. It was the same kind of sudden sweat which he'd had this morning; and he was uncomfortably aware of the proximity, though not the presence, of the pain.

Tim said:

"Full marks to her for her cheek! I bet she was pinching our mushrooms."

"Used to be one of your flibbertigibbets, didn't she?"

Tim smiled. He remembered the trim small girl who had ridden on the pillion of his motor-bike four years ago, and also incidentally on the motor-bikes of most of the other farmers' sons. She had always wanted to go faster. She clutched you by the shoulders as if she were a little monkey perched on your back and with a cheerful disregard of what the wind was doing to her skirts she urged you on. It was a wonder she didn't break somebody's neck. Then there had been tales about her. Tim, at a village dance, had thought he would test the truth of these tales. He had taken her out into the orchard behind the village hall. He had been at the stage when oafish innocence is unsuitably allied to clumsy ardour; and all he got for his pains was a swift and surprising clout, delivered very much as a teased cat lets fly a jab with its claws out, which left four long scratches on the side of his face. These scratches had been a source of entertainment to his friends when he went back into the village hall. That was the last time he had seen Marianne; a week later her running-away had been a seven-day wonder in the village, and then Tim had almost forgotten her. There had been a lot of other girls.

John Sollars was grumbling on:

"I wish the damn fool would pay his phone bill. I'll have to take the car and go up to the Hope, tell him what we've arranged about the rate for the picking." He thought he'd tell Tommy about that hedge, too, and ask him to run a couple of strands of barbed-wire along his side of it. "The Hope," he added, almost to himself, as he looked across the dip towards it. "What a bloody Hope too!" Yet it could be made into a first-rate farm if a man had the capital and the common sense. The land, despite Tommy's neglect, was in "good heart," as the old country phrase went. He'd have been willing to lend Tommy ten thousand on it; indeed he'd half offered to, years ago, before Tommy had casually borrowed that trivial two hundred. But Tommy had been wary, guessing perhaps what was in his mind, and had raised the mortgage elsewhere. No doubt the mortgagor was beginning to squeeze him now; and likely enough the farm would be sold. If so—

Yes; he admitted it to himself, he wanted the Hope Farm. If he'd had the mortgage on it, Tommy would probably have been out by now, and the hedge by the river would have been decently laid, and there'd have been none of those mousy-looking half-breeds off the Welsh hills eating that meadow grass which would certainly give them bellyaches because it was too rich for them after the scant hill pasture. John Sollars wanted the Hope; but why? He was sixty-two, though Tim was only twenty-four; he'd married late, being cautious always, looking round for a good wife, taking his time over it, waiting for the right one to turn up, in just the same way as he had bought his first Hereford bull. At sixty-two, then—and especially after that sharp warning he'd received this morning—why did he want the extra work and worry of another two hundred and fifty acres added to his own four hundred? It wasn't greed in the ordinary sense, but a kind of lust, the last one left to him: the lust for land, not only to possess it but to tame it as he would break a horse, to make it serve him, to bring it back from unruly disorder into the kind of domesticity which he knew as Good Farming. When he died he would leave more than a hundred thousand; so his wife would be well provided for and there would be quite enough capital for Tim to run the farm. What was the point of adding another thirty thousand, which was what the Hope would be worth if it were put into decent order? No point: nevertheless he coveted the Hope Farm.

"Well, I'll go and see the little beggar," he said, reluctant to leave the beautiful green shade of the hopyard. "You'd better hitch on the trailer and fetch in some bales of straw for the varmints. Get yourself something to eat first, though."

Tim drove off along the headland beside the windbreak of poplar trees. From his perch on the Fordson he could see the main road, which was deep-cut here, three feet below the level of the fields. He caught a glimpse of the roof and the little chimney of a caravan. A moment later he recognised the caravan; it was bright green with yellow shafts, and that was Black Barty's! He'd be on his way to the Hope; he had such a bad name that Tim's father wouldn't have him on the place, nor any of his gang, so he always picked for Tommy, camping in the field by the river next to the Sollarshill meadows. The gipsies who picked at Sollarshill, about two score of them, were the band of Wisdom Lee, who was called the King of the Gipsies because he was more powerful and authoritative than the rest. Last year Black Barty had challenged his authority; there had been a fight, and the older man had beaten the younger one, but Tim guessed it had been a near thing. Wisdom, with a black eye and a broken nose, had been very quiet and subdued for the rest of the hop-picking; and though he reigned still, his throne tottered. This year the up-and-coming Barty would doubtless challenge him again; and there'd be a new King of the Gipsies if Wisdom were beaten.

Glancing slyly over his shoulder, to see if his father was watching, Tim pushed open the throttle. He wanted to get to the bend in the road before the caravan did, to see if Sue was sitting beside her father. The tractor gave a lurch, one wheel on the headland, the other in the ditch. Then it roared off, spurting smoke, twelve miles an hour.

At the hopyard gate Tim's father heard the noise and stumped forth angrily. What's the bloody young fool up to now? And yet he grinned to himself, glad that he hadn't got one of those namby-pamby sons, like Barker's two boys, one of 'em sissy, the other playing jazz records to himself half the night and waggling his backside like a nigger. Bill Barker, a tough chap, had told him about it, bewildered. "Makes me want to kick him where he joins." But Tim rode the tractor like a charioteer!

Coming at last to the bend in the road, Tim turned the tractor round, drove it up to the hedge, and waited. In a moment he heard the pony's hoofs and the green caravan came leisurely towards him. There was only Black Barty sitting between the shafts, and Tim felt a sharp stab of disappointment. Then he saw the sun-bleached head of hair beside the pony's head. Of course—the women generally walked, when their caravan was in a district where other gipsies were likely to encounter it. The men rode at ease, to show their importance and superiority.

The caravan was nearly opposite and below him. Black Barty hadn't seen him, because he was on Black Barty's blind side; the gipsy's right eye had been shot out with a catapult. Nobody knew when this strange event had happened, nor who had done the deed; Black Barty wouldn't say. But when he was drunk he would always declare that one day he would get the bastard that done it; then he would produce a knife from one pocket and a whetstone from the other and melodramatically sharpen the knife. That was the kind of fellow Black Barty was: a great boaster, a terrible one for threatening, but some said a coward when it came to the point. Yet he'd fought Wisdom, and nearly beaten him. This season's hop-picking, thought Tim, would probably decide the issue between them.

Sue's head, from above, testified to the strength of the summer's sun. The hair was pale honey-coloured on top, underneath you could see the dark brown. She walked beside the pony as all the gipsy women walked, the hips swinging, the small of the back almost a hollow above the buttocks, the breasts held high, the head quite still, as if she were carrying a pitcher upon it. Yet she was only three quarters gipsy, Tim supposed. Her mother, Betsy, whom he could see now peering out of the caravan window, was the daughter of one of those scrap-dealing gipsies who become townees and marry out of their kind.

Tim wanted to see Sue's face, but she didn't look up; so he whistled.

Then all three faces turned up to him at once: Betsy's, sharp and suspicious; Black Barty's, swarthy, the right eyelid drawn down over the eye, permanently closed—perhaps the hospital had stitched it up like that; and Sue's, with that rather foxy look that was nevertheless so attractive—a sharpness softened by her youth, brown eyes a bit slanting, the lips parted, a profile line from the bridge of the nose down past the chin to her throat, which would have been lovely to draw if one could hold a pencil between thumb and finger and do it in one swift delicious movement!

Black Barty said, sycophant as ever:

"Master Tim! Master Tim! Here we are back again, and they say there's never bin hops like there is this year at Sollarshill!"

"Good hops everywhere," Tim shouted. Forgetting for the moment about the one and tuppence, he added laughing: "You'll all make your fortunes."

"It isn't us that makes our fortunes, Master Tim," said Black Barty. Meanwhile Betsy within the caravan was bobbing her head in what presumably was a sort of curtsy; but Sue had made no sign.

So now he looked straight at her for the first time, as Black Barty, waving his whip and showing off as usual, walloped the pony to make it break into a trot. Sue, at the pony's head, had to run to keep up with it. Running, she looked back at him; but she didn't smile. He couldn't have told whether there was an invitation, a memory, or even a recognition of what had happened between them, in that reticent brief glance.

## 7

Against the annual incursion of the gipsies Mrs. Agnew made ready the Royal Victoria as a prudent captain prepares his vessel to meet an expected storm: the decks cleared, the hatches battened down, everything ship-shape and Bristol-fashion, all loose objects secured. September the first was ringed in red ink on the calendar hanging up behind the bar; and it was a great wonder to Mrs. Agnew that the gipsies who had no calendars, nor the ability to read, contrived nevertheless to arrive so punctually. It strengthened her conviction that they were not quite human, but "creatures," like swallows or fieldfares, or the random moths that came fluttering at the lit windows of the inn, each kind at its appointed season.

Yesterday afternoon she had gone shopping to Hereford and laid in provisions for a month; she would not leave the premises again until the gipsies departed—you never knew what mischief they might get up to, what wilful damage, what thieving, what arson! This morning she had awakened early, dressed in a hurry, patted into place her thin hair, fastened round her neck the black velvet band without which she would have felt quite naked; and she had suffered the alarm of seeing Moggie hunted by the foxhounds. She had comforted and cossetted him, and soothed his ruffled dignity with a tin of Grade Three Salmon; and after that she was all behindhand, and she had fairly bustled about, making her preparations. First she had written out a notice for the hop-pickers' bar (naturally they weren't allowed in the saloon), ALL GLASSES WILL BE CHARGED FOR, 6d; then she removed every scrap of inflammable material from the outhouses, locked them, put a chain on the back garden gate (else the rascals would be after those fat vegetable-marrows) and fixed a good padlock to the hen-run door. Next she had looked to the fire-extinguishers, and the A.R.P. stirrup pump she'd had during the war, filled three buckets with water and stood them in strategic positions, and, for fear of the gipsies' omnivorous ponies, had taken in the flower-boxes from outside the bar windows.

She had just completed this task when Mr. Tomkins drove up in his very old car that had white patches showing through the rubber of its tyres and a windscreen which had gone yellow with age—it was such a hindrance to vision that he generally drove with his head hanging out of the car. He wanted to use her telephone, because his wouldn't work.

"Something's gone wrong with the wahs," he said in his lah-di-dah voice; but of course Mrs. Agnew guessed that he hadn't paid his bill. He didn't seem in a hurry to phone. He ordered a double whisky, and made polite conversation; he wasn't the kind of customer who banged down his money and demanded his drink as if he were buying something from a shop. He treated you as if you were his hostess in her sitting-room.

"Fine fellow," he said, as he tickled Moggie behind his ears. Full of tinned salmon, the huge marmalade cat lay dozing on the counter. "*How* heavy did you tell me he was?"

"Twenty-two and a half pounds," said Mrs. Agnew proudly. "But of course he's been *You know,* and that always makes them heavier."

"Quite, quite."

"But now, poor Moggie, he'll have to be shut away. He hates September. That reminds me, I must fill a tray for him."

Mrs. Agnew suspected that all gipsies were cat-stealers. Whoever saw a cat in a gipsy caravan? *They boil them up in their horrible hotch-potch,* Mrs. Agnew believed. Indeed during the last two years she had become quite sure of it: what else did they live on now that myxomatosis had killed off all the rabbits? Moggie, being so fat, would clearly present a special temptation to them. So every year on the first of September, she shut him up in her bedroom; and there he remained until the end of the month, when the last of the gipsies had gone.

"You're all ready for them, I see," said Mr. Tomkins, noticing the fire-bucket which she'd placed in the corner of the saloon. "One's always afraid of fahs, when the gipsies are about. Dear fellows, they're very careless and happy-go-lucky."

He asked for another whisky, and Mrs. Agnew guessed that he was fortifying himself against some dreaded ordeal on the telephone. Ringing up the bank, perhaps? His cheques generally bounced once, and sometimes twice, before they went through. He was "always a gentleman," nevertheless;

and it didn't seem fair to Mrs. Agnew that he should be so poor whereas all the other hop-farmers were so rich—especially as his poverty was really a consequence of his cleverness. She knew all about the hop-picking machine and she thought it was wonderful of him to have invented it, even though it didn't work. She knew that the prosperous hop-farmers despised him, and laughed at his poor old car as they swept past it in their sleek shiny ones. But they'd made most of their money during the war, when Tommy Tomkins could probably have made a fortune too, if he hadn't taken it into his head to join up, leaving his wife to run the farm with the aid of old and untrustworthy labourers who had let it go to wrack and ruin. He must have been a hopeless soldier; he'd looked quite absurd in his uniform, when he came home on leave. Mrs. Agnew was very sorry for him; and she was sorrier still when she'd let him into her back room and overheard what he was saying on the telephone.

"*Sell me up?* My dear boy! After all, you're pretty well-breeched, you know, and you can afford to wait just a little. . . . It's the Principle, you say? Now George, George, just think of all the monstrous things that are done in the name of Principles. . . ."

Mrs. Agnew had left the door an inch or two ajar. She saw no harm in eavesdropping when she allowed somebody to use her phone, regarding the scraps of information which she gleaned in this way as the perks to which she was entitled in return for the privilege. While she listened attentively, she busied herself writing out another notice: LADIES WANTING TOILET PLEASE ASK FOR KEY—one couldn't have the gipsy women going in *there*.

"Yes, dear boy," Mr. Tomkins was saying, "I do know that, but just at the moment I simply can't lay my hands on a . . . I tell you, as soon as the hops are picked I shall be able . . . A splendid crop . . . You don't believe me? Well, come down and see."

This was said rather defiantly, and apparently it got an unexpected answer, for there was a long pause before Mr. Tomkins admitted with obvious reluctance:

"Yes of course there's a spare room. . . . And Marianne's home, so . . . It'll be rather like picnicking of course. *The day after to-morrow?* Well, yes, it will be delightful to see you after all this time."

But when he came out of the back room he looked far from delighted, he looked a bit like one of those white turkeys he went in for, red-wattled and pale-cheeked. He ordered another drink.

"You couldn't, I suppose, put it on the slate? I changed my trousers before I came out."

Of course they were the same filthy grey ones he always wore; and Mrs. Agnew was aware that his excuse was a kind of convention between him and her, just as he would say: "I missed the bank by five minutes—why on earth do they close so early?" when she knew perfectly well (and he was aware she knew) that he didn't dare go near the bank and wanted to change one of those bouncing cheques. But she smiled: "Certainly, Mr. Tomkins," for he always paid up in the end.

"And that call to London? Don't forget to remind me. My young brother," he added vaguely. "He's coming down to stay."

"Then we shall be seeing something of him?" said Mrs. Agnew politely.

"Not in here." He suddenly grinned at her through his straggly, yellow-stained moustache. "Not in here, Mrs. Agnew! He's one of those *great big black teetotallers that are sent to us for a rod!* Oh dear! Everything seems to happen at once, at the hop-picking. Listen!" he said, going towards the window. "Here comes the first of our troubles, I think."

Mrs. Agnew heard the clop-clop of hoofs and the crunching of iron-shod wheels. She was assailed by that feeling of being all of a dither, half-pleasurable, half-alarming, which always affected her when the gipsies arrived. She followed Mr. Tomkins to the window and saw a yellow caravan, Wisdom Lee sitting lordly within it and puffing at his pipe, while his wife Marta strode beside the pony. She was belligerent, big-bosomed, splendid—rather like a warrior queen as she swung along with her chin in the air and the coppery plaits coiled high on the crown of her head. A second caravan followed, driven by Wisdom's mother, the old witch whose face like brown parchment looked as if it had been kippered in the smoke of a thousand camp-fires. She smoked a very small clay pipe, about two and a half inches long, so that the bowl came almost immediately beneath her long sharp beak of a nose. Mrs. Agnew knew the smell of that pipe, which stank out the hop-pickers' bar on Saturday nights and made her feel sick when she went in to clean out the bar on Sunday mornings.

This second caravan was filled with the assorted brats of Wisdom, all ages, lean rangy youths and elfish-looking little boys, and girls who peered out of the windows with wary, secret and appraising eyes, like wild things in a cage. Hateful lurcher dogs went sinuously beneath the caravan's rear axle —cat-killers, Mrs. Agnew was sure! A sleek dun pony brought up the rear.

This dun pony suddenly plunged and tugged at its halter. Three or four of Wisdom's children, crowding to the rear of the caravan, began to gesticulate and shout. Grannie Lee yelled something to Wisdom just in front. And now the cause of the commotion came into view. Black Barty was on the tail of Wisdom's little convoy; and in order to show off, or for the purpose of shouting insults, or simply out of devilment, he was determined to overtake them. He was slashing at the flanks of his high-stepping pony, standing up and hanging on to the reins, while the caravan swayed and the buckets slung from its tailboard rattled and banged together.

Betsy stood behind Barty, and the little foxy-faced wanton, the one that Master Tim Sollars was said to go with, more shame to him, had jumped up onto one of the shafts and perched there, swinging her legs and putting her tongue out at the Wisdom children in front. Mrs. Agnew disliked the pert minx, and suspected her of an ambition to steal handbags; she also hated Black Barty; but the one she really dreaded was the half-gipsy Betsy, who when she was going to start a fight didn't give warning of it by screeching and screaming, as the whole-gipsies did: she simply seized the nearest woman by the nearest protuberant part and wrung it like a dishcloth, relying on silence and surprise.

Black Barty's caravan now drew level with Grannie's, overtook it, and nearly caught up with Wisdom's; Wisdom, hearing Grannie's yells, looked back over his shoulder and saw what was happening. He promptly pulled out into the middle of the road.

"Oh dear," said Tommy Tomkins mildly. "I do hope they're not going to *start* the hop-picking with an accident and a fight!"

But Barty was too quick for Wisdom. He'd pulled his pony right over to the verge. For a moment the caravans were level, and there were some seconds of wild confusion as Wisdom shouted abuse at Barty, Barty shouted back, Marta tried to seize the bridle of Barty's pony, Barty viciously flicked his whip at her, Wisdom roared like an angry bull, and all the Wisdom children set up a concerted howl which made Tommy Tomkins think of the Death Song of the wolves in the *Jungle Book.*

Then the green caravan was in front. A bucket, knocked off Wisdom's caravan, clattered onto the road and bowled along. Marta, magnificent in her rage, tore in pursuit of Barty, as if she would take vengeance single-handed, but Wisdom called her back. Crestfallen, she retrieved the bucket. Sue, who had jumped down off the shaft, ran back a few paces, shouted a rude word at her, and put out her tongue.

Tommy Tomkins turned to Mrs. Agnew.

"Looks as if we've all got a turbulent month before us," he said. Suddenly he began to laugh, in his funny high cackle, and Mrs. Agnew looked at him in surprise.

"I was just wondering," he said, "what my young brother George is going to make of it all. He leads rather a sheltered life, I fancy. . . . Good morning, Mrs. Agnew."

He went out, and Mrs. Agnew watched him start his old car with the handle; the battery was run down as usual. It started at last with a noise like a pneumatic drill, and Mr. Tomkins drove away. Mrs. Agnew bustled into her kitchen, searched for and found an old baking-dish, went out into the garden, prodded about with a trowel, filled the baking-dish with soil, and bore it up to her bedroom. Black Barty was about; there was no time to lose! So she hurried back to the bar, picked up Moggie, and bore him upstairs. She put him in her bedroom, fetched him a wing of chicken from the larder to make up for his confinement, admonished him: "There you stay, Moggie, till it's *safe*," closed the door and locked it. She breathed a sigh of relief. The gipsies were back, the storm was blowing up, but her vessel would weather it; come hell and high water, the Royal Victoria was prepared!

## 8

Chugging home, Tommy tried to picture his brother George among the gipsies at hop-picking: George for example confronted by Black Barty at one of those moments of sombre reflection when Black Barty was sharpening his knife and particularising how and where he would employ it upon the man who had shot out his eye; or George being kissed by Mrs. Wisdom Lee, who kissed everybody when she'd had a pint or two of cider; or George twitching his long thin nose at the smell of Grannie Lee's pipe. Then he thought of the gaggle of Welsh girls from Pontypridd whose lilting talk as they picked the hops sounded like a twittering of finches; but if George should go near enough to hear what they were saying so prettily, oh my hat, thought Tommy, it would turn even a student of social biology pale! That was the name George used for his horrible hobby, which had resulted in a paper called *Sexual Promiscuity in Relation to the Drink Trade*. Needless to say he knew little about either. In his working hours he was a high-up official at the Ministry of Education. When Tommy had visited him there, to beg for a loan, he had found him sitting in a large office, which had a carpet appropriate to his rank, at a terribly tidy desk upon which a single, neatly drawn graph lay exactly half-way between the "In" and the "Out" trays. The graph was something to do with School Places, and that meant children, but they hardly ever used the word "children" at the Ministry. In the hopyards George would encounter some real ones, by no means School Places, but yelling swearing fighting biting eye-gouging imps of hell. Tommy spurred his imagination across a tall fence of improbability and saw George in their company: trying to stop their gobs with the boiled sweets which he always carried in a paper bag. He thought they were good for his duodenal.

These boiled sweets, tiger-striped stickjaws, had long ago laid the foundation of the Tomkins family fortune, of which Tommy had squandered his portion though George still clung to his, for though he affected to despise money he would neither spend it nor give it away. In the prosperous eighteen-sixties a serious-minded young Tomkins had left his native Herefordshire to seek betterment in the growing city of Birmingham. There he had married a serious-minded wife, of the Quaker persuasion, who disapproved of her husband's only bad habit, which was smoking. She was handy in the kitchen, so she compounded boiled sweets to wean him from his pipe. They were extremely wholesome, as indeed was everything about her—her round face, of which Tommy had seen several portraits, was as wholesome as a suet pudding. The sweets became popular among her friends, to whom she gave away half-pounds now and then, especially if she suspected their husbands of smoking or Taking a Glass. But the Tomkinses were poor, even in that city of soaring profits and ever-multiplying machines, and before long she began to sell the sweets, at a ha'penny an ounce, saving up the money to give her children a schooling. She soon found it an advantage to install a little still in her kitchen, where she made from fresh herbs the peppermint flavouring. The aromatic fumes, however, caused everything in the kitchen to taste of peppermint, whether treacle tart or sausage and mash or the roast beef at Sunday dinner. She asked her husband to build her an outhouse in the back yard. He thankfully did so, out of packing cases, and the Tomkins' Model Factory went into production.

Of course it was not described as a model factory then. It was Tomkins the second who introduced white coats for the workers, hand inspections twice a day, nailbrushes provided in the washplace, and Temperance tracts dished out with the Christmas pay-packets. During the reign of Tomkins III the factory was rebuilt and extended; it covered seven acres by 1910. Its owner became Lord Mayor, and would have been knighted for his good works if he had not believed that Honours were corrupting. He turned his limited company into a trust for the benefit of his employees; otherwise he might have died a millionaire, and he priggishly disapproved of millionaires. His benefactions, however, by no means impoverished him, for he was one of those philanthropists who seem always to strain the quality of mercy through a very fine-meshed sieve, so he cut up for a hundred and fifty thousand, of which Tommy and George inherited equal shares. George put his into safe investments (the mortgage on Tommy's farm was so well secured that it was hardly a lapse from this principle) and studied for a while at the London School of Economics before he became a Civil Servant. Meanwhile Tommy spent his money lavishly on all the indulgences which his forebears had deplored, but he still had forty thousand left when the whim took him to return to his native countryside. He decided to grow hops as a deliberate act of filial impiety; his father when he bought a large country estate had caused his tenants to grub up their hopyards, because of his Temperance Principles. He had compensated them on a miserable scale, which he justified with the argument that by sharing in the sacrifice they would entitle themselves to a share of the heavenly reward. He was a sanctimonious old humbug, and Tommy had no respect for his memory. It was easy enough to find a hop-farm for sale during the bad times of the early 'thirties. Tommy went touring in Herefordshire, looking for a suitable place; and he chose one in the end chiefly because its address amused him: The Hope, Weston Beggard.

He was approaching the crossroads now, and the signpost which though he had bumped it last Saturday night still pointed its arms in the general direction of SOLLARSHILL, STOKE EDITH, WESTON BEGGARD AND THE HOPE. A telegraph-pole stood there, and like most of the poles in the hop-country at this time of year it was fantasticated with the green bines. Some random plant had rampaged over the hedge, swung out perhaps on a friendly breeze, wrapped itself round the pole, and gone up it like Jack's beanstalk. It clung tight, and the green heart-shaped leaves, so fittingly resembling the leaves of the vine, hung in beautiful contrast against the black pole. What lively herbs these hops were! He could swear this bine hadn't been half-way up the pole three weeks ago; now it had reached the top. The rate of climb, in the hopyards when the plants were growing well, was two feet in a week; three inches in a night sometimes in hot moist weather. They climbed clockwise, the opposite way to most plants, following the sun. They were obstinately determined about this. Just after the war Tommy had employed some German prisoners to start the hops—that is to say, to train the little shoots up the strings. He knew no German, and the prisoners knew no English, so his careful instructions had been misunderstood: the Germans had twined all the hops the wrong way. But during the night each one had most skilfully untwined itself. They were spirited things, ramping, puissant, passionate things—what was that phrase of Suzette's? They had *la rage au corps*. She had used it of Marianne, when Marianne was seventeen, going to her first village dances, slipping out of the house secretly after dinner, coming back late from trips on the pillions of young men's motor-bikes. "We must look out, Tommy!" Suzette had said. "*Elle a la rage au corps!*" But it still hurt Tommy to think of Suzette, especially at hop-picking time; for she had loved the hops as he loved them, because they were like the vines. One of his hopyards was hers especially. He'd planted it soon after they were married, and called it "Houblonnière Suzette." As he began to turn the corner, he could see this hopyard as it were hanging on the side of the hill, a thick foam of green, and it suddenly struck him that this was perhaps the last season he would look upon it. George meant business, since he was coming down specially from London: "to inspect the place," he'd said. He hadn't actually used the phrase "sell up"; but he'd talked of "foreclosing on the mortgage" in his precise Civil Service way. The mortgage was for twelve thousand pounds; and Tommy knew that even when the hops were picked and sold he hadn't a chance of raising as much as that. Would George, who didn't need the money, really carry out his threat? He was such a cold fish, he might. Yes, he might do it, more in sorrow than in anger, for a principle. And then—?

There was a screech of brakes. Tommy was aware of a cloud of white dust as John Sollars's Bristol did a dry skid towards him. Then came the crash, and the steering wheel seemed to be plucked out of his hands and did half a turn on its own. His car swung round and bashed into the telegraph-pole. Glass tinkled from a broken headlamp. The Bristol skidded to rest half-way over the crossroads. John Sollars jumped out and began walking rapidly round it. Tommy discovered that his door was jammed, but he was able to get out of the other one. He went over to John Sollars.

"Bloody fool," said John Sollars. "Look at that scratch; and she's practically new."

It was the third Bristol John had had in six years. Apparently it paid him to buy expensive cars: something to do with depreciation and the income tax. It seemed to Tommy that when you were very rich you lived by a paradox: the more you spent the richer you became. John Sollars didn't enjoy motoring but he liked to get quickly from place to place. This car would do a hundred miles an hour. He drove as he lived, arrogantly.

Apparently the Bristol's bumper had hit the offside of Tommy's car and cowcatcher-fashion had thrown the poor old contraption aside in disdain. The scratch on the Bristol seemed a very small one; but John Sollars said:

"It'll mean a new panel, and cost the earth. Still, I suppose you're insured."

"Third party," said Tommy, wondering whether he still owed for the premium.

"Hardly pay you to insure your old rattletrap comprehensive." John strode across to it. He was always a bit lame, arthritis or something, but you couldn't describe his walk by any other term than striding. Tim moved in the same way; it was part of the family arrogance. The Sollarses walked as if they owned the whole blessed earth instead of a few hundred acres of it.

"Headlamp, wing crumpled—or was it like that before? Front members twisted. Blacksmith's job. Nothing that matters."

Tommy thought it was just like John Sollars to think it didn't matter about *his* car, which was a wreck anyhow but the only one he had or was likely to have, while making a great fuss about a little scratch on the Bristol, though he'd got a second car in his garage and Tim also had his M.G. John was now inspecting the old car, walking round it but keeping his distance, rather as he'd look at a beast which he suspected of having foot-and-mouth disease.

"How the hell can you see out of that windscreen?"

"I can't, much. I poke my head round it."

"Well, you weren't poking your head round it when you came up to the crossroads. You were looking up at the telegraph-pole. I've just been to your place," said John Sollars.

"Oh yes?"

"Rate for the pickers: one and two a bushel. I told your girl. We've all agreed to it."

"Except the hop-pickers," said Tommy. He didn't want to argue; he simply stated the fact. But John Sollars fairly snapped at him.

"They must take it or leave it."

"It's not much."

"The hops are thick and picking will be easy. And for once in a way things are in our favour. There are too many pickers, and quite a lot of the growers have gone in for machines. Hate the damn' things myself." He gave Tommy a glance to remind him of his old folly, the monstrosity that looked like Meccano, the endless belt that always broke, the hairpins. And yet, thought Tommy without resentment, it was the very *first* machine. Nowadays they worked, and you could buy them for about five thousand pounds; and of course they didn't use hairpins, but the little bent wires were very like hairpins, that clawed off the hops.

John Sollars went on:

"We don't have to go begging for pickers any longer. They come eating out of our hands. Anyhow, we've settled it: and one and tuppence it is. We've got to hang together."

"Well, I suppose so," said Tommy unhappily.

Then John Sollars began about the fence in the river meadow. Tommy remembered that it was still on his list of "Things to Do To-morrow." Indeed he'd been about to go down and have a look at it after breakfast this morning, but when the postman came, and there was George's threatening letter, and the one from the bank, it had slipped out of his mind.

"Run a bit of wire along it, please," said John Sollars crisply. "Don't want those beasts of yours getting through. Uneven-looking bunch. Where on earth did you buy 'em?"

"Leominster, last Friday." Tommy knew he'd had a bad deal. He was hopeless at chipping with dealers. They had one particular trick which always defeated him. At a critical point in the argument they would suddenly beam at him, say: "Done?" and hold out a beefsteak of a hand. Even though he shook his head the hand remained outstretched, and the word was repeated but this time without the question mark. He always took the hand. The dealer at Leominster was a Welshman from the Radnor border. "A pleasure it is, Mr. Tomkins, to deal with a man who knows a good beast." But of course Tommy didn't. The yearlings had looked quite big in the market; they shrank when he turned them into his meadows. He knew they were scruffy; but he thought they'd thrive on the good aftermath, after being pastured on the high bleak hills.

"It always pays to buy the best," John Sollars said; and of course it was true, but it presupposed that you could afford the best. He gave a last glance at Tommy's car, nodded, said: "Let your insurance know," and strode away. For a moment Tommy wished he were like John Sollars, knowing exactly what he wanted and exactly how to get it, never hesitating, never compromising, driving through life as it were in a Bristol, making everybody get out of the way. Then it occurred to him that if you were like that everybody must look the same to you; you'd see only the least interesting aspect of them: the backsides of their personalities as they scurried out of the way. And that would be dull.

So perhaps it was better to look people in the eyes, and to try to find out or at any rate to speculate what was going on in that mysterious place behind the eyes: to know, for example, that John Sollars wanted the Hope, and exactly why he wanted it—to know he'd have got it by now, if one had accepted that deceptively casual offer of a mortgage long ago, and if he'd got it he'd have bulldozed all the little spinneys and rough corners that one loved best, on the chance they might harbour the last few rabbits that had survived myxomatosis. It was fun to know all this and yet at the same time to recognise the virtues of John Sollars, his love of good land, his sense of dedication to it.

Well, we are as we are, thought Tommy Tomkins; and he started his car, pushing it back from the telegraph-pole first to make room for the handle to go in. He was rather surprised to find that it would go, despite the bent front member and a broken spring. It wobbled a bit, but then it always wobbled. Six months ago he'd taken it into a garage and the garageman had been filled with wonder at a small bracket-fungus which was growing on one of the wooden uprights that framed the door on the driver's side. The car had a fabric body, but of course in places the fabric had come off, and upon this bit of bare wood the fungus had taken root and grown outwards, as if it were on a tree. That was because the car was kept in an open barn which the rain blew into. There was a garage at the Hope, but Tommy used it as a workshop and it was filled with bits and pieces of his unfinished inventions, including the endless belt of the hop-picking machine, prickly as a hedgehog with ten thousand hairpins.

"Shall I chop it off?" the garageman had said; but Tommy wouldn't let him. "I dare say mine is the only car in the world that has a fungus growing on it. Let's keep *that* distinction at least."

The garageman had greased the car and tried to cure the wobble of the front wheels.

"There's not much we can do, sir. Your kingpins and bushes are worn something awful."

Tommy grimaced at the memory of this as he wobbled up the rough hill to the Hope and the steering wheel jumped about in his hands. Without self-pity he repeated to himself: "My kingpins and bushes are worn something awful." It was certainly true, that was the condition they had come to, the kingpins and bushes of his life.

## 9

Marianne came towards the car as Tommy pulled up in the yard, and for a fraction of a second he had an extraordinary feeling that he was seeing his wife again. He'd had it several times during the last few days, since Marianne had come home; he couldn't remember it happening before she went away. It alarmed him a little, and he supposed it was something to do with getting old, or drinking too much, perhaps. She came out of the back door in an apron; the wind which always prowled round the farmhouse on the top of the hill fluttered the apron and blew her hair over her face, and she pushed it away with a gesture which he half-remembered. Then she saw what had happened to the front of the car, and pointed. Her mouth made an O of alarm or surprise.

"You all right?"

"Yes, but I hit old Sollars's Bristol."

"Who won?"

She laughed, and as she did so she put her hands on her hips, which was perhaps the cause of the illusion; English girls didn't do it as a rule. She threw back her head, and she was Suzette then, standing in front of the château in Bordeaux, as he had first seen Suzette when he was touring the vineyards.

The queer feeling ran swift as an electric impulse across his mind; zip, and it was gone. Tommy slowly climbed out of the car.

"His precious Bristol got a bit of a scratch."

"Serve his precious Bristol right. He's been up here."

"I know."

"He leaned on our gate." Even that had seemed arrogant. You leaned on your own gate, an act of possession; you stood before other people's. She went on:

"He looked me up and down as if—"

"As if what?"

"Oh nothing." She gave one of her mother's shrugs. It had been a man's look of academic speculation, and it had annoyed her.

"Then he said, 'Tell your father the rate for the pickers is one and two this year.' Who's he to give us orders?"

"The big fellows fix it between them. We're only tiddlers."

"I don't like him. . . . Look, I've got something cooking," she said, and they went towards the house.

"Well, you held the fort?" he said. It was a joke between them. His was a very precarious citadel.

"A fertiliser man came. I don't think he wanted to sell anything."

"No, he wanted his cheque."

She squeezed his arm.

"It'll be all right when we've got the hops in." They'd been saying that ever since she came home.

Then he told her about George. She ran into the kitchen and began to stir something in a saucepan. "The old so-and-so!" she cried. She could never keep still when she was excited or angry. She swung round, with the saucepan in one hand and the spoon in the other; she waved them both; for the moment she was all French.

"He's coming the day after to-morrow? To stay?"

"Yes. I must remember to meet him at the station."

"In the old car." She came towards Tommy jigging up and down. "Don't have it mended. Just as it is! Hurray! And leave all that woolly white stuff that's growing out of the seat—bugs in it I wouldn't be surprised. There's a broken spring where the passenger sits. It'll stick into his bottom to remind him we're broke. Bet his bum's as skinny as Praisegod Barebones'!" She ran back to the cooker. "The old screwnose! I'll poison him if you like, with toadstools." Now she was pouring the contents of the saucepan into a baking-dish. "I saw a Death Cap this morning, up at the corner by the wood. That'll fix him. And there were a lot of evil orange ones with speckles. But I found some mushrooms too." She turned round and gave Tommy one of her wicked little grins.

"They'll taste extra sweet. Stolen."

"Over the boundary hedge?"

"Worse. Right at the top of old Sollars's slope. What's more he saw me. He was snooping round with a gun. When he came here he asked me what I'd been doing. I said I always went a five-mile walk before breakfast. I don't think he guessed about the mushrooms."

"You shouldn't have done it," Tommy said.

"I know. But I was suddenly tempted." She turned away, and he sensed, but didn't see, the little grin this time.

"I am sometimes, you know."

She began to arrange the mushrooms in the baking-dish and sprinkled chopped parsley over them. "Cider instead of white wine," she said, "and we haven't got any anchovies, but just the garlic will do." There was an evocative smell, and Tommy went to the window and stared out at the untidy lawn, and the white turkeys strutting on it, and the rose-bed all weedy, with big white convolvuluses climbing up and putting out their flowers where the roses should have been. He didn't dare look round at Marianne, for fear he should see not Marianne but Suzette standing there, and cooking *champignons à la Provençale.* He didn't want anything to eat, though he knew he'd have to pretend to like the mushrooms which Marianne had cooked the way she'd learned from her mother. He wanted a drink, with a sheer desperation which he recognised, but there was nothing in the house except cider. It was one of those moments when he felt something was going to snap in him. Then a lucky thing happened. There was a loud clatter in the yard, and round the corner by the cow-house came the green caravan. Black Barty pulled up his pony with the usual jerk, and then two more caravans drew up behind Black Barty's; children chattering like monkeys swarmed out. They belonged to the two Butler families, and were the advance guard of the little tribe that was called Black Barty's gang. Marianne rushed to the window beside Tommy. "That's Black Barty, isn't it?" She put her hand on his shoulder and jumped up and down to get a view of the caravans. "Hurray, the gipsies again!" It was two seasons since she'd seen them.

"But don't call them gipsies," Tommy said.

"Oh no, of course." She was remembering now. "It's Wisdom's lot that are angry when they're called travellers, and Black Barty's that are angry when they're called gipsies." The reason for this curious distinction was that Black Barty had married a half-gipsy. In his view this made him superior: a traveller. Wisdom made the opposite boast, of racial purity. It was important not to forget this.

"They'll want cider," said Tommy. "We'll have to give them cider. Then I'll show them down to the meadows." Thus he would escape from Suzette, the *champignons,* the foolishness of going down to the cellar, where he knew there were only empty bottles, on the chance which didn't exist of finding a half-full one.

"They'll ask about the rate for the picking," he said. "If we tell them to-day we may lose them; they'll try everywhere else, and then when they come back to us perhaps the weather will have broken, and we'll be late starting."

"Must we really stick to one and two?" said Marianne.

"Well, it's a kind of gentleman's agreement."

"Is it fair?"

"I shouldn't think so."

"Let's pick with them to-morrow," she said, "and see."

## 10

It was one of those Garden of Eden mornings when everything is made new; the John Martin picture came to life in Tommy's hopyards. There had been the same heavy mist as yesterday, but it rolled away down the hill, and the sudden sharp sunlight defined each hop-leaf separately, etching them lobe by lobe as they hung down from the strings. The sprays of hops most delicately green looked as if they had been fashioned that very instant. A wood pigeon puffy and huge flapped out of the shelterbelt and as it flew past Marianne with the sun on it, iridescent in violet and green, she felt as if it were the first wood pigeon in the world. She found a furry caterpillar on a hop-leaf, bright yellow with white tufts on its back like shaving-brushes. When she was a child she used to collect these hop-dogs, as they called them, and they would spin up their cocoons in a cardboard box and hatch out into soft grey tussock-moths next spring. But now it was as if she had never seen a hop-dog before, and she perched the quaint thing on her finger and ran with it to show her father.

Tommy had carried one of the bins, which were bags of sacking stretched on a frame of withy-poles, to a part of the field well away from the pickers. He was full of early morning enthusiasm, he was going to pick with Marianne and see how many bushels they got in half a day; thus they would find out if the rate of one and tuppence was fair. They stood at opposite sides of the bin and picked like mad. The sun crept up and warmed them. The trick came back into Marianne's fingers and she found that she could pick without looking; this gave her the chance to stare about her, still wondering at the world in which each thing that grew or flew seemed to spring from a separate act of creation, this moment finished. Even her father was new-made this morning, quaint as the hop-dog, delighted in his absurdity; he was wearing for some inexplicable reason an old straw hat with a cricket-ribbon round it which must have belonged to *his* father. He'd already been the round of the pickers, shaking hands with them all, welcoming them back, rather like an old-fashioned host greeting the guests at a garden-party. Old Sollars wouldn't do that, Marianne thought; he'd stride round with a curt nod here and there. The pickers would respect old Sollars, she knew, and they didn't respect Tommy in the least but they loved him. It was better to be loved than respected, perhaps. She laughed at him suddenly across the hop-bin, and he said, "My hat, Marianne, I believe you're glad to be back." And she was glad; but she couldn't have explained to him why she had come home. London had been fun and it had been foolish, it had been grubby and it had been gay. She wasn't repentant about any of it, except possibly about the panic, the silly unreasoning schoolgirl panic that three years ago had sent her fleeing there. She could look back on that with a rueful smile; otherwise she was sorry for nothing.

It was just ten days ago that she'd decided the party was over. She was walking back to her bed-sitter behind Knightsbridge, because it was too late for a taxi even in town. It was so late that the dawn, or what passed for dawn in London, was coming up over the jagged black housetops. An episode had finished; she had a dry mouth and a bit of a headache, and no regrets about the personal episode that was done with; she shrugged it away. She walked beside the Park railings, and heard the incongruous sound of wild duck going over towards the ponds. An old bonfire of dead leaves was smouldering somewhere in the Park, the smell of it tickled her nostrils, and she thought of the gipsy fires under the hedges where the caravans stood. It was almost the end of August! So already the caravans would be on their way, crawling up the passes over the Malvern Hills, through the Wyche cutting, over the British Camp or over Hollybush, and then moving down as the sun rose behind them into that flowing bowl of light, which was how she thought of Herefordshire. As they dipped deeper into the bowl, the earth would gradually become redder, the grass greener, the stubbles more golden, until at last they came to the hopyards where the light was almost a jungly light and where the scales dropped from your eyes so that you saw the world as Adam and Eve saw it!

That morning she had tried to ring up Tommy, but of course he was cut off, so she had simply caught the next train. He had said, most typically and absurdly, "To think that you should turn up on the *one day* when there's not a bottle in the house to celebrate with!" He had sorted through the empties in the cellar, *dum spiro spero*, but of course it wasn't any use. So they'd gone down to the Royal Victoria, and leaned on the counter and stroked the big cat, and then they'd walked in the hopyards, and it was almost as if she'd never been away.

She had the same feeling now, as the curious dreaminess of the hop-picking began to possess her. If time existed at all it was measured by the volume of hops in the bin; an inverted hourglass, a pale green pyramid that grew very slowly as you flip-flip-flipped along the bines with your finger and thumb, and the bottles fell into the bin in a steady trickle. Sun and speckled shade dappled the red earth, there was a hot hum all round you, hover-flies darted into your vision, hung there for a second, vanished. You heard as in a dream the voice of the busheller, *One, two, three, four,* as he dipped his bushel basket into somebody's bin, counting aloud each time as he filled it. He tipped the hops out of his basket into one of the big hessian sacks, and the total of basketfuls was written on a card and initialled by the picker. This busheller, who was called Jake, had a voice like a corncrake, and as he wandered from bin to bin his cries came now from one part of the field, now from another, as a corncrake's do in the mowing-grass. "Three, four, five," he rasped. A wood pigeon cooed drowsily. Lots of tractors murmured in other hopyards to the south and to the west. Close at hand the insect hum rose and fell in a slumbrous rhythm. The sunlight grew stronger and slanting through the hop-curtains made the whole world seem green. Marianne became for a little while a green thought in a green shade. Thus fishes, floating with sinuous ease among the tremulous waterweed; thus the little deer that flit down forest paths! It was a delicious feeling.

Tommy said suddenly:

"Our tractor's going very badly."

She could hear the engine spluttering as it went round with the trailer to collect the full sacks of hops and take them up to the kiln. She glanced at her father, and nearly giggled, because she realised that like a little boy he'd got tired of hop-picking and was cunningly formulating an excuse to go down to the pub. He bustled off to fiddle with the tractor. Then he came back, very hot with his straw hat on the back of his head, to say he hadn't got a spanner. He went up to the house to look for a spanner. Then he returned, as she'd known he would, to tell her he couldn't find the right one, and he would have to borrow one from the garage in the village. He bustled off with a great affectation of busyness: "Beastly jolly rotten nuisance, *would* happen, just as we were settling down to the job." Of course this didn't deceive Marianne; probably it wasn't meant to. It was a gambit in his awful game. He was so absurd, so impossible, in a way he was so helpless, that she caught herself wondering why her mother had married him, and loved him, and been happy with him, and lent him the last of her own money to launch some foolish scheme he had for growing cricket-bat willows on the banks of the Wye. It had failed like all the other schemes, the Hop Machine Scheme, the Applejack Scheme, the great Melon Scheme when he had decided it would be profitable to grow a thousand melons under cloches. As soon as the flowers appeared they had to be mated; male and female created He them. Marianne remembered how day after day, when she was fourteen, she had got up early with her mother and they had crawled along the rows, each with a little camel's hair brush, pollenating the melon flowers. The fruits had duly appeared, and grown until they were the size of ping-pong balls, and then some mould or fungus had attacked them, and they had begun to fall off. In the end there were only about two dozen cantaloups out of all the thousands, and since they weren't worth selling Tommy had told Marianne she could have them as a reward for performing the marriage ceremony. She'd taken a knife into the garden, and cut thick pink slices, and gnawed deep into them until the two ends of the slices were touching her ears: like a pickaninny in a picture book her mother had, *Temps Passé en Martinique*.

She watched Tommy go off, stepping with a kind of mock briskness like somebody in one of those old silent films—short legs in the baggy grey trousers, jerky quick paces, a bit like Charlie Chaplin himself. How on earth, Marianne wondered, had he contrived to command even a platoon of infantry, in that first faraway war, and in the second one how had he managed to look after himself, let alone elude the Germans, when he was dropped in France to serve with the Maquis? The thought of Tommy dangling from a parachute made Marianne smile. Compassion for him filled her, and she felt very wise.

It was no fun picking on her own, so she wandered about round the hopyard and added a small tribute of hops to each of the other bins in turn. She picked with the family from Oldbury, with the Welsh party from Pontypridd, with Black

Barty's gang. All the time she felt as if she were stepping rather gingerly back across the years: a little bit farther, and she would never have been away! She didn't understand much of what the Oldbury people said to her, but then she had never been able to understand them. Their speech was heavy and laborious and the sentences thudded dully like lumps of wet clay falling into a deep trench. "Yow'm back agun," they said. "Yow'm lukk'n 'n fine fettle. Weerst bin?" They had pale children, hollow-eyed and peaky, for they lived for eleven months of the year beneath the sable wing of smoke that spread out wide from Birmingham. Already the children were beginning to catch the unaccustomed sun, and a four-year-old was crying because she had a raw patch on the back of her neck. Fat Mrs. Towner, the grandmother of this lot, who was in shape rather like a toad, waddled off to the village store to buy some sunburn lotion. All this had happened before.

The Welsh were singing already. They always sang when they were picking, little short snatches as the birds sing, and in the intervals between the snatches the girls talked about their boys in quick chirruping whispers, with exclamations and giggles.

"Evan Jones took you to the mountain!"

"It was only a little way up."

"Now mind what you are say-ing!"

"After Chapel it was."

"Better the day better the deed!"

There was one girl, Dolly, who didn't join in the chatter. She leaned over the bin, picking with automatic fingers, and after a while she said suddenly: "Strange I do feel," and went and sat in the shade close to the hop-row. The other girls glanced at each other, and one whispered to Marianne: "Pregnant she is."

That, too, had happened before.

And there was Mr. Roberts coughing. He was an old man, he must be nearly eighty now, though he didn't look any different from how he had looked three years ago. He had one of those proud, beautiful, hawklike faces which old Welsh and sometimes old Jews have, a tired face and wise-looking as the eagle cock that blinks and blinks. He had dull blue marks speckling his forehead and across the bridge of his nose, and he'd worked in the pit from fifteen to sixty, when the pneumokoniosis had got so bad that he couldn't work any more. He used to tell Marianne (it was all coming back to her!) about the old days when he left home at five o'clock in the morning, walked five miles by road and two miles under the earth to the coal-face, hewed for eight hours, and walked back: six days a week for thirty shillings. He had told her how a roof-fall had killed his mate beside him, and how out of their week's pittance twenty miners had collected the sum of five pounds to give him a "proper good funeral." Not that Mr. Roberts held with the pomp of funerals, save as a demonstration perhaps that a dead miner was as good as a dead lord; for he had read Shaw and Wells in cheap editions which he'd bought, heaven knew how, out of his weekly thirty shillings. He was strong in his disbelief of the Bible, all parsons' sermonisings, the popular press, and the windy words of politicians; but he had one great shining hero, who was Keir Hardie.

Marianne watched him picking the hops with beautiful long fingers, which had the indigo marks on them almost as if they'd been tattooed, and she thought of all the thousands of tons of coal those fingers had got out of the dangerous darkness, and she loved this grave old man, whose occasional brief smile was like a saint's when he suddenly looked up from the bin and saw her opposite him and smiled. But most of the time he was coughing: a very quiet controlled cough, but brittle, as if it came out of lungs of stone.

Black Barty's gang was brewing tea when Marianne got to them. She took a chipped cup from Black Barty's wife, and she smelt the hop-smell on her sticky hand as she drank it, the smell she was going to live with for a month. She glanced at her hand and saw the stain between the forefinger and thumb, the nail-varnish cracking and coming off, and under the nails the yellow powdery stuff like pollen which shook off the hops and was called the Gold by the pickers; the experts called it lupulin, and it was supposed to contain the active principle of the hops, which made beer taste bitter. The particular sort of hops which Tommy grew were called Fuggles and Marianne recollected the odd name with delight. Nothing was forgotten; and when Jake came round with his bushel basket she could have predicted exactly what Black Barty's Betsy was going to say.

"That there bushel basket's too big, Missie. Truth it is. 'Tis not a fair basket. My Barty was saying—"

They always, as a matter of principle, argued about the size of the basket though of course it was a standard size. Marianne laughed.

"I expect it's the same basket as last year."

"Now you wasn't here last year, Missie," said Betsy, with a shrewd glance at her. "Nor the year before you wasn't. I minds just when you left home, it was the hop-picking before that. I minds you standing by me just where you're standing now, and we was saying—"

Black Barty lounged up and Betsy broke off suddenly. She gave Marianne a sidelong glance; then she bent down to pick up another hop-bine from the heap on the ground beside her. Her deft brown fingers flicked along it. She hummed to herself.

Black Barty said wheedlingly:

"What do you think the rate will be, Missie? One and six? Sure to be one and six. The hops pick terrible hard."

"They're a good crop, Barty. They pick easy."

Black Barty fixed her gloomily with his one eye.

"Eight bushels in four hours between five of us. That ain't easy picking, Missie."

Of course there weren't five of them really. There was Betsy, and there was Black Barty who was deliberately going slow as the gipsies always did on the first day, so that the small quantity they had picked might help them to argue that the job was profitless; then there was the girl Sue, who spent much of her time fiddling with her handbag and looking at her face in the mirror on the flap of it; and there were two boys who had a fitcher ferret which they kept in their coat-pockets but released every now and then for the fun of chasing and retrieving it when it ran away.

They now dropped this ferret into the bin and it burrowed down among the hops. They couldn't reach it, so they poked it out with sticks. The quick slinky creature then ran along the edge of the bin towards Marianne, and the boys said: "Stroke it, Missie. It likes being stroked."

They watched her in wicked anticipation.

"No thanks. I value my fingers."

"He never bites nothing except to eat."

"Well, I don't want him eating me."

She found another hop-dog on a spray and gave it to the older boy to keep him quiet. He had an old-young face, very gentle-looking and exquisite with its slightly slanting eyes. He regarded the caterpillar curiously for a while, and then with thoughtful deliberation squashed it between his finger and thumb.

Black Barty suddenly turned and addressed his tribe, the Butlers and their relations, who were picking at an adjacent bin. Alf Butler was his brother-in-law, having married Black Liz.

"We shall be all right," Barty shouted. "Missie says she thinks the rate will be one and six, maybe more."

"I didn't!" But he ignored her, and went on:

"We shall be all right! We'll get paid fair! Mr. Tomkins is always a good boss!"

Marianne was aware of the purpose of this public announcement. Black Barty had seen Tommy go off and he had guessed where he was going, for the gipsies always guessed things like that. When Tommy came back, in a state he hoped of reckless generosity, Black Barty would immediately ask him to fix the rate; and as a kind of reinforcement for his bargaining he had made sure that the whole of the Butler family would chorus loudly: "Missie said we was going to get one and sixpence."

Sue looked up from her mirror and asked:

"What's the time, Missie?"

The gipsies asked this question about twenty times a day.

They didn't use watches but they could tell the time precisely by the sun. Marianne supposed that when the sun was out they nevertheless went on asking the time out of a habit they got into when the weather was dull. She looked at her wrist-watch and told Sue:

"It's five to one."

Sue yawned, and looked languidly pretty leaning with her elbows on the edge of the bin. Marianne wondered about her, whether she who was as young as Pippa had been aware of the newness of everything when she tumbled out of her caravan this morning. But of course not; her eyes had looked on such mornings ever since she'd peeped out of a shawl slung over Betsy's shoulder. She looked bored now, and was probably dreaming about boys. Marianne smiled across at her and Sue's brown face creased in acknowledgement, as if some zephyr of communion had blown between them.

The summer hum had reached its noonday's peak. It buzzed round Marianne, a chorus of innumerable atomies, and drowsed her senses so that Jake's corncrake-voice chanting out numbers at the bottom of the hopyard sounded like a cry heard in a dream. The Welsh girls three or four rows away sang softly, making the latest crooner's rhyme sound like real poetry and its jazzy tune sound like a hymn. The ferret, driven at last to desperation, nipped one of the gipsy boys; he didn't cry, but sucked a bloody thumb gravely, and Betsy said: "Ferrets is poisonous. Get a dockleaf to draw off the poison." The child went away, and everything was quiet again except the insect hum that throbbed like a pulse. Marianne basked in the greenness, a kind of aquarium light, and let her thoughts swim through it, back to the last hop-picking, when she was eighteen. But she knew she could never quite go back; she could never fit into that skin again. The hop-pickers then had been part of a month-long raree show: not quite real. Betsy had been a kind of harmless witch, Black Barty had been an ogre-ish figure of fun; she wouldn't then have been able to see into his little sly mind and to know that he was thinking: *When Mr. Tomkins comes back he'll have had a few, maybe he'll have had as much as he can carry. That'll be the time to tackle him about the rate for the job.*

And now at this very moment she saw Black Barty's face turning slowly, in the questing fashion of the partially blind, the horrible lidded eye towards her, as he looked up at the lane where his sharp ears had heard the rattle of Tommy's car. She saw Betsy dart a glance at him and Sue take her elbows off the edge of the bin and straighten herself. She had an extraordinary feeling of being wary of them. That was the difference, she thought, between now and three years ago. That was why you could never go back: you had grown too wise.

# 11

Tommy left the car in the yard, spouting like a whale through the radiator-cap; the fan-belt had broken, and she'd boiled all the way up the hill. He walked down through the Home Ground towards Houblonnière Suzette, and hugged to himself a small triumph, which was his achievement in leaving the Royal Victoria before closing-time. He supposed that this extraordinary feat was connected with the homecoming of Marianne: for such a long time there had been nothing to come back for. The knowledge that he would find her in the hopyard made him happy, and this kind of happiness was as rare a thing nowadays as his leaving a pub before it shut.

He got to the stile at the corner of the hopyard and climbed over it and suddenly Black Barty and his gang were all about him, they came like Red Indians ambushing a paleface, Barty and Betsy and Sue and the boys with the ferret, and Black Liz and all the Butler children and a wall-eyed lurcher dog. Last of all Alf Butler clawed his way through the hop-curtain with the hook he had instead of a hand. He and Black Barty always went about together, and they made an odd pair, the one-eyed, the one-handed. At hop-picking Alf twisted the bine round his hook, raised a crooked arm so that the bine hung down, and picked very quickly with his good hand. It was grotesque and rather unpleasant.

Barty took a pace towards Tommy and cried loudly: "You're a good boss and I'll knock down the man as says you ain't."

He glanced about him theatrically, as if he expected a hidden enemy to rise up and accept his challenge. Then he shouted: "Three cheers for Mr. Tomkins!" and all his people raggedly cheered. Quite bewildered, Tommy flickered his eyelids with the nervous twitch which always came into operation when he was surprised or embarrassed. Barty now slunk up to his left side, and Alf to his right, and all the children gathered round. Barty in a hoarse whisper demanded earnestly:

"It's true, ain't it, Mister, what Missie said?"

"What's true?" said Tommy.

"Why, as you're going to pay us one and a tanner, because the picking's harder than last year?"

At this all the Butler children clamoured, "Missie said so," but without much conviction; it was like a crowd-scene in a play that hadn't been properly rehearsed. Tommy, blinking fast, looked from Barty to Alf and back to Barty, recognising their cunning yet seeing something endearing in it, as he would in the cunning of children. It never took more than two or three drinks to imbue him with a catholic and comprehensive love of his fellow-humans, especially of the more disreputable ones. He'd had four whiskies: and he reflected that they had cost him two and threepence each (or they would have done if he hadn't asked Mrs. Agnew to put them on the slate). He felt a twinge of guilt for spending so much when these people had to argue about pennies. He knew the gipsies were play-acting, but in a way that made it all the more pathetic; he thought how disappointed they would be, and he hated to disappoint them, but of course there *had* been a kind of gentleman's agreement with old Sollars to pay no more than one and two. He realised now that he ought to have stuck out against John Sollars; he ought to have told him he wouldn't be a party to any private arrangement the big growers might have made between themselves. But it was too late now.

"One and a tanner," croaked Black Barty in his left ear. "Eighteen pence," breathed Alf Butler in his right.

"Well . . ." he began hesitantly.

"Father!"

Marianne came running down the hop-row. She gave him a grin and a rather obvious wink and said: "Father, I want to talk to you." Then she had him by the arm and was walking him away, while the gipsies stood disconsolate. They were tongue-tied now because their play-acting had been interrupted and none of the performers knew what they were meant to do next. Even Black Barty was flummoxed, and he gave Marianne a malevolent look as she led Tommy away.

"They asked you for one and six—?" she began.

"Yes. They said you said—"

"Of course I didn't. You were just about to promise them—"

"I wasn't."

"You were, you were. I could see it!" She tugged his arm. "You are an old softie." Tommy was suddenly aware that he didn't know this Marianne, the one that had come back from London, so different from the one that had gone away. He found himself asking her:

"What *shall* we pay them? I suppose it ought to be one and two, because of John Sollars."

Over her shoulder incisively she said what John Sollars could do with himself. Tommy blinked. As they walked up the road they overtook Mrs. Towner wearily waddling along it, as she returned from the village with the sunburn lotion. She'd been doing the shopping for the whole of her brood, and the heavy basket weighed her down. Marianne said: "I'll carry that, Mrs. Towner," and took it from her. They went on towards the bin where the Black Country folk were talking in their strange tongue which might have been Stone Age talk.

"I should think you've bought up half the village," Marianne said.

"Nay, dook," said Mrs. Towner, "theer's no more 'n theer than'll kep the kids quiet for a coupla meals; and nobbut a tanner change art'v a quid for it."

Marianne glanced down at the basket. It was true enough: two jars of jam, sugar, bread, marge, tea, bacon, wheatflakes, some sweets, and there was a pound note gone. Three years ago, before Marianne went away, Mrs. Towner would have had five shillings back out of her pound; and that year the rate for the hop-picking had been one and three.

Marianne put down the basket in the shade of the hop-row. The peaky children crowded round Mrs. Towner, clamouring for lollies. Marianne led Tommy on towards the bins where the Welsh were picking.

"We're not going to be bounced into anything by Black Barty," she said. "He's a crook and a cleverbreeches. I don't like him. But we want to be fair, don't we? I've had an idea. Let's ask Mr. Roberts!"

Already she was beckoning to the old miner, and Tommy, still bewildered and delighted by this new Marianne, was content to leave everything to her. He recognised at once the rightness of asking Mr. Roberts, the poetic justice of calling in as arbiter this wise and gentle and so-long-exploited man. Mr. Roberts now came slowly towards them, holding himself very straight—his painful straightness was like a silent protest against the years of cramped toil. He was coughing in his quiet way which produced the merest twitch along the line of his jaw and didn't alter his calm expression at all.

Marianne said:

"Mr. Roberts, we want you to help us to fix the rate for the picking. You've been at it all day and you know how many bushels you and the girls have got. What's fair?"

If he was surprised at being asked he didn't show it. He gave Marianne one of his rare smiles and then lapsed into gravity again. He pondered for quite a long time and his Adam's apple worked up and down like a little piston in his throat as he tried to control his cough for good manners' sake. Watching him, Marianne made another excursion into the past, remembering the fearful awe she had held him in because someone had told her, when she was about twelve, *Mr. Roberts says the Bible isn't true.* She would tiptoe down the hop-row until she was in hearing of the Welsh pickers, and sometimes she would listen to him as he preached against the preachers— "Nothing but dope do they dish out to you, man, to keep you content in the station it has pleased the capitalists to call you!" Yet he was not struck down nor shrivelled by a ball of wildfire; and year after year at the hop-picking he continued in proud defiance of heaven, like Milton's Satan, princely though damned, in the frontispiece of that old *Paradise Lost* on the shelf in the dining-room.

Nobly satanic, he brooded now. Tommy's glance went from him to Marianne, trim, compact, hands on hips, awaiting his verdict. Not far back, Suzette's people had been peasants; Suzette herself had had the peasant's passion for a meticulous bargain, when she went shopping she would never pay a penny less nor a penny more than she believed was right, so that the shopkeepers, not understanding, thought her mean. Tommy fancied that Suzette would have approved of Marianne now; and Suzette's mother, when the old man died and left her the vineyard beside the Gironde, might have laid a dispute before some old wise peasant, trusting his sense of what was precisely fair, just as Marianne was doing at this moment.

At last Mr. Roberts spoke. Without any preliminaries or qualifications but with absolute authority he said:

"One shilling and fourpence would be fair."

Marianne turned to Tommy, but of course there was no need. He nodded and said: "So be it," and wondered what the devil John Sollars would say when he came to hear of it. Mr. Roberts still stood before them in his proud humility, as if waiting to be dismissed, so Marianne put out her hand.

Mr. Roberts took it in his long fingers with the blue marks crisscrossing the knuckles. He smiled again, then turned and walked stiffly back to the bin where the girls were singing.

## 12

Wisdom Lee, in the cool of the evening after the first day's hop-picking, put a halter on the little dun pony and, running beside it, trotted it down to the Royal Victoria. Marta and old Grannie Lee and a horde of children followed him. Wisdom tied the pony up to one of the white posts outside the pub and sent Marta into the hop-pickers' bar to fetch glasses of cider. There were a lot of gipsies in the bar, old Manasseh's tribe who were distantly related to Wisdom, and the Smiths who were cousins of Black Barty; they drifted out one by one and two by two to look at the dun pony. Wisdom slapped its sleek quarters and cried, "Worth twenty pounds a leg, twenty-five pounds a leg, wouldn't sell it for a hundred!" And truly he didn't want to sell it, he had brought it down to the pub only to display it and to enjoy the honour and glory which his possession of it brought him. It was a lovely little pony: the trimmest, the most quick-footed, the cleanest-legged little pony he'd owned in thirty years of horse-dealing. Between the shafts, it seemed to dance along; put a saddle on its back, and you didn't feel as if you were riding, you were borne on air! He had bought it for thirty-three pounds ten after two days of haggling with a farmer up in the Radnor hills; ever since then it had been his great delight, three or four times a day, simply to stare at the dun pony, to stand with his hands in his pockets and look at it, or to run his fingers gently up and down its beautiful fetlocks. He might pretend that he was going to sell it, but that was simply part of the horse-dealing game; in his heart he believed that if he and Marta and all the kids were hungry he would go stealing rather than part with the pony for a hundred pounds. He called it by a Romany name, Malona, which meant lightning. He loved it so much that he crooned the name to himself: Malona, Malona, as he stood admiring it now.

It was in his mind that shortly Black Barty would come to the Royal Victoria. Black Barty would cast covetous eyes on Malona, and he, Wisdom, would gain in stature and authority over Black Barty, by reason of his ownership of the little dun mare.

Sure enough, as Wisdom was pointing out to Manasseh how tidily she stood, the strength of her shoulders, the straightness of her back, Black Barty drove up at a canter in a flimsy high trap which belonged to Alf Butler. Betsy and Sue and several of the Butlers perched on it with their legs dangling over the sides. Black Barty pulled up by heaving so hard on the reins that his pony put its forefeet together and slithered to a stop. Flecks of blood showed in the corner of the pony's mouth.

Barty jumped down, threw the reins to one of the Butler children, and swaggered into the pub. His party followed him and when they came out a minute or two later all the men had pints of beer, Betsy had a stout, and Sue carried a small glass of what looked like gin-and-something. Wisdom saw a motive behind Barty's lordly gesture in buying these expensive drinks; it was designed to impress the other gipsies, Manasseh's lot and the Smiths, it was the first shot in his campaign, his challenge to Wisdom's kingship.

With Betsy and Sue he came across to Wisdom and gave a casual glance at the pony.

"What have you got there?"

"Best little pony *you've* ever set eyes on," said Wisdom. "Look at her, man, *look!*"

Barty made a disparaging noise, clicking his tongue, and looked the pony up and down. He stared hard at each of its legs in turn as if he were seeing spavins, thoropins, splints, sidebones, ringbones, navicular in every one. But Wisdom, watching him narrowly, was sure already that Barty fancied the dun mare, he could sense Barty's envy of him on account of it. This pleased Wisdom, and he felt that it cancelled out any advantage which Barty might have got through buying expensive drinks for his women. The drink which Sue was sipping in such a ladylike fashion was assuredly gin-and-something. It even had a cherry in it. Wisdom's mother, old Grannie Lee, had been staring hard at it, and now she puffed her pipe in Sue's face and muttered to herself:

"Whenever I sees a young chai drinking gin it always makes me wonder."

"Makes you wonder what?" said Black Barty truculently.

"Ha," said Grannie, "they do say it brings on miscarriages."

"Look here, my gel's a good gel and—" Barty stepped forward threateningly and Grannie hissed at him like a cat. Wisdom didn't want a fight on his hands, so he untied the pony and cried loudly: "See her trot, see her trot!" He ran her up and down the road outside the pub, and all the gipsies gathered at the roadside to watch. Just then with a noisy crackle a blue sports car shot round the corner, and the little mare reared up, nearly pulling the halter rope out of Wisdom's hand. The car stopped outside the pub and Tim Sollars came over to Wisdom.

"Sorry I gave her a fright," he said. "I say, that's something like." He ran his eye over the pony, and nodded appreciatively. Wisdom beamed. All the gipsies knew that Master Tim was a horseman. They saw him in the early morning before hop-picking exercising the big chestnut hunter which he rode in point-to-points. He would go down to the river meadows and take it over the jumps which he'd put up there, and once last year he had ridden across to Wisdom's caravan when Marta was cooking, had said, "That smells good," and sat down to breakfast with them, while the children proudly led the chestnut round the field and pretended they were stable boys. Wisdom loved Master Tim, and to show him the pony's paces he trotted it up and down faster than ever. Each time he passed Black Barty's group, Black Barty jumped out and flapped his arms like wings to make the pony shy; but Wisdom let him be, well satisfied because he knew Black Barty coveted the dun pony and was also jealous of him because of his friendship with Tim Sollars.

"She's a beauty," said Tim, as Wisdom came to a stop at last and tied her up to the post. He was puffing badly, and he had a stitch. It told him of his years—forty-eight? fifty? he wasn't sure how many; but he knew he was no longer the strongest of the gipsies and that if it came to a fight again this year he might not be able to stand up to Black Barty for ten minutes or a quarter of an hour.

Black Barty watched his chest heaving, looked hard at Marta, and then turning to Betsy said loudly:

"Womanwhacked, that's what he is."

Sue giggled shrilly, and there was a cackle of laughter from the Smiths. Barty lounged up to Wisdom and said:

"I'll bet you a dollar—"

"Free with your money! You'll bet me what?"

"Bet you a dollar you can't jump her clean, then carry her over your shoulders like you used to!"

This had always been Wisdom's boast, when he'd had a few pints, when he wanted to show off his agility and the strength of his broad shoulders. He was the only gipsy who could do it; long ago in his young pride he had sometimes believed he was the only man in the world who could do it. He would stand a quiet pony in an open space, with one of his children at its head; then he would take a run, and jump over her back; he always reckoned he could clear anything up to fourteen hands, which was four foot eight inches. Then he would turn back and lift up the pony and carry her for ten paces. Almost every year he performed this feat at the gipsy horse fair, which they held on Sundays during the hop-picking in the road outside the Royal Victoria. He had done it last year, and after that he had fought Black Barty and beaten him in the field behind the pub.

"Bet you couldn't do it now. A dollar," said Black Barty.

Wisdom stared hard at the dun. She was thirteen and a

half hands, four feet six from the ground to the withers, two or three inches less where he would jump her, at the lowest part of the back. He could manage four feet six, he thought, even though her back was so broad. But she was well made and with those heavy shoulders she must weigh—what? six hundred, six hundred and fifty pounds? No, he dared not try it. He saw Marta shaking her head at him, Grannie Lee's black boot-button eyes turned towards him, warning him not to try. Then Tim Sollars said:

"Don't be a fool, Wisdom. At your age—"

Wisdom for a moment or two almost hated Tim Sollars: Tim had meant it kindly, but when he said, "*At your age,*" Wisdom knew that he must do this thing or he must creep away, in front of Tim, in front of Marta, in front of them all, go back to the empty caravan alone with his shame, and leave Black Barty to lord it in the hop-pickers' bar. So he cried out to Barty loudly and defiantly: "A dollar? No, a quid!" and even before Barty had nodded agreement he was down on one knee undoing his laces. He took off his boots, and then he said to Barty: "Show me your pound note." Barty grinned, and routed in his pocket, and waved a pound note in front of him. "Show me yours." Then Wisdom remembered that he hadn't got a pound, only ten bob and a few coppers, because he'd spent almost all his savings when he bought the dun mare; but Marta with quick understanding brought out the pound he had given her for the shopping, and now she was waving it furiously a few inches from Barty's nose. Wisdom untied the pony and gave the halter rope to his eldest boy. He took twenty paces back down the road, and shouted to the gipsies to let him have plenty of room. Then, in his stockinged feet, he started his run. He saw the dun pony twitching her ears, saw his quick-witted boy move swiftly in front of her head so that she couldn't see him coming, heard his boy crooning to her, "Malona!" and then just three paces from her he sprang, threw forward his left leg, tucked up his right leg, knew that he was clear of her, heard the gipsies shouting, landed on his toes, staggered, recovered himself, and turned to Black Barty with a grin.

The dun pony was standing quite still! he hadn't touched a hair on her back as he cleared it. Womanwhacked? thought Wisdom in his triumph; but he knew the worst part was to come. He turned swiftly and went towards the mare as, puzzled, she scraped the tarmac with her off-hind hoof and tossed her head at him in quick jerks. He put his hand on her mane, ran his other hand down to her nose, tickled it, sang to her softly, "Malona, Malona," until she was standing quite still. Now he had to be quick. He had to be quick but not sudden, or she would shy and perhaps kick, and the thing he was going to do was dangerous as well as difficult. So he kept his right hand, fully stretched out, holding on to the velvet of her muzzle; smoothly he drew himself back and ducked underneath her; then in one motion he dropped his right arm and clasped her round the knees, spread his left arm around her hocks, and before she knew what was happening he had her off the ground. He felt her strong hind legs straining against his arm, but his head was tucked into her belly and he bore the weight of her across his broad shoulders, as a man might carry a sheep or a dead deer. And so, bent double, he tottered along, one step, two steps, three, four, five. She was heaving against him now, there was an intolerable ache in the muscles of his left arm as she fought to kick herself free, one of her forefeet rapped against his ribs but he hardly felt the blow outside because of the pain within. It seared through him as if his lungs were being torn out, there was a thudding in his head and everything was going dark, he tried to fix his eyes on the tarmac road, on his own foot stepping forward very slowly and somehow unrelated to the rest of his body—that was six paces—the other foot came forward—seven, eight, nine. The thudding in his head became a kind of loud surge, like water breaking over him; he took the tenth pace and then he staggered forward, the mare's hind legs touched the ground, she reared up on them, and in that moment Wisdom pulled out his head from under her belly, clutched wildly in the gathering darkness at where he thought the halter rope was, failed to find it, and through the surging water noise, as he pitched forward, faintly heard her hoofbeats as she galloped away.

When he got up, Marta was standing beside him, and she was holding out Barty's pound, Barty's and her own, one in each hand. The boy had caught the dun pony and was walking her back. Tim Sollars was saying: "Are you all *right,* Wisdom? Are you all *right?*" and Grannie Lee was blowing very hard at her pipe, spouting little puffs of smoke agitatedly between her thin brown lips. There was no sign of Black Barty. Marta said:

"The bastard's gone back into the pub."

"Well, so shall we go into the pub," said Wisdom slowly, and heard his breath rasping between the words. Tim Sollars said: "Come on then, Wisdom, and let me buy you a drink; you deserve one." Wisdom took a pace or two towards the pub and stopped; Tim tried to take his arm but he shook him off. "No need, Master Tim, no need." He was getting his breath back at last, and the pounding in his head was dying away; but he couldn't straighten himself and when at last he got into the bar and all the gipsies turned towards him he was still backbent like an old man.

Tim went up to the bar and ordered drinks, a large whisky for Wisdom, but Marta said she'd have cider and Grannie asked for a drop of rum. Sue was standing close to the bar and Tim said very quietly, "Have a drink, Sue?" as he passed her. She nodded quickly and handed him her glass; but he thought she wouldn't want the gipsies to see her accepting a drink from him, so he passed it to her secretly as he went by with the other glasses, and she took it without acknowledgement in a small brown hand that was still stained and sticky from hop-picking, though she'd painted her fingernails bright red.

When Tim, pushing his way through the crowd, got back to the Lees, Wisdom was leaning forward with his hands on a table and Grannie was rattling off to Marta a long list of herbs which she would need to make a lotion to rub into his back, and another list of herbs which he should take internally. She gave most of the herbs their gipsy names, but the ones Tim could recognise seemed sufficient to speed

Wisdom into his grave. "And a brew of black snails," said Grannie. "He must drink a brew of black snails to make him strong again." Wisdom took his whisky, raised himself painfully, and said: "She's a wonder, Master Tim, is old Mami. Cure anything, never been to a doctor in my life, and never shall so long as old Mami's alive and kicking! She'll cure anything, cure the cancer, cure the tubercolossus, cure the ringworm in a kid's head easy as winking. She can do spells too." Wisdom was always extravagant in praise of Grannie's powers as a white witch, but Tim suspected that he had less faith in her than he pretended, and that he sought to persuade himself of her virtues by repetition of them, as he would do if he were selling a broken-winded pony.

The strong whisky was doing him more good, perhaps, than any brew of black snails. He was able to straighten himself now, and to hobble to the bar for some more drinks. He was determined to spend the pound he'd won from Black Barty, and he bought cider for all Manasseh's people and even for some of the Smiths. The bar was now very full and noisy, stinking with the smoke from Grannie's pipe and lots of other pipes nearly as foul as hers. The gipsies were getting excited and argumentative as they always did after a few drinks. The high voices of their women contrasted with the stolid speech of the Black Country folk; a few of the Welsh pickers had come in too and were singing softly in a corner —the neat pretty girls with comehither looks who picked for Tommy Tomkins. Somebody started playing a mouth-organ, and a young gipsy climbed onto a table and tap-danced to the tune. This brought Mrs. Agnew out from behind the bar, to tell him she'd make him pay for the table if he broke it. "Get down!" she said. "Jigging about up there like a monkey—!" He got down. Mrs. Agnew exercised a strange authority over the gipsies, who were much more frightened of her than they were of the village policeman. "Monkeys, monkeys," she muttered to herself, adjusting the black velvet neckband which in her agitation had gone awry. "Mischievous monkeys!" And that was how she thought of them, as creatures with tricks and half-human attributes, partly tamable but never truly domesticated, destructive and all-devouring, on no account to be trusted within reach or even within sight of the huge cat Moggie now safely confined in her bedroom upstairs.

Old Manasseh said it was his turn to buy a round, and sent two of his grandchildren up to the counter to fetch pints of cider on a tray. Tim watched them, a ten-year-old boy and a still younger girl, sneaking empty glasses off the tables as they wriggled their way between the legs of the grownups. Since Mrs. Agnew charged sixpence on each glass, which was repayable when the glass was returned to her, a small stealthy child with his wits about him could make two or three shillings in this fashion every evening. It was a kind of juvenile apprenticeship to theft; but it could be dangerous. The little girl approached Betsy where she stood at Black Barty's side, noticed a glass on the counter beside her, stretched out an eager hand, and got a clout from Betsy's clenched fist which nearly toppled her over. She did not cry; the gipsy children cried as rarely as they smiled. She continued on her way, holding the tray in one hand and clutching her smarting ear with the other. Then she spotted another empty glass, crept on tiptoe behind its owner's back, and skilfully filched it. Betsy's blow had taught her, not that it was wrong to steal, but that cunning, stealth and swiftness must be cultivated by those ambitious to succeed in stealing.

Tim tried hard to catch the eye of Sue; but she had her back to him and she would not look round. She was watching her father sharpening his knife on the whetstone which he had brought out of his pocket. This meant that Black Barty was getting drunk and would shortly start boasting about what he'd do to the enemy who had shot out his eye. Betsy and Sue seemed absorbed in the knife-sharpening. Tim by craning his neck could just get a glimpse of Sue's sharp face tilted up. Before her eyes, in Black Barty's practised hand, the bright blade flickered to and fro.

"I could mix a love-potion for a young gentleman."

Tim started as Grannie suddenly cackled right in his ear. She had perched herself on the edge of a table, with her feet off the ground—for she was very small, so small that it wasn't easy to believe she was the mother of huge Wisdom Lee. She liked to sit up on the table, so that she could see what was going on. She didn't miss much, and Tim guessed that she'd seen him looking at Sue. She turned towards him her little wizened head (like one of those heads which witch-doctors shrink till they are human dolls!) and fixed him with her beady black eyes and hissed:

"Yes, Mami can make love-potions, weak for the willing, strong for the shy, yes, yes, and she knows a young gentleman who might think he could find a use for one now."

"Hold your tongue, Mami," said Wisdom sternly; but the rum had made Grannie Lee garrulous and she cackled on:

"So he *might* think: but Mami wouldn't be party to no such thing, no she wouldn't, for 'twould lead to no good, take heed of Mami, 'twould lead the young gentleman to no good at all."

Marta, smiling at Tim, said: "The old woman talks foolishly. Take no notice of her." She suddenly seized Tim round the shoulders and enveloped him in her capacious bosom. "The young gentleman needs no love-potion!" Chuckling, she kissed him on the forehead and let him go. This happened at every hop-picking, it was a natural hazard if you happened to be in Marta's company when she'd had a drop of cider. She kissed everybody, man, woman or child, who at any given moment had a place in her large and comprehensive affections. Tim had received his first kiss and bunny-hug from Marta when he was twelve. He had gone down to watch the horse fair on a Sunday morning, and Marta, who was about thirty then, finding him close to her and the spirit moving her to loving-kindness suddenly, had pounced and seized him in her splendid brown arms with the gold bangles jingling on them. While the gipsies laughed and cheered her, she had lifted him up, pressing him hard against her breasts, and despite his struggles had kissed him soundly and wetly upon the mouth. She was the first person who had kissed him so; and for years after that he had been wary of her, keeping well out of her way in the hopfield or at the horse fair, for he remembered with dismay the touch of her wet lips on his, and her breath in his face, and her warm earthy smell. He had thought he might get some dreadful disease from her mouth. But the next time she caught him he was seventeen, and she showed her recognition of his manhood by giving him a mere peck on the forehead, most courteously.

As Tim smothered back his tousled hair Wisdom said: "Lord, Lord, Marta, is one man not enough for you? Truly, Master Tim, I think she needs a dozen!" He glanced proudly at her broad hips, and slapped her on the behind. "But her old man ain't done yet, is he, Marta? There's not another could lift the dun pony and carry her for ten yards." All gipsies boast, and Wisdom with three large whiskies inside him squared his shoulders and swaggered up and down, forgetting the pain across his loins, forgetting how each breath had seemed like a stab in his heart, during those last terrible two paces down the road. For a few moments he was in his prime again, and he slapped his chest and repeated loudly: "Not another man could do it, not another man alive!"

Black Barty, hearing Wisdom, moved away from the counter and came sidling into the middle of the room. He still had the knife in one hand and the whetstone in the other; he looked wicked and dangerous. Betsy kept close to him, and Sue came with them until she was standing, by accident, or design, close to Tim's shoulder. She still had her glass of gin-and-It. Tim without looking at her let his hand just touch her bare arm. She didn't move away from him. He whispered:

"Sue."

She looked up, and he just had time to say: *"To-night? At the stile by the Old Wood?"* before Grannie Lee had noticed Sue's presence. Grannie Lee had a particular hatred of Sue, and also she was made argumentative by the rum. So she spat out:

"More gin? Hoity-toity we are getting with our cocktails!"

Sue took no notice, nor did she reply to Tim's urgent

whisper. She took the cherry out of her glass and ate it thoughtfully.

Black Barty said to Grannie Lee:

"You leave my gel alone. What's to do with you what she drinks?"

"There's some folks," said Grannie Lee, "as seems to have money to burn. Wonder where they gets it, at only one and two for the picking."

"Ha!" said Black Barty, and grinned broadly, for though he was drunk he perceived that the Lord had delivered her into his hands. "You wants to get a good boss, Wisdom."

Wisdom looked puzzled and wary. He glanced at Tim. "What's that? We got a good boss," he said. Black Barty, with the knife in his hand, was swaggering so that he seemed almost to prance in front of Wisdom. Betsy was grinning a challenge to Marta, Grannie Lee had jumped down off her table, and Sue, most unexpectedly, had moved closer to Tim, so that she let her arm brush against his hand again. Tim was suddenly excited, by Sue's closeness and by the little dust-devils of anger that were already blowing up among the gipsies. It was like Verona at the beginning of *Romeo and Juliet:* you could sense the hot blood stirring.

"And you wants to look arter your people, Wisdom," Black Barty went on, in the manner of one giving kindly advice to an old fool. "Letting your poor people pick for one and two."

"Well, one and two's the rate, ain't it?" said Wisdom. "Same for all?"

"Not if you've got a good boss. Not if you looks arter your people. Barty's the boy, Barty's the kiddie!" cried Black Barty, still prancing. "I says to Mr. Tomkins, 'You're a good boss,' says I, 'what's it to be?' 'One and two,' says he. 'Not for we,' says I. 'We picks for one and four, or else,' says I. 'Or else what?' says he. '*Strike,*' says I. 'So one and four it is, says he. And we shook hands on it, didn't we, Betsy?"

"They shook hands on it," Betsy said.

There was a sudden silence in the bar. During Barty's speech the Smiths and Manasseh's lot had been gathering in a circle round Wisdom and Harry. They were aware of a challenge thrown out, a challenge accepted. And now they all turned towards Wisdom, looking to him to refute Black Barty. Surely one and two was the rate everywhere? Wisdom had argued about it but John Sollars had said: "Take it or leave it then," and Wisdom with a shrug had accepted one and two. Manasseh's people and the Smiths, picking at other hop-farms, had likewise argued, threatened, and in the end capitulated, reluctantly taking the hard terms because there was no choice. If Barty had really got one and four for his people, then it demonstrated that Barty was cleverer, bolder, more cunning, more powerful than Wisdom. Black Barty went up, Wisdom went down.

"Don't believe it," Wisdom said at last. Black Barty was boasting, Black Barty was shooting his mouth. If John Sollars who was rich would only pay one and two then it stood to reason that Tommy Tomkins who was poor could not pay one and fourpence.

"It's just his talk," said Marta, loyal to Wisdom but, Tim thought, just a shade doubtful, wondering whether Barty would be so foolish as to make a boast that could be easily disproved.

"So it's just Barty's talk. Young missies!" cried Barty, raising his cap with an air as he spoke across the room to the Welsh girls who stood there. "Young missies, you that sings so pretty, what's the rate for the hop-picking up at Mr. Tomkins's farm?"

The Welsh girls drew together, alarmed at the sight of Barty's knife, wary lest they should involve themselves in some trouble with the inexplicable gipsies.

"I'm only asking you," wheedled Barty, "to settle a little argument as I'm having with my old friend here."

The girls chittered among themselves. Tim heard one whisper: "Drunk he is. Come, Megan." She tugged at Megan's arm and they began to move towards the door. Marta in triumph swung round to speak to the gipsies behind her:

"There! You can see he's a liar! I said it was just talk."

She spoke too soon. Barty pranced after the girls, and the one called Megan, perhaps in fear of him or perhaps because she felt safe now as the gipsies parted to let her through the door, called out in a voice as clear as a blackbird's:

"One and fourpence a basket Mr. Tomkins said we should have!"

Then the girls scuttled out; and the room fell so quiet that Mrs. Agnew stopped in the middle of drawing a pint of cider and looked up in alarm, for she had known such silences before and they generally meant that the gipsies were poised for a fight. No one stirred, however, except Marta, who moved swiftly to Wisdom's side. Then Barty let out a kind of yell. It was a horrible squawk of triumph, shattering the silence; as if, thought Mrs. Agnew, some jungle animal had just made its kill.

"Barty's the boy, Barty's the feller, Barty's the kiddie!"

He made a sawing motion with his knife in the air. Alone in the centre of the ill-lit room he cast a long strange shadow. He took two or three mincing steps as he played with the knife and continued to shout: "Barty's the kiddie!" at the top of his voice. His longish black hair had fallen down over his good eye. He looked grotesque and slightly demented. Mrs. Agnew, now seeing the knife for the first time, shouted to him from behind the bar: "Put that away, you monkey!" but Barty took no notice. Wisdom a year ago, or perhaps only a few months ago, would have stretched out his strong arm, and taken Black Barty by the wrist, and given one sharp twist to it; the knife would have fallen to the ground, and Black Barty would have cowered away. All the gipsies as they watched Wisdom now were expecting that to happen; but Wisdom did nothing. He looked smaller than Wisdom generally looked; he was bent forward from the hips and he didn't tower over his tribe any longer; he looked older too. And he said not a word. Instead he turned his head slowly and stared at Tim, and it was still his doglike and devoted look but there were doubts in it. It made Tim very unhappy, for this morning Wisdom had come up to him in the hopyard, straight from the argument about the rate with Tim's father, and Wisdom had pleaded: "Is it really true, Master Tim—as we're only to get one and tuppence?" Hating himself, Tim had to answer: "It's what all the growers have agreed between them; it's the most they're going to pay this year." Wisdom had said: "Very well then, 'tis so if you say so," and had gone back to John Sollars. "We don't like it, Mister John, but we'll take it because we must."

The gipsies were silent still, and their faces were all turned towards Wisdom as if they waited for a sign. Manasseh's lot were puzzled, pitying Wisdom but looking for a leadership that was no longer there. The Smiths, whose allegiance to Wisdom was less strong, were openly resentful and rebellious. Black Barty, with his quick dramatic sense, realised that this was the moment to take his departure. Throwing up his knife so that it turned over in the air, catching it by the haft as it came down, he swaggered away. Betsy followed him, having first put out her tongue at Marta. The gipsies drew apart to make a way for him as he went down the long room. Sue's shoulder brushed past Tim, she glanced up at him and whispered: "*I'll slip away.*" Black Barty turned so swiftly that Tim felt almost sure he had heard her. He felt again that queer pleasurable sense of dangerous adventure.

"Come, gel," said Black Barty. Sue scuttled after him. Marta put her hand on Wisdom's shoulder and gripped it tight as if she were trying to give him some of her strength now that his own was failing. Grannie Lee looked towards Black Barty's back and spat on the floor.

Then Wisdom said suddenly: Malona!" and began to hobble after Black Barty. It had crossed his mind that Black Barty, drunk and with the devil in him, might do some mischief to Malona. Hamstringing, even, thought Wisdom wildly, remembering the knife in Black Barty's hand. And he tried to hurry, but he felt hamstrung himself, it was as if something had snapped across his loins, he put his hand behind him and pressed it into the small of his back as he stumbled along.

As he went out, all the gipsies surged towards the open door. But Malona was standing quietly by the white post as

Black Barty and his followers climbed into the high trap. Black Barty waved his whip and walloped his pony; swaying and lurching, at a full canter, he drove off towards the Hope Farm.

## 13

Full tilt round the corner by Tommy's signpost came the high trap. Tommy and Marianne had to jump aside and press themselves in to the hedge. The trap had no lights of course although the stars were out. Black Barty was standing up between the shafts, the pony was blowing, the springs were squeaking, perched up on the trap phrenetic gipsies shouted and sang. Barty cracked his whip and raised an exultant cry to heaven.

"Barty's the kiddie! Barty's the boy!"

Tommy taking Marianne's hand to heave her back out of the hedge murmured:

"Your Uncle George, you know, is going to find it all very strange. Hereford's like a madhouse in the hop-picking. We catch it from the gipsies; we all go a bit crazy."

"I know," she laughed. "I can feel it coming on."

"Beware then," said Tommy. "Beware old Dionysus. He possesses us, I think."

Tommy himself looked a trifle possessed. He had come out of the kiln ten minutes ago, spluttering and choking, his eyes as red as that wicked little ferret's which the gipsy boys played with. The sulphur fumes gave him a sort of hay-fever; so Marianne had suggested a walk to the bottom of the lane, and he'd been sneezing his head off all the way. He always took charge of the drying of the hops; he couldn't leave it to his doddery old foreman, who was apt to nod off at the critical moment and who had once baked a whole load into the likeness of potpourri. So Tommy, during the hop-picking, worked harder at night than he had ever done by day. He rarely went to bed, but took catnaps in his armchair, woke up every hour or two, and then stiffly hobbled out to the kiln. In between working and dozing he read old books again, fumbling his way through all Shakespeare's tragedies in a month. He smoked about fifty cigarettes a night and chucked the ends into the fireplace where they served as a *memento mori* when he saw them in the cold light of morning. Yet somehow it seemed to suit him thus to turn his life topsy-turvy for one month out of the twelve. He enjoyed being a night creature, the fellow of old Whiteface, the barn owl, who lived in the hayloft; of the mice that scuttled about the hop-floor; and of Tybalt, the black cat, that hunted them. The pub routine was broken, so he stopped drinking, and the torment of asceticism drove his fancy once again towards experiment and wild inventiveness. It was in the still hours, during hop-drying nights, that he had designed his picking-machine with the hairpins stuck in its belting, and had drawn to scale in plan and section the plant which was to turn rough stunnem cider into ambrosial applejack. Crumpled sheets of paper, doodled all over with sketches of futuristic agricultural machines, lay with the cigarette stubs in the fireplace every morning.

The hoofbeats tattooed cloppity-cloppity down the lane; Black Barty let out another howl.

"Why does he always have to go so fast?" Tommy said.

"The devil on his tail!"

"I'm sorry for his pony."

"So'm I. By the way, I've been thinking: I'd like one."

This was so unexpected that Tommy said:

"You'd like what?"

"A pony."

"Well, you must have one! We must buy you one!" Tommy was delighted, because there seemed to be something settled and permanent implied by this wish of Marianne's. If she wanted a pony, perhaps she meant to bide. He hadn't brought himself to ask her how long she was staying; he had scarcely dared to hope that she had come home for good.

"Yes, yes, you must certainly have a pony," he beamed, quite forgetting that he was broke, as he always did in moments of enthusiasm. It was this forgetfulness, and this enthusiasm, that led him so often to buy drinks all round for the labourers in the pub. He would then remember his true situation when he had to ask Mrs. Agnew to put them on the slate for him. He remembered it now.

"When our ship comes home."

It was one of his old-fashioned phrases. He was thinking of the hops as his ships, an argosy precarious as Antonio's, still a month to go before it came to harbour, all the hazards of the weather in between. Marianne startled him by saying:

"How do we carry on until the hops are in?"

With Suzette, when he was very close to her, there had been a kind of telepathy: each had known what the other was thinking. But it hadn't happened before with Marianne.

"Can we just scrape through, and manage to pay the pickers?" she said.

He had thought about that. The bank manager would probably let his overdraft run up a bit higher, knowing that he had the hop-money to come. But the pickers' wages would tot up to more than two hundred a week: nearly a thousand pounds before the hops were finished.

"I may have to sell that bunch of young cattle," he said; and one of his foolish, optimistic sums began to take shape in his mind, fifteen beasts at £40—£600; that was what he had given for them; but perhaps they would have improved, grazing the good pasture in the river meadows—and somebody in the pub had said the trade was better last week. Say, then, fifteen beasts at £45—£695. (When he did these sums in his head he generally got the answers wrong; and they were always wrong on the hopeful, never the pessimistic side.)

He began to feel quite cheerful. Call it £700. That would pay the hop-pickers for the whole month; very nearly.

He suddenly remembered that bad fence against John Sollars's land. He must put it right to-morrow. He didn't know whether it was thinking of the cattle that had reminded him of this, or whether it was the sound of the footsteps coming down the lane; for even in the dark you could recognise a Sollars by his stride. You could sense that goddamed arrogance in it. A tall figure loomed up; Tommy wondered vaguely what Tim was doing walking that way at night, well past the turning to Sollarshill Manor Farm.

The firm footsteps hesitated. Tommy called out:

"Hello, Tim."

"Oh, it's you. Hello, sir."

Tim paused, came up to them out of the dark.

"Marianne—had you heard she was home?" said Tommy.

"Oh yes, I had. Hello, Marianne."

"Hello," she said; and laughed, because she was remembering the last time she had seen him, coming back from the orchard into the village hall, ruefully mopping with a handkerchief at the scratches on his face.

She thought Tim knew why she had laughed. If so he didn't seem to mind, for he had settled himself in a typically Sollars attitude, hands in pockets, legs wide apart, and was regarding her with a kind of amused curiosity. At last he said to Tommy:

"How are your hops, sir?"

It was funny to hear him call Tommy sir. It didn't quite go with the Sollars arrogance.

"They're very good," said Tommy. "And yours?"

"They pick easy," said Tim; and Marianne guessed that he already knew Tommy was paying more than the rate they had agreed. She was poised and ready, if he said anything, to ask him who the hell the Sollarses thought they were, to give everybody orders. But Tim didn't mention the rate for the picking. He said easily:

"And it's just the right weather for the job." He turned back to Marianne.

"Good mushrooming weather," he said.

Then he grinned. Again she was aware of his curiosity, as he looked at her by the starlight. Thoroughly ruffled now, she remembered how John Sollars leaning over the gate had looked her up and down and she had thought: If I were a horse he'd run his hands down my fetlocks. So she stared back at Tim, straight at his face so that she held his eyes and he couldn't make appraisal of her as his father had done. A white moth floated by. An owl hooted. For the sake of something to say she turned to Tommy:

"There's your old barn owl, Father."

"Tawny," said Tim. "Tawnies hoot, barn owls screech."

His correction made her angrier than ever. She ought to have known, of course; she had known once. She saw now that nothing remained of the clumsy boy who had pawed her behind the village hall. Tim was damnably assured. He seemed comfortably rooted in the tarmac of the road and content to remain motionless for ever. Marianne realised it was her own foot scraping as she shuffled. The silence was broken by one of Tommy's fits of coughing.

"That damned sulphur," he said.

"Yes, it gets right down into your wind." Tim ceased to be a feature of the landscape and moved off up the lane. "Good night, Marianne. Good night, sir." He took great leisurely strides.

Tommy put his arm in Marianne's and said:

"Let's walk on a bit farther."

He had intended to turn back home, but that would mean walking with Tim, which might embarrass him if he were up to mischief of some sort, as Tommy thought likely.

"He had you over the mushrooms," Tommy laughed.

She didn't answer. She had her hackles up, Tommy knew, but he couldn't understand why. He liked young Tim; to see him on a horse was something that lifted the heart. He listened to his confident steps becoming fainter up the lane, and wondered again where he was off to at this time of night: some young man's folly of the hop-picking, he was sure.

"Yes, poor George," he said half to himself, "I don't know

what he'll make of us, honestly. The drunks and the fights and the galloping gipsies, the hot pants and all the hullabaloo! He won't understand that something funny happens to people at hop-picking time."

"Perhaps," said Marianne, "it will happen to him too."

"That would be very interesting and extraordinary." Tommy broke off and considered this, in genuine awe at the possibility. But he shook his head. Nothing of that kind would ever occur to George. He lived in an emotional igloo; he was somehow impervious to the wild winds that trouble the spirit. The most adventurous thing he had ever done was to go off alone on a bicycle tour and take brass rubbings in village churches. He sat up very straight on his bicycle, ringing the bell as he approached each corner.

"Perhaps," Marianne went on, "it will make him decent about the mortgage?"

"Not George if I know him."

"*Can* he sell us up?"

"Naturally; unless I can pay off the arrears."

"And naturally you can't?"

"It would take most of the hop-money, and leave us practically nothing to carry on with."

"So he's got us by the short hairs?" she said.

Tommy blinked, then chuckled.

"As you elegantly put it."

"Look," said Marianne, stopping suddenly and pointing over the trees.

The slenderest crescent moon leaned upon their topmost branches. "Let's turn our money," she said, "and wish."

Tommy put his hand in his pocket, and felt the half-crown and the shilling which hadn't been enough to pay for drinks this morning at the Royal Victoria.

"Now you whizzle round."

He turned round twice, and became extremely giddy. She took him by the shoulders and pushed him round again. "Now bow, and wish."

He wished like mad. He thought: I should like to be a real heathen, instead of just a dreary agnostic. I should pray to all the gods of earth and air and sky and water. It's extraordinarily comforting.

Marianne was lightly revolving. "Seven times for me, to make sure! I'm letting you off with three in case you get a cerebral thrombosis." She was in one of her suddenly excited moods, when she couldn't keep still.

"It'll all come right," she said, dancing before the crescent. "I know it'll all come right."

Just then there were more footsteps in the lane. They were small scuttling ones. Peering into the dark ahead Tommy could see a white blur. Then the gipsy girl scurried by without turning her head. Her feet pattered up the hill.

"*Tous les chats sont gris,*" Tommy said. "But I bet I know that little cat. Black Barty's Sue, wasn't it?" And he thought: So that is your bit of mischief, Master Tim.

*My mother said*
*I never should*
*Play with the gipsies*
*In the wood!*

Better mind your step, my lad. I wonder what John Sollars would say. And yet, why not, after all? You're young and she's pretty, that little moon's rising and it's hop-picking time —hot pants and hop-picking go together! He murmured aloud without thinking:

" 'The wren goes to't, and the small gilded fly . . .' "

He felt Marianne stiffen beside him, and he told himself: I shouldn't have said it, not that savage thing. All right for old Lear, all right for a broken-down old drunk like me; but when you're young you shouldn't think of it like that. And he felt oddly ashamed that he had said it in front of her.

"Let's go home," she said. They turned their backs on the new moon, and Marianne was silent all the way up the lane. Tommy didn't know what was going on in her mind; and the desolate thought struck him that Suzette's head close to his shoulder had come just so high, her light step had sounded just as the step that went beside him now. With her he had always known; between him and this one lay the chasm of the years, and he wondered if he knew anything about her at all.

# 14

"What's the time?" asked Sue once again, and Tim had to light a match to look at his wrist-watch in the dark shade of the trees.

"It's half past eleven."

"I ought to go," she said, but with the faintest shade of a question mark. "He'll thrash me else."

They were at the stile into the wood. It was an old stile on which Tim had discovered last year his father's initials, J. S., carved very neatly as a lad might carve them to while away the time as he was waiting for a girl; though it wasn't easy to imagine John Sollars waiting for a girl, or for anybody.

Tim had got there first, and standing by the stile he had seen the lights come on in the farmhouse across the little valley. So they were back from their walk. He had thought of Marianne and that brief unaccountable flare-up in the lane: a moment of conflict which made him curious about her. He had wondered about her running away from home, about her life in London, and other things. Then he had heard Sue coming up the hill. At once he was aware of a difference between their last meeting and this one. Last time she had come flitting out of the darkness as silently as a moth. It was a thing he happily remembered. It was what had given to that meeting a spice of adventure. But to-night there was something ungipsyish in the way Sue minced towards him, picking her way with little steps along the rough path. She was breathless from hurrying up the hill.

"We haven't got long," she had said, putting up her face to be kissed.

The difference still puzzled him; he was still trying to define it as he kissed her. There was a lot of lipstick, which tasted sticky in his mouth. She had some scent on her too: what he supposed in the magazine stories they called "cheap scent." Last year, he remembered, she had smelt of hops! But nothing was quite the same as last year. Even the way she kissed him was different. "We haven't got long," she said again. "We must be quick." It seemed a funny thing for her to say, and Tim without quite knowing why found himself shying away from its practical implications. He had sat on the stile, vaguely uncomfortable and troubled by a feeling that this wasn't the same Sue he had met here twelve months ago; or perhaps he wasn't the same person.

He let the match burn out between his fingers. She leaned against him, her sharp elbows pressed against his thighs while she cupped her chin in her hands. She said again:

"I ought to go."

Tim hedged.

"Tell me what you've been doing all these twelve months?" —and he wondered what twelve months meant to you if you lived as the gipsies did, having no fixed point in your life, drifting to and fro. He thought of being in a boat on the Wye, when you measured your speed by the bridges you passed under or the landmarks you went by, and it struck him that perhaps the months were measured like that by the gipsy people, time for them was a tally of places, Worcester for the pea-picking, Shropshire for the cherries, Evesham for the plums, Hereford for the hops, and so on.

"Talk to me, Sue."

She wrinkled her forehead.

"After hop-picking I went back to the Forest."

Tim's fancy leaped at that. He repeated, for the pleasure of it: "You went back to the Forest?"

The match sputtered out, and left him in the dark with a delightful image, which he thought he would keep for ever, of Sue's face with its slanted eyes and startled look as she said: "I went back to the Forest" and made him think of a nymph or a deer. The Forest, of course, was the Forest of Dean; they wintered there.

"The camp flooded," she said in her short sentences like a child's. "It always does. And I hate it. And we wear gumboots all the time. But there are plenty of buses so you can get into Gloucester to go to the flicks."

Now Tim was wondering what it felt like to go to the pictures if you were a gipsy: what strangeness that fitful screen must hold for you who have never even been inside a house! It was an extraordinary thought that this Sue, who leaned against him now, had perhaps never entered a house in her life; had never once looked inside a bedroom, a bathroom, a kitchen, switched on the electric light, walked upstairs. This thought filled Tim with an absurd awe, and he perceived that the lives of ordinary people, of all the people he knew, were like circles of various sizes, sometimes overlapping and cutting into other circles, but each with a little dot at the exact centre, which was their "place." In contrast with them the gipsies' lives ran like a tenuous thread hither and thither, and only touched the circles of the house-people momentarily at some point on the circumference—as when they sold clothes-pegs to a housewife, or stood in a chattering queue to be paid for the hop-picking, or bought bread.

So at a point on his own personal perimeter Sue's little thread touched him now. He saw that it was a fortuitous thing, as if she barely brushed him in passing, and he wanted to hold her there and keep her there for a little longer. That image was still sharp in his mind, Sue's brown face in the matchlight, the nymph or the deer from the forest, and he responded to it with an intense curiosity. It was a kind of extension of the curiosity he felt about beasts and birds which he could never properly know or understand. Tenderness was mixed up in it, and tenderness reawakened desire. He let his hands run down Sue's thin arms; she pressed closer to him then, and lifted her chin out of the cup she had made for it, and once again as he kissed her he was aware of the new quality in her kiss, the artfulness as well as the eagerness there. He slipped down off the stile and held her against him and for a moment it was the same as it had been last time. Only the merest trivial chance stopped it from finishing like last time. Sue started. "Oh, listen!" Then Tim heard what had made her start. There was a movement in the bracken, a shuffling, a padding, quite close. Tim knew all the woodland sounds by night or day.

"It's only the old badger."

There was always a badger-sett in the wood, and John Sollars would never let the stupid badger-diggers come there with their mattocks and spades and ragtag terriers. "Reckon old Brock's been here longer even than us," he'd say. Tim liked the badger too; he liked all wild creatures, but especially the ugly or quaint ones, the solemn toad, the fenny snake in the river meadows, the show-off magpies prinking and preening, the quick lizards on the wall. The badger was ugly too, in a shaggy and primitive way, and Tim remembered a line in a poem about it: "That most ancient Briton of English beasts."

Quite close to their feet, this one suddenly grunted.

Under Sue's thin dress Tim felt her shoulder-blade move beneath his hand as she stiffened.

"It's just the badger," he said again, and thought it was extraordinary that she didn't know. Surely the gipsies were fellows of the wild woodland things? "I went back to the Forest."

Tim saw the bracken tops moving, only about five yards away. They shook for a moment in the stillness and he could track the beast's course by them. Then the quiet came back, and though he still held her against him Tim knew that it was not for them now, the couch among the fronds. He didn't know why. The little thread of their relationship had snapped. Over her shoulder he saw a light moving among the buildings round the farmhouse on the hill. That would be Tommy with a lantern, going across to his oast. An intrusive thought of Marianne came into Tim's mind; it seemed irrelevant and he wondered what it was doing there.

Sue said: "When it grunted I was frit."

The wood lay absolutely still about them. The light on the opposite hill blinked like a star: the hurricane-lantern swinging.

"You're taller," Tim said, for something to say. "You used to come up only to there." Then it occurred to him that she wasn't taller, it was her high-heeled shoes; he'd noticed them in the pub and thought how ill they suited her and how unnaturally she walked in them. They went with the cheap trinkets and the lipstick and the scent. They were all part of the difference since last year; he understood that he had lost last year's Sue, if she had ever been real. It was finished anyhow, and he thought she guessed it was finished; she had ducked away under his arm and she was saying in a kind of forlorn defensive way:

"I ought to go. But I could come to-morrow. It would be better to-morrow. He's going off horse-dealing, to Leominster and that's miles. I could slip out easy then, honest. What's the time?"

Tom lit another match.

"Quarter to twelve."

He didn't think she listened to the answer. She asked the question repetitively, like a child.

"I'll have to run. He was drunk and he went to sleep quick. But I'm frit of him. If he woke up, he'd thrash me—"

Tim had a horrible picture of Black Barty rising half-drunken out of his bed, Sue cowering back, Black Barty monstrous in the oil-lamp's glimmer, seizing a strap or his horse-whip—and most foolishly Tim wondered whether he ought to take Sue back to her caravan, explain to Black Barty (but how?) and in chivalry defend Sue against him; but of course that would only make it worse for her afterwards. Once again, and more sharply than ever before, he had a sense of the strangeness, the slightness, the remoteness of his contact with Sue, this small brown unknown girl who could say so factually: "He'll thrash me" because that kind of violence was part of the pattern of her life. Melodrama was inherent in all the gipsies did; Tim remembered one night during the hop-picking two or three years ago, when he had walked back up the road from the Royal Victoria with Croft, the village bobby. A series of dreadful screams had rung out suddenly from Black Barty's caravan down in the river meadow. They had stopped to listen, and Tim had been horrified; it sounded like murder.

"Oughtn't we—?"

"No we oughtn't, Master Tim," said Croft. "Just leave 'em to it."

There was another wild and hideous scream, which died away in a gurgle; Tim was convinced that Betsy was having her throat cut.

"But we can't let him *kill* her—?"

"You never can tell," said Croft judiciously—"*I* never can tell, and I've bin here fourteen years—whether they're beating their wives or just making love to 'em. The women screams just the same either way, like vixens; and whichever way it is, I've got an idea they enjoys it. So don't you ever go interfering. You'll have both of 'em on to you else."

Next evening in the pub Tim had observed Betsy with interest. She bore no visible marks, and she and Black Barty seemed to be on excellent terms; he was buying drinks for her.

The match had gone out, but Tim lit another. He wanted to look at Sue once more before she left him. He held it up between them, saw again by its light the sharp foxy face which he still found quaintly moving, the secret eyes that had watched, perhaps, as she crouched in a corner, whatever had happened in the caravan that night when her mother was screaming; that had watched, on all the other nights, the beating or the love-making; she had seen her small brother, Betsy's youngest, conceived and born, had seen her grandfather, Old Black Barty, die in that caravan of the cancer two years ago; the eyes, he remembered suddenly, that he had never seen smile. He thought he knew no more about her than he knew about the old badger in the wood, though he had made love to her twelve months ago, down in that very patch of bracken where to-night the badger had blundered by.

She leaned towards him in sudden impatience and puffed at the match. The neck of her loose dress fell forward a little and by the last flicker of the match he saw the ellipse of her small pointed breasts and thought again of the nymph that went back to the Forest. The match went out, and out of the sudden blackness Sue said in her forlorn voice: "To-morrow?" and Tim moved by her tone and by that last glimpse of her in the matchlight said: "To-morrow," though he knew he would be sorry he'd said it when to-morrow came.

"The same time," she said. "I'll slip away."

She stumbled as she turned, and that was because of those high-heeled shoes, Tim thought. He understood now about the difference which he'd been immediately aware of when she came up the hill. She had made a noise, twigs had crackled, her foot had slipped on the steep path.

By the moon's little light he watched her going down the hill. A light burned steady in Tommy's oast. Tim thought of him coughing and snuffling in the sulphur fumes. Close at hand, suddenly, there was a real snuffle. Pad, pad, grunt. The old badger was lumbering home. Tim stood very still, and saw the feathery bracken fronds grey in the moonlight quivering quite close to him. He wished he could see the badger, wished he could eavesdrop upon it with eyes and ears as it went upon its secret nocturnal business. He was conscious of a world of mystery, the unknown Sue a phantom now as the moonlight touched her white dress half-way down the hill, Marianne across at the farmhouse where a bedroom light still burned, the unknown badger shuffling about his affairs as his ancestors had done long before there were Sollarses at Sollarshill, long long before there were any men upon the earth.

# 15

Tim tumbled out of bed half an hour late next morning, ducked into his shirt, pulled on his trousers, and got downstairs just as the cows were coming in for milking. There were two pairs of gumboots standing by the back door and as Tim stepped into his pair he thanked his lucky stars, for it looked as if his father had overslept too. This was unprecedented in hop-picking time. Tim went out to do his early morning chores. He weighed out the cows' rations and the pig-food, fed Samson and cleaned out his stall; then, as there was still no sign of his father, he thought he'd better go along to the oasts to see if all was well there. It was another misty morning, full of loud invisible pigeons and heraldic beasts, the usual cat rampant on the wall and a ram-lamb salient, Mrs. Sollars's pet, leaping wildly up to Tim by the dairy. It had refused to be weaned from the bottle and hung about there most of the day, butting everybody's bottom to remind them that it wanted some milk.

The oasts in the mist rose up like the guard-towers of a medieval city. They had been built sixty years ago, so they were topped with the outdated cowls and vanes which revolved with the wind. These were no longer needed, but Tim's father when he modernised the kilns had insisted on keeping the cowls "for the look of the thing," and because they were landmarks which he liked to see when he was walking round the farm, and because he didn't want his farm buildings to be "like a blasted factory site." But within the towers everything was scientific and up-to-date. A hoist lifted the sacks of hops off the trailer and whisked them up to the hop-floor, where they were spread out to make a deep-pile carpet of delicate green. Thence they were shovelled into the drying-chamber, where they were cooked for eight or nine hours at a temperature which varied from 100° to 160° at different stages of the drying. Oil-burning furnaces heated a current of air to the proper temperature, and this hot blast was drawn up into the drying-chamber by fans. Old Dave watched over the furnaces and performed his priestly task with the sulphur and swore to himself alliteratively, for a whole month on end.

Tim found him dozing on his truckle-bed. Dave sat up and said:

"We sought for thee last night." He added accusingly: "Thee'd gone galivanting, dessay."

"What was the matter?"

"Frigging furnace. Your father fixed it."

"What was the matter with the furnace?"

"Buggering burner got choked; so I had to fetch the Master."

That's torn it, Tim thought; he'll want to know what I was doing.

"How is he?" asked Dave.

"Why? I haven't seen him yet. He's not up."

"Nor ought to be. He was in here till midnight but he should a-bin abed then rightly. I never sin the Master sick before; but he looked real sick, Master Tim. If I could have found thee—"

Tim hurried back to the house, and went into the big cool breakfast-room. His father was sitting in the chair by the fireplace. His mother and Carol were at the table. His mother glanced up from her boiled egg, which she was tapping with a spoon.

"Oh, Tim, I'm afraid your father's not very well."

John grunted from his chair when Tim said he was sorry. There was an uncomfortable feeling, which Tim shared, that routine and good order were somehow threatened because John was ill. Tim couldn't even remember him having so much as a cold. Mrs. Sollars went on tapping her egg. Carol was doing the *Telegraph* crossword. She looked up from it as Tim sat down.

"You've got half a cowpat on your forehead."

Tim had got dirty mucking out Samson; he ought to have washed. He took out his handkerchief and wiped his forehead. His mother said:

"Carol, I do wish you wouldn't use that word."

Carol was making a funny face at Tim. He didn't know what she meant. Then she scribbled on her crossword and passed it over to him.

"See if you can do that one for me."

She'd written: HANK LIPSTICK HIDE IT.

He put it in his pocket quickly and she winked at him. Mrs. Sollars, having gradually softened the top of her egg, was now able to decapitate it neatly with a spoon. She was delicate and deliberate in all she did. She was as cool as the dairy which was her especial province and from which she banished daily every intrusive speck of dust and dirt. No rewards and fairies there! And somehow she managed to make her own life as hygienic as the dairy, removing from it everything dirty, unpleasant or distressing with a kind of mental scrubbing-brush. If she had known or guessed what Tim had been doing last night she would have used that scrubbing-brush and cleaned it out of her mind. But Tim felt certain that his father had guessed. The old man growled:

"Is the furnace working all right? Have you seen Dave?"

"Yes, Father."

"We had a bit of a job with it," John Sollars said.

"I've told him you can manage to-day," said Mrs. Sollars to Tim. "He had a bad night. I don't want him to go down to the hop-gardens."

She always spoke of hop-gardens instead of hopyards. She came from Kent. John Sollars had met her, in between the wars, when his membership of the Hop Marketing Board had taken him to Canterbury. Her father was on the board too; so John had "married into hops," and possibly he had never thought it conceivable that he should do otherwise.

When he brought his bride home to Sollarshill she had quickly fallen in with all the Hereford ways save that she clung still to her Kentish manner of speech. She called hop-yards hop-gardens, and the bins she called cribs, and the "houses," which was the Hereford name for an area allotted to a group of pickers as their own picking-area, she spoke of as "drifts." John Sollars had never got used to it; but it was the only difference between them, about which they had mildly and lovingly quarrelled for twenty-five years. For the rest, she had submitted herself to him mind, body and soul. Ever since his arthritis began to trouble him she had knelt, every morning, to lace up his boots. On hunting days she tied his stock. Nobody ever brushed or mended his clothes but her. Each special dish which she had discovered to be his favourite she cooked herself, because she knew she could cook it more to his liking than anybody else could. All the time she studied to please him; but it was as if, giving so much love and service to him, she had little left over for the rest of the world. People hardly seemed to exist for her saving in so far as they were the background and the surroundings, the friends or the servants of her John. Tim sometimes felt that he knew her only through his father; sensing, but not sharing, the goodness and the gentleness which she bestowed upon him.

Speaking to his father's back, hunched in the chair before the fireplace, Tim asked him what was the matter. John only grunted, and Tim's mother answered for him.

"It's a pain in his chest." She added: "And of course he won't have the doctor, in case he sends him to bed, in the hop-picking."

Tim could see that despite her care for John she accepted and understood the overriding duty to the hops, because she was dedicated to them too. In her family as in John's it was unthinkable that anybody should be laid up during the hop-picking. Tim remembered that when Mrs. Remington, the wife of one of the big growers, had had a baby in September his mother had said: "I should have thought she could have arranged things better than *that*." She had laughed, but there had been a hint of real disapproval. The hops and the Herefords came first always; and Tim, as he recognised this devoted professionalism, began to feel guilty about last night, —not about meeting Sue, but because he hadn't been handy when he was needed.

"I can manage everything to-day," he said.

"Of course you can." His mother gave him a bright smile, including him suddenly in her gentle benevolence because he could be of service to John. She folded her napkin meticulously, laid it beside her place, and got up.

"They'll be bringing the milk in," she said. (If she wasn't there, they were liable to come into the dairy with dirty boots or to leave the door open so that dust blew in from the yard upon the cream in the pans. Four Jerseys were kept for her cream-making; the Herefords, of course, weren't good milkers. The Jerseys were Mrs. Sollars's very own; she had bought them one by one out of her takings from the sale of the butter and cream. John could have written her a cheque for a whole herd; but she preferred to do it this way. Every penny she had made or spent was neatly recorded in the little blue notebook which hung up behind the dairy door.)

She went out; and going by John Sollars's chair she let her hand rest lightly on his shoulder for a moment as she passed him. Carol got up too. She said:

"It's a funny hop-picking. Father's ill and I've got religion."

"How?"

"It's a missioner," she said. "He's sweet, and he blued two pounds four and sixpence in my shop yesterday. He came in four times. He's at Oxford, but he wanted to spend his vac. doing good. They're going to have a service in the hopyard on Sunday. I shall go. But I expect you won't. You're too unspiritual." And she grinned at him about the lipstick on the handkerchief.

When the door was shut behind her John Sollars said:

"Dave and I were looking for you last night."

He still had his back to Tim. He paused; then:

"I didn't want to mention it in front of your mother."

One never did; nothing potentially unpleasant must ever be hinted at in her presence. It would be like going into the dairy with dirty boots. "But if it's gipsies," he growled, "you'll burn your fingers."

Tim realised that his father had deliberately refrained from asking the direct question. He had said: *If* it was gipsies. Tim suddenly perceived a kind of courtesy in this. It surprised and touched him. No explanations would be asked for or encouraged; and Tim knew he could never have explained to his father about Sue. He couldn't have told him how intimately desire had been mixed up with tenderness and curiosity; he couldn't have made him understand all that foolishness about nymphs of the Forest. Far better let him think what he obviously was thinking: just another tumble in the hay, another bit of skirt that was different only because it was a gipsy skirt, the same unvarying objective underneath it!

"The only good thing I've ever noticed about the diddykyes," John Sollars went on—he always called them diddykyes in contempt—"is that they keep their women to 'emselves. But if they don't—" He turned round in his chair, and Tim for the first time saw how ill he looked; his face was almost grey, that Tim had never known other than ruddy. "But if they don't, they're up to funny business, and it's look out, my lad!"

There was a knock at the door. The little maid Polly came in. Tim thought his father looked almost relieved at the interruption.

"Yes, Polly?" he said.

"Wisdom Lee's at the back door, sir. I said you wasn't well, but he wants to see you special."

"Show him in here," said John; and as Polly went out: "I wonder what the trouble is now."

Tim guessed it was because Wisdom now knew how much Black Barty was getting for the picking and wanted the same rate for his own tribe. He said nothing, however, and his father, harking back, grumbled more to himself than Tim:

"There are a hell of a lot of farmers' daughters."

There were indeed: a whole phalanx of them fresh-faced under their velvet caps out hunting, Remingtons, Ferrers, Revels, Barkers, Johnsons, all mad on gymkhanas and hunt balls. This was an old theme of John Sollars's. He wanted Tim to marry and settle down; preferably to "marry into hops," land to land as well as flesh to flesh joined in Holy Matrimony.

Polly came back, showing in Wisdom. He held his cap in his hand. It struck Tim that he hadn't seen him without a cap before. Bareheaded, he looked older, although he had no grey hairs. It was a boast of the gipsies that they never became grizzled, even in their late years; but perhaps the grey never showed because of the grease they put on their hair or because they never washed it.

Wisdom looked unhappy, twiddling his cap in his hands. Tim wasn't quite sure whether John had asked him into the breakfast-room because he didn't feel like getting out of his chair, or simply to put Wisdom at a disadvantage; for no gipsy is happy under a roof. Wisdom's natural dignity half-hid his discomfiture. He said:

"I'm sorry, Mister John, to hear as you're ailing."

Perhaps it was the word "ailing" that annoyed John Sollars. He said quite sharply:

"You don't look so sprightly yourself."

Wisdom had limped when he came into the room. He was still stiff from the labour of Hercules which he'd performed last night outside the pub. He'd probably torn a muscle in his back, thought Tim; or he was griped by the poisonous potions Grannie Lee had compounded for him! He said:

"We be both getting on, Mister John, you and I."

"Well, what is it?" said John, still sharp with him.

Wisdom laid forth his grievance about the rate for the picking. It took him quite a long time. He had none of Black Barty's fluency. He told John what Black Barty had said in the pub and how the Welsh girls had confirmed it—"I wouldn't have believed it else, Mister John." Tim as he listened uncomfortably was conscious of Wisdom's integrity, the truth that was in him dragged out sentence by sentence, laboriously. It rather shocked Tim when his father turned to him for confirmation.

"Is this true, about Tomkins?"

"I heard the Welsh girls say he was paying one and four."

"You see, sir," Wisdom put in, " 'tis not for me, but for my people. They looks to I, to see as they're used fair."

"You say I'm unfair?"

"I wasn't meaning that, sir. You couldn't have known, when you told me yesterday, as the rate wasn't the same everywhere."

"I didn't know," said John.

Wisdom nodded, as if he were glad of the assurance that at any rate John hadn't deceived him.

"But as to what *I* pay," said John, "that is my business, and none of Mr. Tomkins's. My rate is one and two."

"Yes," said Wisdom, wringing his cap as if it were a wet rag.

"Please tell your people."

"Yes," said Wisdom dully once again.

"That's all, then," said John.

Wisdom turned to go. Tim, feeling miserable and ashamed, went to open the door for him. Pausing beside it, Wisdom said:

"Maybe, Mister John, they won't pick for one and two?"

"Take it or leave it then."

Wisdom slowly went out. Tim walked to the back door with him; he thought that Wisdom, unused to houses, might lose his way in the long corridors of this one, and it would embarrass him if he found himself in the kitchen, say, by accident. But then he wondered unhappily if Wisdom thought he was afraid of him stealing something. At the back door he shook Wisdom's hand.

"I'm sorry about it," he said. He would have liked to say more, but that would have been disloyal to his father.

Wisdom made things worse by looking at him devotedly.

"We ain't never had a strike on this farm before," he said. "And I shan't like it, Master Tim, but it's for my people." He limped off. When Tim got back to the breakfast-room his father was just putting down the phone. Presumably Tommy had paid his bill and was cut off no longer; for John was angrier than Tim had ever seen him. Tim didn't know whether it was his illness, or sheer rage, that made him tremble so.

"Wisdom was telling the truth," he said.

"Did you speak to Tommy?"

There was a short pause.

"No," roared John. "I spoke to his little tart, though."

"And you told her what you thought of Tommy?"

"She told me," said John, "what she thought of me." And, most surprisingly, he began to laugh. He laughed through his anger, as sun comes through a rainstorm. Tim was amazed; his father was a man who didn't laugh readily, and who hardly ever laughed at himself. He wanted to ask him what Marianne had said; but John had stopped laughing and his face was all drawn again.

"Damn," he said. "It's a bloody pain; and it's in my vitals somewhere. I shan't—" He paused, and seemed to be trying to get his breath. "I shan't come down to the hops this morning."

"I'll manage," said Tim.

"You'll have a strike on your hands."

"I think so."

His father said: "Limit it to the gipsies if you can."

"What if the whole lot walk out on us?"

"Let 'em go."

"Wouldn't it be worth it," said Tim tentatively, "to go up to one and four?"

"Of course it would be worth it," snapped John. "But I've agreed with the others to pay one and two: John Revel, Bill Ferrers, the Johnsons. We all agreed. And unlike some buggers I keep my word."

"I'll be getting down there, then."

"Yes. And when they've struck, and you've nothing to do, go and have a look at that boundary fence by the river. He's got some scruffy cattle in there, and I told him to mend it. Hell to pay if his screws get through and mix up with ours.

Christ, what a farmer!" said John. "If I had my way on the County Executive Committee I'd have him out neck and crop."

Tim wondered whether his father had already sounded the committee about evicting Tommy for bad husbandry. It was quite likely; he was tough enough, and Tim knew that for years he'd had his eye on Tommy's farm.

"And there's Sollarshill Sally down in the meadow," John said. "Due in a fortnight, isn't she?"

"September the seventeenth."

"If she has a bull calf it'll be a winner." He broke off and eased himself in his chair. Tim could see the sweat glistening on his forehead. "It'll be one as good as Samson, if I know anything about Herefords at all. Tim," he said suddenly, "I'll have a little game with you, my boy. Get in my hops before the weather breaks and I'll give you Sally's calf!"

He laughed, and yet his face was all twisted with pain. Tim couldn't make him out; it was an unfamiliar thing, this grim-and-gay mood of his father's. But he thought John knew that he wouldn't be able to take part in the hop-picking, and this was his way of saying: "It's up to you."

"You can have it for your own, and show it, and it'll be your first winner. Done?" said John.

"Done!"

"Then go and deal with those blasted diddy-kyes." John leaned back in his chair. "Get to it, my lad. Get to it!"

## 16

The gipsies sat in a long row, having spread themselves out to get the maximum shade from the hop-bines. Tim was oddly reminded of swallows before migration. Now and then a bunch of gipsies would get up and move away towards the gate; then they would change their minds and return to the main body. He wasn't sure whether or not they were going to migrate. They had stopped work, but they seemed unwilling to leave the hopyard. Most of them were brewing tea, or telling tales, or sleeping in the hop-bines' shadows. It was an hour since Wisdom had told Tim, not defiantly but in sad resignation, that they were going to strike. "It's not me, Master Tim; it's my people." Tim thought it was mainly Marta and Grannie Lee, who had probably agreed that Wisdom was likely to lose his leadership unless he held out for the same terms as Black Barty's folk were getting.

The Welsh were still picking, and some of the Black Country families were still picking in a desultory way; but most of them stood in a group round a man in a dark suit called Mr. Comstock. Tim had never seen Mr. Comstock before. He was a new picker this year, one of a score that had come down from Birmingham, and he had emerged from his anonymous obscurity at the very first whisper of the word "strike." He had declared himself the Spokesman of the Workers from the Midlands. Nobody, as far as Tim knew, had invited him to be their spokesman. "It so 'appens as I've 'ad a lot of experience in 'andling disputes," he had said; and he had added that the first thing to do, in the case of a dispute, was to form a committee. He had bustled from bin to bin, canvassing this extraordinary proposition. Wisdom had refused to join, for the simple reason that he didn't know what a committee was; and he had been backed up by Grannie, who took an immediate dislike to Mr. Comstock and spat out at him: " 'Tis between we and Mister Sollars, and we don't want no Mitty." Mr. Comstock had gone next to the Welsh pickers; but they were perfectly happy, singing, laughing and flirting among themselves, and in singsong sentences they told Mr. Comstock exactly where he could stick his committee. He had returned, disillusioned perhaps about working-class solidarity, to the factory folk from the Black Country, among whom shop stewards were not without honour. He was now haranguing them on the theme of Exploitation by the Bosses.

Tim, who thought he would do more harm than good by arguing with Mr. Comstock, joined Wisdom, old Mami and Marta at the end of the hop-row and had a cup of tea with them. The tea tasted so extraordinary that he thought Mami must have tipped some of her herbal medicine into it; and shortly she confirmed this, explaining that she always mixed lime-leaves with the tea, for the improvement of Wisdom's water.

"Often have I cured a stoppage with the lime-tips," she said.

She was in a gloomy and prophetic mood.

"So Mister John is ailing?" she said. "Well, he must be careful. Only yesterday as I looks at him I says to myself: 'There's a man who *looks* hale'; and yet I had a feeling that he was like to be struck down. 'Twasn't a sure feeling, like I had about Old Black Barty afore he took the cancer: when I says to myself: 'You'll be dead, old man, in a year and a day.' And in a year and a day, to the hour, there was Betsy wailing over his yaller corpse. 'Twas not so powerful a feeling about Mister John, but 'twas a feeling all the same. Mister John should go careful."

Wisdom got up and went behind the hop-bine. Mami said in triumph:

"What did I tell you about the lime-tips?"

Tim thought this was a good opportunity to tackle Mami on the subject of the strike.

"What's the use of Wisdom holding out?" he said. "You know my father, Mami."

"Known him eighty years." Mami, like all gipsies, had only the vaguest ideas about time. She believed herself to be a hundred and two.

"Hearken to Wisdom," she said. "It never fails."

"Well, you know my father well enough to know *he* won't give in," Tim insisted.

Mami turned her old tortoise-head towards him. She looked cunning.

"Maybe he'll want the hops picked in a hurry."

"The weather's settled. There is no hurry."

Mami stretched up her wizened claw and pulled down a hop-bine.

"Ah. The hops *looks* good."

"They are good."

"And yet they're nesh," she said, digging her talons into the leaves. "They looks good yet they feels nesh." By nesh she meant tender, too soft and sappy. "They could take the pestilence," she said.

Wisdom returned. Mami peered up at him and said:

"I can smell pestilence."

"Last time she said that," asserted Wisdom, "within a week the green bines was hanging black in the rows, like as if they'd been shrivelled by a fire."

Tim saw that he had been right about Mami. She was the instigator of the strike, and since Wisdom was mortally afraid of her it was likely to continue.

Tim was very unhappy to be up against the gipsies. Wisdom had been one of the great heroes of his boyhood; had taught him how to make his first catapult, to set his first rabbit snare, to tickle his first trout. He had boxed with Wisdom and coursed hares with Wisdom and learned from him some of the secrets of the horse-coping trade. To be at odds with him now over a matter of pennies made Tim feel mean and contemptible. But he was sure that his father would not budge, and he had decided that the best course was to beat the strike if possible and then try to persuade his father to offer better terms as a gesture when the pickers were working again.

Obviously the success or failure of the gipsies' strike hung on whether the rest of the pickers came out with them. If not, Tim could probably manage without the gipsies. It was odd that they did not understand this. They made no attempt to get the others to join them. The idea of having allies was quite foreign to the gipsies; they had never had any allies, in all their long history. They walked alone.

"Look at that Mitty man," said Mami now, and spat.

Mr. Comstock seemed at last to have formed his committee. At the head of it, very absurd in his shiny black suit which was so out of place in the hopyards, he was marching purposefully towards the Welsh pickers: a deputation. Tim decided that he'd better find out what was going on. When he got to the "house" where the Welsh were picking Mr. Comstock was already in the full flood of his oratory.

"Tike a look in the boss's garridge: tike a look at those motey-cars, what was bought eout of the pennies 'e can't afford to pye you!"

One of the Welsh girls said:

"Hot does he make me feel with all his talking."

And indeed Mr. Comstock in his thick serge was a depressing spectacle. But he was a persistent fellow. There were a few young miners among the Welsh pickers, and he had realised that if he could bring them out the girls would ultimately follow. Also the miners were more susceptible to the idea of a proletarian brotherhood, even with the gipsies, who were nobody's brethren of their own choice. So he concentrated on these young men. He went from one to another, trotting out his patter: "Kime 'ere for a 'olidye, didn' you, so myebe you don't keer abeout a fyeow bob more or less in your pye-packet? But them poor gipsies do keer. 'Tyen't no bleedin' 'olidye for the likes of them. Hungry kids they got to feed. Neow look 'ere, you're a miner, and a miner don't let deown 'is pals. All stick together, brother, and we'll win!"

Tim let him be. His own tactics were to jolly along the people who were still working; so he picked for a time with the Welsh girls, and teased them and flirted with them, and then he decided to attack the enemy's stronghold and went across to the Black Country crowd, who in Mr. Comstock's absence had mostly returned to their bins. He kept off the subject of the strike; but he picked with each family group in turn and got them talking about their domestic affairs—Why isn't Peg here this year? Married a sergeant in the R.E.M.E. and went out to Germany? And Margie is having another baby? And Bob doing his National Service? He'd known most of them since he was a boy. "I minds you pickin' at this very bin," said one old woman, "when you cood'n a bin more'n five; and you thought as the hops was good to yut and you nigh choked y'sel' when you swallered one."

"I've swallowed plenty since," laughed Tim.

All except about a dozen of the Dudley folk were picking now, and they had enough hops to keep the busheller busy. Tim tipped him off to be a bit generous when he dipped the basket into the bin; by crediting them with a whole bushel for a basket only three quarters full he raised the real rate to more than one and fourpence. John Sollars might not have approved; but at any rate the letter of the agreement was kept, though the spirit was broken, and the pickers were persuaded that they weren't doing so badly after all. "What we loses on the swings," they said, "we gains on the roundabouts." Mr. Comstock returned, and hung about looking depressed; he seemed to have lost heart and in a last despairing effort to keep the pot boiling he called another committee meeting. His committee of seven rather sheepishly followed him to a shady spot, where they sat down and passed resolutions in conspiratorial whispers.

Tim thought he was winning. Perhaps he would have won but for the inopportune arrival of Carol and the missioners. They parked their old saloon car at the edge of the hopyard and dispersed themselves among the pickers. Carol came up to Tim and said:

"You didn't mind me bringing them? They came to my shop and spent pounds on sweets for the children. They say they've got to get to know people, if they're going to do any good."

Carol was dressed, rather unsuitably, in a strapless suntop with the shortest possible shorts. It was bright green to go with her red hair. Her puppy-fat bulged out of the top of it pleasingly. She was carrying a bottle of suntan oil. Tim laughed.

"If Father was here he'd send you home to put on something decent. Take care you don't overexcite the missionaries."

"Charles thinks it charming," said Carol complacently.

"Well, I think you look like a Jezebel."

"Who are you to talk of Jezebels," said Carol with a bland smile. "Waving hanks covered with lipstick at the breakfast table? I do wish you'd tell me who it was."

"Well, I won't," said Tim; and remembering Sue he wished, as he had known he would wish this morning, that he hadn't promised to meet her again to-night.

Carol said:

"I'll set my missionaries on you, I think. Here's Charles coming over to us."

He was a nice-looking young man with a shy smile and the tense air of one who suffered acute spiritual conflict every time he was about to light a cigarette. Being introduced to Tim, he said earnestly:

"Can we be any *use,* old man? I mean over this strike you're having? If we can do anything, bringing people together you know, well, that's the kind of thing we're here for."

Tim's heart sank as he looked down the hop-row and saw that the other missioners, a girl in slacks and two men wearing grey bags and blue blazers, were already in conversation with Mr. Comstock. He realised that Mr. Comstock, who probably believed in nothing more spiritual than dialectical materialism, would be only too pleased to enlist the forces of Christianity on his side. He explained to Carol about him.

"That little man?" she said. "He came into my shop yesterday, and the meanie only bought one razor-blade, tuppence. Then he asked what happened to my profits."

"And of course you told him you were going to buy a dress?"

"Of course."

"Exploiting the workers," said Tim.

"Do you think he's a *real* Red? Comstock the Commy? A member of the Party, I mean? How exciting," said Carol, "I've never even seen one before."

"If he is one," said Charles, in the tone of a hunter whose attention has been drawn to the spoor of an exceptionally large lion, "he's just the kind of chap we ought to get to work on, isn't he?" He glanced at Carol with an expression in which deep devotion, and the alarm of Saint Anthony tempted in his cell, were nicely intermixed.

The other missioners had got to work on Mr. Comstock already; or perhaps he had got to work on them. They now came hurrying down the hop-row with bright happy smiles that seemed to say: Blessed are the peacemakers. They introduced themselves to Tim. "Bill—Ram—and Pansy only she's called Poppet." Bill was huge, gaunt and bespectacled; his ginger hair rose *en brosse* from his forehead. Ram, who turned out to be an East Indian, was small and sallow and bespectacled. Pansy called Poppet was a very pale girl without spectacles but with a red mark across the bridge of her nose where she generally wore them. They all shook hands with Tim, and Bill's grip nearly cracked his metacarpal bones. Bill said:

"We've been talking to the strikers' spokesman. Hope you didn't mind us butting in. He seemed a decent johnnie. We felt we might bring you together, somehow."

"I don't think it's very much use me talking to Mr. Comstock," Tim said.

Ram said, with a slight sigh and an air of bearing upon his shoulders at least as many of the world's troubles as Mr. Nehru:

"Come, man, come, man, these little troubles are best solved by talking about them. Mediation, man."

Bill put in, as if to excuse him:

"You'll think us frightfully interfering. But we do believe we've found that with industrial problems, with all problems, it never does any harm if you bring God into it. Well, talking to Mr. Comstock, we thought we had a rather bright idea."

"A pellent idea," said Poppet.

Tim looked at her in bewilderment. Charles hastened to explain:

"Opposite of repellent. Sorry, it's Somerville slang. They run a magazine called *Couth.* That means the opposite of uncouth of course. And if I said Carol was pugnant, I'd mean she was, well, jolly nice." And he gave her another long glance of terrified devotion.

Tim was still somewhat confused, but he had taken to Charles, whose shy smile flickered out upon his otherwise grave face in the friendliest fashion whenever one looked at him: as a cat purrs every time it is stroked. The others seemed well-meaning if a bit odd, though Poppet's pale eyes had a look of great intensity which was rather alarming. Tim asked:

"What was your bright idea?"

"Simple, man," said Ram. "They're asking for one and four; you offer one and two. Split the difference!"

Tim glanced from one earnest face to another. He would have liked to ask them if these elementary mathematics were the best that God could do, but he didn't want to hurt their feelings. He tried to explain to them about the agreement which his father had made with the other growers; to pay one and three would be just as much a breach of the agreement as to pay one and four. But it sounded meaner than ever when he put it into words. Bill said: "Isn't that a bit of a restrictive practice, old man?" and Poppet gazed at him with tormented eyes, making curious faces to herself, an ardent face, a disapproving face, an ecstatic face, in turn. This seemed to be an unconscious habit. Tim thought she looked as if she might go off her rocker at any moment; he also thought she was suffering from repressed sex.

Ram said (like Mr. Nehru offering to fly across the world in the interests of peace and good will):

"What would be the reaction of your father if *I* were to go and have a talk with him about it?"

Tim refrained from saying what his father's reaction would be. Carol, who was becoming bored with the whole affair, began to oil her shoulders. Being redheaded, she always burned badly in the sun. She said to Charles:

"Will you please do me where I can't reach?"

She handed him the bottle. Charles gazed at her with mounting alarm. He held the bottle between thumb and finger, gingerly, while Satan and Saint Anthony contended for his soul. Tim felt very sorry for him. At last he poured a minute quantity from the bottle on to the tip of his finger and smeared it between Carol's shoulder-blades with the gesture of one who anoints an ordinand with Holy Oil.

At this moment Mr. Comstock appeared upon the scene. He was a jack-in-the-box of a man. Tim was beginning to have a reluctant respect for him; for in the very short time since the missioners had suggested splitting the difference he had not only persuaded Wisdom to accept one and three but had got an assurance from the other pickers that they would take no less. So he said, at any rate; and Tim could see the members of the committee busy as bees again among the Black Country people and the Welsh. Mr. Comstock was certainly a quick worker. Now he presented Tim with his ultimatum:

"We give wye a bit and you give wye a bit as our good friends 'ere suggested?"

Tim thought hard. He said at last:

"I'm afraid I can't discuss it with you, Mr. Comstock; but I'll go and have another talk with Wisdom Lee." He had been on his way back to the gipsies when the missioners arrived; for it had struck him that his idea of only lightly filling the bushel basket might prove to be the simple solution of the whole thing. It would appeal to the gipsies, who always liked to feel they were getting something for nothing; and a sort of gentleman's agreement, that the basket should never be quite full, would be sure to please Wisdom. He was a man who always preferred to put his trust in a promise and a handshake than in any hard-and-fast bargain. So Tim's plan should satisfy everybody, except Mr. Comstock; it would not break the growers' agreement, or involve Tim in disloyalty to his father, but it would give the pickers more money for a day's work. If only the missioners hadn't put their spoke in, Tim believed he could have settled the strike. He would have liked to wring Carol's neck.

Mr. Comstock was saying:

"I'm the accredited spokesman—"

"You're nothing of the kind," said Tim. "Wisdom Lee is the King of the Gipsies, and therefore he speaks for the gipsies."

Mr. Comstock snorted at the word "king." Probably he didn't understand anything at all about the gipsies' ways. Probably all monarchy was anathema to him anyhow.

"The wairkers are solid behind me," he said. "I warn you that if you turn this offer deown—"

"Yes?"

"Eowt to a man," said Mr. Comstock. "*And* we picket the gates!"

No chance, in that case, of getting the gipsies back again; Grannie Lee would smell victory as well as pestilence, and Wisdom wouldn't dare to stand up to her. On the other hand, if Tim gave way now, Mr. Comstock would be an intolerable nuisance for the rest of the month. Tim had never met anybody like him before; but he recognised his disruptive quality. His presence not only spoiled Tim's good relations with the families that came year after year: it threatened the whole fun and happiness of the hop-picking. He was an alien creature, he didn't belong here, and Tim firmly decided to have no further truck with him. He said:

"There's nothing doing. You can go back to your bin and pick the hops; or you can get out."

Tim saw the unhappy faces of the missioners turned towards him: Ram in pained resignation, his spirit weighed down by all the crosses he had to bear, Poppet making unconsciously the face of one who is caught up in dramatic events, Bill with his mouth half-open showing big teeth, like a startled horse. Mr. Comstock, who perhaps found it difficult to believe that anybody should be ignorant of the importance of shop stewards, seemed stricken dumb. He looked helplessly at everybody in turn as if asking whether none would defend him against this outrage. He looked lastly at Carol, recognised the exploiter who took profit out of the workers' hard-won pence to buy herself an evening dress, was clearly shocked by the exploiter's half-naked appearance, averted his eyes and strode away.

There was a long silence after he had gone.

"Well!" said Bill at last. "I suppose you know your own business best, old man, but weren't you just a shade precipitate, don't you think?"

Ram said:

"Greatly fear such forceful methods out of date in changing world. Think again, man, and let wise counsels prevail."

Poppet goofed at Tim but said nothing.

Exasperated beyond measure, Tim nevertheless found something endearing in their absurd innocence. He wanted to laugh, but that would be unkind. They made him feel old and experienced, and he was surprised that although they were all about twenty, and up at a university, they were still not grown up—they seemed younger even than Carol, who was only eighteen. She was complaining now:

"I say, if they all go on strike there'll be no customers for my shop!"

The extent of this disaster had only just struck her. She pouted at Tim:

"And just as I was seeing myself expanding, like Izaac Wolfson."

"I see you expanding every day," said Tim; and prodded her.

"Beast!"

Charles glanced down the hop-row and said:

"Look."

His quick sympathetic smile flickered at Tim. Mr. Comstock was marching purposefully along the line of the bins. As he passed by each bin in turn the pickers grouped round it stopped work and followed him. Like a kind of vacuum-cleaner he was sweeping the hopyard of its people. He left a long row of deserted bins behind him.

"The Pied Piper," said Carol. Suddenly she cocked her head on one side. "Good Lord, listen. That's the Bristol."

Tim heard the unmistakable hum in the lane; then he saw it turn into the hopyard through the gate where the missioners had parked their car, but it didn't stop there. It came bouncing and bumping along the hop-row at about twenty miles an hour. John Sollars believed in treating his cars rough. That was why he bought expensive ones. If he struck a very deep rut and broke his back axle he'd simply buy another car.

He drove the car right up to Tim. He got out very slowly and Tim noticed that he held on to the open door as he stood beside it. He looked around him at the departing pickers.

"So they're off," he said.

"Yes, Father."

Carol's bare shoulders caught his eye. He shook his head in disapproval; but he had no time for her now.

"Get 'em back," he said.

"Back?" repeated Tim in astonishment.

His father looked at him for quite a long time in silence.

"You did right, my boy. But now I want you to get them back for me." All the peremptoriness was gone. "You see, Bill Ferrers rang up. They've got the downy mildew on Temple Farm."

Downy mildew was a fungus disease of the hops. It came sporadically. In some seasons the hops were quite free of it, in others only a few here and there were affected, but occasionally it would take hold, and spread far and wide, and run like wildfire through the hopyards from farm to farm. The experts from the Ministry of Agriculture talked learnedly about it, but they didn't know what caused it to appear nor how it was spread. They called it by a grand scientific name, *Pseudoperonospora humuli;* but the growers knew it was still the same downy mildew which had plagued their fathers' hops, though it seemed to have become more frequent lately, and more virulent. The old farmers put this down to the modern artificial fertilisers which perhaps made the hops outgrow their strength. John Sollars believed that the invisible spores of the mildew were carried on the wind.

"Remington's got it too," he said. "Just at the edge of his hopyards, nothing much yet; but he's taken on extra pickers in case it spreads. We'll have to pick quickly too." He leaned heavily against the car door, and he glanced again at the backs of the pickers streaming out through the gate. He was beaten, and perhaps it was the first time in his life he had ever been beaten. Tim thought of Napoleon upon the stricken field.

"So, in view of what that rat Tomkins has done," John Sollars said, "we feel we've no choice but to put up the rate. We've all agreed to pay one and four."

## 17

The battery was flat as usual; but Tommy said, as one who counts his blessings, "The great thing about living on top of a hill is that the battery doesn't really matter." He had to meet George's train at Ledbury at half past two. So Marianne pushed, and the half-witted youth who worked for Tommy because nobody else would give him a job pushed heartily with grunts and giggles; they got the car out of the yard and into the lane, where she could run down the hill. Tommy let in the clutch; the tyres scraped on the road, the car jerked to a stop, Marianne and Stan pushed till they were breathless, and Tommy with his head over the side said:

"Most awfully sorry; she was in reverse."

They had another go, and this time she was in the right gear but there were only coughs from the engine. Tommy got out and opened the bonnet and took off the cover of the magneto. He searched through his pockets for a nail-file, found one, and inserted it between the mag. points; he rubbed it briskly up and down. Marianne stood watching and considered his ridiculousness. He was still wearing the straw hat with the Free Foresters' ribbon. His complexion was bright red and dead white in patches. His awful wispy moustache was stained ginger by tens of thousands of cigarettes. He was smoking now, and the hot ash was falling upon the overflooded carburettor. His sheer incompetence was infuriating. Marianne knew that in 1944 he had taken a wireless transmitter to France. It had immediately gone wrong; he had taken it to pieces and naturally had made it worse. The Germans had hunted him. With all the bits in his pocket he had made his way into Provence, sampling the wine at any inn or café where the Germans were not in evidence. "In a bit of a daze," as he put it, he had found the Maquis at last. He had then put his wireless set together again, it had worked, and Tommy had told the men in England what it was necessary for them to know.

So Marianne was quite sure that he would make the car go. In the end he always did. His whole life was an obstacle race in which he climbed and crawled and wriggled over and round and under the obstacles his own folly had created for him. He smiled happily at Marianne:

"I'm sure she'll go now. But will you and Stan run *very* fast behind her, please, and push like mad?"

They tore down the hill. One of Marianne's shoes came off. "Push, push!" cried Tommy. He let out the clutch and Marianne felt the exhaust chugging out hot smoke against her leg. The car made its pneumatic drill noises. "Hurray!" cried Tommy, waving his thanks to them. Marianne limped back up the hill to pick up her shoe. Putting it on, she looked round to make sure the car was still going, and saw Tommy turn the corner by the signpost. Across the road just beyond the corner were John Sollars's river meadows; Tommy's adjacent pasture was hidden by the shoulder of the hill. She looked down upon the beautiful bend of the river, where it lay like a huge shining scimitar dropped by a war god in the valley between the farms. John Sollars's Herefords were standing hock-deep in a shallow place at the tail of his salmon pool. It struck her that there were an awful lot of them; then with dismay she realised that there were some brownish ones among the red. She remembered about the fence Tommy had meant to have mended. She called to Stan and pointed down at the meadow. He nodded vigorously.

"Yes. Master's cattle."

Marianne was horrified. There would be a big row about it

and the Sollarses would have a genuine grievance this time. It would put Tommy in the wrong and give them a kind of moral advantage over him. But there was much more to it than that. It was an unneighbourly thing. It was not only a breach of an unwritten country law, that each man must fence against his own beasts; bad manners came into it too. Marianne didn't know much about the law, but she had an instinctive feeling about the unneighbourliness, as if the peasants she had sprung from were speaking to her across the years.

"We must get them back!" she said to Stan.

"Yes, Miss," said Stan, grinning happily because it would be fun to chase them back. "Must be big hole," he said. "Driving them back will make it bigger. Then they'll just go through it again when we're gone." This was as far as his reasoning would go, and he looked pleased with himself but a bit puzzled.

"We must mend the hole. Is there any wire?"

"Big tangle."

"Listen, Stan," she said. "You must get the wire and some cutters and some stakes and something to hammer them in with." She heard the tractor in the yard; it was taking a load of hops to the kiln. "Then you must come down on the trailer and we'll mend the fence. Tell Robbie I said so." Robbie drove the tractor. He was an elder brother of Stan's but he was much more intelligent; he had been sent to an approved school for stealing. It was just like Tommy to give the pair of them a job because he was "sorry for the kids."

Stan shambled off, and Marianne hurried down towards the meadows. She went by way of the hopyards, to collect some help, and found Black Barty's two boys playing with the ferret. As they trotted beside her, the owner of the ferret said to his brother: "Throw it to me," and deftly caught it as if it had been a ball. Marianne wondered why it didn't bite them; it was probably too exhausted, and wished only for death.

They got to the meadow, where Black Barty's caravans were parked by the river; the whole tribe had been doing their washing, and old-fashioned underclothes, of strange shapes and mysterious purposes, hung on the line in striking contrast with some pink frilly knickers which obviously belonged to Sue. Now Marianne could see the hole in the hedge. It was wide enough to let a wagon pass. The stream beyond it was very shallow, and still muddy where the cattle had crossed. Yesterday the hole had probably been only a little one through which Black Alf's seventh child could just crawl; to-morrow if nothing were done about it most of the hedge would have disappeared. The gipsies devoured hedges. The grownups took the stakes to burn on their fires, but the smallest children had ways of their own with even the stiffest quickset; Tommy held that they gnawed their way through, like rats.

The two boys ran purposefully through the gap, pulling out two big sticks on their way. Marianne followed them, splashing ankle-deep through the stream, and now she was on the Sollarses' land and she felt uncomfortable about being there. She looked all round but there was nobody in sight; she hoped she could get the cattle back before she was caught. The gipsy boys raced on and plunged into the shallows under the willow trees, noisily splashing to drive the cattle out. They were very happy now they had something to beat, and although Marianne yelled at them they thumped the cattle impartially, John Sollars's as well as Tommy's, so that the whole lot stampeded round the field. Marianne tried to remember how many there were of her father's. She thought there were fifteen. It was fairly easy to tell them apart, for the Sollarses' beasts were bigger and their coats were a deeper red; but both lots were still mixed up together, and it was difficult to count them as they ran round the field. Marianne thought that, if only she could get them into a corner and keep them there, Robbie and Stan when they arrived might be able to sort them out. She tried to explain this to the boys, but they were completely out of control now, and they took no notice of her at all. Whenever she shouted at them she was afraid that her cries would bring John Sollars down in fury from his hopyard or his farm at the top of the hill. She felt vulnerable and incompetent, and angry with herself for being so helpless; she was thankful when she heard the tractor coming down the hill. But the gipsy boys, who could run faster than the cattle, had now got in front of them and were hitting their noses with the sticks. This caused a new stampede in the opposite direction; the whole herd came back straight at Marianne, swishing their tails as if they had the bree behind them. She saw a chance to head them into a corner and held her arms out wide, flapping at them. They took no notice until the very last moment, when they shied away and parted into two separate cavalcades, tearing by on each side of her. Their hoofs made such a noise on the hard ground that she didn't hear the other hoofs thudding behind her. The great chestnut horse seemed to come from nowhere. Tim pulled it up from the gallop and shouted:

"Can't you see she's in calf, you bloody little fool?"

He stood up in the stirrups and yelled at the gipsy boys: "*Stand still!*" To Marianne's astonishment they fetched up in mid-career and became immobilised in curious attitudes, like runners in a film which is suddenly stopped. Tim said more quietly: "Drop those sticks," and they dropped them, first one, then the other, plop into the grass. Then for the first time Marianne saw the cow. It had been running in front of the boys. Now it came to a stop with head thrust forward and forelegs wide apart. Its deep sides heaved. In panic Marianne wondered if it was about to drop its calf. Tim jumped off his horse. He didn't even glance at Marianne when he held out the reins to her.

"Hold him, please."

He went towards the cow, planted himself Sollars-fashion beside it, and stared hard at the barrel sides; as if, thought Marianne, he could see through to the inside of the cow, the dark womb with the embryo lying uneasy there. The skin on top of the cow's withers gave little twitches. At last Tim shrugged his shoulders and came back to his horse. He looked straight at Marianne this time. He said:

"I'm sorry I called you that."

"I was being that, wasn't I?"

"Sollarshill Sally. She's due quite soon; but of course you didn't know."

"Oh, Tim, has it hurt her?"

He took the reins.

"Not very good for her; but I dare say she'll be all right." To Marianne's surprise he gave her a kind of half-smile, and she was aware of a gentleness which she hadn't known about; she was in touch with him for a moment, then he put both his hands on the saddle and vaulted up, and once again he was right out of touch, miles away, formidable and remote and she hated him as he said: "Go back through the gap please and leave it to me." He rode over to the gipsy boys.

Stan by the gap like Hercules with the Hydra was trying to disentangle a roll of wire. Marianne told Robbie to move the tractor out of the way so that the cattle could come through. She watched Tim leaning down from his horse to talk to the gipsy boys. They were showing him their ferret; and they who hardly ever smiled were grinning like imps at something he said. Then they all three went among the cattle, Tim on his horse and the boys one on each side, a few yards wide of him; the boys hadn't got their sticks. All the time they kept their eyes on Tim, and now and then he signalled to them by waving or holding up his arm. Marianne could see that he had made it a sort of game for them, more fun than using sticks. She felt a fool. There was no shouting and the cattle never moved out of a walk, but soon all the big Herefords were back on the river bank and all Tommy's were standing together in the middle of the field. Then Tim nodded to the boys; they went ahead on the flanks as he rode up behind the cattle, which now ambled up to the stream, squelched noisily in the muddy water, and crackled through the gap in the hedge on Tommy's side. Tim told the boys to drive them on to the far end of the meadow. He sat on his horse and watched Stan struggling with the wire. He was thinking, Marianne supposed, that it was typical of Tommy to have such a roll of wire and such a nitwit as Stan to work for him. She glanced up at him and thought how the common people in the old days must have detested the knights; being on a horse gave a person an unfair superiority, a sort of you-be-damned air whether the person really felt like that or not. Robbie with a beetle was clumsily driving in the stakes; one of them broke off in the hard ground and Tim said: "You'll find it softer nearer in to the hedge." It sounded like an order, because he was on horseback. Robbie almost jumped to obey it. Tim was still watching Stan, and at last he could stand it no longer; he slid down off his horse and said: "Here, for goodness' sake, let me have a go." Once again he threw Marianne the reins; her only part in all this seemed to be that of horse-holder. Tim with his bare hands took the end of the wire and began to thread it in and out of the tangle. After a minute or two he let go of the end and the roll sprang apart like an uncoiled spring. Stan smiled and nodded like a child who has seen a conjuring-trick and pretends it knows how the trick was done. Tim went across to Robbie and held the stakes while Robbie hammered them in.

The horse impatiently tossed its head. Its big forefeet threatened Marianne's toes. It tugged at the reins. It was a very bright chestnut, unclipped, and its coat in the sunlight shone like a nut just out of its shell. It had a long mane and now as it arched its neck and flexed its ears and rolled its eyes towards Marianne it looked wild and beautiful, an out-of-this-world horse, an earth-spurner, a mount for a valkyrie or one of Phæton's, *Gallop apace, you fiery-footed steeds!* Marianne suddenly conceived a crazy ambition to get on its back. She'd ridden since she was four. She had hunted with Tommy, on a little black mare he'd bought her, for three seasons after he came back from the war. He went hard, in a desperate way, as if he were trying to get away from his debts. Marianne, back from school in the Christmas holidays, had kept up with him on her black. Then the debts overtook him and the horses had to be sold. Marianne wondered what it would feel like on the big chestnut's back. She stood lower than its withers even on tiptoe.

Tim was preoccupied about where to put the stakes. She called to him:

"Do you mind if I walk your horse round?"

He said: "Of course not," without turning his head. She put her foot into the stirrup and the horse revolved in rapid circles. She stood on the stirrup and somehow wriggled up into the saddle. The horse danced about, she couldn't find the other stirrup, and the horse's shoulders as it lifted both its forefeet off the ground felt so powerful beneath her knees that she thought it could shoot her off like a stone out of a catapult. Just then Tim looked round and said:

"Good lord, I thought you meant lead him."

The second stirrup conveniently swung itself over Marianne's shoe and she began to feel more at ease. Tim was watching her amusedly.

"Don't let him gallop," he said, "because I race him, so he'd pull your arms out."

She walked the horse for a few yards and then it started throwing up its head and taking unpleasant little mincing steps which jigged her up and down. She seemed extraordinarily far from the ground, and she didn't feel part of the horse, as she used to do when she rode the black hunter. She thought it might be more comfortable if she let the horse trot rather than tittup; so she eased the reins and immediately it began to trot very fast. It threw out its forelegs and took immense strides. Its pace changed from an ordinary trot into a kind of run which swung her from side to side, and she felt as if she were on a camel. This action had the effect of working up her skirt so that it was somewhere about her thighs and when she took her hand off the reins to try to deal with her skirt the horse with a terrifying plunge went straight into a canter. She leaned back and pulled hard at the reins but the horse simply threw its head forward and lifted her out of the saddle. She was standing up in the stirrups, and there was a great wind in her face, and now she tore past the two gipsy boys and had a fleeting impression of their great happiness at her plight and their eager anticipation of even more joyous things to come. Then she was among Tommy's cattle, which scattered before her, and then she was approaching the hedge at the end of the field. She thought the horse was going to jump it, and that would be the end. It turned away, however, and during this change of course she lost her offside stirrup and felt the iron thumping against her shin. Before her now lay the gipsy caravans, with Betsy's washing on the line.

The horse shortened its pace as it approached the washing. It swerved, and went parallel with the clothes-line, twisting its head sideways in a most alarming way and warily eyeing some combinations, a shirt and Sue's knickers in turn. Then some large flapping thing in the nature of a camisole bellied out in the breeze. This was too much for the horse. It gave a tremendous bound and at the same time seemed to go through the air sideways, throwing Marianne onto its neck. She now lost the second stirrup and the reins, and she was tenuously attached to the horse by means of one hand which grasped the cheek-strap and the other clasping a long lock of the creature's mane. The river came into her view, flowing apparently at torrential speed, as the horse galloped upstream along the path which the salmon fishermen used. The path was baked hard by the sun and the hoofs thumping upon it made a loud and menacing noise. This so terrified Marianne that she gave a convulsive wriggle, rather like the last despairing protest of a fish on a line. This wriggle, against all probability, got her back into the saddle; at the same time she found the reins and seized them gratefully. In doing so she gave them a jerk to which the horse promptly responded with another change of course; it headed towards the gap where Tim and Stan and Robbie stood close together making incomprehensible signals with their arms. As she came nearer to them they stopped waving and all three stood quite still, in somewhat awe-stricken attitudes —she saw Stan's dumpling face with his mouth wide open, like a hole in the middle of it. She thought that probably as far as her hinder part was concerned there wasn't much to choose between her and Lady Godiva. She couldn't do anything about it for she needed both hands on the reins; but fury at her ridiculous situation now took the place of her fear and gripping the saddle until there was a sharp pain in her thighs she leaned back and pulled at the horse's head. At first it seemed immovable; then it came up slowly like a boat's anchor dragged out of the depths. As it came up she continued to shorten the reins; this gave her a better purchase, and feeling she would be quite pleased if she could pull the hateful beast's head off she put all her strength into one terrific heave. The effect was surprising.

The horse, which had not taken the slightest notice of her previous efforts and perhaps had not even been aware of them, was now apparently persuaded that she wanted it to stop. It was a well-trained animal. It put both forefeet together, slid for a yard, and stopped dead. Marianne continued upon her way, over its ears. Tim was there almost as soon as she met the ground. He fielded her half-volley just as she was rolling over for the second time, scooped her up, set her on her feet and firmly held her there as he said, "Hurt?" She didn't know if she was really hurt or not; her behind felt as if she'd taken all the skin off it. Her hands went instinctively to smooth down her skirt. They encountered Tim's hands, enormous round her waist; he didn't take them away and he continued to regard her with serious concentration, in the same way that he'd looked at the incalf cow. But there was a twitch of laughter behind his concern, and as soon as she shook her head he let the laughter go, Marianne in release from terror started laughing too, and for an extraordinary moment she wasn't aware of Stan and Robbie looking on, or of Tim's hands round her waist, or of anything at all except a quite irrelevant happiness. Then Tim stood away from her and she looked round and saw Robbie grinning and Stan still gaping and the horse with the reins hanging over its head, grazing peacefully as if nothing had happened.

The sudden strange happiness vanished. It had come out of the blue like a visitation of the spirit, now it left her feeling oddly forlorn. Its irrelevance still puzzled her. She was angry with Robbie and Stan who were still goofing at her as if she were a kind of exhibit. And now Tommy's cattle trotted up, with the inquisitiveness of young cattle, and stood in a half-circle, a dozen stupid white faces all turned in her direction. The gipsy boys came after them, and stared at her in a resentful way, disappointed she supposed because there were no spattered brains or bones sticking out at curious angles. They nudged each other and whispered. She thought how silly she must have looked on the horse. She remembered about her skirt.

Suddenly Tim called to the gipsy boys: "Catch my horse, you two, can't you see he's going to step into the reins?" He spoke sharply, and they ran to pick up the reins. Now Tim turned to Robbie and said: "They'll be wanting you with the tractor, won't they, up in the hopyard?" Robbie took it as an order, and though as a rule you had to tell him three times before he would do anything he started the tractor straightway. Stan jumped up on the trailer. Tim said to Marianne: "Are you O.K. to walk back?" and she wondered how he had guessed that after what had happened she didn't want to ride with that grinning oaf on the trailer. He took her arm and led her away from the gipsy boys. He said:

"We've fixed the fence."

"Thank you."

He went on rather hesitantly:

"Yes, but look, there may be a bit of a row."

"Your father?" she said.

"I don't want to tell him about it but I've got to."

She couldn't see why he had to tell John Sollars.

"Must you?" She was thinking that it would mean more trouble for Tommy, on top of everything else. She thought of John Sollars as an enemy still.

"Well, yes," said Tim. "Your cattle aren't T.T., are they?"

"No." It had been silly of her not to understand. The Sollars herd was pedigree, of course, and tuberculin-tested. It mustn't come into contact with untested ones.

"It could mean reinoculation, and all sorts of things." He looked round at Tommy's cattle and said rather apologetically: "They are a bit scruffy, you know, Marianne."

"The hoi polloi," she said. "I'm truly sorry about it; about chasing that cow too."

"I expect she'll be all right. We're expecting an extra-special calf from her, on September the seventeenth."

"September the seventeenth? That's my birthday."

"How old?" He smiled at her.

"Twenty-one."

He was still holding her arm, just above the elbow. She could feel the palm of his hand, rough and hard, against her skin. She wondered whether he was doing it consciously, and, suddenly amused at herself as she remembered that village dance ages ago, she thought: It would be pawing if I didn't like it. But she did like it, and to show him she pressed her elbow against her side, where he was holding it.

He was still staring at the cattle. He said:

"That one like a highwayman with the dark patch round its eyes—" He broke off as he realised what she was doing. He looked surprised for a second and then he gave her a quick smile of acknowledgement. It was a completely un-reticent smile, and it said without wasting any time at all: If that's it, right you are. Hurray! He squeezed her arm. Marianne, her whole spirit adance, looked up at him and grinned. There was no need to say anything, and neither of them spoke for quite a long time. Then Marianne said:

"Yes, that highwayman—?"

Tim turned back towards Tommy's beasts. He looked at the one with the dark patch thoughtfully.

"Keep an eye on that one," he said.

"Why?"

"I don't know." He looked puzzled. He had let go of her arm, for they'd told each other all they needed to in that way for the time being. He went towards the beast and shooed it. He watched it carefully as it ran away.

"Just something not quite right," he said. "Nothing I could explain."

"Just a bit more scruffy than the rest?"

"I expect so."

They went back towards the gipsy boys who were holding Tim's horse. Marianne said:

"What's he called?"

"The Joker," said Tim.

"Why?"

"Chestnut. Not my pun. He was that when I bought him."

"Does he win races?"

"Just point-to-points. Would you like to ride him again?"

"What, after my performance!"

"Oh it wasn't too bad," said Tim. "You must wear breeches next time." He gave her one of those serious looks with the smile just twitching behind it. She giggled. She could have giggled at anything; her spirit felt like a kite tugging on the end of a string, up, up—it was flying away with her!

"I must get back," said Tim. "Father's not well and I'm in charge; we're picking in the top hopyard."

"But why on horseback?" It was puzzling her why he'd suddenly charged up on the chestnut when she was chasing the beasts.

"I was up in the farmyard when I saw your rodeo. The Joker was in the paddock, I just chucked a saddle on him. It was quicker on a horse."

"Well now you've wired yourself in," laughed Marianne, looking at the double strand neatly stretched across the gap in the hedge. "You'll have to go round by the road."

"Not I," said Tim, as he jumped up on The Joker. "Just you watch." He trotted a little way out into the field. Then as he turned his horse he gave her a grin and a wave, and cantered fast towards the part of the hedge where the wire ended. The chestnut's shoulders lifted gloriously and Marianne felt her heart lifting with them; Tim went over the hedge with hardly a crackle, easily flew the little stream beyond it. She watched him trot across the meadow where the Herefords were and stop for a moment to look at Sollarshill Sally. Then he went through the gate and he waved to her again as he cantered up the hill. It struck her that they hadn't said anything about meeting again; but it didn't matter, indeed it was right and proper, it was all of a pattern with what had happened when he was holding her arm. Marianne began to run home; she was much too happy for walking. The inside of her thighs, where she had gripped the saddle, felt as if they were on fire: but she was still running when she came to the gate by the crossroads and saw Tommy's car, with Uncle George sitting up very straight beside Tommy, turning the corner towards the Hope Farm. The back seat was piled with many suitcases, and a bicycle was lashed on to the back of the car.

# 18

George liked buns, Tommy had said, as if he were speaking of an animal at the zoo. So Marianne had spent most of the morning baking them and thinking how dull it was to cook for a teetotaller; he was said to like suet puddings too, which would make their boiled-rag smell in the kitchen—how much more fun it was to devise tasty little savoury dishes to titivate a drunkard's palate! Because she had little interest in the buns they turned out heavy and horrible; but George's non-smoker's non-drinker's appetite was sharpened by privation. He had obviously been too mean to buy himself lunch on the train. Marianne in awe as one who watches an ostrich eating nails counted to herself, two, three, four, five, as he gobbled up the buns. It was astonishing that he was so thin. He was just as she had remembered him, a lanky stooping Praisegod Barebones, all angles, knobbly; it was painful to imagine what his knees looked like. His bones looked as if they would burst through the skin stretched tight as a drum over them: an anatomist's delight. The newspapers, Marianne thought, would have described him as "balding"; that was what they called any man who hadn't got a complete mop nowadays. The receding hair gave him a high forehead which shone and which even George's multitudinous worries had not been able to wrinkle. He worried about his health and about his job and about his money and about the world. It was no wonder he couldn't sleep. He was saying earnestly to Tommy:

"The insomnia gingers up the ulcer, and the ulcer in turn increases the tendency to insomnia. It's a vicious circle, you see."

Tommy was looking distraught already, after only two hours of George's company. When George, replete at last, went upstairs to unpack, Marianne said:

"How long's he staying?"

"I don't know. He says he wants to put himself in the picture."

"What does he mean by that?"

"He wants to find out all about the state of the farm and my finances, he said."

"Well, I should think that would take him simply ages," Marianne said.

"He's a rather difficult person to entertain," said Tommy, "and of course we must try to keep on the right side of him, whatever happens. He's brought his bicycle. I suppose you wouldn't, between now and dinner, care to take him for a bit of a ride?"

Marianne cocked an eye at Tommy and read what was in his mind. If he could get George out of the way he could slip down to the Royal Victoria at six and fortify himself against the dreaded discussion with George which would obviously take place after dinner. But her bicycle in the shed had two flat tyres, and she was much too sore to sit on any more saddles. She told Tommy about her ride on Tim's chestnut. This cheered him up, and he laughed in his high squeaky way until the tears came into his eyes and made them red.

"But wasn't he very angry? People are fussy about their horses," Tommy said.

"Tim? No, he laughed too." And she remembered Tim laughing, and his hands round her waist, and hugged to herself a secret delight.

"So I can't bike," she said. "I can't even sit down properly. In any case I hate bicycling; it's waggling your legs to give your arse a rest."

Tommy blinked swiftly.

"But I'll tell you what," she said; she was sorry for him about the appalling prospect of talking business with George. "I'll take him a walk round the hopyards, then you can go down to the pub for an hour without him knowing."

"The pub?" said Tommy vaguely, pretending that no such thing had crossed his mind. "As a matter of fact, I rather thought I ought to Do My Money, as George will want to ask questions about it."

She knew he was playing the awful game he played with himself; it must never be admitted that he needed a drink, it must always be contrived that he had a drink by accident.

"Of course," he said, "we shall need some *soft* drinks for George, won't we?—lemon squash, tomato juice? Got to be hospitable even to a teetotaller. . . . Yes, I suppose I *ought* to go down to the pub. And of course if I take a notebook I can Do My Money while I'm there."

He smiled at her happily. George came in at that moment. He looked very depressed. He said:

"It's extraordinary how one always leaves the most important thing behind."

"Razor-blades I bet," said Tommy. "I can provide."

"No, phenobarbitone."

"What?"

"My sleeping pills."

"I'll be going into Ledbury to-morrow morning," said Tommy brightly, and Marianne seeing through him knew he was thinking of the Talbot and the Feathers. "I'll get some from the chemist's there."

"Good of you," said George. "Meanwhile I must put up with it." He sighed with a kind of "this-would-happen-to-me" resignation. "I shall stay awake all night with curricula running through my head."

"With whats?" said Tommy.

"In the Ministry," he said, "we are working out some new schedules. They probably won't get adopted; the teachers always oppose anything new. But we're trying to introduce some sort of uniformity into the curriculum. It's terribly untidy at the moment." The untidiness of everything was a great worry to George. "We could learn a lot from the Younger Countries," he said. "Do you know, in New Zealand, a man in my position in the Ministry of Education could take out his watch at a given time, and say to himself: At this very moment, in *both* islands, *every* child in a given grade is doing arithmetic."

"What is happening to the teachers who don't teach arithmetic?" said Marianne.

George looked at her in mild reproof of her stupidity.

"They are teaching the other grades," he said. He turned back to Tommy: "There is something about curricula which is peculiarly tantalising at three o'clock in the morning. Without the phenobarbitone I shan't sleep a wink."

"You ought to try a hop-pillow," Tommy said.

"What's that?"

"In these parts we believe it's a cure for insomnia. Marianne will make you one if you like. Perhaps it's just an old superstition, but you never know."

George shook his head.

"I hardly think an old superstition will do me any good. Even the pills don't work as well as they used to. I think I shall try a psychiatrist next," he said seriously.

"New superstitions for old," murmured Tommy. "Have it your own way; but all our people hold that hops are soporific. Maybe it's simply the beer they drink after hop-picking."

"Alas, yes," said George.

Tommy said after a pause:

"You know, George, you're going to find our hop-pickers a rather rough lot, I'm afraid."

George said surprisingly:

"For that very reason I'm looking forward to meeting them."

You could never say that George beamed, but he came pretty near to it now. It was an expression of smug beatitude which tightened the skin over his cheek-bones and caused pale patches to appear where the tension was greatest.

"In my job, inevitably, I lead a rather sheltered life. I get few opportunities of coming across other kinds and, ah, classes. The study of a community such as your hop-pickers will be very useful to me, I think. The rougher the better," said George, in the tone of one who girds up his loins. "You needn't think I am capable of being shocked. On the Social Biology Council—it's one of my interests, you know—we freely discuss subjects which would make even *your* hair stand on end, Tommy." He gave Marianne a glance that was almost arch. "And which you, my child, have never heard of."

She thought: Pansies and tarts I bet my bottom dollar; and she knew she would giggle if she caught Tommy's eye.

"We speak of them," said George, "as doctors do of diseases, quite objectively. We take the clinical view."

Marianne wondered how one would take a clinical view of Black Barty. She said:

"Well, what about coming down to the hopyard with me and having a look round? I think Father wants to put in an hour or two at his accounts."

"Accounts" sounded very grand for those hieroglyphs on the backs of bill-envelopes. Tommy gave her a wink so grateful and obvious that she was afraid George would have noticed it; but he had shambled across to the tea-table where he now stood staring in a contemplative way at the plate of buns. Is it possible, she thought, that this Bear is going to devour another? He fumbled in his pocket and pulled out of it an empty paper bag.

"If it's going to be a *long* walk—" he said; and he took a bun off the plate and popped it into the bag.

"Forgive me: but my doctor told me little and often."

Marianne marvelled that anybody should be able at will to

produce a paper bag out of his pocket. Then she realised that it must have contained the buns with which George had sustained himself in the train. He said:

"By all means: let us go down to the hops."

Just then the telephone rang in the hall outside. Some imp intruding into Marianne's mind gave her a nudge and whispered that it might be Tim; then she realised it was much more likely to be John Sollars, furious about the cattle. In the interval before Tommy got to the phone she had time to take a cool look at herself, she recognised all the symptoms, admitted that she was a little fool, and was happy to be so. Then she heard Tommy saying: "My dear fellow . . . it completely slipped out of my mind. No, alas, they're not T.T. . . . Is it really as serious as all that?" George was listening, and she thought it would give him a bad impression of the state of the farm if he learned about the cattle breaking through the hedge. The sooner she got him out of the way the better; she said:

"Come along, Uncle, or the pickers will have finished for the day."

He followed her into the hall. Tommy with his agitated turkey-cock look had the telephone to his ear by the John Martin picture of Adam and Eve in Eden. She could hear John Sollars's voice angrily crackling away. She slipped by quickly and opened the front door for George. They were out in the garden, and she was shutting the door behind her, when Tommy began again:

"I'm *really* sorry . . . yes, yes, I do realise . . . good fences make good neighbours . . . I wouldn't have had it happen for worlds."

She thought George hadn't overheard; but when they got to the farmyard he turned to her with a slight sigh:

"I know little about farming, but I should have thought it was one of the fundamental things."

"What?"

"Good fencing I mean."

He looked gravely round the farmyard. It was a muddle, of course, as all farmyards are. There were the two old carts with the shafts broken, a ladder lacking half its rungs, a gate off its hinges and tied to the post with wire, a pile of rusty paraffin cans, the old sow at large, Tybalt with a live mouse in his jaws, some grubby-looking ducks, three white turkeys perching on the remains of a wall that had fallen down long ago and had never been mended because it wasn't a very important wall.

"I could swear," said George, "that wall was down when I last came here, on VJ-Day."

Marianne retained a lively recollection of George's visit on VJ-Day. He had come down from London to escape, he said, from "the mass hysteria and the flags and the crowds." Pacifism, plus seventy-five thousand pounds, was his inheritance from the Quakers. He hadn't been able to escape from the church bells merrily ringing in all the towers from Sollarshill to Tedstone Wafer, and Marianne's mother, exasperated by his long face, had said to him angrily:

"For heaven's sake, George, don't look as if they were tolling for a funeral."

"In a sense they are," he had said. "*Hiroshima.*"

Tommy was still in France. Suzette as she got the lunch ("No garlic in the salad, he doesn't like garlic") whispered to Marianne: "We're going to drink Papa's health to-day in spite of the old misery," and she had put a bottle of red winc on the table. George, of course, wouldn't touch a drop and drank water with his Spam. Suzette, though she was abstemious as a rule, proceeded to drink half the bottle on her own, because it was VJ-Day and she was lonely without Tommy. Flushed and a little tipsy, she had suddenly jumped up and cried:

"Come on now, George. *À la victoire!*"

At first George wouldn't get up. He said something about his Principles. Suzette had almost dragged him to his feet, and to humour her he had taken a perfunctory sip of his water, murmuring: "Very well: to Peace—at last."

"That's not good enough," said Suzette. "Victory—and Tommy!" She had picked up the bottle and splashed some wine in Marianne's glass. George had protested: "Suzette!

Remember she's only a child!" and then Suzette in defiance and devilment had filled Marianne's glass to the brim. George had said in a pained whisper: "Only think what it may *lead* to"; but Marianne catching her mother's excitement was on her feet fairly shouting, "To victory—and Papa!" as she drank the wine that was hot and mysterious and sacramental on her tongue, like the cup at Communion. Soon after that George bicycled off to catch his train to London, and Suzette had a headache and cried because Tommy wasn't there.

Marianne had asked:

"Why didn't Uncle George go to the war? Was he afraid of being killed?"

"Oh no, I don't think so." They were speaking in French, as they often did when they were alone together. "People like George aren't afraid of death as a rule," Suzette went on. "It's life they're frightened of." She suddenly laughed through her tears. "I always think you can judge a man by his taste in food. You will generally find, my child, that people who are afraid of garlic are afraid of life."

## 19

Life throbbed and pulsed in the hopyard, with a rhythm that quickened towards knocking-off time. The Welsh girls sang snatches of song, and chittered and giggled together about the dates they'd made for the evening. Even Dolly, who looked, thought Marianne, almost as near to her time as Sollarshill Sally, seemed to have forgotten her unbecoming pregnancy and had joined in the fun. Marianne saw George's bleak gaze turned towards her and then swiftly turned away; she fancied he nodded to himself, as if to say that he had expected no less. At one bin, where the girls had stopped work already, one of them was teaching three others the steps of a new dance. She held up her skirt and did quick light steps on the sunbaked ground; the other girls followed suit, and suddenly they all spun round in a whirl. They had slim brown arms and pretty legs and neat little breasts scarcely concealed by their thin dresses; against the green of the hop-bines they looked like a rout of dryads. Marianne in her new-found happiness would have liked to dance too. She stood and watched them, forgetting George, and as the warm sunshine fell on her neck she had a sense of life humming and pulsating all round her, life lilting in the Welsh girls' chatter, adance with their quick feet, abuzz among Mrs. Towner's Black Country brood, new life astir in Dolly's big belly, the eager life of the children all swallowing experience like trout gobbling flies, life angry and murmurous somewhere down at the end of the hop-row, where some of the gipsies seemed to be having a row—she heard Black Barty's voice crackle like a whiplash and Betsy or Sue utter a sharp cry.

She glanced at George, and she thought her mother had been right. She could sense his alarm even though he was looking singularly determined and purposeful, with a kind of *Bring me my bow of burning gold* expression in his eyes. He said: "Let us continue our tour of inspection," and Marianne took him down the row and introduced him to Mrs. Towner. She gave him a sticky hand to shake, then she turned to Marianne:

"Ah'm real glad you'm coom, dook; the kids 'as all brukk out in spots sooden-lake—Lizzie!" She seized a ten-year-old girl by the arm and said, "Show the lady and gent your rash." She unbuttoned the front of the child's dress and held it open. "Theer," she said. "Am it chicken pox or maysles, dook? Ah'm crossin' me fingers it ain't maysles. See 'ow red it es, and she ain't bin scrattin' it neether. It's all over her fanny too."

Marianne glanced sideways at George; she remembered Tommy saying that he was mortally afraid of germs and that he washed his hands in Dettol three times a day. He had retreated several steps backwards and from that distance was presumably trying to take a clinical view of Mrs. Towner and the rash on Lizzie's chest and the unwiped snotty nose of Lizzie.

"It's probably just the heat, or something hasn't agreed with them," said Marianne. "But to-morrow if it's no better we'll send for the doctor."

She turned to George:

"Perhaps you'd like to meet the gipsies now?"

George marched at her side with the air of an earnest anthropologist setting forth to study the habits of head-hunters. At the bottom of the row, where the gipsies worked, there was an ominous silence. Marianne could see that Black Barty was in one of his thundery moods; he was darkly confabulating with Black Alf, so that the pair of them looked rather like the two Murderers in *Macbeth*—"Ay, in the catalogue ye go for men." Every now and then Barty turned his head to glower at Sue, who was clearly in disgrace for some reason and was picking with unusual industry, her honey-coloured head bent low over the bin. Even the gipsy boys were dutifully at work, and Betsy was brewing a pot of tea to put her lord and master in a better temper. She gave some to George in a grimy cup that still had traces of Sue's lipstick round the edge of it. He didn't notice the lipstick until he had the cup in his hand, and then he stared at it in dismay. Marianne wondered if he was thinking about V.D., which was no doubt one of the subjects earnestly discussed by the Social Biology Council. He managed to pour away the tea when Betsy wasn't looking, and munched his bun instead. Marianne thought he had suffered enough for one day, so she took him home by way of the path that ran round the edge of the hopyard. He was quite talkative and cheerful now that his initiation was over. When they encountered a small boy, one of the Welsh children, walking along the path, he greeted him most genially, "Hallo, young fellow-me-lad," and presented him with one of Tomkins' Boiled Sweets which he produced from a second paper bag he had in his pocket. He asked the child if he was enjoying his holiday. "Happy? That's the spirit," said George. "But I suppose in a week's time you'll be going back to school, and that will be nice too?"

The boy looked very hard at George, as if to discover whether he was making a joke. The Tomkins' Boiled Sweet formed a large lump in his cheek; he rolled it over with his tongue and transferred it laboriously to the other cheek. He spoke thickly but with emphasis.

"Bug-ger schoo-ul," he said.

After this George walked for a time in thoughtful silence. At last he said to Marianne:

"*I'm* quite unshockable, of course; but I'm sorry he said that word in front of you."

They got back to the farmyard. Marianne picked her way round the midden; George minced like Agag, trying to keep his shiny shoes clear of the brown liquid that had seeped out of the muck. He sniffed. The midden smelt strong and sharp and ammoniac and Marianne rather liked the smell. Pungent in her nostrils, it matched the impression of rank and throbbing life which the hopyard had given her. They came to the oast, where a sweet whiff of the hops was mixed with a tang of sulphur, and there by the door of the oast was Tybalt playing with his mouse, letting it run for a yard or two and then picking it up, like a child with a clockwork toy.

"Horrible," said George, averting his head from the spectacle of nature red in tooth and claw.

Tybalt then picked up his mouse and trotted towards them. With the perverse sycophancy of cats he went straight to George and rubbed against his legs, purring throatily through the mouse's fur. Sensing George's distaste, he proceeded to offer him the mouse, laying it neatly between his feet. George gave a shudder. "I hate cats," he said; and Marianne chalked it up as another mark against him, for she loved them and felt a kinship with them in some of her moods. Suzette used to call her "the little cat." "See, she goes prowling already," Suzette would say, half in laughter, half in reproof, when Marianne at sixteen or so used to slip out at night to go down to the village dances. When the moon turned the green grass silver-grey, and the trees' black shapes etched woodcut-patterns upon it, she would wish she could be Cat for an hour: what fun to scurry there on swift silent pads, pupils dilated, each nerve a-quiver—to know the ripple that runs between the shoulder-blades and down the spine and along the tail until it ends in a little twitch at the very tip of the tail—to hear the night's dark voices that speak to the nose as well as to the ear! And when she was feeling lazy she liked to lie in the sun like a cat, and to open and close her sleep-numbed hands like the paws of a cat in contentment.

The slanting sun was warm as toast, reflected off the brick wall of the kiln. She stretched herself and yawned and basked in it. She thought how awful it must be to be afraid of life, like George: life that was the sun on your neck and the hum in the hopyards, little Welsh wantons dancing and dating, gipsies quarrelling, kids with rashes, muck reeking, Tybalt's unknowing cruelty, pitiful heartbeat in poor frightened mouse, womb swelling in Dolly and in the Hereford cow, Tommy drinking down at the Royal Victoria, nappies hung out to dry outside the barn where the pickers slept, the fleas in their straw, the song in their hearts, the booze in their bellies, Tim on his chestnut, Tim's hands touching you, the things that touch did to you, O splendid, squalid, gross, generous, boisterous, beautiful Life!—And she stretched up her arms and smiled at George for no particular reason, sorry for him as he stood lanky and drooping like a long wry question mark, displeasure written all over him as he looked down at Tybalt purring and rubbing against the turn-ups of his trousers.

# 20

"Bed, Father," said Mrs. Sollars; she always called him that, never John. She took both his hands in hers and helped him out of his armchair, pretending that it was just a joke and he didn't really need helping. Tim went with them to the bottom of the stairs. A few steps up, John Sollars paused, with his hand on the banisters, getting his breath. "Go down to the meadow to-morrow," he said. "See that he's properly mended that fence." He'd been grumbling all the evening about Tommy's cattle getting out; he'd always despised him, but he hated him for this. "*My deah fellah,*" he said, imitating Tommy's voice. "That was what he called me."

"What did you call him?" said Tim.

"A rotten little bastard."

One step at a time, John Sollars went upstairs. Then Tim slipped out by the back door, and the small moon was high over the black vanes of the oast. He was late already, and now Carol appeared from nowhere; she trotted up to him out of the dark, eager and confidential as a fat little spaniel puppy.

"Where are you off to?"

"The oast."

"I'll come too."

"It's time you turned in." Damn Carol. "What have you been doing, anyhow?"

"Cashing up at my shop," she said grandly. "Four pounds seventeen and eightpence: I'll be able to buy that dress soon. . . . I say, where *are* you going?"

"I told you. To see Dave."

"Whopping lie." She made a face at him. "It's that girl."

"What girl?"

"I'll just make one guess." Tim wondered how she could have found out about Sue; but she said, astonishing him:

"Marianne T."

"Now why the devil should you think—"

"Deduction," said Carol. "She's supposed to be very naughty, and you've never been known to waste time with a good one. I wonder if she really had a baby, when she ran away? I wish I could meet her; I'd get her to tell me the Facts of Life."

"You'd better ask your missioners," said Tim.

"Charles is too sweet; he wouldn't know. We talked about God this afternoon. He said he thought there was a Purpose in everything that happened to us: him joining the mission, and changing to come to this particular farm instead of all the other farms, and meeting me. I say, Tim—"

"Yes?"

"Tell me something seriously," she said. "Do people always feel religious when they're in love?"

Tim looked down at her, and Carol in the moonlight was as grave as a nun; she made him feel about fifty, and wicked and wise. He said:

"Yes. Yes, in a way I think they probably do."

"Hurray," said Carol, and laughed and scuttled back towards the house. "Remember to wipe the lipstick off this time."

Tim went across the Home Ground and through the gate at the end of it. Then he hurried up the hill. Sue would be waiting by the stile into the Old Wood; and he thought what a damned fool he had been to make that promise last night, not to end it then and there. It did not occur to him that he needn't keep the date; it would be hateful to think of a person waiting for one in vain. But there would be no lipstick on the handkerchief this time (You're wrong there, young Carol! he thought); he must just tell Sue that it was finished and say goodbye. Tim believed that dead love-affairs should always be given a decent burial. He hoped it wouldn't hurt Sue; and then he realised with surprise that he didn't know enough about her to know if she would be hurt. Another odd thought came to him as he climbed the steep path: that Sue and he had never once laughed together. There was surely something wrong there. Loving, with Tim, was never very far from laughing. Laughter was the cleansing wind, and without it there might be shame. Fun shared together, bodies' play and the play of minds, was Tim's private and personal justification for love; and it seemed to show up the slightness and the tenuousness of his relationship with Sue, that they had never held hands and laughed. He remembered Marianne in the meadow, smoothing down her skirt, meeting his hands as he held her waist; and how all at once they were both laughing and in that brief moment, heaven knew why, he had been closer to the girl he'd never kissed than he had ever been to the little gipsy he'd made love to in the wood.

So as he went to meet Sue, he thought of Marianne. He tried, for his delight, to see her in his mind's eye: yellow dress, dark hair all over the place, eyes a sort of sage-green? But the heart didn't catalogue and particularise; and mainly Tim remembered small absurd things: a smudge on her nose, probably cowpat, from her fall; lipstick a bit slapdash on a full lower lip; a sort of compactness, trimness, within the yellow dress that made him think of a crocus or a candle flame; a quick look, almost comic, of "Wonder-what-you're-up-to" when he held her elbow; and then the elbow pressed hard and quite deliberately into her side so that his hand was right under her breast. She had glanced up at him when she did this, and it was that glance which was bright in his mind now, as he turned his head to look across the valley towards Tommy's farm. He saw, like a star very low on the horizon, a light in one of its windows. Heigh-ho, Marianne! He smiled to himself and then, as it were for good manners' sake, he put Marianne out of his mind. For he could see the Old Wood very black in front of him; he could see the lighter patch where the stile was, and where Sue, perhaps, was cocking her head on one side, sharp-eared as a fawn, hearing his step. He must get this thing over quickly and decently; he must clear the decks. So he went up the hill with great strides, and came to the stile, and stood with his hands on the top of it, looking for Sue. Beyond the stile the ride, overhung with trees, was pitch-dark and he thought Sue was playing a game with him, hiding, pressed against a tree trunk, lying doggo until he got over the stile. He didn't want to go into the wood, and perhaps be caught up in her game, for that would make it more difficult, afterwards, to say what he had to say. So he whistled. He knew she was there, though he wasn't sure whether it was eyes or ears that had told him so, whether he'd seen some movement or heard a breath. Even as he called her softly—"Sue! Come out!"—he thought it wasn't like what he knew of her, to play such a game. But then he heard breathing quite distinctly and very close at hand; she must be in the bracken, only a yard or two off, on his left. He was about to call again when the bracken rustled and then, sudden as a jack-in-the-box, a figure loomed right in front of him at the other side of the stile, a figure that had been crouching and now swiftly stood up.

"No, Master Tim," said Black Barty softly. "My Sue couldn't come to-night. My Sue's in the caravan where a good gel ought to be. 'Tis late for night-walking."

Completely taken by surprise, Tim heard himself say, "Well, Barty!" and thought what a foolish thing it was to say. Black Barty moved closer, and put his hands on the top of the stile close to Tim's. There was a little pause, during which Tim had time to collect himself, and a feeling of extraordinary alertness took the place of his surprise. Black Barty was breathing rather hard—it was the sound Tim had first heard—and Tim could smell the beer in his breath. He sensed, rather than saw, that Black Barty had staggered slightly as he held on to the stile. He was drunk, but not very drunk; and Tim remembered something that Wisdom had once said about Black Barty: "He's a fool when he's sober, and he's a mad fool when he's drunk; but in between he's real dangerous."

He said steadily:

"I see: Sue couldn't come, so you came up to tell me. That was nice of you."

He sensed that Black Barty was smiling. He was quite at ease now, and it gave him a kind of pleasure to feel how sharp his perceptions had suddenly become. In the silence he listened to the night noises in the wood, and part of his mind, quite detached, separated them one from another, mouse's soft chirrup from grasshopper's chirp. The other part was occupied with Black Barty: trying to find out exactly why he had come and what he wanted.

Black Barty said:

"We ought to have a talk, you and me."

"What's the game, Barty?"

Black Barty stiffened. "Game? It's you that bin up to games. See here, Master Tim, we gipsies ain't like other folk: we're strict. We has our ways; and some of our ways is different from your ways; but they're strict, and we keeps to 'em."

It sounded like a practised speech. Indeed Tim knew his gipsies well enough to be sure Black Barty had thought it all out beforehand. But he still didn't know exactly what Black Barty was driving at.

"When a gel's married, the chap as marries her has to be sure as she ain't bin up to anything beforehand, see? He likes," said Black Barty with a cackle, "to see the evidence."

Blackmail? thought Tim. It sounded like that. Old Grannie Lee, in her cups, would sometimes tell long meandering prurient tales of gipsy marriages long ago; of the jealous care of old matriarchs that their son's bride should prove her virginity on the wedding night: "blood on the sheet." But Black Barty wasn't a thoroughbred gipsy, he was simply a traveller, and his mongrelly tribe, if you could call it one, was very far from being strict about anything. Barty's fine words were part of the play-acting, and Tim felt sure he'd rehearsed them to himself as he walked up the hill. But there was menace behind them, and Tim wondered how much Black Barty had guessed, how much he actually knew.

"So if anyone was casting eyes on my Sue, her father would want to know, wouldn't he, Master Tim?—he'd want to know what was going on, and have a talk to him as was casting eyes, man to man."

Black Barty moved a little, and for the first time his face came into the moonlight; his blind eye, with the lid drawn over it, was in the shadow, and it looked like a cavity, a hole into his brain.

"Man to man," he said again.

"Say what you've come to say," said Tim. "Get on with it."

"There's no call for us to lose our tempers." His tone had a suspicion of a whine in it now. Tim's quickened perception told him that Black Barty was sobering down. He'd probably taken the drink to give him Dutch courage. He was less confident as its effect lessened and as he lost his initial advantage of surprise.

"The way we folks live, a good son-in-law could be a prop for a man's age." Tim noticed that Barty moistened his lips. He was coming to the point now, and it was surely blackmail. "So you see why my Sue's got something as is worth something, in a manner or speaking, to her father that has kept her and brought her up decent. If she lost it—" said Black Barty, and gave a long pause appropriate to melodrama—"I'd thrash her to within an inch of her life, if I thought as she'd lost it!"

Tim thought: Then he hasn't found out *everything* about Sue and me anyhow, or he'd be taking a different line. Nevertheless it was hardly conceivable that he didn't know Sue for the little wanton she was; so this was a kind of build-up, presumably, for some demand or threat which he was going to utter in a few minutes. Seeing through Black Barty, Tim still couldn't make out what form the blackmail would take. He thought he was going to threaten to tell John Sollars, and he was ready with his answer: Go and tell him and be damned. He was quite sure about one thing, that Black Barty was not feeling by any means as truculent as he pretended to be. He heard him take a deep breath; now it's coming, thought Tim, he's going to threaten me and then I shall have the pleasure of telling him to go to hell. But what came was completely unexpected. In quite a conversational tone Black Barty said:

"That's a nice little pony as Wisdom has got, Master Tim."

"Yes. But what's she to do with what you were saying?"

"Nothing. I was just thinking. I was over at Leominster last Friday. Chap there name of Loveridge, a dealing chap, has got a four-year-old, black, black as night, Master Tim. You ought to have seen her. She's a match for Wisdom's, but she trots neater an' she's got better shoulders. The chap wanted too much for her; but maybe I'll go along there to-morrow and have another try." In his haste Black Barty almost gasped for breath, his words tumbled over each other. "You could buy her for fifty-seven pun ten."

If this was blackmail, Barty was taking a long way round. There was no threat stated or implied; he went on in a wheedling voice:

"You're a horseman yourself. We all knows you as a horseman, Master Tim. If only you could see that little black, clean as a whistle she is—though they ain't clipped her out, she's rough, and it'd take a horseman to know how she'd look if she *wasn't* so rough—if you could just see her you'd say she was a sight better than that fat dun of Wisdom's."

Listening alertly, Tim understood many things. There really was a little black pony, and Black Barty really wanted her, for he spoke like a man possessed with covetousness; it was almost pitiful to see how much he wanted her, so that he could be even with Wisdom.

Tim also understood that he was trying to sell his daughter, for fifty-seven pounds ten.

"I thought we might kind of go shares in the little pony, you and me."

"Why should I go shares?"

"Well, of course, it's something between us, ain't it, you casting eyes upon my Sue?"

An unpleasant thought crossed Tim's mind: Was Sue in this? He didn't think so; but she might be. He remembered the difference in her which he'd noticed last night: the hint of artfulness, the scent, the high heels. So goodbye to the fawn in the Forest, the shy unknowable nymph! Serve me right, thought Tim, as Black Barty whined on:

"Fifty-seven pun ten is nothing to a gent like you; and of course she's only a slip of a gel, Master Tim. No man ain't ever touched her, 'fore God they ain't, I'd have cut the living daylights out of any man as had touched her."

And Black Barty put his hand in his pocket and brought out his knife.

The moonlight fell on its blade. Black Barty threw it up into the air, and it flashed like a silver fish as it turned over. He caught it cleverly by the haft. He threw it up again.

"She's only a slip of a gel," he repeated, "and no man ain't had her, Master Tim, 'fore God." I wonder, thought Tim, in horrible fascination, how far this monster will go? He stood still and listened, while Barty played abstractedly with the knife and meanwhile offered the freehold of his daughter, as it were inch by inch and foot by foot, each part particularised, for fifty-seven pounds ten.

He stopped at last, and slowly he turned his good eye away from the bright blade and looked at Tim.

"You could maybe run me over to Leominster to-morrow and have a look at the pony?"

"Get off my land in three minutes," said Tim, "*or I'll run you into gaol.*"

Black Barty stared at him. He looked genuinely astonished; also, Tim thought, he looked afraid. He began to whine again: "We was just talking man to man and there ain't no call . . ." but he came over the stile, rather reluctantly, and Tim stood back a pace or two, to let him come by.

"Now," said Tim. "Three minutes down the hill and into the lane. You'd better go fast or I shall help you along with my boot."

Black Barty stood hesitant. Tim thought he was going to run, but he seemed to change his mind.

"It wouldn't do you any good," he screamed suddenly, "if I was to tell some of the things I know—"

Tim took two quick steps towards him. It occurred to him afterwards that he ought to have remembered Black Barty was afraid; for a frightened man with a knife could be dangerous. He saw Black Barty raise the knife, and perhaps it was no more than a defensive gesture or a theatrical threat; but Tim hit him, with his right, as hard as he could on the side of his jaw.

Black Barty grunted. Tim saw the knife fall to the ground. Black Barty put up his fists, but Tim poked with his left, then swung his right again, and realised, with a kind of devilish satisfaction, that Black Barty was blind on that side; in the dim moonlight, anyhow, he couldn't see what was coming from Tim's right hand. This time he hit him just beneath his blind eye. He had boxed at school and been pretty good at it, but he had never known what it was like to hit a man with his bare fists when he was angry. He slammed again with sore knuckles, and Black Barty suddenly dropped his guard and began to whimper:

"Master Tim, Master Tim . . ."

"Get going, then," said Tim; and he put both his hands in his pockets.

Black Barty half-staggered, making little snivelling noises. Then he bent down and began to grovel in the grass. Tim thought for a moment that he was going to be sick; then he understood that he was hunting for his knife. Black Barty's bottom, as he leaned down, was an irresistible target, and Tim kicked it, not very hard, so that Black Barty toppled over. He got up quickly, still whimpering, and Tim saw that he'd found his knife. He put it in his pocket furtively; then he began to shamble down the hill, looking back over his shoulder every pace or two, his knees bent as he ran. He looked rather like an ape in the moonlight, he looked so funny that suddenly Tim burst out laughing. He leaned back on the stile and laughed; and when he stopped he heard extraordinary noises, almost animal noises, coming from half-way down the slope where Black Barty still shambled on. Tim realised, with distasteful pity, that Black Barty was sobbing.

He jumped up on the stile and sat there for a minute or two, while the shameful noises gradually died away. Instead he heard the usual badger in the wood behind him, snuffle, snuffle, grunt, and he thought: When the moon's full I must come up here, and make a hide close to his sett, and spy on him going out or coming in. The badger noise made him think of Sue, stiffening in his arms only twenty-four hours ago. How did she fit into Black Barty's little plot? He thought it more likely that Black Barty had found out somehow about Sue's meeting him and on the spur of the moment, encouraged by a bellyful of beer, had tried to turn the discovery to his own advantage. But of course Sue could have been in it too, a not unwilling bait for the trap set by Black Barty, planned and plotted for weeks in his crazy, cunning, fantastical little mind. Tim would probably never know; for the foolishness was finished, he'd done with Sue, he'd cleared the decks.

He rubbed his right hand, which was sore with a satisfactory soreness. A strong excitement filled him, and as he got down off the stile he looked across the valley towards Tommy's farm. The shine was still in the window at the very top of the black hill. He recognised it among many stars with the peculiar pleasure of a mariner who as he approaches harbour distinguishes from all the little luminaries the one expected, necessary light.

## Part Two

*First Quarter*

# 1

Tommy had gone off to Ledbury at mid-morning, trotting out the plausible excuse that he must see his bank manager. Even Marianne, who understood his little tricks, had to believe him this time; for it seemed that his special necessity to go to the bank arose out of his discussion with George last night: there were some deeds or documents which George wanted to see. Marianne didn't know how Tommy had fared in his talk with George; she had gone to bed early and left them to it. But this morning George was looking grimmer than ever, and Tommy, who was always terrified of the bank, was in a mood of deceptive jauntiness which she recognised as ominous. He had made all the wrong jokes at breakfast: jokes about bouncing cheques and duns; George had looked horrified. Then Tommy had taken George a walk round the farm and clearly they hadn't got on very well, for at about eleven o'clock Tommy had come down to the hop-yards alone. "I can't stand him in more than small doses," he said. "He drives me mad, maggoty-mad." He added, wild-eyed and conspiratorial: "So I'm going to toddle off now. But I'll be back by lunch-time, honestly. One thirty, not a minute later! You'll see to it if anything goes wrong? But nothing will go wrong, I'm sure."

Almost everything did. Robbie drove the tractor into a deep ditch and it took six of the pickers half an hour to get it out. The gipsies, who were all in murderous tempers and frequently fought among themselves, took advantage of Tommy's absence to bully Jake, the busheller, saying that he was cheating them by filling the basket too full. Three of Mrs. Towner's grandchildren went to the doctor, who confirmed that they had measles and must go home. Then the Welsh girl, Dolly, fainted. When she came to she said she had shooting pains inside her, so Marianne took her up to the house and let her lie down in her own bedroom. She wondered whether she ought to fetch the doctor, and asked Dolly when her baby was due. Dolly said: "Two weeks it might be, or more than a month. I cannot be certain."

"But, Dolly, *when—?*"

"I know, Miss," said Dolly, contrite and pitiful. "To work it out I do try so hard, in my head. Butt I am in a mud-dle."

While she was upstairs with Dolly, the rice pudding burned. George had demanded plain food, because of his ulcer, and Marianne hated cooking plain food. She had also done him a hash, and after waiting in vain for Tommy they sat down to lunch at a quarter past two. George ate the hash inordinately slowly; noticing that she had already finished he said: "The doctor tells me to chew everything three times." It was horrible to watch him chewing everything three times. He found a bay-leaf on his plate and removed it carefully, laying it on the side of the plate and apparently disapproving of it. He also found three peppercorns, which he examined suspiciously and placed in a row beside the bay-leaf.

"What are we eating?" he asked.

"Why, beef."

"I thought it was something that had been shot."

"No, those are peppercorns."

"I'm glad to know," said George. "They would be fatal for my duodenal."

He'd been prowling round the hopyard and talking to some of the children.

"They tell me—but I can't really believe it—that they're *not going back to school* till the end of the hop-picking?"

"Of course not."

"But don't their parents realise that they will be fined—heavily?"

"They're always fined," said Marianne. "But we pay the fines. It's worth it."

"You—your father—*pays the fines?*"

"All the farmers do."

George stared at her, masticating slowly.

"What's more," said Marianne, fed up with him, "I bet they learn more that's useful, in a month's hop-picking, than in a whole term at school."

"Learn more?" said George. "Ah yes, indeed. I hate to think of some things they must learn."

He found another peppercorn and added it to his collection. Marianne thought: "Tinker, tailor, soldier, sailor," and wanted to laugh. She was under the impression that she'd only put four peppercorns in the whole stew; it was odd that George should have them all. He said:

"That terrible gipsy fellow—"

"Black Barty?"

"He's been fighting, I suppose?"

"Looks as if he got the worst of it," said Marianne. "Serve him right."

George sighed.

"Well, *there's* your children's useful education!"

Marianne excused herself and made some tea and took a cup upstairs to Dolly. The shooting pains had subsided but Dolly was crying. Marianne sat on the chair by the bed.

"You poor kid," she said.

"Punished I am."

"You mustn't think of it like that. What about the chap, Dolly? Won't he marry you?"

"He asked me."

"Then why not—?"

"I do not like him."

Marianne left her with the cup of tea and went down to

serve George with the least-burned part of the rice pudding. He was beginning to chew it three times when she heard the garden gate open. She hoped it was Tommy, then she saw Stan coming down the path. More trouble, she thought; but at any rate it was a good excuse to get away from George. She went to the back door, and Stan, oafishly serious, gaped at her, nodded his head three times, swallowed and said:

"Miss, there's a beast down in the medder."

"Yes, Stan, there are fifteen," she said, not understanding.

"No, Miss; one's down and it can't get up."

"Sick?"

Stan nodded vigorously.

"I saw it when I went home for my dinner."

"I'd better have a look."

She ran back into the dining-room and told George she had to go out; he mumbled, with his mouth full, in reply. Then she hurried down the lane with Stan, and past the crooked signpost into the meadow. Opening the gate, she suddenly remembered what Tim had said yesterday: *Keep an eye on that one.* She followed Stan across the field, and sure enough it was the one with the dark patch, the one Tim had called the highwayman. But it wasn't lying down now; it was standing with its head lowered and its forelegs wide apart. When she went near it, it moved a few paces awkwardly, and as it walked a long drip of saliva swung from its nose. It flicked its tail in little jerks. Its hindquarters were all mucky, and in the thin excreta running down its legs Marianne saw with horror there were streaks of blood.

She thought at once: My God, if it's infectious—Sollarshill Sally and all those pedigree Herefords! They'd all been running together when she was chasing them yesterday afternoon, the highwayman among them—and Tim had noticed that it was sickening even then— "Just something not quite right. Nothing I could explain." It seemed important that Tim should be told at once. In any case she didn't know what to do about the sick beast, and with Tommy away Tim was the only person she could turn to. "Look, Stan," she said. "It's only a little way up the hill to Mr. Sollars's hopyard. The one they're picking in—you know. I want you to find Mr. Sollars, young Mr. Sollars, and tell him what's happened and ask him to come down quickly. I'll wait here."

Stan nodded energetically.

"And run, Stan, please."

Still nodding (like some lolling doll with its head loose, she thought) Stan went off at a gangling lope. While she waited Marianne walked round the sick beast in circles. She had no idea what was the matter with it. Foot and mouth? she thought. She didn't know the symptoms, but when it had walked those few steps it had certainly seemed to go lame; and there was that stuff coming from its mouth and nose. If it was foot-and-mouth the farm would be shut up—in the middle of hop-picking!—and that would finish Tommy. But John Sollars's farm would be shut up too, and perhaps all those beautiful cattle would be destroyed—he'd lose thousands. And it will all be our fault, she thought: our fault, because of that fence which should have been mended.

She looked at the beast again, and now its hind legs seemed to be sagging beneath it as it stood there. It had been rather a pretty little beast, with its white face and that queer dark patch like a mask running across its forehead. But now it looked grotesque and terrible, its eyes rolled and what should have been the whites were a kind of dull scarlet. Its breath came quickly and its sides heaved. When she went behind it she saw more blood in the fæces which made pools on the ground. She nearly trod in them by accident, and shied away. She wondered what awful things were happening inside the beast, what flux, what writhing spasms, what searing pain. Some violent fever, she could see, was working there, burning it up inside.

Then Tim came, well ahead of Stan, through the gate by the signpost. He crossed the field with those damned great arrogant strides. She said, rather foolishly: "It's the highwayman"—as if that weren't obvious. Tim stopped dead and gazed at the beast. It was just the same as yesterday when he was looking at Sollarshill Sally; he grew roots. This was an extraordinary thing about him: that wherever he took up his stance he looked as if he had been there always. She thought she had never known anybody else who could stand so still. It was almost frightening.

As Tim gazed at it, the beast's hindquarters suddenly gave way. It toppled over and lay with its forelegs crumpled, half on its side. Its mouth was open and its soft brown eyes, strangely gentle against the fierce scarlet which rimmed them, were turned towards Marianne. She could fancy a helpless plea in those eyes, and instinctively she stepped towards the dying creature. Her hand was outstretched to pat its head, an absurd and futile gesture, a solace to her own pity rather than to the beast's extremity. She had nearly touched it—she could hardly have sworn, afterwards, that she hadn't touched it—when suddenly Tim's hands were about her waist and she felt herself lifted clean off her feet as he swung her round.

*"Don't touch it,"* he said. *"Come away."*

He held her, so hard that it hurt, and carried her back with him, three or four paces. When he set her down again she looked back at the beast and knew that it was dead. She hadn't believed that anything could die so quickly; but that was a foolish thought, for of course everything died quickly in the end. It was an immeasurable moment between living and dying. She turned to Tim: "Why did you—?" and Tim without saying anything pointed to the beast, so very dead now with one foreleg sticking out straight and the eyes glazed over. She saw what she hadn't noticed before, a lot of blood on its nose and in the drools of saliva.

"*Did* you touch it?" said Tim.

"No . . . I don't think so. . . . No."

"You didn't tread in its—"

"No."

"We must get the vet. I'll come up to your house and phone him, if you like." He turned to Stan: "Stay here, keep the other cattle away from it. Don't go near it yourself." He was watching Stan as the youth gaped at him and he was obviously impressed by the half-wittedness of Stan, for he put a hand on his shoulder.

"I mean that, my lad; or maybe you'll be as stiff as that one in a few days."

Marianne said:

"Oh, Tim, what—what is it?"

"I'm not quite sure," he said. "But it could be something pretty beastly."

They went up to the house. Tommy's car wasn't in the yard. There was no sign of George. Marianne showed Tim the phone and he said: "Does it work?" and suddenly they both laughed. She said: "Yes, he's paid." Tim got the number and asked for the vet; he turned to her and said: "We're lucky. He's in his surgery." Then he said: "Hallo. Tim Sollars, but I'm speaking from the Hope Farm. They've got a dead beast here. Can you possibly come out straight away? It might be blackquarter but I think it's anthrax. . . ."

Marianne said:

"O Lord, how awful. Your cattle, Tim? How infectious?"

"Not very. Only the blood, I think. Are you sure you didn't touch it?"

"Yes . . . You were so quick, I couldn't have."

"Well, to be on the safe side, wash like mad. Got some disinfectant?"

"No, but I bet my Uncle George has. Wait a minute."

She ran upstairs and knocked at George's door. There was no answer, so she went in. There were about a dozen different bottles ranged on George's dressing-table: tonics and vitamin pills and aspirin and Dr. J. Collis Browne's Chlorodyne and stomach powders and hair restorer. On the washstand there were gargles and a bottle of Dettol. She took it with her and went down into the little washplace under the stairs. She left the door open and Tim came in with her. "Scrub," he said.

"Fusspot."

"These are rather special bugs, that's all."

"My Uncle George will be terrified."

"Who's he?"

"Father's brother. He's got the mortgage on the farm. He's down here because—" she paused for a moment: but there was surely no harm in telling Tim. "Because he's thinking of selling us up."

Tim didn't say anything. He looked at her gravely and nodded. Everyone knows the mess Tommy's in, she thought. She dried her hands.

"But he's frightened of bugs, so perhaps he'll go away."

"Now you smell like a nurse," said Tim. He smiled suddenly and put out his hands and took her by her elbows. He drew her towards him and she put up her face and he kissed her lightly on the mouth. He held her for just a moment, and then they both went out of the little washplace and neither of them spoke, nor needed to. Tim picked up his hat off the hall table—it was an old green felt one, with fishing-flies in it—and Marianne watching him thought that it was just the same as yesterday when he'd held her arm; it was something predestined and proper and neither of them must make any comment upon it, this was the way it had to happen, just like this.

Tim said briskly:

"I must get back to the hopyard. Father's in a flap—we're picking in a hurry because of the downy mildew—you've heard about it? He'll be in more of a flap when I tell him about this. But I'll come over as soon as we've finished picking and hear what the vet said."

He shoved the old hat on the back of his head and was gone.

## 2

The vet, who was small, bespectacled and without assurance when he got out of his car—Marianne had thought he was a commercial traveller at first—pulled a pair of wellingtons over his well-creased trousers, put on a white coat and rubber gloves, picked up his black bag, and was suddenly transformed into a figure of authority; as if his personality had put on the garb of professionalism too. They had driven down to the meadow, where Stan faithfully and fearfully stood guard over the dead beast. A mongrel collie, originally a stray, which had attached itself to Stan and followed him everywhere, was sniffing at the carcase. It was a disreputable and scavenging dog, and it had apparently been rolling too: there was muck and blood on its coat. It hadn't occurred to Stan to stop it, but now the vet said sharply: "Call off that dog," and Stan whistled it to heel. Then the vet walked round the carcase slowly and said: "Young Tim's made a good diagnosis, I should think; let's see if we confirm it." He bent over the beast and took one of its ears between the tips of his forefinger and thumb. He pricked it with a quick stab and smeared some blood on a glass slide. Then he went back to his car and Marianne watched him staining the blood with some blue stuff out of a bottle. "Now we'll have a look," he said, and set up a small microscope on the bonnet of the car. He peered through the eye-piece and adjusted the screws. At last he said: "Well, there they are. Beautiful."

"The bugs?" said Marianne.

"Yes. The methylene stains them blue, and the capsules go purple."

"Can I look?"

"You're not dressed for the job and *B. anthracis* is a nasty character."

"It's anthrax, then?"

"Yes. You must fence off that carcase. Bit of wire and some stakes. I'll notify the police and they'll come along with flame-throwers and burn it."

"What about the other cattle?" she asked.

"Not much risk. Your father bought them at market? Contaminated foodstuffs is the usual cause; and sometimes the bugs lie dormant in the ground. It's generally just an isolated case. But I shall have to destroy that dog."

"Oh . . . Stan's collie?"

"I'm sorry. It was licking the thing's nose."

"How awful. Look, can you wait a few minutes? He's rather fond of it. I shall have to talk to him."

The vet nodded. Marianne took a few steps towards where Stan stood, then she hesitated. He was playing with the dog, throwing a stick for it, trying to make it retrieve. She went back to the vet and said:

"This is really horrible. Stan's not quite . . . you know . . . and I think that dog's the only thing he cares about. *Must* you? Couldn't you wait and see if it—"

"No. It's been rolling in the stuff. Coat, pads, mouth, all infectious. It's a walking menace. Anthrax is a killer and I'm not prepared to take any chances with it. Sorry."

He was sharp and professional, putting away his microscope, packing the things into his black bag. Marianne knew it was no good saying any more so she went and told Stan but he didn't understand; she told him again, and then again, and all the time the dog was a few feet away, sitting on its haunches, looking up at him. She tried to use very short words: The vet thinks he may catch the illness from the dead beast: then he would die and it would hurt him very much. And he might give the illness to people—to you, Stan, and then you might die too. . . .

Stan's lips began to quiver and he looked at her not in anger or resentment but in fear, as if she were the agent of the Power that had taken all the things he wanted away from him always.

She said: "The vet won't hurt him. I promise he won't be hurt."

Stan leaned down with his arms bent protectively, as if he would defend the dog. "Don't touch it!" she cried, and Stan at last stood up. She said urgently: "He's your dog and you're the one who's got to let the vet have him. Please say yes, Stan." She wanted him to make the sacrificial decision, because then it might not seem to him that the world was always taking away. But she knew it was an impossible thing to ask him, and she could hardly believe it when he looked up at her and swallowed and said, "Yes." She called the vet, and he came quickly, and took away the dog. It hadn't got a collar, but he had his rubber gloves on and he pulled it along by the scruff of its neck. Stan began crying, noisily and not quite as ordinary people cried. She had always thought how silly it was when she read "Boo-hoo" in children's books, but Stan really made a noise like Boo-hoo. She put her arm round his shoulders and she didn't care what the vet thought, she hugged this child and tried to stop him crying. Then she heard the vet's car going away. She thought, not for the first time in her life, how bloody unfair God had been to some people; and when He was unfair He went on being unfair, which was extraordinary. He didn't square the thing up with a few compensations. The Lord has given, the Lord has taken away. She thought with painful humility what a lot of things she had: wits, health, fun; and this Stan had damn-all until a mongrel came along and unaccountably wagged its tail at him.

Stan sobbed, and she tried to comfort him but she knew that in his world commanded by devils called "They" there was no comfort she could give. "They" won't let the girls dance with me at the village hop, "They" make fun of me in the pub; "They" talk about things I can't understand and blame me for not understanding; "They" took away my dog Petunia. Why Petunia? She would never know; but that was the name which out of some fantasy of his imagination Stan had given to the collie.

" 'Tunia," he sobbed, " 'Tunia."

## 3

Tommy had emerged from the bank manager's office at half past twelve feeling as if he had escaped miraculously from a fiery furnace: Shadrach, Meshach and Abed-nego rolled into one. He boldly cashed a cheque at the counter, which he was now able to do because the limit of his overdraft had been increased by three hundred pounds; and this, as always, gave him the sense of being richer by three hundred pounds. It hadn't been an easy interview and the bank manager had said: "You know, we're not moneylenders, Mr. Tomkins" —which Tommy thought was a taradiddle if ever there was one. But in the end he had promised to sell the fifteen cattle next week at Ledbury Market, and on that condition he was permitted the extra overdraft. He had also got the documents for George; but he was persuaded, at any rate after he'd had three stiff drinks at the Feathers, that if only he could avoid a bad financial crisis until the hops were in George might relent about the mortgage. The extra overdraft would keep the wolves at bay for a week or two; then he'd sell the cattle, and perhaps scrape through until the end of hop-picking. In the Feathers they were saying the cattle trade was very good; they were also talking about downy mildew, which had broken out on two more of the hop-farms. That was ominous, but after another drink or two Tommy realised that the price of hops might go up if there were a shortage. The ill wind might blow him a lot of good so long as the Hope Farm escaped the pestilence; and Tommy in his present mood, feeling marvellously reprieved by fortune, simply would not entertain the possibility of such a catastrophe happening to *him*. So he went to the Talbot, and because it was market day the bar didn't shut at two; the pubs were open all the afternoon. A man in the Talbot told him he had heard they had the mildew badly in Kent; good hops were going to be at a premium this year. Tommy began to see a fortune in the offing. At half past three he tore himself away and the car seemed to go much better, as it always did when Tommy had had a lot to drink: as if it had been round the pubs, too, and had secretly poured a few whiskies into its petrol tank! Pleasant fantasies of a Drinking Car played through Tommy's mind as he roared and rattled along the Hereford road, past the pub called the Trumpet wishing its doors weren't shut, past the busy hopyards, past (by a lucky inch or two) three gipsy caravans which he overtook on a corner. He had his foot right down all the time, because it suddenly seemed tremendously important to get back to the hop-picking, to urge on the pickers, to institute overtime, to gather in the hops before the downy mildew came any closer: the hops which might be worth a packet this year if half the crop both in Kent and Herefordshire was going to be ruined.

So he came at last, in a cheerful daze, into the farmyard at the Hope. Tim's M.G. was parked by the gate, and this vaguely puzzled him. He went through the gate and saw Tim and Marianne and George and four figures that looked like visitors from Mars. They wore black shiny suits and sou'wester hats and rubber boots. In their gauntletted hands they carried the kind of guns which spacemen had in the comic strips. The whole scene bewildered Tommy, who suddenly began to feel very drunk indeed. George came up to him first, George smelling oddly of disinfectant, and he was saying: "For heaven's sake pull yourself together. A terrible thing has happened. . . ." One of the spacemen spoke to him: "I'm real sorry about this, sir," and Tommy, more confused than ever, recognised the spaceman as Police-Sergeant Croft. Then Marianne was at his side, a ray of sanity amid the confusion, and she had him by the arm and was leading him away. He heard her say, "One of those cattle down in the meadow. . . . Everything's fixed and the police are going to burn it. . . ." Then he heard the word "Anthrax." "But you mustn't worry, the vet says the others aren't likely to get it. Uncle George is in an awful flap, of course. . . . I say, are you all right, Father?"

He tugged himself away from her and leaned on the gate and for a few seconds the whole farmyard cakewalked about him. He retched, and through smarting eyes saw the blurred Martian figures with their short blunt flame-guns swaying and swirling; white turkeys gobbling; George out of focus, attenuated, long-faced like someone in a distorting mirror; Tybalt irrelevantly walking by with his tail in the air. Waves of nausea broke over him. Then suddenly the scene was bright and clear again, and he felt the sweat icy-cold on his forehead. Marianne was close at hand but it was Tim who held him up now and who was saying quite cheerfully and naturally:

"Bit of a shock, sir? I don't blame you. It's a nasty thing; but everything will be all right, and if I were you I'd have a lie-down. . . ."

It was Tim who took him into the house and who saved him from falling when he stumbled over the hall table. Tommy held on to the table and in a brief moment of clarity he contemplated himself with loathing and contempt. He saw ruin lying all about him. George—and who could blame him?—was surely going to sell him up. Marianne would leave him; and serve him right. He couldn't send that bunch of cattle to market, so he'd be in trouble with the bank. And he remembered the broken fence yesterday.

"My God," he said to Tim, "what if your cattle get it?"

"We'll worry about that when it happens." Tim smiled.

The brief clarity faded; and just then Dolly appeared on the stairs. Tommy looked up at her, uncomprehending, and she came down a step at a time, rather gingerly. Reaching the hall, she paused for a moment and said: "Beg pardon, sir . . . grateful I am," as, big with child, she squeezed past them. She opened the front door diffidently, shut it very quietly as if she did not want to attract any more attention. Tommy looked in bewilderment at Tim but Tim offered no explanation. He shrugged his shoulders and smiled.

Tommy said: "I'm as tight as a tick," and stumbled again. This brought him opposite the John Martin picture, and he stood staring at it, smitten by an awful awareness of sin.

"Tim," he said.

"Yes, sir?"

"Look at that bloody picture."

"Yes."

"Have you," said Tommy with deliberation, holding on to his senses as if they were a runaway four-in-hand tearing at the reins, "Have you ever seen the world looking like that?"

Tim smiled and was silent for quite a long time. He said

at last: "Well, yes, I have."

"Often?"

"Quite often."

"Do you," persisted Tommy, wagging a finger at Tim, "still wake up on bright mornings to such a vish-vish-vision?"

"Yes."

"Then for Christ's sake," cried Tommy, "hang on to it; for when it goes you're damned." Speech left him and he began to sway; Tim caught him as he subsided and carried him upstairs.

## 4

The road, like all the little roads of Herefordshire, went round the haycock hills or between them, trickling like a stream; easy-going folk had made the road, not single-minded and purposeful like the Romans, but men of the west who saw life as a winding lane. For many miles the road turned and twisted as if he whose feet trod out the first track here had said: Shall I take that delightful way, or would the other be nicer? But at last, upon a long gentle slope, it straightened: a mile-long ribbon stretched white and taut between the car and the skyline; and Marianne stood up beside Tim and held on to the windscreen and said: "Fast now! Fast! Faster!"

She had a glorious feeling of escape and truancy. The hop-pickers had finished for the day. George, perhaps to get away from the germs, had ridden off on his bicycle; she had left him a cold supper. Tommy wouldn't want anything to eat; he was sleeping uneasily, twitching and now and then whimpering like a dog that has bad dreams. She had thrown open his bedroom window to let out the stale whisky smell and pulled the eiderdown over him as he lay fully dressed on his bed. Down in the meadow the four policemen, motionless as sentinels about the corpse, poured into it four ceaseless roaring spouts of flame. Beneath each searing stream the dead flesh seemed to become live again, tissue writhed in torment. But the solid bulk of the beast remained, only its edges blurred, the tail gone, the ears gone, the hoofs reduced to smoking stumps; it would take hours yet, Tim said, to consume it all. It was then he suggested: "Let's get away from this? Drive somewhere in the M.G.?"

"Where?" he had said, as they got into the little car.

"Anywhere. Follow the signposts with the nicest names."

Ocle Pychard had beckoned them; Evesbatch, Maidenhyde; Edvin Loach, which Marianne said sounded like a character in Dickens.

"He's a little wan man with a scolding wife. He goes muffled up into the inn and sits shivering in a corner and sips his negus or something and then always before he's finished it his great gaunt wife comes in and calls him out—'Edvin Loach, Edvin, you wicked villain!' "

Stretton Grandison, Stretton Sugwas. "Oh, I love these Herefordshire names!" she said. "It's having Christian names as well as surnames makes them seem so friendly." She had forgotten them while she was away; she relearned them now. Mansell Gamage, Mansell Lacy. Stoke Edith.

"Somehow," she said, "it always sounds to me faintly rude." Tim leaned back behind the steering wheel and laughed, and Marianne got the giggles, and the wind of their speed snatched away their laughter and seemed to sprinkle it behind them like confetti from a wedding car. How Caple set them off again; Marianne thought it sounded like an exclamation by a very superior duchess provoked by the decline in polite behaviour. Much Marcle pleased her; and there was Much Birch, the home she thought of some awful flagellant schoolmaster. They drove through it, but too fast, she said, to hear the howling of his victims, and now Much Birch was far behind them and the straight road lay ahead and Tim said: "Seventy on the clock," and still Marianne cried: "Faster!"

A passionate wind assailed her, seized her by the hair till it stood up like Struwwelpeter's, battered and buffeted her, frantically strove to undress her as she stood up in the car. Then in frustrate rage it blew her dress so flat and tight against her breasts that she seemed to wear it as another skin, she had a sense of splendid nakedness, she gasped and gulped and shouted for joy, Tim said: "Eighty on the clock," and the wind with a *woof* carried his words away. He looked up at her and grinned and yelled, "Figurehead!" and she nodded, knowing what he meant, feeling indeed as if she stood on the prow of a ship, ocean's great winds and waves breaking about her.

Soon, so soon, the straight mile lay behind them. They raced past a tall clump of pines which only a moment ago had been a plume on the horizon; there was a sign which said: BENDS FOR HALF A MILE, and Tim shouted, "Hold tight," as he jammed the brakes on hard. The speedometer needle jerked back, sixty, fifty, falling, falling, forty as the tyres squealed on the first bend. Then the wind, mischievous now, its passion spent, played a last trick on Marianne, swept round her in an eddy and, getting into a tactical position behind her, gave a great puff beneath her skirt which lifted it and held it out quite straight all round her, like the skirt of a ballet dancer. She let go of the windscreen and sat down with a bump and Tim, his foot firm on the brake as they approached another bend, chanted happily:

> *"The Devil is kind*
> *And sends the wind*
> *That blows our skirts knee high;*
> *But God is just*
> *And sends the dust*
> *That blinds the Bad Man's eye!"*

"Where did you get that from?"

"Some old rhyme."

"And was there any dust?"

"No, Ma'am," said Tim.

Marianne leaned back luxuriously. Her spirit was always purged by speed. All the restlessness and the fidgets had left her, and now she wanted to be quiet and to enjoy the new strange happiness that surged through her. This was one of the times when it would have been nice to be able to purr. So she who had urged Tim: "Faster, faster!" now said: "Slow, slow! As slow as you like," for they were headed for home, and it was twilight, and she did not want the drive ever to finish.

They were compelled to go slow, anyhow; for the road wriggled here like an endless eel among steep rough commons, broomy and birchy, and now and then the twin green lamps of a sheep's eyes glowed in the headlights. A road-sign said: BEWARE ANIMALS, which pleased Marianne, for she had a quick visual imagination, and she could never pass such a notice without conjuring up a whole jungle hidden behind the polite English hedgerows. They weren't ordinary animals, though; they were unicorns, griffons, wyverns, cockatrices. She described them to Tim and he said:

"Yes, I know. Like BEAR LEFT: a growling grizzly round the corner."

It was fun to share the same silly fancies. It was fun to sit right back in the rakish seat with your knees drawn up and the cool evening air playing about them, and to listen to the engine doing your purring for you, and to know for sure—but how, in heaven's name?—that Tim was going to pull up at that little pub with the lit windows the merest fraction of a second before you had made up your mind to ask him to. Because this was the moment, Marianne thought, the predestined and proper moment, when they had to drink their first drink together. It would have been premature five minutes ago; it would be tardy five minutes hence. For this was the way the thing was happening to them, step by step, inevitably.

# 5

On a switchback road of small hills and hollows the head-lamps' beam went before them like a sword, dropped now in watchful defence, raised now as if to parry a thrust from the overhanging branches. Behind the shining sword it was pitch-dark, the dash-lamp was turned out, and in the little black box which they inhabited together Tim could not see Marianne's face. But he did not need to see it. Because of what had happened in the pub—the extraordinary, inexplicable thing—it was printed in his mind, it was firm there and fadeless; the image rode with him through the night, wonderfully companionable.

They had been leaning against the bar. Tim never drank anything but pints; he thought halves were fiddling, and he liked the solid feeling of a pint in his hand. Marianne said she would have one too, and looked small behind it as she lifted it up. She was flushed from the wind, and her hair was all over the place. Not looking at Tim, she regarded the pint contemplatively, as if it were something important, to be gravely considered. Tim watched her. It seemed to him that now for the first time he saw her whole, an entity, a complete person, no longer just a jumble of impressions. He made the odd discovery—yet it was a happy one, somehow reinforcing his delight in her—that she wasn't really pretty; at any rate she wasn't as pretty as most of his other girls had been. His objectivity (which included the admission that her face was a little bit spotty and her lipstick as usual was dashed on anyhow) lasted for just so long as she studied the pint before her; then she suddenly turned her eyes up to him, and that was that. All the prettier girls were whisked into limbo. He picked up his glass and they toasted each other, without speaking, face to face; and Marianne with one brief look over the top of her pint delivered herself up to Tim, handed herself over: Here I am, take me, all of me, everything. Tim recognised this with amazement and humility. Nothing remotely like it had ever happened to him before. There had been plenty of girls who had given lightly; Marianne herself, he was quite sure, in fun or folly before now had given lightly too. But what she offered across her pint, deliberately, this very first time they had drunk together, was not offered lightly, and it was not simply love, but herself; and what she asked was not simply love but himself. No reservations, quibbles, half-measures, no faintest shade of dubiety: the whole shooting-match: the lot, or nothing.

It seemed that the landlord had been speaking to them. They both realised this at the same moment; they turned towards him politely, and they both said, "What?" Surprised, he repeated: "I was saying that with these clear skies we shall likely get an early frost." They had neither of them heard a word of it. Marianne behind her enormous drink grinned at Tim like a little cat, and they both burst out laughing. The landlord looked at them as if they were mad.

That bar, in the wayside pub of which they would never even know the name, was dirty and dreary, and though sanctified by the thing that had happened to them there it smelt mysteriously of mice and stale biscuits; so they finished their drinks and took themselves off. They went out into the sweet night, arm in arm; and there was a quarter-moon, with crisp stars. The air had a bonfire tang of autumn in it; and the mist was thin and patchy, fleeting ghosts in the hollows between the hills which shied away from Tim's headlights. At last these very bright lights, scouting ahead as they swung round a bend, glinted briefly on water. That would be the scummy pond by the ruined mill. Hazel bushes beyond it indicated to Tim the corner of Crowhill Copse. They were back now where he knew the contours of the hedgerows and could name each field as he passed its gateway. They were a mile from home.

Tim drove very slowly, two fingers on the sensitive wheel. They hadn't spoken for quite a long time; Marianne, tucked into his shoulder, lay so still that he wondered if she were asleep. She hadn't stirred since she had leaned forward to press the button which turned out the dash-lamp. That was when he first put his arm round her. Then he, or she, or perhaps it was both of them, had undone the front of her dress. His left hand as he drove now rested on her bare breast.

There was a place, a gateway without a gate, where a rutted track used by timber-hauliers ran off the road for a little way into a half-cleared wood. It was in Tim's mind now, as he approached this place, that he would turn the car into it, run on for a few yards, switch off the engine, switch off the lights. . . . Indeed he had taken his foot off the accelerator and tightened his grasp on the wheel ready to swing round into it. Then he hesitated.

He knew beyond any doubt what would happen if he parked the car. In token she was his already; her hostage lay beneath his hand. He did not hesitate on that score, but for an absurd and private reason. He'd parked before in that gateway. It was after the Farmers' Hunt Dance. Nothing much had happened. The girl was Jill Ferrers and between unimportant kisses they had talked about pony clubs. She was one of those girls who looked pretty in a velvet cap and incomplete without it; their affair had been arid and casual. It lent no special significance to the rutted track into the wood. Yet somehow, thought Tim, it would make an unhallowed beginning if he stopped there. The recollection of that fiddling and fumbling, however faint and irrelevant, might seem to mock what must not be mocked. He and Marianne must find their own landmarks, and it must be a new path all the way. So Tim who had chucked his morals out of the window of a parked car often enough, but never his manners with them, said to himself even as the wheels began to turn:

No I'm damned if I do! He jabbed the accelerator, the engine gave a yowl, and Tim, surprised at himself, half-angry with himself because he urgently wanted her, squeezed Marianne hard as the car jumped forward; then, seeing something comic in Miss Jill Ferrers's unwanted intrusion, he suddenly laughed out loud.

"What's the joke?" said Marianne.

"Perhaps I'll tell you some time."

"You'll tell me now." And quite fiercely, with a small tight fist, she jabbed three times, as hard as she could, into his ribs. It was half in fun, but it hurt. It was a small demonstration of toughness; a reminder, if he needed one, of the terms of her bargain. The whole shooting-match, the lot or nothing.

He said, driving fast and rather recklessly, the wheels screaming on a bend: "I had been there before."

Marianne had released herself and was sitting up rather straight beside him. She was silent for a moment; and then she said softly and entirely to herself it seemed: "Hurray, he loves me," and without more ado tucked herself into his side again. She fitted there so aptly, no Siamese twins could have been closer, thigh to thigh and rib to rib, than they.

"As the bark is to the tree," she said. And Tim started humming.

"Faster!" she cried. "Hurtle along! Hurtle and let's sing!"

They sang together:

*"Does she lie as close to thee*
*As the bark is to the tree?*
*And my Nancy kittled my fancy*
*O my darling Billy Boy!"*

"Go as fast as my happiness!"

"How fast is that?" he said.

"Too fast, my love!"

But he had to put the brakes on now. The road joined the lane which ran uphill from the village; there were people coming back from the pub, and the usual latewalking couples of the hop-picking time. Tim exclaimed suddenly: "Good lord!" There was no mistaking that chubby little figure that went hand in hand with the tall young man.

"Who'd have thought it? My young sister, with the Mission to Hop-pickers!"

The couple moved into the side of the road, but he thought they had not recognised the car. They were talking earnestly, of love or God he supposed; or most likely of both!

"Bless 'em all," said Marianne; and they started singing again:

*"You'll get no promotion*
*This side of the ocean*
*So cheer up, my lads, bless 'em all!"*

"We sing well together," said Tim.

"We sing horribly; but I like it. You ought to hear our Welsh girls. There's Megan."

"With Dave Huggett's grandson, who's supposed to be a slowcoach."

"She'll hurry him along!"

The Welsh girls, with their aptitude for pairing off, seemed to be neatly spaced at fifty-yard intervals, a boy and a girl at each gate. The peeping Tom headlights, though Tim dipped them courteously, picked out the couples as the car turned the corners, and sometimes they quailed before the menacing sword, surprised in a kiss.

"And that's Robbie," said Marianne. He was walking with the little dark one from Tonypandy—the conventional courting walk, very slow and uncomfortable, arms round each other's shoulders, the inside legs stepping out together, as in a three-legged race.

Robbie hadn't wasted much time, she thought; and then a sudden dismay clouded her happiness as she thought of Stan. No girl for Stan, ever. And now no dog for Stan. *Hell.* Cuddled up to Tim, she had an awful and frightening awareness of her own riches. This was the only guilt she ever felt about anything; having so much when some others had so little. She told Tim about it, and about Stan.

"No answer," he said at last.

"There isn't, is there? Except, of course, for saints."

"Saints?"

"Chucking up everything, for just that reason."

Tim said (and she almost laughed, because of the tinge of wariness in his voice, a bit frightened of this talk of saints, she thought):

"You're a Catholic, aren't you?"

John Sollars would have told him that, delightfully equating foreigners and Catholics and heathens.

"Born so," she said, "and so I suppose for ever."

But she thought that she wore her faith, if it was one, as lightly as her clothes; and as for saints, she could love them and glimpse their splendour, even Saint Mary of Egypt running about naked and Saint Simeon Stylites standing on one leg to the Glory of God: splendour shining through their absurdity. She could understand the compulsive renunciation; how the guilt of riches or of loving might become intolerable, because there were others hungry or without love. She could understand but one share; and for her part she thought that the only way of expiation, if you were given so much, was to take it with both hands, to cherish it and to delight in it, to thank heaven feasting not fasting, glory be!

They had come to the farmyard gate; and there was room for Tim to turn here, no need to open it and let him in. So Marianne bundled poor Stan out of her mind and, jumping out, thanked heaven for its moon which showed her Tim's slow smile as he bent down to kiss her, and for all the outrageous naughtiness of her body when he kissed her, and for the rightness of the little renunciation he had made—little enough (thank heaven!), for she knew that as sure as the moon shone, one night or another night she'd be his, and he hers.

## 6

On Sunday afternoon John Sollars went down into the hopyards, and walked through them in the stillness which he loved. There was no picking on Sunday, never had been and never would be as far as he was concerned. He cherished the quiet of Sunday, when he held it sacrilege to fire a gun or even to let off those noisy bird-scarers that banged every five minutes to keep the pigeons off the crops. Indeed he had lost ten thousand cabbage plants last summer, because he insisted on stopping the bird-scarers; three hundred pigeons, knowing nothing of Sunday, had descended on the field and eaten out the hearts. Next day John had replanted the field. It had cost him twenty pounds or so to keep the Sabbath and he felt it was worth it: not because he supposed it pleased God particularly, but because it was one of the traditions by which he lived.

The pain went with him, keen between his ribs, as he hobbled across the lower hopyard towards its southwest corner. He walked slowly along the last row, and every few paces he pulled down one of the bines and examined it carefully. He was searching for any signs of the mildew, and he was searching on the windward side because he believed, perhaps unreasonably, that the pest was wind-borne. He'd heard yesterday that the Johnson brothers had got it, only four miles away as the crow flew. His own hops, however anxiously he studied them, showed no taint; but he feared for them still, and he turned towards the west, looking across the Hope towards the Johnsons' big farm which lay beyond it; he felt the light breeze in his face, and he said to himself: That's the way it will come from, if it comes.

He could smell, or he thought he could, a faint whiff still of the sour-sweet smell which had been in his nose yesterday: the burning hide and flesh and fat of the beast which had died of that filthy disease down in Tommy's meadow. Anthrax! His father had had a cowman who had died of anthrax when he, John, was a boy. They had said his blood went black, and thick as tar. And ever since then he had regarded anthrax with particular horror, thinking of it not as an ordinary disease but as something obscene. He'd had the vet up, yesterday, to inoculate Sollarshill Sally and the other Herefords; he thought they'd be safe enough. But the fact that Tommy's unclean beasts had run with his, down by the river, still deeply troubled him. Restless because of the pain, he had lain awake last night and the names of all the dreaded cattle diseases had run through his head, beastly names like blackquarter and lumpy-jaw and wooden-tongue, *foot-and-mouth.* That sickly smell, blowing over from Tommy's farm, had taken him back to a February day in 1924: a day so still that the plume of smoke from the top of the hill had gone up straight and cylindrical as a Norman pillar in the church. On that day he had shut himself in the house. He had closed all the windows, but he couldn't shut out the dreadful burnt-offering smell, nor the sound of the humane killer dully thudding as the herd he had built up were slaughtered one by one—he could remember their names now, Sollarshill Seraph, Sharon, Sheba, Sollarshill Saracen his first bull.

It had broken him, heart and pocket but chiefly heart; and then after the proper interval, when the farm was clean again, he had gone off to the cattle sales and built up once more. Now he had the best herd in the Three Counties; the third-best, perhaps, in all Britain; and the little rat next door, his drunken, feckless, always despised and now hated neighbour, had put them in jeopardy.

Glaring across at Tommy's farm now, he saw it as a kind of reservoir of pestilence; his hand shook in the crook of his thumbstick as he contemplated it. And yet he still wanted that farm. He would plough it and fallow it field by field; grub up the rotten old pasture, put down new leys, until at last the land was clean and sweet again. Maybe he'd get it yet. He'd heard that the little fool's brother was staying there, looking into things, worried about his security. If the farm came into the market in consequence, John would have it, whatever it cost him: for he desired it beyond all reason, the covetous passion possessed him; so that he wondered, sometimes, whether he was not going a little mad.

Meanwhile, he thought grimly, as he went back from the hopyard, on slow feet up the unwelcome hill towards the farmhouse—meanwhile young Tim, mad after a skirt as usual, was sniffing round that little bitch of Tommy's. Well, that was his affair if he liked it easy; but what had infuriated and also considerably puzzled John Sollars was that Tim should have asked her to Sunday afternoon tea. Sunday afternoon tea, at Sollarshill, was ceremonious: the wedding-present tea-service, not a piece broken yet after twenty-five years, Molly's special walnut cake made from the nuts which showered down in bushels from the great tree near the back door; crumpets and brandysnaps. There was a tradition about Sunday afternoon tea; you wore your best clothes for it. And the people you asked to it, in strict rotation according to a list in the back of Molly's diary, were your *good* neighbours, your fellow hop-growers and Hereford breeders (you always took a walk round the farm afterwards), their sons and daughters, and your numerous cousins, scattered about the county, who were all dignified by the title of their relationship, Cousin Edith, Cousin Minnie, Cousin Geoff. You would also ask, thought John, for inspection and approval, after long deliberation and most careful assessment of her qualifications, the girl you intended to marry. But, by Heaven, you didn't ask your flibbertigibbet! To-night, after dinner, John intended to give Tim a piece of his mind.

It would be a peculiar tea-party anyhow; as if it wasn't bad enough that Tim should bring along that girl from the unclean farm (John would have liked to ask her whether she'd had the grace to disinfect her shoes) Carol had asked those God-botherers, as he always called them, who even now, at the bottom of the hopyard, were holding their service for hop-pickers. It was a wonder if they got anybody to go to it; but they were certainly making plenty of noise. John paused half-way up the hill to get his breath, and pretended to himself that he only paused to listen. He resented their intrusion into the Sunday stillness which he loved: caterwauling away—and Carol caterwauling with them! There was a place for everything, he told himself, and the place for hymns was in church. Howling in the open air was downright heathen.

# 7

They sang with the fervour of lonely defiance; for there were only thirteen of them. Carol had counted three times, but she could only make it thirteen. There was the clergyman, who was a friend of Charles's at Oxford and had driven down for the day; there were the four missioners; Carol herself; three Welsh girls, who had come for the singing and who, when they weren't singing, were making eyes at Bill and Ram and Charles; two Black Country children, sucking bootlaces of liquorice which they'd bought in her shop yesterday; the half-witted boy from the village called Stan; and one gipsy girl, whom Carol recognised as Black Barty's daughter, got up to kill in a scarlet cotton dress with a white frill of *broderie anglais* round the low neck, long earrings, and high-heeled shoes. She had drifted into the service more or less by accident, apparently on her way back from Wisdom's caravans in the next field; Carol couldn't think what she'd been doing there, since she knew that Black Barty and Wisdom were enemies. At any rate she made another at the hop-pickers' service. She stood shyly on the fringe of their small company, and she was the only one who wasn't singing.

Ram had gone over to her and pressed a hymn-book into her hand; he had opened it at the right page and pointed to the right place:

*And hath bid the fruitful field*
*Crops of precious increase yield,*
*For His mercies still endure*
*Ever faithful, ever sure.*

But still Sue wasn't singing.

Only thirteen: out of several hundreds. And it wasn't for want of trying on Carol's part that the service was a failure. Last night with Charles she had gone round the pigsties, Dudley Mansions, where the Black Country people were housed; into the barn, Abertillery Hall, to see the Welsh—and most of them had promised to come, but of course the Welsh would promise anything because they loved to please. Then she had been across to the Hope Farm, to invite Tommy Tomkins's pickers, and down to the gipsy caravans, though without much hope, for they were surely heathens.

She's expected fifty people at least; and she was sorry for the clergyman who'd come such a long way to preach to a mere handful. But as Charles had said last night: Where two or three are gathered together. . . . It had all begun with two or three, come together in those catacombs, at the peril of their lives.

Charles had said:

"It's difficult for us to imagine, nowadays, the sheer guts of those chaps who kept the thing going against all the might of Rome. The risk they took! Think of it, Carol—that lonely great arena; tier upon tier the crowd, all worked up—legionaries on leave from Africa or Gaul, citizens on holiday, chucking oranges, women of the town, drunk I dare say, all the goggling oafs who liked to see the blood and hear the screams; then the trumpets, then the Emperor—a bit bored, he'd watched it all before. And *you're* there, right out in the middle, all alone, and you say: Christ! *and mean it,* when the trap-door opens and something tawny, not so big as you thought it would be, comes out. . . ."

That was in the lane, walking arm in arm.

If it was like that nowadays, would we be standing here doing this, thought Carol? She had some private reservations about being eaten by a lion; but the others would be here, she felt sure, and her heart went out to them in her certainty of it: they'd all be here, Charles singing all the louder as a kind of challenge, and Bill with his squeeze-box which played the right tune when he'd got properly started but made the most curious noises beforehand; and Poppet, whom Carol tried so hard to like though she was so strange-looking and tormented—you could see she'd almost be *glad* to be a martyr; and little Ram with his soft voice and gentle manners, still politely holding Sue's hymn-book out in front of her, although Sue hadn't opened her mouth yet and wasn't likely to. Ram didn't understand, of course, that Sue couldn't read.

## 8

Wisdom, Mami and Marta sat on the steps of the caravan in the sun. They heard the singing, a hundred yards away, but it meant nothing to them; it was but another of the strangenesses of the gorgios. But Mami whose old eyes missed nothing spotted Sue's scarlet dress and hissed:

"What's she doing there, that chai of Barty's?"

"There are some men there, maybe," said Marta.

"*Tchk!*" said Mami. "And why did Barty send his chai over with that message?"

"He wants to buy Malona," Wisdom said.

"But he has no money."

"'Let Wisdom come to the pub to-night to talk about a horse deal,'" quoted Marta. "That was his message."

Wisdom said again, as if he tried to persuade himself of the truth of it:

"Barty wants to buy Malona."

"But you will not sell her?" spat Mami.

"No, no. Never."

"Then why will you go to the pub?"

Wisdom was silent for quite a long time. At last he said almost wearily:

"You know well why I must go there, Mami."

Marta said suddenly:

"Don't go, Wisdom. Don't go to-night. You are not strong."

"You know too, Marta, why I must go."

Mami turned her tortoise head very slowly towards Marta.

"Yes, girl," she said. "He must go. He must go because I am sure Barty has told all our people, and Manasseh's people and the Smiths, that he has sent Wisdom this message. And if Wisdom does not go they will say he is afraid."

"Wisdom," pleaded Marta. "Do not go."

Wisdom shook his head.

"He must go," said Mami decisively. "But if there are blows, let Barty strike first; and then remember his blind side." Her eyes were as bright as a girl's as she looked at Wisdom. "*Remember his blind side, my son.*"

"It is not Barty I fear," Wisdom said. "It is Black Alf."

"Black Alf?"

"They are very thick together. I have something in my mind, about Barty and Alf."

"*We* will watch Black Alf," said Mami, and glanced at Marta. She got up and went into the caravan.

Marta said: "You go because Mami says so."

"She is my mother."

"I am your wife."

Mami came to the door of the caravan. She spoke sharply to Marta.

"*Tchk.* No more! Drink this," she said to Wisdom. "It will make you strong."

## 9

Marianne opened the white drive gate, which swung easily upon its hinges, so unlike the gates at the Hope, which were opened by a complicated trick: at exactly the same moment as you pulled back the latch with one hand you had to heave up the whole gate with the other, using your shoulder for extra purchase under the top bar.

The drive was long, straight and intimidating. As she walked up it Marianne seemed to shrink, an Alice in Wonderland feeling. Her apprehension, on the other hand, grew. There was a garden gate at the end of the drive, new-painted bright green and equally well-oiled as the other. The garden was beautifully kept, with beds of multicoloured nemesias and regimented salvias in a row. Behind these scarlet salvias, trained upon a south wall, were apricots and peaches, and Marianne was uncomfortably aware that in contrast to what went on at the Hope everything here blossomed, fruited, ripened, everything "worked." At the Hope there were peach trees too; but they all had a peculiar disease which made their leaves come out in pink warts and ultimately shrivel up. If any of these trees bore a peach it was a matter for comment, and you kept an eye on the precious fruit, felt it every day, and had to pick it half-ripe to save it from the wasps and the birds. But here, against the farmhouse wall, were scores of sun-flushed peaches which nobody had been in a hurry to harvest. The *assurance* of everything alarmed Marianne; and her memory stretched back across the years to the only other time she had been here, with her mother to Sunday afternoon tea. She had been seven years old; and even then she had been impressed by the assurance. It was at

Dunkirk-time, which was probably why they had been invited. It was a time when everybody felt they had to be nice to neighbours. Suzette had been crying that afternoon. The Boches, as she called them, were tearing the very vitals out of France, and the spirit of France seemed to repose precariously in old weary Weygand or in old frail Petain, if there was any spirit left at all. Tommy had joined up already and was training somewhere to handle rifles that wouldn't shoot. Yet on that Sunday afternoon at the Manor Farm they had scarcely mentioned Dunkirk. It was like a peace-time tea-party, with peace-time talk. Carol was a toddler, playing with dolls; Tim presumably was away at prep-school. Mrs. Sollars talked about Jersey cows and John Sollars talked about crops. It was a good year for the wheat.

"But will you harvest it?" Suzette had said.

Marianne could remember still the frozen silence which followed this remark. She hadn't known the meaning of the silence, but she had understood it since. Wars were properly fought on the Continent, and on no account were permitted to spread across the Channel and interfere with harvests in Herefordshire. A monstrous suggestion, the Sollarses would have thought: sheer panic, but understandable in the French. They wouldn't have had the News on at six, unless Suzette had asked them to. Her request had seemed to surprise them, as if it were a foreigner's whim. When the News was over Suzette was trying hard not to cry, and Mrs. Sollars looked at her with the kind of sympathy one gives to someone who has lost a fairly distant relative. John had been more kindly, perhaps because Suzette was very pretty then, but he made it clear that he didn't understand what she had to cry about.

"It will be quite all right, you know," he had said. "I mean you haven't got anything to worry about really. One or two little things may have gone wrong but this is just a setback. We weren't quite ready, that's all. We'll knock 'em for six when we've sorted it all out."

And so they had. *Damn them,* thought Marianne, as she rang the front-door bell.

The only other thing she remembered was the walnut cake.

She had eaten three slices. And now, as the trim little maid showed her into the room, the walnut cake caught her eye, in the middle of the table, uncut. Bread and butter first, then hot scones, then the cake: that would be the order of things. Of course they had Sunday tea in the dining-room and all sat round the table, and to-day there seemed to be dozens of them. Then, for a second, there was only one, as Tim came across to her and led her towards the empty seat between him and Mrs. Sollars. John Sollars got to his feet. He did so not easily, and in a way resentfully, but with a kind of desperate courtesy; and he put out his hand. As she took it she had a quick intimation of his illness and his pain; and then of all the things he could have called her he called her Miss. It didn't sound as if it were meant to be rude, the way he said it. It seemed to come quite naturally, but it had a cold unfriendliness. He looked at her through pale blue eyes angry with pain and "Afternoon, Miss; sit down," he said.

Mrs. Sollars with her cool smile said:

"It's a long time since you were last here, er, Marianne?"

"Yes."

"Of course you've been away a lot"—and she gave her a quick, brief, birdlike glance. Then her eyes began to travel round all the plates, seeing whose was empty—"Carol, please pass the scones to Mr. Ramcharan. . . ." She became very busy replenishing tea-cups. Now and then she glanced at Marianne, but always briefly, always with a ready excuse for that split-second appraisal: "Milk in your tea?" She looked away and then swiftly back again: "And sugar?"

For the very first time in her life Marianne was socially afraid. It had never occurred to her that she could be; she had a natural, comprehensive liking for people which was part of her general enjoyment of life. For this reason most people were nice to her; if by any chance they were nasty the little bit of toughness in her make-up came to her aid and she gave as good as she got. She had always been sure of herself; but sitting beside Mrs. Sollars, subject to those swift glances which somehow made her think of pecks—feeling John Sollars's eyes upon her as he sat slumped at the head of the table—she was frightened, unhappy and devilish unsure. When Tim rang her up yesterday to ask her to tea, though she had said "Yes" eagerly, glad that he had asked her, she had already begun to be afraid. It was too soon, she had thought. They should have allowed their love to go along, step by step, for a little longer in its wonderfully inevitable way. They were still learning together the lessons of love; they were neither of them ready, yet, for the interrogation in other people's eyes. We should have waited, thought Marianne miserably; maybe we should have waited until we'd made love; for then, belonging and bonded to each other, we should be unassailable. That was a queer thought, though, in the middle of the Sollarses' Sunday tea-party; and Tim, who happened to glance at Marianne then, said: "Penny for your thoughts," as he glimpsed her momentary and secret smile.

"That one was worth much more than a penny," she said.

She knew Tim was trying hard to defend her against his mother's pecking glances. He began talking to her, not quickly or nervously, not making conversation, but in the easy way he always talked, and it was as if some extension of himself enclosing and shielding her shut her off from all the others. He spoke so quietly that she had to lean a little towards him, and thus as it were he drew her close to him, and away from his mother. He explained about the missionaries and told her who was who. "Ram's the Indian. Charles is the one we saw with Carol last night." He punctuated his sentences with that slow half-smile which made her happy. "Yes, she's going to be pretty, isn't she, though she's a bit of a pudge at the moment . . . I want you to talk to her after tea; she'll love you. The other girl, next to the parson? They call her Poppet or something. . . ."

Poppet was staring at the clergyman with that odd look of hunger sacred or profane, Marianne wasn't sure which; on the other side of her Ram sipping his tea with a kind of delicate primness sat next to Tim's father, and Marianne again had a sense of the courtesy of these Sollarses, a reluctant courtesy perhaps and rather an uncomfortable one:

hating foreigners, they nevertheless gave the foreigner the place of honour at their table. Moreover, John Sollars most unexpectedly had discovered a subject in common with Ram: cricket.

"No, man, with great respect you are in error," Ram was saying. "That was not Duleepsinghi; with respect, sir, you are thinking of Pataudi, the Nawab of Pataudi, who was playing for Oxford at that time. . . ."

"Believe it or not," whispered Tim, "the old man was the best forcing bat in Herefordshire; he once hit a hundred in thirty-nine minutes: sixty of it in sixes. D'you like cricket?"

"Hate it," she said. "I go all French if I'm made to watch a cricket match. Have I got to watch you hitting sixes?"

"Yes," he said.

"There's something about those great pads and gloves that make you look like animals: peculiar, silly, lumbering English animals."

Tim looked straight at her and said:

"You needn't watch, but of course at village matches you'll have to organise the tea."

Then, as if he hadn't said anything extraordinary, Tim reached for a plate and offered her a buttered scone. Turning towards him as she took the scone, understanding suddenly the implication behind what he had said, she realised that in his different way he had done exactly what she had done over her pint in the pub on Friday night. Their love didn't proceed by question and answer; it leapt to its great assumptions. The splendour of it caught them up as they looked at each other; and for a moment they were the only people in the room. Then Marianne heard Mrs. Sollars saying, with a suggestion of sharpness in her cool remote voice:

"Tim, please pass the scones down the table."

The world came back to Marianne with a vengeance then: with a sense of vulnerability, with an awareness of people's eyes, John Sollars's eyes the colour of starlings' eggs, Poppet's staring at her with that queer hot unassuaged look, Carol for some reason throwing her a small smile across the table, Mrs. Sollars at her shoulder:

"Marianne: let me give you another cup of tea."

The tea-party dragged on. Marianne nibbled her scone, which she didn't want, and then the walnut cake was cut, as if this were a small ceremony, and the missioners, who all had vast appetites, demolished it piece by piece. It seemed hours before Mrs. Sollars got up and said:

"Let's go into the sitting-room to give Polly a chance to clear away."

It was better in the sitting-room. Carol came straight across to Marianne and sat on the arm of her chair. She said:

"I say, I'm awfully glad you came."

Tim said quickly:

"Look, I'd better talk to some of the others. Then I've got to do the milking; cowman's off on Sunday."

"Can I come?"

"Of course."

He went over to talk to the clergyman.

Carol said: "I love your dress."

It was grey and white candystripe, and this was the first time Marianne had worn it. She said:

"I only finished it this afternoon. At half past two I was standing on the kitchen table, getting Father to measure the hem."

"What, you made it yourself?"

"Yes."

"Oh dear," said Carol. "I try, but I think the patterns don't suit my bulges or something. I zipped myself into the last one and couldn't get out."

"It's quite easy really. Next time, if you like, I'll come over and help you cut out."

"Will you? I say, I couldn't make an evening dress, could I?"

"Bit more difficult, but I'm sure you could."

"You'd help me?"

"Of course."

"We'll have to be terribly quick. I want it for the hop-dance. You know, we always have one. We dance in the oast when picking's over. It'll be about the twenty-seventh of this month I expect. You'll come, won't you?"

"If you ask me."

"Well, I wanted to buy a *special* dress, but now I don't think I'll have enough money and if Mummy pays for it she'll insist on choosing it, which means it'll be one that makes me look about sixteen."

"Well, let's make one then," Marianne laughed.

"But quick?"

"Quick as you like."

"Then to-morrow morning we'll borrow Tim's car and go to Hereford and you'll help me choose the stuff? Promise?"

"Will Tim lend you his car?"

"Not me; but he'll lend it to *you*," said Carol, and tossed Marianne another of those smiles which she seemed to throw about like a ball, as if she said, "Catch!" and when you smiled back you had caught it. "Hurray! Let's start early and go to *all* the shops. What colour?"

Marianne turned sideways to look at her. She was altogether taken by Carol, whose red hair was as warm as her character—it was a colour that seemed to have firelight reflected in it. She considered the problem seriously; it would be fun to dress her.

"With that red hair—what shall it be? Cream, or a midnight blue? Green?—but not an obvious green, rather a dark one, I should think. Are we going to be extravagant?"

"Oh yes, *frightfully*. I was saving up to buy a dress, you see."

"A good stiff taffeta, then? Set you back about six quid?"

"Will all of me go into six yards?"

"All of you."

Carol giggled; and then, falling sharply between them as if it were a clean cut with a knife, separating them most surely, came Mrs. Sollars's voice. Marianne didn't know how long she had been there. She was standing just behind her shoulder, on the opposite side from Carol.

"Carol: don't you think you ought to get back to your guests?"

It was said so gently; but the knife was as sharp, thought

Marianne, as Mrs. Sollars's knives would always be, to carve a chicken, say, efficiently, coolly, with the minimum of force. Marianne felt that she, not Carol, had been dismissed; and indeed as Carol jumped off the arm of the chair she got up too, despite Mrs. Sollars's thin hand on her shoulder: "No, no, not you, Marianne; please sit down."

But then Tim was there. He was at her side, like an infallible ally, appearing through the murk of battle upon a crumbling flank. Only a moment ago she had noticed him, by the fireplace, deeply engaged with the clergyman and the Indian. Perhaps their thoughts flew to each other right across the room!

"Coming?" he said. "Five-thirty, and the cows can't wait."

Then, as she was saying her thank-yous to Mrs. Sollars, he put his hand on her arm. It was firm and proprietary; and she saw Mrs. Sollars's glance dart like a robin's, from her face to her arm where Tim held it, to Tim's face, back to hers—in disapproval, reproof, bewilderment? You couldn't tell, Mrs. Sollars's eyes were inexpressive as a bird's.

They went across to John Sollars's chair. "Please don't get up—" she began, but he was on his feet already, one hand still holding the back of the chair, turning to her with that "Damn you but we don't forget our manners" air.

He looked her up and down as if he studied the points of a Hereford; and all the time Tim's hand still on her arm proclaimed *This is my girl, like it or not,* as plainly as any gesture could. John Sollars turned his angry eyes towards Tim, and for a second or two they faced each other, both of them so still, with that Sollars trick of standing still, that it made every other person Marianne had ever known seem to have been a fidget. Then John turned back to her, and put out his hand.

"Good night, Miss," he said.

# ☙ 10

The sodding sulphur, said Dave Huggett, ain't what it used to be. He was on duty in the kiln, although it was Sunday, because the pickers had worked overtime yesterday so there were several loads left over to be dried. Tim on his way to do the milking had taken Marianne to see Dave. They had climbed the steps up to the hop-floor so that Tim could show her where they would have their dance when hop-picking was finished. "It takes Dave a whole day of brushing and scrubbing to get the stickiness off the floor." Dave, who was uninhibited in the presence even of Master Tim's new wench, grumbled alliteratively about the floor. Tim had a look at the hops in the drying-chamber, and Marianne put her head into it too. "You can tell by the stink as the sulphur nowadays ain't the same," said Dave.

Their eyes were streaming when they came out of the oast into the honey-coloured sunshine of the late afternoon. Tim said:

"Dave's grandfather, believe it or not, worked for my great-grandfather and was the hop-dryer here in 1851, when we sent a sample of hops to the Great Exhibition. Dave's grandson, the boy we saw last night with the Welsh girl, works for us as a labourer. That's six Huggett generations we know of, that have worked or are working at Sollarshill."

"How long have your people been here?" Marianne said. They were standing together in a broad beam of the sun that fell between the two oasts, stretched right across the yard, and lay warm upon the wall of the farmhouse beyond. The brickwork was bright orange-pink; the half-timbering, great oak boughs rough-hewn with the adze, was very black by contrast, so that the side of the house had an exquisite pattern of light and shade. How old was the house? Three or four hundred years, Marianne supposed. The dove-cot beside it looked almost as old.

"Oh, we've been here always," said Tim casually. "Let's go and fetch in the cows."

Some pigeons flew out of the dove-cote and circled round; Marianne remembered a line from a poem by Edward Thomas, about Lob-lie-by-the-fire: He has been in England as long as dove and daw. That was what the Sollarses meant by "always"; and of course they believed it, because they could not imagine Herefordshire without Sollarses, hop-growing without Sollarses, indeed England herself without Sollarses farming at Sollarshill. Marianne felt desperately afraid of them—afraid of this place, of its order and its seemliness, afraid of the future because of the way they had treated her at tea. She couldn't have sworn, as she dabbed her wet face, whether the tingle in her eyes was just sulphur fumes, or tears. Tim said, as they crossed the yard:

"Yes, it does make your eyes run when you aren't used to it."

He went into the Home Ground, while she held open the gate. The four Jerseys, like little deer, trod daintily past her. Tim walked after them, as each went into her own stall and waited there. As he hung up his coat on the cowhouse door Tim said:

"We haven't got a milking-machine because it wouldn't be worth it for so few. But I shan't take long, if you don't mind waiting."

"It would be quicker if we did two each," said Marianne.

"What? You can't milk, can you?"

"Where the hell do you suppose I was brought up?" She was still smarting from that "Good night, Miss" of John Sollars's. The oppressiveness of the tea-party lay heavy on her mind. Loving Tim, she hated his father and feared his mother—"Carol: don't you think you ought to get back to your guests?"

"Naturally I can milk," she said. "Unless of course your

father would be afraid of my touching your precious cows."

Tim was putting on his dairy coat. He turned round sharply. She stood with her feet wide apart and her hands on her hips. Something in her attitude reminded him of the time when she'd scratched his face behind the village hall. He almost laughed, remembering that; and he wondered what she would do now, if he did laugh. He remembered, too, the encounter in the lane when she was with Tommy, a few nights ago. He responded, as then, to the challenge.

"Get on with it then," he said cheerfully. "There's a stool and a bucket in the stall, and a coat hanging up behind the door."

She hesitated for a moment; then she went into the cow-house. A few moments later he heard the milk drumming on the bottom of the bucket: a rat-tat-tat, angry-sounding, then a steady stream. He called out to her:

"Bet you I'll do three while you do one."

Marianne didn't answer. She tucked her head into the flank of the cow and milked as hard as she could. The cow, not used to her, turned towards her its small head, so like a gazelle's, in curiosity or dismay. It lifted its hind leg two or three times, as if it were going to kick. She heard the splash and patter into Tim's bucket, and she thought: Damn you, if only I can get *started* on my second one before you've finished both of yours! Soon her wrists began to ache. It was years since she had milked a cow; but during the war, when Tommy was away, she had helped her mother with their six shorthorns, morning and evening, every holiday. She remembered a letter from Tommy, one of his rare letters, which he'd written in the late summer of 1945: "Mummy says how good you are with the cows. There was a big battle here last week and I did only one useful thing in it. All over the place there were cows in trouble, that hadn't been milked for a couple of days. Their udders were so full, it was pitiful to see them. I went through the fields, a funny sort of soldier, just milking the cows wherever they stood, on to the ground. . . ."

Suzette had said:

"When war's so beastly, it makes me happy to think of Father doing that."

Marianne, with sudden affection, thought of Tommy now. He had committed himself to spend a whole afternoon and evening with George, going through his accounts; and George had said that to-morrow, when he had considered the figures, he would make up his mind whether he ought to call in the mortgage. Tommy was frightened of figures: much more frightened of them than he had ever been of Germans. He panicked when he was confronted with a whole column of them, became confused, and lied wildly and foolishly, in self-defence. Probably he was lying to George at this moment; and George with his hurts-me-more-than-it-hurts-you air would be probing and prodding among the figures, discovering the lies.

She felt, with her pity for him, something akin to homesickness as she thought of Tommy. That's where I belong, she thought, among the fecklessness and the incompetence and the muddles and the mess; certainly not here, where everything's so tidy, efficient, accustomed, certain; where they're sure of themselves, have never been in debt, aren't afraid of bank managers and duns, believe that God contrived the world entirely for their benefit, worship their ancestors, and look at you as if they were just a little bit sorry for you because your people haven't owned the same piece of land for five hundred years; where they call you "*Miss.*" She heard Tim picking up his bucket and moving into the next stall. Her wrists seemed on fire now, and her fingers hurt sharply, the teats felt hard and unyielding in her hands. You didn't forget how to milk, any more than you forgot how to ride a bicycle; it would have been easy enough if she'd taken her time over it. But she was possessed by an angry determination to keep up with Tim.

The cow was nearly dry now; the milk came in short bursts, then suddenly it stopped altogether. She picked up her stool and nearly upset the bucket in her hurry to get into the second stall. The new cow's skin twitched over its withers as it became aware of a stranger. She patted it and sat down, her legs apart, the bucket between them; her head was against the cow's side, in her nostrils was the earthy cow-smell and the warm sweetness of the milk, and all at once the habit came back into her hands, she forgot the ache in them, even forgot her fear of the Sollarses, she was happy in the homeliness of her task. *My* people, she thought, have been doing this kind of thing just as long as *his* people; and probably a bloody sight longer! She remembered holidays in her childhood, when Suzette had taken her "home": the slow-treading Percheron horses, the ponderous deep-sided cows, fawn with white patches, their udders gently swinging as they came in for milking, the old women with wrinkled-walnut faces, the strong brown girls carrying the heavy milk pails; she remembered with pleasure and pride the impression it had made upon her, of the slowness and sureness in man and beast, everything of the earth earthy, the plodding peasants under the sun, the hard, hard weekdays and the church bells in the sudden Sunday quiet.

She didn't mind, now, when Tim finished before her; it would still be two apiece when she'd done her second cow. She heard Tim carry his bucket to the door and pour the milk into the churn. She worked steadily on, and the milk made a pleasant rhythm in the bucket, and as if to match her memories she heard suddenly the bells pealing for evening service down in the village. She sang to herself:

> *"Je donnerais Versailles,*
> *Paris et Saint-Denis,*
> *Les tours de Notre-Dame,*
> *Et les cloches de mon pays!"*

and she didn't look up when Tim came and stood in the stall beside her; she went on milking.

"Lost my bet," he said. "Well done, Marianne."

"What do I win?"

"A pint at the pub? We'll have to take the milk across to the dairy first."

They carried the churn between them. They put it down in the appointed place, and Marianne looked about her at the orderly contrivance of everything there, the little account book hung open on the nail in the door, the silver pencil hanging on a string beside it, the neat precise entries which Mrs. Sollars had made in the book: 13 galls. milk, 7 lbs. butter, 4 pts. cream. Marianne thought of poor Tommy's accounts, and it was her flicker of a smile, springing from that thought, which brought Tim to her side suddenly.

"Feeling better?" he said.

He put his arm round her shoulder. "Not here!" she said. "No, Tim, not here!" Tim didn't understand. He bent to kiss her, and she pulled herself free. "Oh anywhere else in the world but here!" She ran out of the dairy and when he followed her into the sudden sunlight he still did not understand.

"Marianne, what's the *matter?*"

" '*Cet animal est très méchant: quand on l'attaque, il se défend!*' "

They were face to face in the yard.

"Do I have to translate it?" she said.

Tim's fifth form French caught up at last; his understanding began to catch up too. He shook his head. "I love this animal."

"And I love you," she said, "oh so much that I know now I've never loved anybody in my life before; but for God's sake take me away from here, Tim, *quick.*"

The M.G. was parked against the shed which had YE OLDE FARME SHOPPE over its door. Marianne almost ran across to it and jumped in. Tim as he got in beside her said: "I'll show you a short cut, then, to the pub." He swung the car round and drove up to the Home Ground gate. "Open, please."

When Marianne got back into the car he grinned.

"You said quick: hold on."

The car went bumping down the rutty steep track. The hopyard lay immediately below them, the river meadow beyond, then the shining river with the village in the bend of it, huddled houses, church tower, thatched roof of the pub. Marianne said:

"If the car had wings we'd take off and glide there!"

"We're going to do something better than that," said Tim, "if you'll open the hopyard gate for me."

The hop-bines were blowing about in a fresh evening breeze. A green turbulence lay ahead as Marianne came back to the car. "Now," said Tim. "This is a little game of mine. Father does it too. It's bad for the springs."

He took the car along the grass at the edge of the hopyard until he came to a place, untouched yet by the pickers, where the hops had grown so lush that they shut out the sun. He nosed into the little space between the rows and gingerly opened the throttle. The car began to leap and bounce on the rough ground; Marianne held on to the door with one hand and tucked her other arm under Tim's shoulder as the seat bucked beneath her. They now entered a tunnel of green; and the light here was extraordinary—Marianne thought of the deep Sargasso, the hops were as waterweed draping old wrecks there! They swayed and tossed in the wind as in the currents of the sea. Marianne had the illusion that the hops were closing in about them and that there was no way through; and then again the hops seemed to retreat and the rows to draw apart as the long bonnet of the M.G. shot between them. The car gathered speed. A wild whirl of colours, made luminous by the sun, danced before Marianne's eyes: the hops green and yellow, patches of blue sky, bright pink earth, and kingfisher-blue of the car's bonnet plunging and rearing. Light and shade came and went in flickering alternation. Successive waves of green broke over the car, dissolving into sunlit spray. Errant bines like tentacles, dipping down, brushed the bonnet, flicked the windscreen, touched Marianne's hair with a butterfly touch and were gone. She was caught up in a huge exhilaration. "Hurray! Hurray! Hurray!" she yelled; down the green gallery, through the green grotto—and then suddenly they were out in the sunshine at the other end of the row, and Tim was laughing at her as he pulled up the car before the gate into the road.

"All right now?" he said; and she laughed back at him and threw back her head as he kissed her, the first time they had properly kissed, he asking and she answering: Take me whenever you will.

## ☙ 11

They went into the hop-pickers' bar, and Mrs. Agnew, obviously disapproving, glanced from Tim to Marianne and back to Tim. She said: "It's ever so quiet and cosy in the saloon; and as you know, Master Tim, it's apt to get rough here on a Sunday night, with all those monkeys playing up daft-like."

Marianne shook her head at Tim.

"I'm not in a quiet and cosy mood."

Indeed she wasn't; the drive through the hops had put her in a wild and crazy mood. She had almost forgotten the oppressiveness of Sollarshill. Her body was wakeful from Tim's kiss; she could hardly keep still. She wanted, to-night, the crowd and the shoving and the swearing and the laughter, singing Welsh girls, smoke and stuffiness, the fierce hot life of the gipsies surging all round her; plenty to drink, and Tim.

"Now buy me something expensive," she said. "I'll teach you to bet me I can't milk a cow."

Mrs. Agnew said primly:

"It's as you like, but I'd have lit a fire for you in the saloon. Here they come, the monkeys." She pointed out of the window.

Marianne cried:

"Oh, Tim, look! Isn't that the most beautiful pony you've ever seen?" A small boy of Wisdom's was trotting the dun pony up and down. Wisdom and all his tribe stood round, admiring it. Marianne stood on tiptoe to get a better view.

"It's perfect!"

"Wisdom thinks so," said Tim, "and he's been horse-dealing all his life. But why do *you* think so?"

"I was saying to myself the other day I'd like to have a pony again. But now I've seen that one I wouldn't want any other." She watched it through the window, arching its neck as it tugged at the halter, dancing a few steps in play or impatience. Wisdom's boy coaxed it, rubbing its nose; and at last it stood obediently while two other boys, as if they were experienced horse-copers already, ran their small hands professionally down its hocks and fetlocks. Wisdom had groomed it and plaited its mane; the neat's-foot oil which he'd painted on its hoofs made them shine like steel.

"Well, that's one you *won't* have," laughed Tim. "See what Wisdom says when I try to buy it."

Wisdom appeared at the entrance to the bar. He hesitated there for a moment, and seemed to straighten himself with an effort. Then he came on, with slow strides like a man who goes to meet his destiny. He glanced covertly round the room, and Marta and Mami, as they followed him, made the same anxious appraisal, as if they sized up the company and counted their friends and their foes. A full dozen of Wisdom's tribe came after them; and Tim, looking over his shoulder as he bought Marianne her drink, was aware of the murmurous tension and was puzzled by it. He heard Mami say:

"Tchk! He is not here."

Wisdom shrugged his shoulders and said: "He will come, I think. We shall see."

Tim beckoned to Wisdom. He thought if he bought a round of drinks for Wisdom's tribe it might help to ease their feelings about the strike; he knew they still thought his father had tried to cheat them. As Wisdom came up to him Tim could see from the way he walked that he hadn't recovered yet from the hurt he had when he lifted the pony. He was hipped, and his step had none of the gipsy spring in it.

"Wisdom," said Tim, "what'll you take for your dun out there?"

Wisdom stared at him, surprised, almost resentful.

"But I told you, Master Tim. . . . Even to you I wouldn't sell her."

"I was pulling your leg. You love her, don't you?"

" 'Tis like this," said Wisdom. "In a man's life, there are a lot of horses; maybe a lot of dogs, or whatever else he fancies. But when he looks back on his life he can see that there was only one, one horse, one dog—"

"One woman?" laughed Tim.

" 'Tis so," said Wisdom gravely. "Maybe there were many but it's only the one he'll remember when he's dying."

Marta joined them, and old Mami. Tim ordered the drinks, and Marta took them across to the other gipsies. Mami said she'd have a drop of rum to warm her. "That'll make you chatter," said Tim, and she turned her bright mischievous eyes towards Marianne's glass. The most expensive drink Mrs. Agnew could provide had been a whisky and ginger ale.

"When you're old as me," said Mami to Marianne, "it's only your tongue that the drink sets wagging."

"And when you're young as me—?" Marianne grinned.

*"Tchk!"*

Tim asked, as he'd often done before:

"How old *are* you, Mami?"

"One hundred and two."

"You're a wicked old liar."

"Impidence! I can remember the Jubilee."

"Whose Jubilee?"

" 'Tis no matter whose. It makes me one hundred and two. A man with booklearning reckoned it." Mami cackled at Tim; they loved teasing each other. "Any more impidence and I'll tell your young leddy what I know about you. She's too good for you, I think." She had taken to Marianne because Marianne knew how to treat her; teasing back when Mami teased, but never forgetting the courtesy due to her years. "It's a pleasure to talk to a well-mannered gel. Too many pert gels nowadays."

Soon Wisdom ordered a round of drinks. He said, "The

same again, Missus," and Mrs. Agnew gave Mami another rum, poured out a whisky for Marianne. It crossed Tim's mind that Marianne, not knowing the gipsies as well as he did, might make the awful mistake of saying, "Leave me out this time," or "I'll just have a half-pint now," as she would probably have done if one of the farm workers had offered to buy her an expensive drink. Then it would have been proper and tactful; but the gipsies were different, Mami would have taken offence and Wisdom would have been hurt, though perhaps he had no more spending money than a labourer. A moment later Tim felt ashamed of his doubts. Marianne accepted the drink without question, gave Wisdom one of her quick smiles, said: "Good luck, Mr. Lee," and raised the glass to him. It had cost Wisdom half a crown, but Tim would find a way of making it up to him later. *This is my girl,* thought Tim, *she will never put a foot wrong anywhere;* he could almost have cheered, he had such pleasure and pride in her.

And now Mami, possessively clutching to her bosom her second glass of rum, was tracing with a grimy forefinger the life-line on Marianne's outstretched palm. She delighted in telling fortunes when she'd had a drink or two; but though the drink cheered her it in no wise brightened her vision of the future of those whose fate she foretold. After an evening on the rum Mami had but to take one brief look at your palm and she who could not read a printed page would see debts and dishonour, sickness and shame, most plainly written there. Dark strangers? Yes, but they would bring you nothing but sorrow. Fair ladies? Aye, but you had better beware of them. All manner of perils, both spiritual and physical, lurked like adders in your path; evil dreams would trouble your nights and misfortune dog your days; so that the early death which she lightheartedly prophesied had the character of a blessed release. For Marianne, however, there seemed to be happier things in store; presumably because Mami liked her, or because the old woman was still fairly sober. Tim could not hear what Mami was whispering—Wisdom was standing between them—but Marianne was giggling and

Marta, who had a deep and dirty chuckle, suddenly embraced her and gave her a smacking kiss. Now Marta had started she would kiss everybody within reach of her fine brown arms, until it was closing time. She still held Marianne in a powerful bunnyhug as Mami shuffled round in front of Wisdom and came cackling up to Tim. She put down her drink on the counter beside him.

"What have you been telling her, you bad old woman?" Tim said.

"Something I can read in both your faces without looking at your hands. 'Tis not for your ears, oh no." Her little black eyes were fixed upon him, shrewd and knowing. "I told you the gel was too good for you. You have done with foolishness, now?"

"What foolishness, Mami?"

"Ah. Mami knows many things. They say Black Barty has been fighting."

"What of it?" said Tim. "He often fights."

"Maybe . . . Now let me read your fortune as I read your gel's, and I will see if there is as much foolishness in the future as there has been in the past."

"Have a good look, then." Tim stretched out his hands to her, palms upwards. Two brown paws darted out from under her shawl. Her head was thrust forward on her scraggy neck, and more than ever Tim was reminded of a tortoise, as those hands popped out like paws from beneath a carapace. They were little and gnarled and knobbly, but they had an astonishing strength. They seized the ends of his fingers and deftly turned them over, twisting his wrists so that his hands were palms down. "Ha!" Mami was gazing at the knuckles. "Ha!" A long talon, with two gold rings on it, prodded the puffy bruises on his right hand. Tim said quietly:

"You don't tell fortunes that way, Mami."

"No, but you sometimes see the past. . . . A man who is handy with his mauleys wouldn't forget to use his right, would he, against someone we both know?" She let go of his hands. "Get on with you! No more foolishness, now you have got a good gel!"

Wisdom, all this time, spoke little, drank little, and frequently glanced towards the door. Now, at the sound of its opening, he seemed to start, and straightened himself suddenly. Tim saw Mami turn, Marta turn; every eye went towards the door. He couldn't make out what was going on, but he was aware of the tension and of the sudden relaxation afterwards, as if a breath long held had been let go by all the gipsies simultaneously.

At the door stood the missioner called Bill. He paused there for a moment, hesitant to enter what must have looked to him rather like a thieves' kitchen, thick with smoke, stinking from Granny's pipe, and full of swarthy faces turned fiercely towards him. The light glinted on his big horn-rimmed glasses; his ginger hair stood in a tuft above his forehead; in his rather neighing voice he spoke to those who stood behind him:

"I say, it's a bit thick in here, isn't it?"

But he was pushed into the room by Charles, followed by Poppet, Ram and, to Tim's horror, Carol, whom his father had expressly forbidden him ever to take to the Royal Victoria. She came bouncing across the room, pursued by a rout of missioners, to whom she said:

"I knew we'd find them here, didn't I? They can introduce us all round."

Mrs. Agnew said, in a tone of despair:

"It's ever so nice and cosy in the saloon."

"Yes, let's all go in there," said Tim to the missioners, making the best of a bad job.

"That's not the idea at all," said Carol. "We've been thinking about our service this afternoon, and why it didn't work. Bill said, and we agree with him, that if they won't come to us, *we* ought to go to them. So we've come." She went close to Tim and wheedled: "Be decent and give them a chance. Introduce them to all your gipsy friends."

"What the devil do you imagine Father will say?"

"Father mustn't know. Anyhow I'm eighteen. Oh, Tim, please don't do your stuffy old elder brother act! I promise we won't barge in on you and Marianne." She gave Tim a wink. "Now let's meet the gipsies."

"On your own head, then, you little devil . . . Wisdom!" he said.

"Yes, Master Tim?"

"These young friends of mine would like to meet some of your people."

There was not much need for introductions. The gipsies, scenting free drink in the offing, had gathered round already. They now fell upon the missioners as eagerly as cannibals, each determined to obtain the juiciest Christian for his pot. Ram was borne away by some upstanding young rascals, the sons of Manasseh, and Charles was collared by the Smiths. Marta seized hold of Bill, kissed him on the forehead, allowed him to buy some rum for herself and Mami, and then hugged him to her bosom in warmhearted gratitude. Poppet became the victim of six small children clamorous for Britvics. Mrs. Agnew, torn between disapproval of all these Goings-on and a powerful profit motive, took more money in ten minutes than she generally took in an hour; for every gipsy in the room who had been drinking cider at tenpence a pint immediately switched over to best bitter at one and sixpence. Tim had known this would happen, but he thought it was only fair that the missioners should pay for their footing. The gipsies among friends were generous, proud, and disdainful of charity; strangers were fair game, pigeons for plucking.

The door opened at the end of the long room; and once again Tim was conscious of that queer brief hush, that breathless moment of expectation; then the chatter broke out again as the Welsh girls streamed in, with an assortment of their boy-friends. Very soon they started singing, and Bill was reminded of his concertina in the car outside and went out to fetch it. Marianne said to Tim:

"For a missioner he's got a jolly good capacity. He's downed three pints in ten minutes."

"Good for him. How are *you* doing?"

"Mad as a March Hare to-night," she said. "I was half tight with happiness before I started." She tucked her arm in Tim's. "I've stopped counting how many drinks I've had. I've been swigging away with Marta and Mami."

"You're feeling all right, though?"

"A bit airy; as if I might fly up to the ceiling if you let go of me. So hold me tight, my love, my love!" she whispered to him. "I'll try not to disgrace you."

"You won't do that. But we'll have to keep an eye on Carol."

"She's drinking ginger beer with a dash of cider in it. Nasty, but it won't hurt her. That's the one I'm alarmed about," said Marianne. Poppet, very wild of eye, went by with a tray of drinks which she had bought for Manasseh's sons. "Darling, what pugnant people!" she said over her shoulder to Tim. She offered the tray to the young gipsies, who seized their pints and rapidly retreated, like timid birds taking crumbs from a bird-table. Marianne said in Tim's ear:

"If someone doesn't *rape* that girl soon she'll blow off her top."

"They're an odd lot," said Tim, "but harmless. They seem to be enjoying themselves, anyhow."

"D'you suppose they'd ever convert anybody?"

"The other way round," laughed Tim. "Look at Bill."

Bill, having fetched his concertina, was popular with the Welsh girls. He had overcome the preliminary brayings of the instrument, which sounded like a donkey predicting rain, and he was sitting on the edge of a table, swinging his legs as he played, with a pint of beer on each side of him and a bevy of nymphs singing like nightingales all round. It was a happy situation, which inspired him to virtuosity: for he played whatever tune came into his head, changing rapidly from "Shenandoah" to "I Got a Robe," from "Frankie and Johnnie" to "Ilkla Moor," from "Widdecombe Fair" to "Barbara Allen." Sometimes the airs got mixed up. "It makes you feel tight even to listen to him," Marianne said. However, the Welsh girls being so quick of ear seemed to enjoy the game; when they didn't know the words they were content to hum the tune, softly and sweetly in chorus, making a delightful lullaby sound. The gipsies, who didn't sing, began to shuffle their feet; and Tim said: "Watch them: in a minute they'll be dancing."

The shuffling became a recognisable stamp, in time with the music. It grew louder, and the floor shook, and even the glasses rattled on the shelf behind Mrs. Agnew, who shouted in vain, "You monkeys! You'll bring the ceiling down!" She couldn't make herself heard above the din of the stamping boots and Bill's Welsh chorus humming high and clear and Bill himself singing atrociously:

> *"Sally Brown is a bright mulatta,*
> *She drinks rum and chews tobacca,*
> *Put my money on Sally Brown!"*

A tall youth, one of Manasseh's, ran into the middle of the room and started tap-dancing. He was swift-footed and clever; slim-hipped and lithe as a cat. He wore a tawny shirt with a red-spotted handkerchief tucked into the neck; his lean face with its high cheek-bones shone coppery under the lights; he seemed all aflame as he danced there. Then, on Tim's right, Marta started; and old Mami, prancing up to Marianne, lifted her skirt and kicked her legs, quite forgetting that she was a hundred and two years old. She had very small feet and trim ankles, almost like a girl's. Marianne's feet refused to keep still any longer. She whispered to Tim: "It's something I can do. May I?" and letting go of Tim's arm she cried: "Come on, then, Mami!" But Mami, out of breath, shook her head and sat down to watch Marianne. "Marta! Wisdom!" she called. "See the young leddy! She dances better than that chal of Manasseh's!" All at once—Marianne didn't know how it happened—there was a clear space all round her, the gipsies had formed a circle, Manasseh's chal had joined her within it; side by side while the gipsies roared approval they tap-danced like mad.

Tim, on the fringe of the circle, found Marta and Wisdom beside him. Marta gathered him to her, pressed him against her bold breasts, planted a wet kiss on his cheek, whispered: "That's your gel; and you'll never kiss another save her and Marta?" Then old Mami, wriggling weaselly through the crowd, reached Tim's side and scolded crossly: "You're in the way, I can't see, I want to watch them." Tim seized her by the waist, one arm beneath her bony buttocks, and raised her up above the heads of the crowd. "There, you old witch," he said. "Riding on your broomstick." She was as light as a child. Stench from the pipe which she still held in her toothless jaw filled Tim's nostrils, with other smells, of ancient dirt, herbs, rancid ointments. She gripped him by the hair to balance herself and from her point of vantage yammered encouragement to the dancers.

They went faster. The young chal took off his cap and flung it into the crowd. Marianne, mad as a March Hare indeed, flushed and laughing, tossed her head back to keep her hair out of her eyes; the gipsy's black locks flopped up and down, making a weird crest for him. Their feet went quicker still. Bill changed his tune suddenly: now it was: *Merrily we roll along—roll along—roll along*—and the clear Welsh voices were like a mountain stream now rippling, now pouring in a torrent. The gipsies were yelling, Wisdom and Marta were stamping—there was so much noise that Tim didn't hear the door open for the third time. He was only aware that the stamping had abruptly ceased, and then of Mami hissing as she struggled in his arms: "*Wisdom, they have come.*" He put Mami down, the gipsies fell suddenly silent, the concertina uttered a last, long, excruciating wail. For a fraction of a second there was still the tapping of the dancers' feet; then the gipsy stopped dancing, and Marianne followed suit. They stood in the middle of the circle, looking at each other in bewilderment. The circle parted and all the gipsies shuffled back towards the wall. Right up the middle of the room, between the two rows of gipsies, strode Black Barty.

Black Alf followed him; then came Betsy, Black Liz, ten or twelve of their people. Wisdom at Tim's side spoke very quietly:

"I think you'd better get your folk away."

"What's the trouble?" Tim said.

"There's none yet, but there's someone looking for it."

Tim said:

"O.K. Thank you, Wisdom. Good luck."

Black Barty, with his people keeping close together in a bunch, had gone up to the counter. The other gipsies watched them in silence. The room that had been so noisy was extraordinarily still.

Tim wasted no time. Out of such a silence, the gipsy brawls would sometimes blow up like typhoons in the calm Pacific. He had seen the gipsies fight, with the bottles in their hands and the boots on their feet; he knew he must get the girls out quickly. He caught Marianne's eye where she stood with the chal, and she was with him in a flash, close to his side as if she belonged there, her arm tucked in his, no questions, a quick nod of understanding. "Now Carol," he said. She was standing by the bar with Charles, and luckily Charles was sensible and sober. Tim smiled to see how the young man's arm went defensively round Carol's shoulder at the mere hint that there might be some trouble. Poppet was more difficult; she declared that she didn't want to go home yet because it was such a pellent party. When Tim told her there was likely to be fighting she wailed absurdly: "But oughtn't we to try to get *between* them?" Charles, who now turned out to be a person who would stand no nonsense, swept her up with his free arm and said: "We're not the United Nations, so don't be a fool." There remained only Bill and Ram. The Welsh girls were looking after Bill. They always made themselves scarce at the least sign of brawling, like a flock of chittering birds startled by a distant gun. They and their boy-friends were on their way out already, and Bill, with a girl on each arm, was squeezing a valedictory wail out of his concertina. But Ram was nowhere to be seen, and Charles thought he'd probably walked back to their camp, which was half a mile away, on the bank of the river. He didn't like pubs, Charles said, and had only come with them to-night reluctantly. Outside, in the bright moonlight, they called him, but got no answer.

"I'm sure he must have walked home," said Charles. "I haven't seen him for ages. . . . Bill, aren't you coming with us?"

"I've got the same idea as Ram," said Bill. "It's a nice night for walking; I think I'll just come along in my own time, old boy."

Inside the missioners' car, Poppet said:

"Darlings, I don't know how you feel, but I think we've laid the foundations for doing some really good works, somehow."

Tim shouted to Charles: "See you get young Carol home safe," and he heard Carol giggle as she settled herself against Charles's shoulder. Charles acknowledged the admonition with a cheerful toot on the horn. The old rattletrap drove away. Marianne leaned against Tim.

"All right?" he said.

"The world's whizzing round a bit, but it's a very nice world."

They stood outside the bar and listened. Far away, down the road, was the sound of singing, and Bill's concertina, pleasantly muted by distance, was playing "Greensleeves." But within the bar, all was silence. Not a sound; and then, sudden and brief and angry, a little murmur, a buzz, as if a hive became agitated, nothing more. The buzz died down; and there was silence again, as Tim and Marianne tucked themselves into the M.G.

# 12

Ram raised his head slowly. The painful thudding had ceased. The night air smelt sweet again. Stinging nettles prickled his hands with a not unwelcome asperity. The heavy dew, soaking through his trousers, bathed his knees. He struggled to his feet and dared to look up at the stars, which were fixed once more in their courses and blinked reassuringly. Ram addressed himself sternly: Moderation in all things, man, excellent motto of wise Greeks.

He had never liked beer. Its taste did not please him, its smell offended his nose, and to guzzle it in pints, quarts, gallons till it lay heavy on your belly, as rowing-men did after boat races, seemed to him a kind of English barbarity. Why, then, had he drunk three pints, no, three and a half, in that horrible smoky public-house? For the same reason, alas, that he had drunk a great many pints, and made himself sick, with the rowing-men in Eights week: for the sake of the brotherhood of man. Ram loved his fellow-humans with a determined, self-conscious, and generalised love. In particular he felt it incumbent upon him to love most those who displeased him or those whom he had displeased. That had been the cause of his downfall after the boat races. He hadn't really liked those muscular toughs, and he thought they didn't like him because he was far from muscular, and because he had become overexcited when he was coxing the boat and lost them a race which they ought to have won. Therefore he had gone to the pub with them, and got drunk to please them, and suffered greatly in body and mind.

Now, in the case of the gipsies, it was something else which had moved him to this extravagant and sacrificial love. It was their strangeness, and the fact that he didn't understand them. Ram believed that all peoples ought to understand each other and that the more different they were from each other the more important it was to discover the common denominator. He often indulged in beautiful daydreams in which he encountered, generally by chance and always in the oddest circumstances, Bulgars, Jugoslavs, Dutchmen, Filipinos; Siamese, Hawaiians, Indonesians, even Eskimos. Always in these daydreams he sought and found the common denominator, and not only made and cemented wonderful friendships but fostered separate friendships between the different people he met. (The most heart-warming fantasy of all concerned an American and a Russian, shaking hands after having been brought together by Ram.) Sometimes these multi-racial companions of his imagination were men; more often, it must be admitted, they were women. Chinese girls with flower-faces; hefty English girls bashing tennis balls; olive Italians; splendid swim-suited Swedes! The universal brotherhood surely included a sisterhood too; and so Ram permitted himself a kind of platonic polygamy in his dreams.

To-night, as soon as he entered the Royal Victoria, he had recognised that the gipsies were not only very different from himself, but from the English too; and it had greatly encouraged him to see these English friends of his, whom also he loved, setting themselves to make merry with the gipsies and so by devious routes to find the way into their hearts. He had felt himself bound to assist in this process; so he had taken a little beer, a half-pint only, for companionship's sake. Although he didn't like the taste of it, he had recognised its virtue as a kind of loving-cup. So he had taken another, and another; and the more he drank, the more eagerly his spirit sought to cross the frontiers of race and environment, questing, exploring, stretching forth towards these people, seeking as it were to embrace *their* spirit under the banner of love. . . . And then, ah then, even as he declared his faith in the ultimate triumph of man's reasonable mind to that wise old Manasseh, reason had suddenly deserted him. The room had swung round him in a haze of nauseous tobacco smoke and a whirl of bright electric lights. Manasseh's face was a brown blur; and speech became impossible owing to the dreadful things which were happening to Ram's inside. Some power of locomotion, however, remained; he staggered to the door, across the yard, through the gate at the bottom of the yard. There he cast himself down, and his belly, violently revolting, demonstrated most cruelly the temporary victory of body over mind.

The attack didn't last long. On his feet again in the moonlit orchard, Ram looked at the gold wrist-watch which his father had given him before he came to England and which was his most precious possession. It showed ten to ten. So the pub would still be open, and soon his friends would take him back to the camp. Purged in body and spirit, clear of head and steady on his feet, Ram returned to the hop-pickers' bar.

The tobacco smoke, which he loathed, made his eyes smart; tears blurred his vision as he looked in vain for his fellow-missioners. As he peered round the room, which was curiously hushed, his eyes lit upon the gipsy girl with whom he had shared his hymn-book at the open-air service. He recognised her bright scarlet dress, low-necked, with white frills on it. She walked across the room, from the bar into the far corner, and the way she walked, straight-backed, narrow-hipped, head held high, awoke in him a memory of home. No English girl walked like that; they slummocked or if they didn't slummock they bounced. But Sue treading but a few paces seemed to Ram to write a little line of poetry with her feet; the hollow of her back, the frankness of her breasts, the delightful swing of her skirt's hem, captured and held his eyes. She walked as the girls with the pitchers walked, going to the river or returning; and this memory made Ram homesick and aware of being a stranger in a strange land. He closed his eyes to shut out the smoke-filled room, and for a fraction of a second he was home again, in the village near Bangalore. He saw the girls in their saris walking at evening, and smelt the hot smells of the village, the burnt-dung smell and the tang of a faraway forest fire; and he was Shri Pattabhi Ramcharan and no longer Ram. Then he heard a sharp sound, a crash, a tinkle—and there was a cry, too, as he opened his eyes and saw, in the very middle of the room, the two tall gipsies facing one another: the square one they called Wisdom and the lean one who had lost an eye. Wisdom stood with his hands at his sides; the other raised a fist threateningly. There were broken glasses on the floor by one of the tables, and pools of spilt beer. The woman behind the bar—it was she who had cried out—was shouting something about the police. Everybody else was silent and still. Then Ram caught Sue's eye as she stood against the wall. She began to walk towards him, but warily, on tiptoe, as if she did not want to draw attention to herself.

Wisdom's voice cracked like a whip:

"*Barty, get out.*"

One-eye stood quite still and laughed. He said:

"Put me out."

"I will not fight in here," said Wisdom.

Then One-eye hit him, not hard, across the mouth.

There was a moment's absolute silence after the blow. In that moment Sue reached Ram's side. Then from all directions came a sudden uproar, shrieks and shouts and curses. It seemed to Ram, as he peered shortsightedly at the confusion through blurred spectacles, that he was looking into the murky maw of Hell itself. The gipsies were as fiends. They grimaced, spat, clawed, swore. One-eye's wife, a little spitfire of a woman, confronted the wife of Wisdom whose great bosom magnificently shook with passion. One-eye's wife seized it, seized them, Ram suddenly realised with the utmost dismay, seized both of them and began to twist them, using each hand as one would use a monkey-wrench to loosen an obstinate nut. But now One-eye half-ran, half-pranced towards the door, looking over his shoulder and laughing at Wisdom who came more slowly after him. Behind these two came their wives, still locked in a deadly embrace, and a very old woman hobbling fast and cursing. Then all the gipsies ran towards the door in a rout which reminded Ram of Kipling's Bandar-log—barging into each other, knocking over the tables, breaking the glasses. Ram was very frightened, and he thought Sue put out her hand to him—anyway he clutched it and held it while the gipsies milled in the doorway and the woman behind the bar yelled to someone in the other room: "Phone for the police."

Then the room was empty save for Ram and Sue; Sue went slowly to the door, and Ram went with her, still holding her hand. Outside Ram gasped gratefully, drinking in the cool clean air. In the yard, where there was an electric lamp on a tall pole lighting the parking-place, the gipsies had formed a kind of circle around which they seethed in confusion; within the circle two men were fighting, and Ram could hear grunts and thuds. He shuddered.

"What's happening?" he said to Sue.

"It's Wisdom Lee and my father, Black Barty."

"Your *father?*" said Ram. That made it all the worse. "Oughtn't we to—" He was going to say "try to stop them" but Ram knew his limitations, and the sound of the blows and the bestial grunts produced in him a physical horror, he began to feel sick again. Now was the chance, the heaven-sent chance, for some splendid act of reconciliation. This was the very stuff of his daydreams. He should push his way through the crowd—but gently, by some method of non-violence which for the first time presented itself to Ram as not so simple as it sounded—he should interpose himself between the fighters, armed only with love he should ward off their blows; with sweet reason he should mend their differences and then, humbly triumphant, watch them shake hands. Mahatma Gandhi might have done that; Jawaharlal Nehru might do that; but not he. At the very thought of such a deed his knees turned to water and his hands began to tremble. With miserable honesty he said to himself: Shri Pattabhi Ramcharan, you are nothing but a coward.

Sue said:

"They will fight until one is beaten, or the policeman comes."

Ram had a horrible vision of blood and pulped faces and broken teeth. Sue had taken a step or two in the direction of the crowd.

"You don't want to look at it?" said Ram.

"N-no," said Sue hesitantly.

"I should think not, indeed!" He took her hand again. She turned towards him, and the moonlight glinted on her hair, shone soft and pale upon her face and neck, leaving little shadows under her cheek-bones and between the delightful small tumescence of her breasts. Ram thought again of the girls in their saris and powerful emotions stirred in him, concerning brotherhood and sisterhood and the universality of love. He turned away from the distasteful clamour and took a tentative step or two in the direction of the gate and the orchard with its moon-washed trees. Sue seemed to hang back for a moment; naturally, he thought, she is concerned for her father; then, to his delight, she was walking at his side. Emboldened, he said:

"I was sure you would not want to watch it. Resort to fisticuffs affront to dignity and reason, no substitute whatever for logical argument. Come away!"

# 13

Beneath the electric lamp the fighters cast grotesque and murderous shadows. These shadows smote and parried, were grappling giants, savaged each other, staggered apart, only to leap back in renewed fury.

The gipsies howled. Mami, right in front, clenched small fists, shot out lefts, rights, short-arm jabs, hooks, uppercuts in passionate dumbshow. Marta was at Mami's side, both hands clutched to her bosom, stone-still.

Wisdom's tribe formed half the circle; Barty's folk the other half. In the forefront of those who shouted for Barty was Black Alf; indeed he had broken the circle and intruded a little way into the space which had been left for the fighters. As the fight surged to and fro, so Black Alf ran this way or that. Always he seemed to be in a position not far behind Wisdom. Marta's eyes never left him.

Barty's Betsy was yelling:

"Fix the bastard! Fix him!"

Wisdom, breathing hard, reeled back before a rain of blows. The retreat took him almost into the crowd. There he stood defensive, his left leg well forward, his body beautifully balanced, swaying a little from side to side. Black

Barty, thinking victory near, was unwary of Wisdom's poised readiness; he came on, flailing with his arms, and Wisdom, choosing his moment, let fly with his left and right almost together. There was only the fraction of a second between the two blows; and they did not merely thud, as the previous ones had done, they sounded like two sharp cracks of bone on bone. Black Barty staggered, and there was a great shout from Wisdom's people; some of them surged forward, thinking the fight was nearly over, and these impetuous ones for a moment obscured Marta's view. She could not see Black Alf, though she knew he was somewhere in the crowd behind Wisdom. Then she saw the shadows on the ground, and she screamed.

Wisdom's shadow was of a tiger in mid-spring; he was leaping in to finish Barty. Barty's shadow, long and spidery, sagged backwards from the knees. There appeared suddenly a third shadow with arm upraised. But the arm had no hand; it ended in a kind of elongated claw.

The claw struck even as Marta screamed.

Wisdom for a moment stood absolutely still. Then he swayed, first backwards, then forwards, and as he fell Black Barty stepped aside and hit him with all his strength on the side of the jaw.

Wisdom lay upon his face. As Marta ran to him Black Barty turned to his people and pointed to the crumpled heap on the ground and cried: "The King of the Gipsies!"

Marta knelt by Wisdom. She put her hand upon his head, and it was wet. She turned her hand palm upwards to the light and saw the blood. Kneeling there, with the crowd all round her, Barty's people and Wisdom's pushing and peering, she looked in vain for Black Alf. He was not among them. He was gone, with his shadow.

Mami came and knelt with Marta. When she, too, felt the wetness she did not need to hold her hands to the light. She knew.

"The hook," she said.

Marta with the gentleness of her great strength took Wisdom by the shoulders and turned him over and propped his head in her lap. She leaned close to Wisdom, and felt his breath on her mouth, and after a while he moaned a little and stirred. She felt his blood running between her thighs, as if it were some flux of her own. He moaned, and Mami said:

"I have sent the boys for a gate."

"A gate?"

"They will lift it off its hinges. We shall need it to carry him."

When Marta looked round her now, she saw that Black Barty's people were gone. They had gone silently, knowing perhaps the evil they had done; but a long way down the road Black Barty was shouting, his voice was the only voice upraised:

"Barty's the kiddie, Barty's the boy!"

Mami said:

"They are coming with the gate."

Wisdom's eyes were open now. As Marta put her face down to his he spoke at last.

"My head, my head."

# 14

Police-Sergeant Croft, as he bicycled up from the village, heard Barty's triumphant cry repeated a dozen times in the lane down by the river meadows. Off home to their caravans, he thought, and was glad that the fight was over. When he first came to the hop-country, as a young constable in the nineteen-thirties, he had thought it his job to intervene when the gipsies were fighting; he'd had three days in hospital and three weeks off duty in consequence. Since then he had always been a little frightened of the gipsies, and it was his policy as far as possible to let 'em be. So long as they didn't smash up the pub, or raid the henroosts, or set somebody's barn on fire, he was unconcerned about their goings-on. If they all murdered each other, he sometimes thought, there would be less trouble in the world.

He got to the Royal Victoria and saw a light in Mrs. Agnew's bedroom. He rang his bicycle bell several times, and at last she came to the window in her dressing-gown, holding her cat in her arms.

"Those monkeys," she said, "they went mad, you know how they do, like wild beasts, sudden. They've been fighting out there. One was hurt, I think." Croft wasn't bothered about that. He asked the practical question:

"Did they do any damage, Ma'am?"

"A few glasses and chairs. That Black Barty was the ring-leader."

"He generally is. Well, I'm glad it wasn't worse."

She had closed her window, and drawn the curtains, when Croft saw the blood. Broken bottles, he thought; maybe even knives.

He wheeled his bicycle a little way up the road, following the blood-trail in the moonlight. Then he lost interest in it, for there were six stray cattle grazing on the verge, and the gate was missing from a field-entrance near by; it looked as if the gipsies had been thieving as well as fighting, a much more serious matter. He penned the cattle in another field, and thought with annoyance that to-morrow he'd have to make investigations, which he hated. Then perhaps there'd be a charge, a lot of writing, maybe a prosecution, a day at Hereford police court.

He got on his bicycle and coasted down the hill. Coming round a corner he nearly ran into a couple who were canoodling in the middle of the road—a funny place to do it, he thought; and as they jumped out of his way he recognised Black Barty's girl and that foreign-looking chap who had come down with the mission. Well, it don't quite go with hymn-singing, he thought; but foreigners has funny ideas.

It was a wild season, was the hop-picking. Maybe 'twas

the smell of the hops made 'em all so harum-scarum, what with fighting and frigging, thought Sergeant Croft.

Then on a grass verge, close to the Hope turning, he saw a parked car. It was under some trees, so he didn't notice it until he was nearly past it. Otherwise he would have known whose it was. But you could never be sure that a stationary car in a country road at night hadn't been stolen and abandoned; so he stopped and shone his torch towards the driving seat, and then he saw Tim Sollars with a girl.

"Sorry, Master Tim. It's me, Croft. I wouldn't have—" and he jumped on his bicycle and pedalled quickly away.

# 15

When Croft had gone, Tim laughed and said:

"Has it stopped going round?"

"Except when I shut my eyes. Then it's like that thing at the fair."

"I'd better get you home, I think. Try sitting up straight." He started the car and drove it slowly off the grass verge. Marianne said:

"Aren't I a little fool? To get tight because I was happy. I've only done it once before, and that was because I was miserable. It was just after I ran away from home. You know why I did that?" she added after a pause.

"No," said Tim firmly.

"Tim, you mustn't ever tell me lies."

"Well, I *don't* know, honestly."

"Not that I got into trouble and ran away? Everybody knew that, didn't they?"

"That's what they thought."

"It's what *I* thought." Marianne laughed, and her hand

found Tim's hand. "I had jolly good reason, too. So I panicked. Eighteen, and Mummy had just died. No one to tell."

Alone with Tommy, thought Tim; and Tommy on the booze because of Suzette.

Marianne went on:

"I even tried taking something. It was in the hop-picking three years ago. I told Betsy I knew a girl who was in a mess. She got me some gipsy stuff, very special, five bob for the bottle. It tasted like a horse drench. It made me sick, but it didn't do me any good." She laughed; then she said:

"Anyhow, it wasn't a baby. It was one of the tricks nature plays on us. Perhaps a little joke, to serve me right."

They had come to Tommy's crooked signpost. Swinging the car round it, Tim said:

"You know, you needn't tell me all this, sweetheart."

"No. If I thought I needed to I wouldn't tell you, would I? And I wouldn't love you, and you wouldn't love me." Her voice sounded dreamy and far away, but when she laughed it was an ordinary laugh, easy and happy and assured. "After that, lots of wild oats in London."

"Yes."

"As a farmer," she laughed, "you'd say it was a good crop."

"As a farmer," Tim said, "I've sown a good one too."

"Gipsy girls?"

He started. Then he remembered: of course Marianne would have seen Sue going up to the wood to meet him, Sue would have passed her and Tommy after he'd left them in the lane.

"Yes," he said.

The lights picked out the white gate of the Hope. As Tim stopped the car Marianne said.

"All square. Hurray. I'm glad I'm tight, I'm glad I told you. I mightn't have, otherwise. I'm going to try shutting my eyes."

She leaned back, and at once she was tucked into his shoulder, as the bark is to the tree. She murmured sleepily:

"*Finis les autres.*"

"What?"

"You must say it too."

"*Finis les autres.*"

"It sounds nice in a Hereford accent," she said. "I say, Tim—"

"Yes?"

"It's still no good with my eyes shut."

"I'll help you out of the car."

When they got to the gate she leaned against it.

"Still no good," she said.

"I'll carry you."

At the front door there was a problem. He put her down on the step. The house was dark and still. He sat on the step beside her and whispered:

"Are you O.K. to explain which is your room?"

"Brain fine, legs hopeless. First on the left at the top of the stairs."

"Good."

He took off his shoes. Then, very gently, he opened the door.

"Light?"

"Just inside, left."

He felt for it and found it.

"Now we're all set. Here goes." He put one arm under her knees, the other round her shoulders.

"Seven stone twelve," she said.

"That's less than a pocket of hops."

The stairs creaked noisily. Tommy's stairs would, he thought. On the landing, still holding her, he had a job with her bedroom door. He managed it at last, and carried her in. There was moonshine coming in through the window; he didn't need to switch on the light. He laid her on the bed and whispered:

"All right now?"

"Gently passing out I think. Happy though."

He could just make out her drowsy smile. She was all crumpled up on the bed. He couldn't leave her like that. He whispered:

"I'd better do the job properly."

"Nightie under the pillow."

He pulled it out while she was fumbling with her dress.

"This is silly," she said. "I'm sorry, Tim." She laughed softly. "We both had other ideas for to-night, I dare say."

"Another night . . . Shall I help?"

"Please." She pulled her dress down over her shoulders. "Skin a rabbit," she said.

Then she lay naked in the dim moonshine. Tim slipped the nightdress over her head.

"Pop you inside now."

When he'd tucked her in he leaned down to kiss her. She was asleep already when his lips touched hers.

He tiptoed to the door and went out. There was moonlight dappling the landing, as well as a glimmer from the electric light downstairs. He was closing the door, and trying to do so without making a sound, when he heard the stairs creak. Damn; Tommy, he thought. His first instinct was to go back into Marianne's room; then he thought it might be better to explain things to Tommy—it wouldn't be difficult. As he hesitated a figure much taller than Tommy's appeared at the top of the stairs. It was white-shrouded like a ghost; and silently as a ghost it came towards him. Too late now to hide in the bedroom. Tim stood face to face with a gaunt man in a nightshirt who bore in his hand a glass of water containing false teeth.

Tim said:

"Good evening."

The man stared at him, glanced at the bedroom door, then back at Tim. His nightshirt was rather short, and knobbly legs showed beneath it. He looked as if he had stepped out of an old print.

"Good evening," he grunted. Then on bare feet he shuffled past Tim and opened the bedroom door next to Marianne's. He paused there for a moment looking over his shoulder. He seemed to shake his head. At last he entered the room and shut the door behind him.

Tim went down the creaking stairs, into the hall, past the

hatstand where Tommy's panama with the cricket-ribbon round it rakishly hung, past the picture on the wall of which Tommy had asked him: "Have you ever seen the world looking like that?" He hadn't noticed the title then. He now saw that it was called "Adam Sees Eve for the First Time."

He went out into the night, through the garden, into the yard. A white owl beautifully glided out of the loft above the barn, on downy wings that made no sound. A black cat trotted up to him purring, and rubbed against his legs. The air was full of the smells of the night, roses in the garden, late meadowsweet, old hay, wet earth, dewy grass, and to Tim in his joy they smelt as fresh as if he had never smelt them before. The moon, riding high above the oast, was bright enough to cast dark shadows. It had been only a wafer that night he met Marianne in the lane; it was growing up with their love.

# Part Three

## *At the Full*

# 1

A moister air, which had sharpened and sweetened the smells of the night for Tim as he crossed the Hope farmyard, blew in from the west and brought a sprinkle of rain. It wasn't enough to hold up the picking; but there were dabbly days when the work was interrupted, the hops were often wet when they reached the kiln, and drying became more difficult. Old Dave at Sollarshill, steadily swearing, and Tommy at the Hope, coughing and choking, spent anxious nights as they checked and rechecked the temperature in the drying-chamber.

The moisture in the air seemed to revive and rekindle the hop disease, downy mildew.

During the hot spell it had spread only slowly. Indeed it had died out altogether in some of the hopyards where it had first appeared. In others it had been patchy, taking a tithe of the crop only. The majority of the farms had so far been spared. But now, suddenly, it became epidemic. John Sollars blamed the wind that came with the rain clouds; he was convinced that the spores which caused the disease were wind-borne. There was still no sign of it at Sollarshill or at the Hope; but on the other farms, to the west and to the south, it scorched the hop-leaves and withered the bines —even the hops themselves hung limp, and were speckled and flecked with reddish brown. It seemed to be a more potent virus than either the hop-growers or the Ministry of Agriculture's experts had ever known before. Bob Barker, on the phone to John, told how he had walked round his hopyard late one evening and congratulated himself on the state of the bines, which were sturdy and vigorous and green as grass in the light of the setting sun; early next morning the hops along more than a dozen rows were drooping and dirty-looking, shrunken and blotched. Some of their leaves had a brownish bloom which rubbed off, like a powder, on his hands.

Day after day, in sunshine and shower, and night after night under the fitful moon, the hop-disease spread through Herefordshire. It did not always destroy the hops altogether; but even where they were partially affected they would be a bad sample, and the brewers would look askance at them. The value of a good sample would be correspondingly increased.

So the hop-pickers worked long hours, sometimes from dawn to dusk; it was a race with the downy mildew. John Sollars took on more pickers. He went into Hereford one morning and did something he had never done before—with distaste he scoured the pubs for pickers, a ragtag and bobtail lot, hiring a bus to bring them out every day. His own sickness lay heavy on him; and that morning he went to his doctor for the first time in twenty years. Mollie had threatened that she would phone for the doctor if he would not go to see him; and John persuaded himself that perhaps there might be some simple explanation of his pain, it might turn out to be something which could be cured by magic pills or potions, or at least eased until the hop-picking was done. After that, if necessary, he could lay up for a while. But the doctor wouldn't give him any pills. Instead he spoke of X-rays and a specialist. John to whom fear was an uncommon experience felt the chill of it then. He tried to speak casually:

"There's no hurry, I suppose?"

"Obviously we ought to make a diagnosis as soon as we can."

"When the hops are in," said John obstinately. It would be a little time, in any case, before the doctor could make the appointments; and within a fortnight, John thought, he should have at least three quarters of his crop safely stored in the long white pockets in the barn. So they compromised; the doctor would fix things up with the radiologist and the consultant, and meanwhile John would carry on.

"Take it easy; and don't worry," the doctor said.

When John got home, and Mollie, hearing the Bristol, ran out from her dairy to ask him what had happened, he told her about the specialist but he didn't mention the X-ray. He thought it would upset her; and by that thought he acknowledged his own fear of the mysterious camera and what its prying curiosity might discover. So he came face to face with his fear, and angrily brushed it away. *He must get in his hops;* and until the hops were gathered, nothing else would matter, not even the pain. He cursed every scud that stopped the picking even for a quarter of an hour; he cursed Tim if a load was late at the kiln, holding up the drying; he cursed Dave, and Dave cursed back, the sodding sulphur, the buggering burners, the new-fangled nonsensical frigging furnace, we'd have done a sight better with the old-fashioned frigging coal.

Each evening he counted the pockets in the barn, which in the half-light looked like the carcases of pigs hanging up there.

As for Tim, John's mantle had fallen on him; and he drove the pickers as he drove himself, relentlessly. He bullied the Black Country people, cajoled the Welsh, went to see Wisdom where he lay in his caravan and took back Wisdom's word to the gipsies when they idled as gipsies always do in the noonday sun. From breakfast to supper-time he never left the hopyard; and at night when his mother had sent John willy-nilly to bed he was in the kiln so late and so often that Dave told him: "You're wuss nor the old man for fussin' around." Whether the harvest was hops or corn, the Sollarses were like squirrels in their hurry to garner it. *Like father, like son!* thought Dave.

# 2

So Marianne had her first letters from Tim. Carol was the postman; she brought one on the Monday morning after the party in the pub, when she picked up Marianne in the M.G. to go shopping in Hereford. It was only a little letter, scribbled in a round farmerish hand on John's business paper, with JOHN SOLLARS FMR. AND HOPGROWER printed with yeoman plainness across the top of it. If your head's awful, it said, Carol will buy you a Pimms in Hereford on me. Her head was awful, and her recollection of last night was a bit blurred. Between sleeping and waking, as she lay in bed, she had blinked in the sunlight which flooded in through the undrawn curtains. The bright beam had shown her the clothes in a heap at the bottom of the bed, her dress and underclothes. Only then she realised how she'd got to bed, and it made her laugh despite her headache, she hugged to herself a secret, absurd and improper delight because of it.

In Hereford they bought six yards of dark green taffeta and a pattern for Carol's evening dress, and then they had a Pimms together at the Green Dragon Hotel to celebrate it. Carol had to get back early; Tim had roped in the missioners as extra hop-pickers, and Carol wanted to work with them, so that she could be near to Charles.

"Shall I tell him about my dress?" she said on the way home.

"No, I should let it be a surprise to him."

"If I made it myself it'd be a surprise to him," said Carol. "How on earth do you make a strapless keep up?"

The next evening Carol came over to cut out the dress. Marianne had suggested they should do it at the Hope; she didn't want to go to Sollarshill again, so she made the excuse that it would be easier to work in her room, where they could do the sewing on her own machine. Perhaps Carol guessed the real reason. She said: "We're not always so sticky as we were at Sunday tea," and threw Marianne one of those small swift smiles, *Catch!* Marianne loved her; and it was fun making the dress after hop-picking every evening. Always she brought a brief letter from Tim, and took one back to him, and it was as if they had found a new path in the progress of their love, and were exploring together along it. For while there are things lovers must speak to each other when the time and the place and the mood are apt for them, there are also things which should be set on paper, and read with the wonder of new discovery, and read again, and read yet a third time to make sure that every heart-warming nuance and implication is understood. Sometimes Tim phoned, but the letters were better, somehow. Twice, in the late evening, Marianne rang him up because he had asked her to. The first time Mrs. Sollars answered. She said: "Are you *quite* sure Carol isn't being a nuisance about the dress? Oh, *Tim?*"—she even contrived to sound surprised. "Yes, of course; I'll go and fetch him." The second time it was John Sollars who had picked up the telephone:

"Oh, it's you, Miss."

After that she told Tim she would not ring him up again; and next evening he came over with Carol, for a few minutes snatched between picking and drying. He'd come straight from the hopyard, in dirty old corduroys and an open shirt. His face and neck were deep-tanned by the sun. "I'm mucky and sweaty and sticky with hops," he said, "and there's another load on the way up to the kiln. I'll have to help Dave spread 'em on the hop-floor."

"Have you had supper?"

"I'll get something when we've finished."

"There's a bit of steak in the frig. Five minutes!" She didn't ask him how he liked it to be cooked. She fried it very quickly, well browned on the outside, red within; she gave it the least smear of garlic. Tim wolfed it and was apparently unaware of the garlic. "Better than at home," he said with cheerful disloyalty. "What did you do to it?"

"Something French, you English oaf."

Then she walked as far as the drive gate with him, and there was no one about, so they kissed in the open there, briefly and lightly, lest more than that token should make them impatient.

"Soon?" she said.

"Jolly soon . . . Friday's your birthday?"

"How did you know?"

"You told me, down in the meadow." She had forgotten that. "The same day that Sally's due with her calf. We'll see if we can go somewhere on Friday. We ought to be pretty well on with the hops by then. How's it going with you?" he said.

"No disease yet. We're keeping our fingers crossed."

"Uncle George?"

"Relenting a bit. He may give us another chance if we get the hops in safely and pay off his precious interest. . . . Till Friday?"

"Till Friday!"

He went off down the hill. Four days till Friday! Too long for love's eagerness; but her confidence shortened it. For she was sure in her happiness, sure as the sunrise, no faintest shadow of doubt or dismay.

## 3

Something strange seemed to be happening to George.

He had been through Tommy's accounts, such as they were. He had given it as his considered opinion that Tommy had been "morally bankrupt" for at least three years, and that his situation was getting worse every day. He had lectured him about his fecklessness, about drink, about his responsibilities to Marianne; and he still seemed determined to call in the mortgage, conceding only that he would wait until the hops had been harvested and sold.

"You realise, after that, it may mean selling the farm?"

"It's still a good safe security," said Tommy. "Hop-farms are at a premium, because of the quota." The Hop Marketing Board controlled the growing of hops as well as their sale to the brewers. The "quota," which varied from year to year according to the demand, was a percentage of the quantity of hops which any given farm had been producing before the board came into being. It was attached to the farm, and not to the owner of the farm. Nobody could set up as a hop-grower unless he bought or inherited a hop-farm; so such farms as possessed a "quota" were much more valuable than ordinary agricultural properties.

"I know all about the quota," said George; and indeed in a very short time he had contrived to find out about everything. "But if I do face the painful necessity of selling the farm I shall first surrender the quota. Naturally."

"*Surrender?* But it makes a difference of thousands of pounds!"

"Of course. But you know my views about the Drink Trade, Tommy. It would hardly square with my conscience if I took a profit out of it—or saved myself from a loss. I'm sorry," George said, "but it really is a question of Principle, old man."

And it really was, of course. George had inherited from the pious Tomkinses not only the meanness which was so curiously mixed up with their piety but their special brand of bleak integrity as well. They who had never been moved by a generous impulse would nevertheless have put their whole fortune in jeopardy for the sake of a principle; and George who was probably reluctant to give half a crown to a beggar would accept the loss of a thousand pounds rather than compromise his conscience on the question of beer. It might not even cross his mind that in making his own sacrifice he offered up Tommy's last asset with it.

You couldn't argue with such unshakable integrity. Tommy sighed and said:

"So be it. But if my hops should earn me enough to pay off the arrears—?"

"In that case," said George primly, "the conduct of your farming would be your own affair, and the quota would no longer be any concern of mine."

All this had happened last Monday. More than a week had gone by; and, although his business with Tommy was apparently finished, George showed no inclination to return to London.

Marianne was heartily sick of him; Tommy could scarcely tolerate his company; but George was oblivious of this and he seemed to become, if not exactly happier, at any rate less miserable as the days went by. His ulcer, he said, had quietened down; he ate enormously and, it seemed to Marianne, most horribly—she made him a soggy steamed pudding, which he enjoyed so much that he demanded another, and thereafter he devoured a steamed pudding every day, over which he poured spoonfuls of syrup. He was still ravenous for buns at tea. He had two cups of cocoa in the middle of the morning, and another at night. He declared that he was sleeping better; perhaps there was something in that old superstition after all—perhaps being among the hops all day *did* have something to do with it. So Marianne made him a hop-pillow, lumpy and uncomfortable and teeming no doubt with biting insects and little red mites. George laid his head upon it and had the best night he had known for years. Next morning at breakfast he quoted:

" 'Sleep that knits up the ravell'd sleave of care,' " and gave Marianne the first smile she had had from him since the night Tim put her to bed. George had never mentioned his encounter with Tim coming out of her bedroom; but every time he looked at her she knew he was remembering it. His eyes never quite met hers.

This morning, however, he was almost genial.

"There's only one little thing. Would it be possible, my dear, to *bake* the hop-pillow—?"

"*Bake* it?"

"It's just the spiders," he said. "They tickle me. I think perhaps they become active and crawl out of the hops when my head makes the pillow warm." He got up from the table. "And now I'll go down to the hopyard and join my young friends."

There were four of them: the two gipsy boys who owned the ferret and two Welsh boys, including the one who had observed to George: "Bug-ger schoo-ul." George fed them on Tomkins' Boiled Sweets and devised means of testing their intelligence quotients. His discovery that the gipsy boys were illiterate had at first shocked and then fascinated him. He had spent hours every evening inventing simple puzzles by which the I.Q.'s of illiterates could be infallibly determined. "It opens up," he said, "a whole new field of study. I am thinking of the possibilities with African natives and aboriginal tribes."

"What the devil *is* happening to George?" said Tommy when George had gone out.

"It's the children, I think," said Marianne, who had been watching him in the hopyard yesterday. "It's rather pathetic in a way. He's been dealing remotely with children all his life; but he's never talked to them before. They fascinate him. You wouldn't think George could love anything; but he loves those brats, and he hasn't got a clue how to deal with them. That's why the old wretch won't go home. I suppose I'd better make him another pudding."

# 4

The younger gipsy boy stared hard at the puzzle which George had made with toy bricks of various shapes and sizes. George had bicycled all the way to Hereford to buy the bricks. The puzzle was laid out on the ground in a clear space between the hop-rows. The gipsy boy shook his head and kicked it over with his foot.

"Tell you something," he said. "There's a rabbit in the hedge down by the river."

"A rabbit? Really?" said George.

"Bet you it wasn't a real rabbit," said the Welsh boy who was called Dai. "They all died of the myxie."

"We saw a rabbit," the gipsy boys said.

"At home they all had the myxie. Pegged out they did. They was lying on the roads all swelled up and stinking. And their insides came out of their backsides. You ought to have seen them," Dai said to George.

The gipsies were called Nat and Dan. Nat said:

"It was a rabbit, and live-o. If we could find its hole we could get it out with the ferret."

"We could chase it with a longdog!" said Dai. "My dad's got a longdog. Over there."

"Which is your father?" asked George. The Welsh were picking at the other end of the row. He could see the longdog tied up to one of the hop-strings.

"That one in the blue shirt. Coal miner he is. That's my sister sitting down under the hops."

"She's always sitting," said the other Welsh boy, Evan. "Sitting and crying. Tell you why, too."

"She went up the mountain," said Dai to George. George didn't understand.

"Up the mountain?"

Dai nodded gravely. "Up the mountain with a fellow. After Chapel on a Sunday evening. Most of the girls do go up the mountain."

Evan sought to make the matter clearer to George.

"And look, when she came down from the mountain, her fellow had given her a babby."

"Silly it is," said Dai, with manly superiority towards the frailty of women.

Evan nodded gravely; then, dismissing the silliness: "Let us borrow the longdog and look for the rab-bit," he said.

George was picking up his bricks. The gipsy boys watched him unsmiling and played with their ferret. Dai said diffidently—the Welsh were oddly shy of the gipsies, aware of a difference, unable to understand it:

"Shall we let *him* come?"

"He can come if he likes," said Nat.

"You can come with us if you like," said Dai kindly. "Do you know how to kill a rabbit?"

"I've never killed a rabbit," said George.

"You pull its neck out so it goes *click*. We'll show you."

## 5

It had been their worst day so far at Sollarshill, heavy showers in the morning, an hour's steady rain in the afternoon, and towards evening a strike fomented by Mr. Comstock, who took advantage of the general discomfort, wetness, muddiness and depression to start a row about overtime. Tim was able to settle the strike at last, with some help from Mami, who loathed Mr. Comstock. Wisdom was still laid up with his wound; Tim thought he should have had it stitched, but Mami would have no truck with doctors. "It must stay open," she said "to let out the p'ison." She made pads of rank herbs and tied them on to the back of Wisdom's scalp. They were "drawing the matter," she said; but meanwhile Wisdom must lie abed, and old Mami ruled the gipsies with a rod of iron. "Take no notice of that Mitty man!" she ordered; and the other pickers, when they realised the gipsies were not going to strike, came to terms quite quickly. But by then it was six-thirty, and too late to re-start picking. There would be only six pockets added to the stack in the barn tomorrow; half a ton of hops, instead of the usual day's harvest of two tons. John Sollars, still counting the pockets every evening, reckoned the tally at ninety-nine. He wanted to see two hundred and fifty there before hop-picking was finished. Each pocket, this year, would be worth about twenty-seven pounds. But the hops had been costly to produce. A year's work would be lost if, even now, the downy mildew took them. You played for high stakes when you went in for hop-growing. Upon the fortunes of the next ten days depended whether John made two thousand profit, or lost fifteen hundred pounds.

Now on this bad day, somehow or other, John heard about Carol going to the Royal Victoria. Tim never knew how he got to know these things; he didn't often go down to the village, and he was nothing of a gossip when his business took him there. Probably Dave Huggett told him; for Dave, though he was immured in the oast during the hop-drying, managed to learn all the village news from the tractor-drivers when they brought him the loads of hops. At any rate, John knew that Carol had been to the pub and he tackled Tim about it. Tim didn't like to let Carol down so he took the blame for taking her there. John said:

"They tell me that girl of yours was tap-dancing with the gipsies! If that's the way you like 'em, well, it's your look-out. But at least I don't expect you to mix your own sister up in it.

That was the night of the fight, too. What if she'd found herself at the wrong end of a broken bottle?"

He left Tim in the yard and stumped into the house. Mollie was in the sitting-room, darning the sleeve of one of his old coats. John didn't tell her about the pub. Carol drinking with the gipsies came into the category of unpleasant things which one kept from Mollie. But he did say:

"Where's Carol? Over at the Hope again, I suppose?"

"Yes, she goes there every evening."

"I'm not happy about it," said John.

"No? I wasn't either; but I've been wondering—"

"Wondering what?"

"Whether we might have misjudged that girl a little."

John looked at her in surprise. He was about to say what he thought of Marianne, but he checked himself; one didn't use those words in front of Mollie. And Mollie was saying:

"According to Carol, she makes all her own clothes."

"She'd go threadbare otherwise!"

"And she's an excellent cook."

"What's that got to do with it?" John demanded.

"Nothing; but somehow it makes her seem less of a—well, what we've always thought her. Anyhow it's quite clever to make an evening dress."

"I'll say when I see it," said John. "One of those half-naked ones I suppose. . . . I wish Tim hadn't taken up with her. It's time he settled down; high time he thought of getting married."

Mollie glanced up quickly from her darning.

"Who were you thinking he might—?"

"There are lots of decent girls. There's Pam Johnson, Diana Revel, Jill Ferrers—I thought he had his eye on her once; Enid and Joy Barker—we'll be seeing them all at the hop-dance. But the Barkers are second cousins, of course." A Sollars long ago had married a Barker and joined two fat farms together, the other side of Leominster. Most of the hop-growers were related to each other, and their big acreages bore witness to the fact that they had often found it convenient to match farm to farm as well as man to maid.

"I've always thought I'd like him to marry into hops," John said.

"Well, dear," said Mrs. Sollars, "I expect he will."

John was still looking at her, puzzled by her tone and wondering about her meaning, when Carol came in. He would have liked to speak to her straightway about going to the pub; he must keep that for later. At least he would let her know what he thought of Marianne.

"Your mother and I have been talking. When you've finished this dress you're so busy with I don't want you to make too close friends of the Tomkinses."

"But, Father—" Carol interrupted.

"She's not your sort; and he's a drunken good-for-nothing."

Carol was standing by the window, and when she tossed back her hair it was bright as an ember in the last of the sunlight. She said:

"Good-for-nothing or not, he's making a jolly good fight for his farm. Marianne told me. His brother who's staying there is going to sell him up—"

"Oh, is he?" said John, and leaned forward a little in his chair.

"—unless the hops come to enough money to pay off what Tommy owes him. He'll auction the farm."

"That's very interesting," said John.

"It's touch and go with them. He may be drunken but he's got guts; and so has Marianne. They *deserve* to keep their farm."

"Not the way he farms it."

"He went to the war," said Carol, "and fought with the French Resistance because he speaks the language like a Frenchman. That's why his farm went to pot. He needn't have gone. The other farmers didn't."

Mrs. Sollars's quick glance went to and fro between them; she was aware of John straightening himself, of Carol's defiance, and she tried to catch Carol's eye. She said:

"Somebody had to stay behind and do the work; or we'd have starved."

"We'd starve to-day," said John Sollars, "if all of us farmed like Tommy Tomkins. When's the auction?"

"I told you it depends on the hops," Carol said.

"What's he like, this brother?"

"Why?" Carol went towards her father. Her eyes were on his face, and it was as if she saw something there she had never seen before. "Why do you want to know?"

"I'm wondering if he'd think of selling the farm privately."

Carol stopped dead.

"Oh!" She flushed suddenly, one of those hot flushes that go with red hair and a pale skin; standing in a patch of sunlight she was all aflame. She had spoken before Mrs. Sollars could lift her warning hand. Her clear young voice rang through the room.

"Like Ahab?" she said.

Mrs. Sollars had got up from her chair. "Carol, please."

Carol stood looking from one to the other. Her flush faded and she was very pale.

"You didn't mean that," said Mrs. Sollars.

"No." She hesitated. "I'm sorry." The bright evangelism, Joan of Arc, all gone now: she threw a hesitant little smile to her father. "I shouldn't have said it."

"It was fair enough," said John grimly. He looked hard at her for a moment, watched her smile fade, and then suddenly before it left her he smiled back, rekindling her smile.

"Come here," he said.

She went over to him. He held out his hands.

"Heave me up."

She gave him a strong pull and he stood over her. He regarded her gravely. At last he said:

"If you're going to go on hitting the right nail on the head you'll have to remember your manners." He bent and kissed her.

"Good night," he said. It was earlier than he had ever been to bed; still light outside, the Welsh hills black on the skyline with the red sunset coming through the window. He was very tired, and the pain was tearing at him. He went slowly upstairs. Ahab, he thought; and he didn't remember much about him, except of course Naboth's vineyard. There was Mollie's Bible on the table by her bed; she didn't often read it but she always kept it there, perhaps because she'd been brought up to have a Bible by her bed. He picked it up and thumbed through it. Then he thought Mollie might come in, and he didn't want to be seen looking at the Bible, it would be an embarrassing thing, like being caught saying your prayers. So he took it into his dressing-room and sat down and tried to find Ahab. He didn't know which book he came in. He thought it was Judges, but Judges seemed to be mostly about Samson. There was the bit where Samson went to Gaza and saw there an harlot and went in unto her; and on the same page there was Samson tying together the tails of the foxes and putting firebrands on them to burn the corn. John didn't believe that: "Samson went and caught three hundred foxes." How? We ought to have one like that for our M.F.H., John thought.

He tried the Book of Samuel. His big fingers were clumsy with the thin rice-paper pages. It was mostly about Saul and David: *David marrieth Michal* on the top of the page. John glanced down the column and read: "And Saul said, Thus shall ye say to David, the king desireth not any dowry, but an hundred foreskins of the Philistines, to be avenged on the king's enemies." Well I'm blowed, he thought: that's a damn' funny price to pay for a wife. He chuckled and forgot his pain. Enjoying himself now, he read on to the end of the chapter. They were a roughish lot, those Israelites.

At last he found Ahab in the Book of Kings. "And it came to pass after these things, that Naboth the Jezreelite had a vineyard. . . ."

He read the chapter all through with a kind of grim pleasure, seeing not a vineyard but a hopyard hanging on the side of a hill. Then he heard Mollie in the bedroom next door. He shut the Bible as she called to him.

"I'm putting a hot water bottle in for you."

He left the Bible in the dressing-room and came through into the bedroom. Mollie looked at him in surprise; he was laughing.

"That little devil," he said. "She hit the right nail on the head."

## 6

Black Barty sat on the steps of his caravan, and the sun that had been creeping up behind Malvern was bright suddenly over the sepia hills. By its light he examined the hop-sprig in his hand. The leaves were brown and withering; the hops were brownish red—but carmine when he lifted them up in the rays of the sun. Holding them so, Black Barty smiled. That sprig, which he had pulled off a drooping bine at the very first light of dawn, represented power. Slinking down the edge of the hopyard, with the sack heavy on his shoulders, furtive, secret, turning his head this way and that as quickly as Dan's ferret, he had noticed that one of the bines was different from the others, sick among all the healthy ones. You had to be very clever to notice such a thing; clever to pull a sprig off it so that you could examine it later in the better light, and be sure. But Barty was clever. Wisdom was down, Barty was up, soon they would acknowledge Barty King of the Gipsies, he would lord it over the mall. With this little sprig he would prove his cleverness; at the very start of hop-picking to-day, when Mr. Tomkins came down to the hopyard, he would show them. Black Barty had power! Ever since the defeat of Wisdom he had been conscious of it. He had only to stretch out his hand and take what he wanted; just as in the blackness before dawn he had stretched out his hand, through the door of the henroost, heard the sleepy clucking, felt the scaly cold legs, taken . . .

Barty's the boy, Barty's the kiddie, Barty's the King of the Gipsies, ho! He stood up and held the hop-sprig high before him; with his other hand he tossed up his knife, for fun, delighting in the shine of it as the blade turned over in the dazzling sunlight. The knife was a weapon, but the hop-sprig was a better weapon, for anyone who knew how to use it. You had to be clever to know how to use it. Barty's the boy!

A little breeze, the last of the dawn-wind, ruffled the grass. Among the grass something fluttered. It caught Barty's eye. He stared at it and watched the wind turn it over, the tiny speckled thing. He swung round and called through the door of the caravan:

"Sue."

She came out, half-dressed still, the naked bird in one hand, in the other the little knife she'd been using for drawing it.

"Come here."

Betsy called from within the caravan:

"What's the matter?"

"Come here, Sue," said Barty again.

He pointed. "Look." The wind, still blowing gently, stirred the speckled feather.

"Pick it up."

Sue looked fearfully up at him. Then she put down the bird on the steps of the caravan and went slowly towards the feather. When she had picked it up Barty said:

"There's another."

She went on a few paces and found it. "Another!" said Barty. "Just in front of you." She had to go down on her hands and knees to find that one. At last there were no more, and she came back to the caravan. At the step she leaned down to pick up the bird. Barty pounced at her then. He caught her by the arm and twisted it behind her back. "In," he said. She went into the caravan before him. Betsy looked up, startled; she was drawing the other bird. Barty said:

"I told her to pick up all the feathers."

He tightened his grip on Sue's arm. She whimpered a little. Betsy did not move.

"Lazy little bitch." He struck her hard, with his open hand, across the shoulders. "Take that; and that." The blows came in swift succession, almost rhythmical; they were loud in the little space. Sue did not cry out at all. Betsy left the chicken, and cowered in a corner.

"Teach you!" Barty cried. He let go of Sue's arm, and she reeled across the caravan. Black Barty strode out into the sunlight. He picked up the little hop-sprig where he had dropped it. He held it up to the sun again; the hops were red as blood. He saw Black Alf, sleepy, with an armful of wood, outside the next caravan. He shouted to him:

"Barty's the kiddie! Barty's the boy!"

## 7

Barty and Betsy had gone up to the hop-picking. Barty had called terribly through the door of the caravan: "Come, Sue!" and she had said she was just coming. But they had gone without her, and she still lay on the bed, face downwards, until she felt the sun through the window warm on her burning shoulders. Then she stirred, and sat up on the bed. After a little while she went across the caravan to get her dress; a small mirror hung there, and she turned her back to it and looked over her shoulder to see the red weals between her shoulder-blades. She pulled on the dress and did her hair. She thought of Barty's cruel hands and then she thought of Ram's hands, small and manicured and nervous and tender; they were the only gentleness she knew.

She looked out of the window. She could see the hopyard on the hill, and the little coloured figures moving about in it; but there was no one in the meadow save a child of Black Alf's playing with a lurcher dog. Sue became busy suddenly; she ran about the caravan collecting her things. They were very few: her bag, her other dress, some underclothes, two pairs of stockings, hairbrush, lipstick, scent. There was also a doll she had had as a child. She added it to the pile, simply because it was hers; then taking a last look round the caravan she found the tobacco tin into which Barty sometimes put some money, to pay for bread and milk from the farm. There was six and threepence in it, which Sue put into her bag.

She went to the window again and saw Mr. Tomkins's girl coming through the gate at the bottom of the hopyard. Sue watched her as she strode fast and purposefully across the meadow towards the caravan. She supposed she'd come to look for those chickens. Well, let her find them.

She wanted something to put her things in and her eye fell on the old sheet which she'd spread on the ground to catch the feathers in when she plucked the birds. It was lying in the corner, where she'd put it down. Sue carried it to the door of the caravan. She shook it, and all the feathers blew out, a shower of them flying away on the wind. Some fell in the grass, and others floated gently for quite a long distance, so that when at last they came to earth they made a trail of feathers leading towards the caravan. Sue took some pleasure in this. Then she laid out her belongings on the old sheet, tied them into a bundle, and tucked it under her arm. She went to the door. At the step she paused for a second and looked all round to make sure that the coast was clear; Marianne coming over the meadow was more than a hundred yards away. Sue jumped down off the step and began to run, down to the river, along the path beside it, into the lane.

## 8

Marianne hadn't seen Sue leave the caravan. She didn't notice her until she was nearly at the gate into the lane. She ran like a fox, Marianne thought, stopping now and then as if she listened for the pursuit, then darting off again. Thus she stopped for a second as she approached the gate; her attitude was poised and eager, almost as if she sniffed the air. Then she was through the gate, and Marianne caught a glimpse of her red dress in the lane.

A moment later, approaching the caravan, Marianne saw the first of the feathers in the grass. She spotted another, then a whole heap of little neck-hackles, then the bigger wing-feathers; so she followed the trail to the caravan door.

She had guessed right. There had been no eggs this morning when she went to collect them; otherwise perhaps she wouldn't have counted the hens. They hadn't been laying well, but they shouldn't have stopped so suddenly, in mid-September. The hen-house door was open, but Tommy often left it open; there were two hens missing, and when she told Tommy he said at once: "That blessed fox." Last spring a fox had had six hens in a night, because when Tommy came back late from the pub he had forgotten to shut them up. But Marianne knew that a fox wouldn't take just two of the hens and leave the others unharmed; unless it was disturbed suddenly it would kill the lot, and later carry one or two away.

"Two-legged fox!" she said.

"The gipsies?"

"I bet. Anyhow, I'm going to see."

She wouldn't wait until she'd had breakfast. She had said: "We must find the culprit *now*," and Tommy, as he watched her run across the yard, had seen Suzette again, Suzette who would have cared about the loss of two old hens, the peasant coming out in her, possessive, mindful of property, quick and angry in defence of it.

Now Marianne, triumphant, went back to the hopyard. She hadn't gone into the caravan; it would have been a mean intrusion, somehow, and in any case she had all the evidence she needed. She was determined to make Black Barty bring back the fowls.

All the gipsies were standing together at the end of one of the hop-rows. They were in a circle, with Tommy in the middle of them, so that Marianne wondered whether Tommy had somehow found out about the theft of the hens and had tackled Black Barty with it. But now she saw that there were others beside the gipsies there; something was going on, some argument, because the Dudley people and a few of the Welsh were leaving their bins and hurrying along the row to join the crowd round Tommy.

Old Mr. Roberts was with them, and Marianne pushed her way through the gipsies and stood by him. Tommy was face to face with Black Barty, and he was blinking in his embarrassed way, while Barty waved a spray of hops just in front of his face and said:

"But if we picks quick, extra quick, even now we may save 'em. We got a good boss and we knows it. We won't let you down." He spoke over his shoulder to the gipsies behind him. "What do you say? We won't let a good boss down!"

The gipsies chorused:

"Won't let him down!"

"A terrible thing is the downy mildew," said Barty. "Goes like wildfire when it catches hold. We'll need to pick real hard, no time off for dinner, no time off for tea. We won't let Mr. Tomkins down!"

"No!" shouted the gipsies, and Marianne saw that this was a prearranged chorus; obviously Barty had rehearsed the gipsies in their parts. She caught sight of Betsy staring at Barty with an expression she couldn't understand. Fear? Unwilling admiration? Perhaps a little of both.

Tommy said: "Well. Thank you," and then there was a rather odd little silence while Barty twirled the hop-spray round in his fingers. At last he spoke, half to Tommy and half to the gipsies, very softly, as if he were thinking aloud.

"O' course, picking so hard, without dinner or tea—picking all day, picking late—that'd be worth a bit more than one and four a bushel? But we've got a good boss, and he'll *see* as it's worth more to us, worth one and eight, worth one and nine maybe. . . ." He raised his voice suddenly and spoke directly to Tommy.

*"Worth one and nine to you, Mister, to save your crop as is withering before your eyes?"*

Blinking hard, Tommy said mildly:

"Hey, come off it, Barty! You can't take advantage of us like that."

"One and nine," said Barty. "You was always a good boss. One and nine."

"No."

"One and eight, then—" A threat now instead of a whine. "One and eight, or else—"

Tommy shook his head. There was another hush; the only sound was Mr. Roberts's coughing next to Marianne, that dreadful quiet cough that was nearly a purr.

"—or else we strike," said Black Barty.

Marianne put her hand on Mr. Roberts's shoulder and squeezed by him. Tommy hadn't seen her until now. He thought she'd only just come.

"Black Barty's shown me some disease in the hops at the edge of the hopyard," he said. "Yes, it's downy mildew I'm afraid. Naturally we need to pick in a hurry. But he's asking—"

"Yes, I heard." She raised her voice a little. "Barty sees we're in a jam so he wants to make a better bargain for himself. But we're not going to make any bargain with a thief."

There was a sudden quick stirring among the gipsies, and Black Barty took two paces towards her.

"Yes, a thief," she said.

He screamed at her then, and she saw Mr. Roberts step forward out of the crowd, as if he thought Black Barty were going to strike her. Tommy had come to her side. But she wasn't afraid of Black Barty. She was much too angry to be frightened.

"Where are the hens, Barty?"

He didn't answer. The Dudley people were crowding nearer, enjoying the show; Mrs. Towner gave Marianne a broad, comfortable grin. Some of the gipsies, she noticed, were already beginning unostentatiously to creep away.

Marianne glanced at Tommy. He looked bewildered and rather embarrassed, but he gave her a nod as if to say: "It's your show, you can do what you like."

She spoke again to Black Barty.

"You'll bring back the hens," she said. "Otherwise we'll get the policeman to search your caravan, and you'll go to prison, I dare say. But we won't get the policeman if you bring the hens up to the farm in ten minutes' time. Instead we'll pay you off, and you'll clear out."

Black Barty faced her for a moment, and in that moment for the first time she realised that he was mad. She watched his fists opening and shutting, and as her anger went she was at last a little frightened, and glad of Tommy's hand on her arm. Then Mrs. Towner laughed. She had a loud and raucous laugh; and she let it go in sudden delight at the discomfiture of Barty. Then all the Dudley people were laughing; and Black Barty who had been so fierce and bold was abject all at once, and the other gipsies, like animals that hate to be laughed at, were swiftly melting away. Black Barty turned on his heel, and Betsy followed him as he pushed through the crowd, nearly knocking over a child who stood in his way.

"Thieves!" shouted Mrs. Towner; and the Dudley people and the Welsh all took up the cry, "Thieves! Thieves!" with Marianne joining in as Black Barty shambled down the hop-row, turned his head to look behind him, and broke into a run as the cry was repeated and Mrs. Towner let loose another yowl of mocking laughter.

## 9

George was not a witness of the shame of Black Barty; nor did Nat and Dan see the disgrace of their father. The three of them, with Dai and Evan, were on their knees half-way into the hedge on John Sollars's side of the boundary fence. Dan scouting up the hedge last night had at last found the rabbit's hole. First thing this morning Dai had borrowed his father's longdog. They had lain in wait for George. When he came down to the hopyard they had all trotted up to him and as usual he had given them sweets. They had told him about the rabbit's hole. They had said, kindly, "You can come if you like."

And now the ferret had been introduced into the hole. The longdog, held on a leash by Dai, stood quivering and uttering its very high whimper, almost as high as a bat's squeak. George's middle-aged ears could not hear it. George's middle-aged and knobbly knees were prickled by unkindly thorns. Dan, with his ear to the hole said:

"He's there. I can hear him a-thumping."

"Git ready," said Nat to Dai.

"I am ready. Loose the lurcher I will."

"He's coming," shouted Dan. But it was only the ferret, yellow-brown and smeared with the red earth.

"Put him in again," said Nat. Dan seized hold of the ferret and turned it round so that it faced the hole.

George heard somebody shouting:

"Hey, you!"

Several things happened at once. The shout was repeated. Four pairs of eyes simultaneously looked to George for leadership. Dai whispered: "Farmer!" Dan seized the disappearing ferret by its tail, pulled it back out of the hole, and popped it into George's pocket.

A voice said:

"What the devil are you doing?"

The Under-Secretary of the Ministry of Education backed out of the hedge upon his hands and knees. He stood up. He faced the tall young man whom he had last seen coming out of his niece's bedroom. As he did so he was aware of a convulsive movement in his pocket. He said:

"Good morning."

Tim said:

"This is our land, you know; and the kids break down the

fences. That was what all the trouble was about. What *were* you doing?"

Dai and Evan on one side of him; Dan and Nat on the other: all looking at George. There was a violent twitching in George's pocket. He sensed that the ferret was about to escape from his pocket. It was probably half-way out already, for Dan was urgently tugging at his sleeve. He said evenly:

"We were looking for a ball."

He heard a tiny breath, emitted by four small boys. His pocket twitched again and there was another tug at his sleeve. He dared not look down at his pocket; but he put his hand there, and felt a furry head which caused him profound revulsion. He shoved the head right down into his pocket and held it there. Tim, fortunately, wasn't looking at his pocket. His grey eyes, full of laughter, were on George's face. He said:

"Well, I suppose I must let you find your ball; but please don't tear down the fence looking for it."

He turned away and at that moment George felt the little teeth sink deep into his finger. There was no pain at first, only the awareness of the teeth and the horror of them; then a warm flow of blood, and then the pain, which made George jump, though he uttered no sound.

Tim was walking away with his loping strides. He was calling, "Sally! Sally!" and a great red cow, heavily in calf, waddled out from under the willow trees by the river and walked in front of Tim. George withdrew his hand from his pocket, and the blood dripped from it, in little drops on to the ground. He thought of a dreadful picture in *Struwwelpeter* which had frightened him when he was a child.

Dai and Evan stared at the blood. Dan extracted the ferret from George's pocket. Tim had opened the gate at the far end of the field and was driving the cow up the hill.

George brought out his handkerchief and tried to stanch the flow. The sight of blood always made him feel faint. The sweat was chilly on his forehead, and the world was already whirling about him, when he heard Dai's voice that seemed to come from miles away: "Brave he wass." It was as if the

Minister himself had written on a docket: "The Under-Secretary's minute is to be highly commended."

George said:

"Don't be alarmed, children. He just nipped me. It's nothing at all."

## 10

It was probably Betsy who crept up to the farm unseen and laid the two plucked hens on the back doorstep. Tommy was unhappy about this. He said:

"I say, don't you think we ought to have let 'em keep 'em—sort of gesture?"

"No I don't," said Marianne flatly.

"Their kids could do with a good square meal."

"Their kids would hardly have got a smell of them. Betsy might have picked the carcase; a wishbone for Sue; and my lord would have had the rest."

Tommy laughed. The little streak of toughness in her never failed to surprise him—though she had obviously got it from Suzette. He hadn't forgotten—he could never forget—that Suzette had lent him every penny of her money, and that he had lost it all before she died, and that she had never once reminded him of the loss. Marianne, he knew, had the same large generosity; but over little things, like those two boilers, she acted as Suzette would have acted: both of them as hard as nails.

"But what are we going to *do* with them?" said Tommy.

"Cook 'em and eat 'em," Marianne grinned.

Black Alf had come up for the gipsies' pay; Barty hadn't shown his face since the scene in the hopyard. Tommy had put the money in separate envelopes, and Black Alf with his left hand had made his mark, a scrawled X, on the receipt. Now all the gipsies were packing up, down in the meadow. Tommy would be twenty pickers short, and the race was on against the downy mildew. They must try to get some more pickers from somewhere, and so Tommy was off to Hereford to see the man at the Labour Exchange. Marianne had been against this; she had no illusions about what might happen if Tommy went to Hereford in his present mood of frustration and despair. But he took the wind out of her sails by saying:

"As a matter of fact I was going into Hereford anyway. Little job I want to do there."

"That's a good story."

"D'you bet me?"

"Yes. What's your little job?"

Tommy blinked rapidly, showing the whites of his eyes. He coughed his embarrassed cough, a little sharp barking one, like a fox terrier.

"Birthday present for somebody I know."

And now he insisted on having a stirrup-cup before he started. "I was keeping this to celebrate your birthday," he said. "I found it in the outhouse yesterday." He showed her the four bottles hidden in the sideboard. "I went into the outhouse to have a look at my patent distillery; I'd had an idea for improving it. I picked up a sack out of the corner, and the bottles were underneath it." This was the daydream he often had, that he would discover by accident a full bottle or at any rate a partly full bottle among all the empty ones. It was the first time the dream had ever come true. With incredible self-denial he had refrained from drinking any of the applejack; but now the downy mildew in the hopyard, coupled with the loss of twenty pickers, provided a good excuse for breaking his resolution.

"*You're* looking a bit down in the mouth," he said. "Never mind. Have a little drink. Buck us up. Make us feel better."

He opened one of the bottles and poured himself out a full glass of the greenish yellow applejack. Marianne wouldn't have one; she couldn't face the stuff so early in the morning. Tommy raised his glass.

"This'll do us good," he said.

Marianne felt depressed. She wondered now if she'd been foolish to get rid of the gipsies; would it have been better to have kept them on, in spite of the thieving, so that there would have been at least a small chance of getting in the hops before the mildew spoiled them? But Black Barty had demanded one and eight a bushel and had threatened to strike otherwise. If Tommy had given in he would have had to pay all the other pickers at the same rate; he couldn't have afforded it—there would probably have been no profit in the hops at all. But now it looked as if he might lose a good part of the crop altogether. There certainly wouldn't be enough money to pay off the arrears of the mortgage; and that would be the finish of the Hope Farm.

But Tommy, having poured himself out another drink, was already seeing himself as a sort of Pied Piper, leading scores of hop-pickers through the streets of Hereford.

"We may even finish up," he said, "with more pickers than we had when we started."

He downed his drink and poured out another. He drank this one very quickly, in about three gulps. He beamed.

"Well, what did I say?" He gave Marianne a little pat upon the shoulder. "We feel better now, don't we?"

And the extraordinary thing was that she did feel better. She burst out laughing at his utter absurdity; and Tommy nodded at her in approval.

"Just what I said. A little pick-me-up, a wonderful thing."

Marianne had to push his car down the hill. It was going worse than ever and it made some new and alarming noises when it started. Also Marianne noticed that one of the back wheels was wobbling. She shouted to Tommy to tell him about it, but he replied with a cheerful wave. Perhaps the back wheel always wobbled.

# 11

In the early evening it began to rain. All afternoon she had watched the dark clouds pile up in the west, over the far blue Radnor hills. In front of those clouds a thin white veil was drawn slowly across the blue sky. It was translucent, and a watery sun shone through it for a while; then it grew thicker, it was like a film, a cataract, that slowly blinded the sun. Now the clouds with teased-out edges crept up in sable companies. The first big drops fell about tea-time; the hop-pickers had to give up ten minutes later and they were wet through before they reached the shelter of the barns. Marianne could see that this was no mere storm; it meant a big break in the weather, and it might hold up the picking for days. Tim rang up at dinner-time; she had hoped that because of the rain he would come over to-night, and she longed for him, she was miserable about the hops and vaguely worried about Tommy, and eager for Tim's arms. But it was no good.

"Sollarshill Sally," he said. "It's any moment now I should think; but you never know, she may keep me up all night. She's making heavy weather of it."

Soon after dinner George went to bed. He said his finger was throbbing, and did she think it was poisoned? She had dressed and bandaged it after examining it with due gravity, though she had nearly laughed when George said he had been bitten by a ferret. He wouldn't tell her how it had happened; but he was smug about it and seemed curiously pleased with himself, self-consciously brave when she dabbed on the iodine.

"Naturally it smarts a little; but it's nothing at all."

He became alarmed, however, when it started throbbing.

He began to think of tetanus and septicæmia. "A ferret's teeth could be specially dangerous, I suppose?" Marianne gave him Ovaltine and aspirins, and he went to his hop-pillow.

Marianne lit a fire and sat by it, waiting for Tommy. To cheer herself up, she tried a drop of Tommy's applejack. It tasted faintly of apples, but otherwise it was rather like vodka or schnapps, so rough and fiery that it made her choke when she sipped it. The aftereffects were encouraging, though. She felt a pleasant glow spreading all over her. She finished the glass leisurely, sip by sip. The rain beat a tattoo on the window and the wind was so loud in the chimney that she didn't, at first, hear the knocking on the back door. It startled her when she heard it, and she thought of Black Barty, drunk perhaps and crazy for revenge. That was a rather uncomfortable thought, as she went through the kitchen, and heard the urgent knocking, and wondered what she'd see when she opened the door.

A small boy stood there, with the rain glistening on his face.

"It's Dolly, Miss," said Dai. "Bin took she has."

Marianne got a torch and put on a mackintosh and went with Dai to the barn. The electric lights were on and the Welsh girls were chittering round Dolly's bed. Megan was holding her hand. She whispered fearfully to Marianne:

"The labour pains is on her."

Dolly was wide-eyed and frightened upon the mattress laid on top of the straw bales. The girls had taken off her dress, and only a blanket covered her. Her belly's contour was plain beneath the blanket, and as Dolly drew up her legs and began to moan the contour seemed to become steeper, the mound was rising up in the bed. Marianne leaned down to her.

"You'll be all right, Dolly. I'll get the nurse. When did the pains start?"

"This afternoon, in the hopyard."

"Wish you'd told us then. Never mind. I'll phone the nurse now." She told Megan to boil a kettle; there was a Calor-gas stove in the barn; the girls did their cooking on it. "Be back in five minutes," Marianne said. She ran to the house through the pouring rain. There was obviously no point in waking George; he'd only be a nuisance. She rang up the District Nurse. It was quite a long time before the nurse answered and while Marianne stood in the hall listening to the burring of the phone she noticed a strange thing: the Adam and Eve picture was gone from the wall. There was a dark oblong on the wallpaper where it had hung. Tommy must have taken it down. But why? To sell it, perhaps? She didn't know whether it was worth much; but Tommy loved it and it was awful to think of him hawking it round, trying to raise a few pounds on it. . . .

The burring stopped. A sleepy voice said:

"Nurse here."

She sounded not only sleepy but cross when she asked:

"How do you know she's about to have her baby?"

"Well, she thinks she is."

"That means to-morrow or the next day. Still, I'd better come along."

"As soon as you can!"

"My car's in dock. I'll have to bicycle."

"Lord!" said Marianne. "What if it comes before—?"

"Well then, it'll come," said the nurse. She was fully awake now, and better humoured. She laughed, and her laugh sounded close and comforting.

"You'll manage. Just boil up some tape or string and tie the cord in two places and cut between the knots!"

"What if—?"

"That's all you'll have to do. I'll pedal up in half an hour. It's raining cats and dogs. Bother your Welsh girls!" The nurse chuckled. "Don't they teach 'em the facts of life in Pontypridd? I'm all for contraception on a night like this."

Marianne went upstairs and collected some spare sheets and blankets, and a length of tape. She was half-way across the yard when she remembered the scissors. She tore back for them, and collected a pile of old newspapers at the same time. In the barn, however, Dolly lay quiet and still. The only sound was the kettle hissing on the stove. Megan came up to Marianne and said:

"The pains have stopped. Dolly thinks it's hanging fire."

Dolly's eyes were closed as she lay back exhausted. Marianne thought perhaps the nurse had been right; this might go on for hours yet. However, she used the respite to make things ready. With Megan's help she slipped the sheet under Dolly, and the newspapers between the mattress and the sheet. Megan was sensible and intelligent, and she was obviously going to be a help if anything happened. Marianne couldn't make up her mind, at first, what she ought to do about the other girls, who were in various stages of excitement, agitation and alarm. She could have sent them up to the house, but they were company for Dolly and their dismissal might seem ominous to the frightened girl on the bed. Marianne decided it was better for them to stay. There was no shame about this thing that was happening to Dolly's body. So she gave them little jobs to do. They filled hot water bottles to warm a blanket, and they boiled so much water that the whole barn seemed to be thick with steam. Marianne suddenly remembered that she ought to sterilise the scissors. She had just dropped them with the tape into a saucepan on the stove when Dolly's labour started again. She gave a loud moan. Megan breathed, awestricken, to Marianne: "It makes you think, Miss." Marianne grinned: "Makes you think till next Saturday night, Meg!" and they went across to Dolly. Before they reached her she was crying, "Oh, please come quick!"

"Here we are, Dolly!"

Holding her hands Marianne could feel the stress and rhythm of the labour, she had a sense of the little life within Dolly's life, she was aware of nature potent and inexorable, the body obedient, the mind rebellious, fear, revulsion, and fierce joy alternating. Marianne had thought she would be frightened, but she was more awed than frightened; she had thought it would be sordid but it was somehow splendid, the power and the glory at work between Dolly's legs. She stopped being sorry for her and she almost wanted to cheer her on. Minutes passed. Once, when she leaned down to wipe the sweat off Dolly's forehead and Megan had had the same idea at the same moment, she found herself face to face with the pretty dark girl, and was astonished to see that Megan wasn't frightened either. She was smiling. Then Dolly drew up her legs, and gave one brief cry, and pressed the palms of her hands so hard against Marianne's that she dragged herself up in the bed. It was Megan who realised first that the baby had been born. She gave Marianne a quick nod, and ran to fetch the warm blanket. Marianne said: "The scissors in the saucepan, too." She scalded her fingers picking them out. She lifted up the blanket and tied the tape twice and then she snipped the cord that separated the new life from Dolly's, as the nurse had told her to. Then she picked up the baby, and Megan was there holding out the blankets. The baby gave its first cry, and the Welsh girls, all huddled together at the other end of the barn, heard it and a kind of concerted soft cry from them, *Oo!,* echoed the baby's. Under the electric light which hung above Dolly's bed the baby was rose-petal pink, not at all the colour Marianne had expected, it had none of the darkness of the dark womb, it was pale and glowing. Then it wriggled, quite strongly, and Marianne had a delightful sense of life kicking in her hands. Her delight was mixed with alarm when it wriggled a second time and she discovered how slippery it was, so she laid it in the blanket; Megan, who had provided herself with some cotton wool, dabbed away the queer greasy stuff which covered it, and then they wrapped it up. Its tiny face just peeping out of the blanket looked comic and Megan laughed. They gave it to Dolly, and Dolly laughed too; Marianne called the other girls, and they came tiptoeing over with an air of being in church, and peeped at Dolly as she lay there in great content, with the sweat all over her face, holding her baby. Marianne had a huge wonder now that it was over, washing her hands that had felt life give its first kick in them, something she thought those hands would remember always. She couldn't keep her eyes off Dolly, who looked so pretty now, as pretty as doubtless she'd looked to somebody that night nine months ago, "up the mountain." A cry and a spasm then, maybe, began it; a cry and a spasm now completed it, an immortal soul!

The nurse should be here soon: she could deal with the afterbirth and bathe the baby. Marianne looked at her watch, and it said two minutes past midnight.

"It's my birthday too," she said.

# 12

Tommy came round the corner by the signpost as fast as he could and as he drove the old car at the hill he knew that if she reached the top it would be the last time she ever climbed it. There would be no starting the engine again when soon it ground to a standstill. The noise was appalling, a kind of angry clanging like a fire-engine's bell. As the car breasted the hill, this noise became less frequent but much louder, every clang sounded as if it were the last.

A series of ridiculous accidents, culminating in what was surely the final disintegration of the works, had attended the homecoming of the car. Its battery had been flat when Tommy tried to start it in Hereford; that was because he had left it too long outside a pub with the lights on. When the self-starter failed to work he had hunted in vain for the starting handle. His search had betrayed a hole in the floor-boards which looked as if rats had gnawed through them. Presumably the handle had fallen through this hole. Getting back into the car, Tommy tried the starter once again on the chance that he might extract a dying kick out of it, and he pressed the starter-button so hard that it went right through the dash-board and disappeared into the mysterious regions that lay between the dash-board and the engine. Tommy felt for it in the pocket under the dash, where his fingers met a confusion of wires; there was immediately a shower of sparks and the horn started blowing. It made a mournful lowing sound, like that of some despairing ungulate, until Tommy in panic tugged at the wires, causing a small explosion. This blew the fuse of the horn and silenced it, but also (as he subsequently discovered) put out of action the windscreen-wiper and the headlamps. Tommy went back into the pub in the hope of finding somebody who would help him. "Anybody here who knows about motors?" he said. He had several more drinks with a man who earlier in the evening had said he knew a pub where one could engage a dozen hop-pickers. They had been to that pub, and to a second and a third, and Tommy had bought a lot of drinks for this man and for other men who said if only he'd been there yesterday they could have provided him with hop-pickers galore.

At closing-time some of these men belatedly repaid Tommy's hospitality by pushing his car. It started, most unexpectedly, and Tommy drove back on his sidelights, without a windscreen-wiper, through the rain. He had to go very slowly, and frequently found himself on the grass verge or in the entrance to gateways; once he stopped at the very edge of a pond. The journey took more than two hours. From time to time the space beneath the dash-board was illuminated by faint blue flashes, rather like faraway summer lightning behind the Welsh hills. By these flashes Tommy could see the raindrops coming through the roof onto the oblong brown-paper parcel which was propped up on the seat beside him. With his free hand he shifted the parcel out of range of the drips.

It made him doubly miserable, to be reminded of the presence of the parcel. Taking it to Hereford had been bad enough; but then he had been uplifted by the sacrificial nature of his act. He had determined to sell it, on the spur of the moment, because it had seemed to him to be the only readily negotiable possession he had left; also, perhaps, because he loved it and the circumstance of Marianne's twenty-first birthday demanded some such gesture from him. His state was so parlous, now, that he dared not write a cheque for even ten pounds. George had been to see Tommy's bank manager and had agreed to guarantee his overdraft on condition that he drew no more than the minimum needed for the housekeeping and the wages. This was to be paid back out of the hop-money when it came in. In Hereford he had cashed the weekly egg cheque, which he had managed to conceal from George; this had paid for his drinks. But in order to buy a birthday present for Marianne he had to sell the picture. Feeling like Abraham as he went up into the land of Moriah, Tommy had taken the picture to the shop.

Now if it had been a little bit earlier or a little bit later, said the picture-dealer; or if it had been in a different style. And Tommy had recognised the shrug of his shoulders. If you are one of those people who have it in their natures always to buy dear and then later, being squeezed by unforeseen necessity, to sell cheap, you learn to recognise that half-apologetic shrug. It is the shrug of the garageman as he listens to your old engine; of the bookseller looking at your Dickens first editions, the plates a trifle foxed, damp spots on the binding; of the antique dealer regarding the doubtfully Hepplewhite chair. The same excuses always accompany the shrug. The Devil would use them too, thought Tommy: Once upon a time we paid quite a lot for Souls, Mr. Tomkins. It sometimes ran into seven figures, with Helen of Troy chucked in as a makeweight. But nowadays, well, you've only got to look at your *News of the World*—Souls are a drug on the market! Offer me a bishop's and I might possibly be interested. . . .

"Those Impressionists—" said the picture-dealer, "if you can rout me up a Renoir or a Degas out of your attic, I'll promise you needn't worry about the dibs for quite a long time. But this Victorian stuff, well, it's just a matter of luck if you can find somebody who collects the particular painter. All I could do is to offer you a couple of quid for the frame."

He had handed the picture back to Tommy.

"*Adam Sees Eve for the First Time.* Nowadays you could

just go to the Windmill Theatre."

Hating him for that, Tommy had snatched back the picture. And now, just out of reach of the raindrops, it lay beside him, a rejected sacrifice, as Abraham's was.

Just before he got to Sollarshill village, the thumping began. This was nothing to do with the other troubles; they had been as mere measles, mumps, minor disorders of the car, compared with this mortal thing. It was clearly associated with the fact that the oil-pressure, which Tommy was able to read whenever the wires shorted, had suddenly gone down to zero. It was a thumping as of a worn-out heart, failing through aneurism; but it rapidly became a clanging, a sound resonant and bell-like as Tommy put his foot down on the accelerator at the approach to the hill. It seemed important, somehow, to get to the top of the hill, and when Tommy saw the white gate in front of him he had the sense of a small triumph. The gate was open, and as Tommy went through it there was one final clang, which suggested that the connecting-rod had smashed through the crank-case; and the ensuing silence was broken at last by the slow, glutinous plopping of oil.

Tommy sat in the car for a little while. He addressed a silent valediction to the car: You have brought me home drunk or sober for nearly twenty years; you have brought me home for the last time. He was, in fact, sober, but with a wretched post-drinking sobriety. The rain drummed steadily on the roof. There would be no hop-picking tomorrow; and the downy mildew would spread all the faster through the wet bines. No chance of paying back George; no hope, no Hope Farm; bankruptcy, and then—? But after that, Tommy wouldn't care; Marianne would presumably leave him, and make her own way, and the last little bit he had of Suzette would be lost to him, so it didn't matter what happened then.

Tommy got out of the car, and listened to the loud plopping—yes, all the oil was running out under the engine; the finish of the car, coinciding with the final collapse of his fortunes, seemed fitting, though sad. He took out the picture and went towards the house. He was surprised to see a light on in the sitting-room.

Marianne came running out to him as soon as she heard the front door. He was bewildered by the chatter in the sitting-room, laughter and girls' voices, and, to his greater astonishment, George's voice. Marianne kissed him. She said: "We've started my birthday party rather early! We're drinking your applejack, d'you mind? We were making rather a noise, and George came down. *And George has had some applejack and I think it's doing him good.*"

Excitedly she clutched him by the lapels of his coat and told him about the baby.

". . . Then I picked it up and held it," she said.

She held out her hands in front of her, and looked down at them almost as if she were surprised that they were the same hands.

"I held it in my hands and it *kicked!*"

It was at that moment, Tommy didn't know why, that the whole splendid solution came to him in a flash, about her birthday present and about the picture. He should have thought of it before, of course; he couldn't imagine why he hadn't thought of it before. Even now he didn't know whether she would like to have the picture; but he knew why it was fitting that he should give it her now. It was something to do with the baby, turning its eyes for the first time to the light; something to do with the way she'd looked at her hands; something to do with creation and innocence, dimly and confusedly perceived in Tommy's muddled mind. He couldn't have put it into words, but he was happy as he hadn't been happy for years at his perception of the rightness of it. Glory shone around as Marianne, glancing at the parcel in his hand, said:

"Why did you—?"

And he on the spur of the moment, with splendid nonchalance, replied:

"I took it into Hereford to get it reframed, for your birthday present; but the man hadn't got a suitable frame, so you'll have to take it as it is."

After that they went into the sitting-room, and Tommy still blinking in bewilderment saw the Welsh girls, flushed and perhaps a little bit tipsy, all as pretty as nymphs; and the nurse, broad-faced and smiling, sitting in the armchair and drinking tea; and George in his dressing-gown, smiling too, George holding a glass in a hand from which his bandaged finger stuck out awkwardly.

"I had a little accident . . . with a ferret," explained George, as if it were quite a common thing to have accidents with ferrets. "And my finger was throbbing so I couldn't sleep. I came down, and heard of the—er—happy event, and the nurse was here, and she was good enough to look at my finger, she doesn't think it's actually poisoned, and then—"

It occurred to Tommy that George was extraordinarily talkative.

"They were all drinking this stuff you made out of apples," George went on. "It has a curious flavour, but pleasing when one gets used to it. Why on earth didn't you tell me you'd invented it? It might have great commercial possibilities, you never know." George nodded his head three or four times, and repeated: "Great commercial possibilities," very solemnly. "I imagine," he said "that one could describe it as a teetotal drink, by stretching a point, couldn't one?"

"By stretching a point, undoubtedly," said Tommy.

George closed his eyes contentedly:

"It makes an excellent nightcap," he said.

## 13

At three o'clock in the afternoon on Marianne's birthday the rain suddenly stopped; the sun came out in a sky new-swept by a housewifely wind that brushed away the last clouds busily, and the washen world looked just like Eden in the painting which Tommy (fussing for an hour about exactly where it should go) had hung in Marianne's bedroom this morning. Each small leaf shone; each draggled autumnal flower stood up smartly again; the daisies on the lawn were white as laundered linen; and bright as a kingfisher's back was the bonnet of Tim's M.G. when Marianne in that first blink of the sun ran out of the house at the sound of the engine.

He had rung her up, breakfast-time this morning, to wish her many happy returns; she had told him about Dolly's baby, and he had told her about Sollarshill Sally:

". . . She had a bull calf early this morning. Father thinks it's the best—"

"What time, Tim, what time?"

"I don't know, just after midnight"—and already it seemed to Marianne that this was a day of fulfilment. She had gone with Dolly to the hospital to keep her company in the ambulance which the nurse had arranged for her; and Dolly hugging her baby all the way had looked like a cat that had had five fat kittens. She was kindly disposed even towards the begetter of the baby.

"Write to him I shall; tell him it's a boy."

"You jolly well make him pay for it, Dolly!"

"Marry him I might," said Dolly dreamily. "After all."

The friendly ambulance driver had brought Marianne home. Then Carol had turned up, with presents: a jumper from herself, Edward Thomas's poems from Tim (but that was a token gift, for Carol said: "He's getting something else for you and he won't even tell *me.*"). Carol had a fitting of her dress. Then Tommy opened another bottle of applejack, and George drinking Marianne's health (he had certainly taken to the applejack) had rather shyly put an envelope into her hand. When she opened it later, she had found a cheque for five pounds. Judged by the yardstick of George's meanness, this was princely, and being touched by it she had subsequently kissed George and had been struck by his rather extraordinary smell.

"Uncle," she had dared to say, "haven't you put something special on your hair?"

"Fancy you noticing it, my dear." (He seemed quite unaware that he stank like a badger.) "It *is* something rather special, as a matter of fact. Have you ever noticed that gipsies never go bald?"

She hadn't, but now she realised that she had never seen a bald one, nor even one who was a little thin on top, like George.

"One of my young friends told me the secret," said George.

"What is it?"

"*Hedgehog oil.* Dan got it for me from his mother. I thought I'd try it."

Shortly afterwards two small boys, Dai and Evan, came to the back door asking for George. Although it was still raining, he went off with them cheerfully, having first borrowed some jam jars from Marianne. His metamorphosis was complete. "We are going to look for caterpillars," he said. "Of course the children ought to be at school; but perhaps they will teach *me* something. Haven't you got a phrase for it in French? *L'école buisonnière,* the school of the hedgerows?"

And now Tim got out of his car and gave Marianne her birthday kiss, a kiss hugely possessive in broad daylight that said, You-be-damned, to anybody who might happen to be watching. Tim was dressed, most strangely, in shiny black waders that came up to his waist. He was urgent and excited.

"We've got to be quick! There's a salmon in the Willow-tree Pool!"

Marianne had fished with Tommy when she was a child, but she had never caught anything except a wicked-looking pike, about two feet long, with an expression rather like that of Black Barty when he was smiling. She ran into the house and fetched Tommy's old waders, which were certain to leak. She looked very odd in them. They went down to the river, and Tim rigged up his rod. They took it in turns to fish, casting a spinner across the big pool below the willow trees. The salmon didn't show itself, but Tim swore he had seen it.

"I came down to the meadows to fetch up the cattle, in

case there was going to be a flood. It jumped out head-and-tail, just in front of that smooth rock. Of course it may have gone on up, in this heavy water."

The river was noisy, singing many songs; in between fishing they walked along it and watched the dippers. They were drab birds with very clean white shirt-fronts; they made Marianne think of shabby Soho waiters seen in the street in the morning. They found flowers, and Tim knew the names of all of them, old sweet names like helilot and plowman's spikenard. As they went hand in hand up the river Marianne thought that for her birthday she wanted nothing but this; but the gods had a gift for her in store.

She was sitting on the bank looking over the Willow-tree Pool. They had come back there towards evening. Tim was saying:

"The river's up three inches since this afternoon. You can tell by that rock in the middle." It was loud too, its song now was a savage and mountainy one of Wales whence it sprang. "Damn," said Tim. "I wanted that salmon for Father. It's what he likes best; and he's so sick now, he hardly eats anything at all."

"Oh! Look!"

Just in front of the smooth rock the salmon leaped. It hurled itself into the air straight as a javelin, argent in the sun. Tim was down the bank before the boil in mid-river had died away.

"Quick!" he cried. "You try for it."

"No . . . You."

"Come on. It's *your* birthday."

She took his rod and waded out as far as she could. She felt the angry river tugging at her legs. She cast towards the smooth rock.

"Upstream a little," said Tim.

Then the fish showed itself again. It was a big one, at least twenty pounds. Marianne's hands were trembling so much that she could hardly hold the rod. She cast upstream of the rock, twice, three times, four times: nothing happened. The fifth time she felt a little pluck. The spinner had swung round almost onto the rock, and she thought it had hit the rock, and she gave a tug to clear it. Just as she raised the point the rod jumped in her hand just as a water-diviner's twig is supposed to do, and the butt hit her hard in the pit of her stomach. Tim was shouting, and the rod was bent like a swan's neck, and her finger was smarting where the runaway line had ripped across it. The reel gave a loud protesting screech. Then Marianne saw the fish, going upstream like a torpedo, its back out of the water. She kept the line tight but the salmon cruised at will round the top of the pool; after a minute or two it came back towards her so that she had to reel in fast, and then in a sudden access of panic, the first alarm it had shown, it shook its head, tore away from her, leapt twice ("Dip your rod-top!" shouted Tim) and then plummeted down, down, down into the depths of the pool. It felt so heavy on the arched rod that Marianne was sure she would never get it up again; it must be right on the bottom now, sulking and lying still. She put on as much pressure as she dared, and although there were sixty yards of line between her and the fish she could still feel it shaking its head. That was a rather eerie feeling. Tim came out into the river and stood beside her. Just then the salmon set off once more, downstream now and very fast, so that the line made a little hissing sound as it swished through the water, cutting a V there and throwing up a tiny spray. The reel began to scream again as the line ran out. The fish felt heavier than ever with the current to speed it along. Tim said:

"Can you manage? You'll have to run."

She nodded and set off downstream after the salmon. Tommy's waders were steadily filling with water, and as the buoyancy left them they felt as heavy as lead. She stumbled twice on the rocks, and once she thought she had lost the fish as the line went slack suddenly. Then it became taut again, and Marianne was off in pursuit of the fish, twenty yards of splash and scramble, right down to the bottom of the pool. There was shallow water here, and a lot of jagged rocks were showing; if the fish went between them the rocks might cut the line. So Marianne leaned back and raised the rod-top and hung on. There was an awful moment when she thought something must surely break; she was pitted against the salmon, it was now or never, the rod-top dipped, dipped towards the river. And still she held on. Then the strain gradually became less and she knew she had won. Tim had run down the bank to her, he had the gaff in his hand, and he was pointing to the slack water at the edge of the shallows. She looked where he pointed and there was the salmon's back fin, like a little boat's sail, moving very slowly in a semi-circle towards the bank. Marianne reeled in, and the brown sail came tacking across the current until it was directly downstream of her, and not five yards from the rod. Tim went down the bank and stood above the fish. It plunged when it saw him and that last plunge took Marianne unawares,—the point of the rod went down until it was nearly touching the water. But the long tug-of-war in the turbulence at the tail of the pool had tired out the salmon; now it began to come up out of the deeps it had been desperately seeking, inch by inch, foot by foot, as Marianne fought it. She remembered riding Tim's horse and heaving its head up when it ran away—this was just the same feeling. As it came to the surface the fish turned over on its side, lashing feebly with its tail; Tim with the gaff at arm's length struck like a heron, then he was struggling up the bank with the fish dangling from the gaff and Marianne was squelching after him, reeling in the line as she ran. Tim carried the salmon well into the meadow for safety's sake before he laid it down. Marianne's heart was thumping, her legs ached, she felt the water in the waders cold about her knees. She threw herself down in the grass beside the salmon. It lay there gasping, deep-sided, enormous, bright as a new-minted coin. She slid her hands beneath it and lifted it up to feel its weight; it gave a kick in her hands, and she thought again of the slippery baby kicking. It was queer how that memory still delighted her. But the salmon was three times as heavy as the baby.

Even as Marianne balanced it in her hands, trying to guess the weight of it, the hooks came out of its mouth and the artificial minnow fell to the ground.

"Who's lucky?" Tim picked up the minnow and dangled it in front of her, so that she could see how one of the hooks had straightened, pulled out perhaps during the salmon's last plunge; like that, it could have had only the flimsiest hold. "Just one more wriggle," said Tim, "and you'd have lost him."

"It's my birthday! Nothing can go wrong to-day," she said, and on their hands and knees, with the salmon on the grass between them, they looked into each other's eyes and laughed. Then Tim got up and pulled off her waders as she lay on her back and kicked her legs in the air. "Skin a rabbit!" Pints of water poured out of them. Tim said:

"I'll take you home to change in ten minutes. I've got something I want to show you first."

# 14

Nothing could go wrong to-day! From now on it was as if Tim took her by the hand and led her down paths of happiness along which he had prepared and cunningly hidden for her a surprise round every corner.

They went across the meadow and into the field below the hopyard where the caravans stood. They had pulled handfuls of grass to wrap the salmon in before they laid it in the back of the car. They had taken the rod to pieces and put it in its case. Marianne had taken off her wet stockings and she went barefoot through the caressing grass. Tim was in a hurry; he almost pulled her along. He wouldn't tell her what he was going to show her; but as soon as she saw Wisdom sitting on the step of his caravan, and saw him turn his head to call Marta out, she knew that the gipsies had been expecting them. She couldn't guess why, and when she glanced at Tim, questioning, he only said: "Wait and see." Hand in hand they went towards the caravan as Marta and old Mami came out of it. Wisdom stood up and took off his cap; Mami's grubby bandage was still on his head. Marta gave a little curtsy to Marianne.

"The birthday lady," she said.

Mami hobbled up and said:

"What's twenty-one? A chit of a child! You wait till you're a hundred and two." She looked hard at Marianne, and her little face cracked into a toothless grin as she said:

"A chit of a child to send Black Barty packing!"

Marianne wondered how they knew about Black Barty; but the gipsies had their own ways of hearing things.

"He's off back to the Forest," said Marta. "With all his folk."

"All except his darter!" cackled Mami. "She's left him, so we hear tell."

"He's off," said Marta again, and gave Wisdom a long glance. Marianne thought she knew what Marta was thinking: Wisdom was King of the Gipsies still!

"See," said Mami, and stretched a brown paw towards the village below. The sun glinted on the roofs of caravans drawn up in front of the Royal Victoria. It was astonishing that the old woman could see so far.

"They'll drink there till closing-time," said Wisdom. "Then they'll be away."

"Maybe." There was something in Mami's tone which caused Wisdom and Marta to look sharply at her. She had gone back to the caravan and was sitting on the step. "Not like Black Barty to go so quiet." Something was puzzling her; her face was wrinkled up like an old russet apple that has hung all winter on the tree.

"What is it, Mami?" Marta said.

"I smelled trouble." She smelled things in her mind, pestilence, death, fire, flood, fleeting fantasies; they floated through her consciousness like scent on a wind. "It is passing. Maybe it was nothing at all. Black Barty is going. But I shall sleep sounder," said Mami, "when I know he has gone."

Tim had been looking round, seeming puzzled, at Wisdom's dun, tethered with two piebald ponies beyond the caravan. Now he turned to Wisdom.

"But where is she?"

Wisdom smiled cunningly at Tim. Marta said:

"Give me your handkerchief."

"Lucky it's a clean one," Tim said, as Marta merrily chuckling stepped behind Marianne and threw the handkerchief over her eyes. While she knotted it Wisdom went round to the space between the caravan and the hedge.

"You're not cheating?" said Marta.

"No, I can't see a thing."

"Wait till I tell you. *Now,*" said Marta, almost dancing with excitement. Marianne took the handkerchief from her eyes and the jet-black pony pirouetted in front of her. It was newly clipped and Wisdom must have just groomed it; it shone like ebony in the sun. Wisdom gave Marianne its halter and she ran her fingers through its long mane. "You couldn't have Malona," Tim said (and Wisdom shook his head vigorously), "but Wisdom went to Leominster for me yesterday to have a look at this one which I'd . . . heard tell of." He gave Wisdom a quick glance then, and Marianne didn't know why they were smiling. "Wisdom thinks it's the next best thing to his dun."

"Better!" cried Marianne. "Oh, better!"

It was surely the very spit of the dun pony barring its colour; and she was glad it was black, like the mare she used to ride out hunting.

Tim said:

"We hope she doesn't kick or buck or run away. We got no guarantee with her. Wisdom liked the look of her so much, he bought her w.a.f.—"

"What's that?"

"With all faults."

"Like a man takes a wife," laughed Marta. Marianne gave Wisdom back the halter and kissed Tim in front of the gipsies. The example was too much for Marta; she promptly seized Marianne and cushioned her against her big warm bosom. Then she laid hold of Tim and hugged him too. Mami wasn't going to be left out. "Don't forget old Mami on your birthday!" Marianne had to bend down, to kiss her on her grimy forehead.

"You got a good gel," said Mami to Tim. "She'll keep you in order, a gel who Black Barty's frit of!"

Wisdom promised to take the black pony up to the Hope to-morrow. Then Tim and Marianne went back to the car. He took her home to change her dress, she put something in the oven for Tommy and George, and they were off again; but he wouldn't tell her where they were going. He turned the car due west, into the setting sun.

This was the light Marianne loved, when the slanting beams threw long shadows and fields, hedgerows, trees, seemed to belong to an old woodcut that had been lovingly hand-coloured in red and green and gold. The whole world shone and glowed about them as they drove towards the sunset. There were rose-pink fields where up-and-doing farmers, taking advantage of an early harvest, had ploughed in their stubbles; but there were many stubbles still, golden as sand new-washed by a tide. Great Hereford beasts, Siamese twins with their black shadows, moved with the leisure of evening across fields so green they assuaged the dazzled eye. Hopyards made a frieze on the side of every hill, and the road went between hazel hedges still shining from the rain.

Here and there were apple orchards, with Worcesters scarlet as sin.

They passed the Welsh girls, "walking out" with their boys, two by two, at tactful hundred-yard intervals. Tim suddenly recited:

> *"Apples be ripe,*
> *Nuts be brown,*
> *Petticoats up*
> *And trousers down!"*

Marianne looked sideways at him and grinned.

"A naughty little rhyme."

"But seasonable." There was Megan, holding hands with

Dave Huggett's grandson in a gateway. Marianne wondered whether Megan was still saying to herself: "It makes you think!" Not for long, on such a night. It was warm and still, not a fleck of cloud in the duck-egg blue above the sunset, over the indigo hills.

"*Cymru am byth!*" cheered Tim, as they waved at Megan.

And there was Wales, not thirty miles away, beyond those hills. This land was borderland, not quite English as the stolid comfortable counties were English. You could make it sound so, thought Marianne, if you repeated to yourself the lovely arrogant syllables: *Harry of Hereford, Lancaster and Derby!* And it looked so, lying easy in the sun. But it had been fought for too often to be an easy land. It had been fertilised with blood, died for time and again—a dead man to each acre, a ghost to every field! Tim's ancestors, perhaps, had fought for it; walloped the Welsh for it, lost it, won it again; raided, slain, mated, married, across that disputed border—

"Bet you're half Welsh yourself," she said, to tease him.

"Me? Good lord no! We've been here always."

So he thought; so let him think. When they planted their feet in the ground and seemed to grow there they were stern West Midland stuff. They liked to pretend they hadn't the flyaway fancies that came from over the hills.

"How long's always?" laughed Marianne.

"I'm hoping to show you," he said, "when we go home to-night, the only folks that have been at Sollarshill longer than us." She didn't know what he meant, but he wouldn't tell her any more, and she mustn't ask any more, she must let this birthday of hers go along with its beautiful inevitability, step by step as their love went along.

# 15

So she didn't question it when beneath the full moon Tim drove straight back to Sollarshill and parked the car in the yard; though she was still frightened of Sollarshill, and she thought it might spoil everything if he took her in to see his father and mother now. They had been expected by the gipsies; they had been expected at the little country inn where the landlord had come bustling out to meet them—where Tim, ringing up beforehand, had already chosen the dinner and the wine. They weren't expected here: there was one light in a bedroom, but it was dark downstairs. Tim took her hand and led her, not towards the house, but through the yard; into the Home Field; up the hill.

The short grass was crisp with dew. The harvest moon showed them the way up the path between the bracken. They had seen it rise to-night, through a window at the inn while they had a drink before dinner. While the sun went down due west over Wales, the moon had come up due east over Malvern. Tim had explained that this only happened when the harvest moon was at the full. "Twenty-four hours' light for your birthday!" he had said. Looking down upon the river now, Marianne could even make out the rock where she had hooked her salmon. Tim said:

"It's just the night for what I want to show you."

"What are you going to show me, Tim?"

"Shan't tell you yet," he whispered. He helped her over the stile. "I reckon it's five to one against you seeing them anyway; but perhaps being your birthday it's only evens. I've been up two nights lately, and both nights they were here."

He'd brought a warm coat for her, and he put it over her shoulders; but there wasn't a hint of autumn in the air tonight. They went into the wood and there was a space between tall bracken where Tim had beaten the ferns down. "How long can you stay quiet and still?" he said.

They lay down in the hide among the bracken, side by side, Tim's arm round her lightly, and she didn't know how long it was they waited, hearing just each other's breathing, looking at each other sometimes in the moonlight, seeing each other's faces dappled with leaf-shadows, close with a companionable closeness; she was only a little aware of the promptings of that closeness, not discomforted, secretly laughing within herself at her sureness of what would happen in the fullness of time.

It might have been twenty minutes before they heard the padding and the rustling in the ferns. Tim's arm tightened a little round her. He turned his head away from her, willing her to look where he looked. There was an open space between two big tree trunks. It was about six yards away. A broad moonbeam lit it. In this moonbeam there appeared, suddenly, a pattern of black and white: a broad white streak separating two black ones, V-shaped, then more white behind them. It wasn't until Marianne saw the ears, whitish as their undersides were turned towards her, that she realised she was looking into a face. It came a little nearer, and she saw the muzzle, questing close to the ground, grey shoulders behind the head, hunched, then a second black and white face moving towards her beside the first one.

She had guessed that Tim was going to show her beasts. She had thought of foxes. She had never seen a live badger before, only a dead one which the hounds had caught out cubbing when she was a child.

The two badgers came on, very noisily, snuffling and grunting, and suddenly they were so close that when one of the faces was turned towards her Marianne could see its eyes. It looked surprised, but that was a trick which the moonlight played with the black and white pattern. The pattern, Marianne thought, was like the make-up of a clown.

It made a tragi-comic face. Some animal Grock was turning its painted mask towards her. Behind that lay the mystery. You would never know what went on there, in Brock or Grock, behind the mask that made you laugh or cry. The grave, ridiculous face turned slowly away from her. The beast had not seen her; and it shuffled off, ponderous, with the other badger close behind it. Marianne saw the sett now, a little cavern among tree roots laid bare at the other side of the open space, with a mound of freshly turned soil like an earthwork all round it. One of the badgers climbed up onto this mound, and had a quick look round before it went into the hole. The other paused there for quite a long time before it went in; it scooped up some earth with its forepaw, as if it were in some way dissatisfied with the state of its front door. It did this two or three times, rather angrily, and the earth fell with a light patter behind it as it scooped. Then with sudden unexpected and out-of-character friskiness it flicked its tail and disappeared into the black hole.

Tim said:

"That's all."

He jumped up and took both Marianne's hands to pull her to her feet. "Cold?" he said; but she didn't feel cold. She was glowing all over with the excitement of eavesdropping on the beasts. She trembled when Tim kissed her, and he thought she was shivering and he led her fast to the stile and down the path with its tickling bracken fronds. She had believed, when he kissed her, that they were going to stay in the wood; she wanted him now, and she was a little puzzled because she didn't know Tim's reason for not staying in the wood. She didn't know that he had met Sue there. They went down the hill and she put the unanswered question out of her mind. What matter how, when, where?—she was pliant to his will and content that he should lead her along the way of love towards its imminent fulfilment. Twice on the way down the hill, and once at the gate between the hill and the Home Ground, they stopped and kissed again, and tight in his arms her whole body spoke to his: Yours for the having! The moon was so bright that they could look into each other's eyes almost as if it were day. Tim said: "You look like a cat with cream." Then they were off again, through the Home Ground, Tim's arm was about her, love and laughter were kindled between them at every touch. She caught his hand and laid it on her breast. She pressed it there till it hurt.

"I'd like to shout," she said.

"Shout what?"

"Just hurray."

"Wake up the badgers."

"We'll let them snore. But Tim," she said, as they came to the last gate, the one into the farmyard, "when I think of all the people who whine about love—crooners and such—moaning and *bellyaching* about it—"

"Yes, it's worth a good holler, isn't it?" And bending swiftly he lifted her up, held her level with the top bar of the gate, swung her, one, two, three, pretending he was going to throw her, kissed her on the mouth while she laughed and struggled, then heaved her over and put her down on her feet at the other side. The car was silvery in the moonlight at the far end of the yard. As they went towards it Tim said: "Show you something else." He led her to the loose-box where she could hear the cow munching. The moonlight went in with them as he opened the door, and the little calf's face, with its broad white forehead, was just visible under the belly of the cow. It was still not quite strong on its legs. Tim went into the loose-box and Sally tossed her head restlessly as he picked up the calf. He carried it to Marianne, and it looked like a toy, its legs stuck out so straight and stiff.

"Samson's son," he said. "It's mine."

"Yours?"

"Father promised it to me. Look: those shoulders; look at the breadth there across its loins. We'll win a championship with it if we're lucky." He looked straight at her when he said "we"; she thought he didn't mean himself and John Sollars.

"Born on my birthday," Marianne said.

"It's still your birthday," said Tim, looking at his watch.

"What time?"

"Ten to twelve."

Tim gave the calf back to Sally. It began to suck, clumsily, noisily. Tim came back to Marianne.

"Still your birthday." He took both her hands, very gently, and she stood on tiptoe to kiss him; it wasn't a real kiss, like their others had been to-night, it was just a brushing of his lips across hers, yet somehow this kiss meant more than the others, and she knew it would be now. She knew, too, that Tim hadn't planned or plotted that it should be now, but he had simply waited as she had waited until the gods should say Go; and why they should say Go, here and now, was irrelevant and inscrutable. There was a haystore next to the loose-box and Tim picked her up and carried her into it. She was kissing him as he carried her, and his hand was under her dress, and the heap of loose hay sank beneath them both as he laid her down. She could see, over Tim's shoulder, through the open door, a sort of luminous veil of moonlight between the loose-boxes and the barn. There was straw in the barn, stray ends of it sparkling in the moonlight, and she saw among these little scintillations one speck of light more fixed and steady, which for the merest instant startled and troubled her, because she thought it was somebody's torch shining there. Then Tim's shoulder moved in front of it, and she forgot it, and there was nothing but Tim. They were one now, and all the speech which man in his million years had taught his tongue to utter couldn't say to them what they were able in silence to say.

But at last she cried his name, for the splendour of love, and then they lay very still, and Tim's shoulder had shifted a little, and she saw the light again. It burned its way into her consciousness very slowly, it was a distraction trivial but insistent, intruding into the vast quiet and the immeasurable comfort which were suddenly hers. It would have puzzled her if she had let it puzzle her; so she closed her eyes and shut it out while Tim's hand, easy now, lay between her breasts. She said:

"If all days could be such days."

She was thinking of the baby, the fish, the pony, the badgers, the little calf, Tim. It must be nearly twelve.

"No," said Tim.

"Why no?"

He laughed so comfortably that she wanted to be nearer to him, she rolled over to be in his arms.

"Because," he said, "the sun doesn't always shine or the moon either. It's not special days I want with you but ordinary days." He couldn't possibly have said anything happier. "Me mucky and tired, gumboots when you go to feed the chickens, cold hands, mud on the carpet, log fire, brats."

He broke off suddenly.

"I say, we took a chance on it, didn't we?"

"We took a jolly good chance." But they were both laughing as he drew her still closer to him, and then that funny light came into her view again and she said:

"Tim."

"Yes?"

"Look."

"Well, what is it?" he said at last.

She didn't want to get up from the bed of hay. But Tim sat up, and she saw him staring at the light, and then he rose and caught her hands and pulled her up beside him. They went out into cold brightness, and Tim suddenly urgent almost pulled her across the yard.

Just under a bolting of straw that jutted out from the rest of the straw was an old battered tin. Marianne thought at first it was the moonlight glinting on this tin that had caught her eye. So she was laughing when Tim picked up the tin, and held it to her, and she saw the candle.

A candle end burning inside the tin; and, as it burned, floating in something that looked like water.

Marianne said:

"I don't understand."

Tim dipped his finger in the liquid and put it on his tongue. The candle was burned down almost to the level of the liquid.

"Petrol," Tim said.

"Why petrol?"

He blew out the candle. There was about a quarter of an inch between the guttering top of the candle and the petrol in the tin. "See how it would have burned," he said, and looked at the straw. Next to the barn there was another building, and a sudden loud snort made her jump.

"Samson in there," said Tim.

She felt a spasm of fear in the pit of her stomach; she remembered old Mami sitting on the caravan step, smelling trouble.

"Black Barty," said Tim, and he put down the tin on the ground beside him.

"They said he was going back to the Forest—?"

"I dare say he's gone, by now. It'd take two hours for the candle to . . . He probably slipped up here when the pub shut.

She clutched Tim and shutting her eyes she saw red flames licking the straw in the barn.

"It's all right now," Tim said.

And then they heard the footsteps. Very slowly the footsteps came round the corner by the loose-box and she didn't know why she expected to see Black Barty, because of course Black Barty wouldn't be likely to return after he had put down the tin. John Sollars had a torch, and he shone it on them; but by the moonlight she could see who it was standing behind the torch. He said: "Oh, Tim," and he switched off the torch as he came towards them.

"I thought I saw a light—"

Tim's hand tightened on Marianne's arm as he said:

"I was showing Marianne Sally's calf. I expect—"

She knew he wasn't going to tell his father about the tin.

John Sollars looked at her. She wondered if he were going to say: "Oh, it's you, Miss." But she wasn't frightened of him now. She was defensive, but she no longer felt insecure. She would never be frightened of John Sollars again.

He said at last, with a kind of tired but savage irony:

"Are you interested in calves?"

"She'd better be," said Tim, "if she's going to marry me."

John Sollars took a step forward. He and Tim stood face to face, and she wondered if this was the first real conflict they had had. Tim was standing very straight. She was aware of anger and love between them. Then Tim shifted his arm so that it was firm and possessive round her waist, and with triumph and a marvellous joy she knew that the gesture was telling her of how they had lain together: telling anybody else who might be interested, too. Come hell and high water, it seemed to say.

John Sollars turned his head towards her, and there was something about him that reminded her of the badgers on the hill. His hunched shoulders, perhaps? Or the strange mask which the moon had given him? It had taken all the expression out of his face. The eyes were deep craters, the mouth was a gash, there was a black shadow under the heavy jaw. She didn't know what was going on behind the mask.

"Is that true?" he said sharply.

"Yes!" she almost shouted, and she was so little afraid of him now that she could have laughed when it suddenly occurred to her that Tim, up till now, had not asked her to marry him.

John Sollars moved out of the brightness of the moon so that the mask seemed to fall away from his face. She saw anger there, and pain, and something else which she couldn't recognise. She believed that he knew, by some old intuition, that they had just made love. She didn't care. Because of it, she felt invulnerable.

Then, to her astonishment, John Sollars put out his hand. He seemed to do so in response to the compulsion of an inescapable courtesy; she knew he did not want to shake her hand, and a little anger flared up in her as she took his hand. There was nothing of congratulation in his gesture; it was a kind of acknowledgement, no more. But anger left her, and she felt pity for him now, and with pity, respect.

He said:

"There it is, then. So good luck."

He turned, and he went slowly towards the house, and

there was pain in every step. Marianne had the impression of a man fiercely and resentfully dying, as he half-strode, half-hobbled across the yard in the moonlight.

He had just got to where Tim had left the car when Tim said to her:

"Your fish."

"What, Tim?"

"Go and give him your fish."

She hesitated for a second, then she ran after John Sollars. Tim stayed beside the barn and watched them. He saw his father stop and turn round to Marianne. She looked very small beside him, and a little defiant still; as she stood face to face with him her hands were on her hips. Some trick of the moonlight made John look immense; immense but ruinous like an oak broken by a storm. Tim couldn't hear what they were saying to each other. His father went to the car and looked at the salmon in the back seat. He came back to Marianne, and Tim could see that she was still defensive, she glanced up sharply because of something John said to her. Like challengers and challenged, they were both tense and still. Then John laughed and she laughed and Tim saw his father bend down and kiss her.

John Sollars called:

"Tim."

Tim went towards them.

John said:

"So they've got downy mildew at the Hope?"

"Yes. She told me."

"And they've lost half their pickers—those varmints?"

"Yes."

"Well, it would be a neighbourly thing if you took up half of our pickers to-morrow, to give 'em a hand." He looked at Tim hard, almost fiercely. "Since you're going to marry the girl," he said. He turned to Marianne, half-laughing, half-angry still. "Come along in and bring that salmon with you. We'd better have a drink on it, I suppose."

# Epilogue

## *Last Quarter*

# 1

They had pulled the longest bines they could find from the very last hop-row of all; Carol would decorate the inside walls of the oast-house with them to-morrow, ready for the dance on the hop-floor. Then they had all climbed into the trailer heaped high with the last load, and the tractor had set off up the hill, through the desolate hopyards which looked now as a fairground looks after the fair has moved on. The tracks worn by the pickers crisscrossed them; there was hardly a grassy patch left. Litter lay everywhere. The poles stood gaunt, and the crosswires and the bare strings were as spiders' webs between them. The bines that had been so green were withering and had already been heaped up for burning. A shrill wind, whistling through the wires, blew about the débris which the pickers had left behind them and wherever the tea-makers had built their fires a little plume of wood-ash streamed away from the top of the heap as if it were a miniature Vesuvius. The first raindrops splashed down, heavy and cold.

It seemed strange that they wouldn't be picking to-morrow. For ten days—ever since Marianne's birthday—they had worked from early-breakfast-time until the last light, which fell a little sooner every evening. The untiring sun had shone for them: and in five days, with the help of John's pickers, they had raced and beaten the downy mildew which had been spreading through Tommy's bines. Only six rows had been spoiled. Then Tommy, returning John's compliment, had taken his pickers across the valley to give a hand at Sollarshill. The hops were still clean there, without a trace of disease; but the nights were getting chilly, you could not always tell when the sun rose whether there was dew or white frost on the grass; in the barns and in the caravans the pickers woke stiff and cold to another day's labour. As they flicked the hops into their bins with calloused fingers that smarted as the life came back into them they had a sense of winter peering over their shoulders, grimly watching the race.

But the Welsh girls still sang, rock 'n' roll for preference, which set the gipsies' feet stamping. The Black Country people still threw their earthy jests at one another, as if they cast clods of speech from mouths which dropped open to expel them and then unsmilingly clamped to again. The gipsy children kept up their monkey-chatter, while Mami trotted round boxing their ears if they grew lazy.

The missionaries made a team on their own, and picked as many bushels in a day as most of the old hands could do. Now there were always seven at their bin instead of five. Sue, fleeing from Black Barty, had taken refuge with Ram. Nobody, least of all Ram himself, knew what to do with her; so she shared a small tent with Poppet, who found her pellent though not overclean; she was apt to wipe the make-up off her face on to Poppet's towel. What might happen to her when hop-picking was finished greatly troubled the missionaries. Sometimes after supper at their camp they would set her to do the washing-up, or send her off in the dusk to fetch wood for their fire—anything to get her out of the way while they earnestly debated the problem, trying to plan the future for Sue. But she had a habit of stealthy eavesdropping which inhibited them. Whenever she heard them whispering together she would creep up silently out of the shadows, establish herself unseen just within hearing, and startle them at last by announcing in her small voice: "I'm frit to go back to him; he'd thrash the hide off me if I went back." They would turn round, startled, to see her exquisite grave face, tawny in the flickering firelight, and they would be moved to fresh pity for her and would draw her into their circle, Ram on one side of her, Poppet on the other, holding her hands. "Of course we won't let you go back, Sue," Poppet would say; and Ram—less comfortably because he was heavy with the responsibility of Sue— "Imperative to find niche in happier environment, where loving-kindness can erase memory of cruel past." But how and where to discover a niche for Sue?—who couldn't read or write, had no inclination to work in a factory, had never known a roof over her head and showed the greatest alarm at such a prospect, and whose only apparent talent, apart from one the missioners didn't mention, was for unlawful acquisition. She had already stolen Poppet's lipstick, and a jar of face cream, and "borrowed" a brassière which Poppet thought she would now be unwilling to wear again.

Poppet herself was responsible for their other camp-follower. Stan, who had been one of the little congregation at the first hop-pickers' service, came again the next Sunday, because he liked the noise Bill made with his concertina. Poppet had asked Carol about him, and Carol told her the tale, which she had heard from Marianne, of how his dog Petunia had been destroyed because of the anthrax. This story had awakened all Poppet's compassion, which took the form of a perpetual gnawing hunger to do good; she had conceived it her duty to make life happier for Stan. To this end she had bought, at a pet-shop in Hereford, a pedigree poodle pup. Any mongrel, probably, would have served the purpose equally well as far as Stan was concerned; but Poppet's pity for him demanded some heavy sacrifice to assuage it, and she spent six guineas on the poodle, which she could ill afford. She therefore gave up cigarettes, thus achieving a double martyrdom. Stan called the poodle Petunia, perhaps because his one flight of fancy had left him bereft of any other ideas; or perhaps because he thought all dogs were called Petunia. It took to him at once and followed him round everywhere with dumb devotion; with dumb devotion the half-wit followed Poppet round everywhere; and Poppet, driven to distraction both by Stan's company and by her lack of cigarettes, of which she used to smoke thirty a day, suffered deeply and found a tormented happiness in doing so.

## 2

Even the gipsies did not idle, during those last few urgent days. Wisdom, through Mami's ministrations or despite of them, had recovered from his wound; and when he walked down the hop-rows now the spring was in his stride again and his broad shoulders were thrown back. He was King of the Gipsies, with none to dispute it! When he spoke now it was with the authority of a king. Mr. Comstock, the Mitty man, had tried to start another strike on the morning when Tim first took his hop-pickers up to the Hope Farm. He'd heard that Black Barty had been sacked, though he knew nothing of the circumstances, and he worked hard on the loyalty of the Black Country people and the miners to the solidarity of the working class. "Are we blacklegs," he asked, "to tike the plice of some poor iggerant gipsies who's been victimised by the boss?" On his errand of mischief he came at last to Wisdom.

"Brother—" he began.

"No brother of thine!" said the Gipsy King in his majesty; and Mami came screeching: "No brother of that bastard! No brother of that Mitty man!" Marta joined in, warlike, Boadicean, and Marta's children, the three strong boys, the four big girls who were like well-grown sprigs of Marta, the two little ones spitting like the kittens of a half-wild cat.

Mr. Comstock fled before them; and there was no strike, nor any hint of a strike, for the rest of the hop-picking.

## 3

On that last day of all, when the sky lost its bland patience at last with these summer-folk lingering on into winter; when the wind stirred uneasily from the northeast and a great anvil-shaped thundercloud rose in awful majesty over the Welsh hills, even Mrs. Sollars had joined the pickers in their final desperate bid to get in the last of the hops. She had gone straight to the bin where Marianne was picking with Tommy and George. She picked very swiftly and proficiently, though her thin hands, so smooth and white, obviously hadn't touched a hop for years. She was cool, remote, courteous as ever. She had written a cool, remote, courteous letter to Marianne on the day after her birthday. She had said: "In view of what Tim has told us we send you our best wishes and hope you will always feel very welcome at Sollarshill": no more.

Now she observed:

"You pick almost as if you were brought up to it, Marianne."

"Well, I *was* brought up to it, Mrs. Sollars."

"So silly of me to forget that— You've been away so much, haven't you?"

A little later she said:

"It was clever of you to catch that fish."

"Tim would have caught it; but he let me try first and it hooked itself on."

"John—" said Mrs. Sollars (it was the first time she hadn't spoken of him as "my husband")—"John was very pleased with your present. He ate a little of it."

"Yes?" said Marianne, puzzled by a difference in the tone of Mrs. Sollars's voice.

"It's the only thing he's fancied for . . . a long time."

Mrs. Sollars turned away, and Marianne knew she was crying. It was all the more painful because Mrs. Sollars, she was sure, would never forgive herself for crying in public. She made no sound, but her shoulders were twitching. Marianne saw that Tommy and George were looking away. She took Mrs. Sollars's arm and led her up the hopyard. Mrs. Sollars said at last:

"We've been married twenty-five years, Marianne."

She had stopped crying and now she turned her face to Marianne. The tears were dry; she was self-possessed as ever. She said, astonishingly:

"I hope and I believe that you and Tim will be as happy."

## 4

And now in the trailer Carol squealed because the raindrops were cold on her bare shoulders. It was the last time she would wear the sunsuit this year. She said:

"I say, Marianne, I hope our dress is low in the same places; otherwise I shall look piebald like Wisdom's ponies."

Her shoulders and legs were burned a delightful brown. She picked up one of the long hop-bines and said: "Volunteers for helping me decorate the dance-room to-morrow."

"Me," said Charles.

There were six of them in the trailer: Charles and Carol, Tim and Marianne, Tommy and George. George was as brown as the others. He had been picking hard for the past ten days, despite his bandaged hand. The ferret-bite had festered; and while this had been painful for George, Marianne had the impression that he got a smug satisfaction out of his suffering, he wore the bandage as a badge of courage, by no means unostentatiously. It greatly impressed the children, who followed him about everywhere now, and when they asked how the bite was feeling he would put on an expression of brave disdain: "Well, naturally it throbs a little; ferrets are extremely poisonous creatures, you know, and the teeth sank in almost to the bone; but it's nothing to worry about, children, nothing at all." Heroism had settled like a mantle upon unheroic George; for it was he during one of his hedgerow-hunting expeditions with the children who had spotted, chased, caught and been scratched by Mrs. Agnew's cat Moggie; it had escaped from her bedroom and had been missing for days—she was convinced that Black Barty had eaten it. George had restored it to her personally, entering a public-house bar for the first time in his life and finding there, not a den of iniquity, but two old men grave as bishops playing dominoes in a corner. Experience crowded thick and fast upon him: this afternoon he had been kissed by Marta. Until now he had eluded her embraces; or perhaps his forbidding expression had imposed an unwonted restraint upon her. But when the last hop-row was finished, and the pickers were bidding each other goodbye till next season, Marta had approached George with the innocent intention of shaking his hand. Holding it in hers, and being suddenly overtaken by an access of general affection, Marta had dragged him into her bosom; and there he had remained, clamped firmly in the vice of her powerful arms, feebly struggling, while the gipsies cheered and Marta made up for her previous abstinence by kissing him soundly, three times, upon his smooth and domelike forehead. He had borne the ordeal with a good grace; indeed he now looked rather pleased with himself, as he smoothed into place his ruffled hair which he regularly anointed with hedgehog oil. ("It may be imagination," he had told Marianne, "but I got the impression, in the looking-glass this morning, that the stuff may really be doing some good.")

He smiled across at Carol, who was playing with the hopbine which she dangled in her hand, and he said:

"They'll look nice, hanging round the wall, won't they? They're beautiful things."

A few days ago he had borrowed from Tommy a book about hops. He had learned from it many surprising facts about them, that they were related to the stinging-nettle, for instance, that the male and female flowers were borne on separate plants, that the males were planted in the hopyards in the proportion of one to a hundred females—an enviable polygamy, Tommy had told him. But George's great discovery, which he had made in that old textbook of hop-growing, was that hops were not in themselves "alcoholic," as he put it. This revelation had altered his whole view of them. He had previously believed that in some way they were responsible for the potency of beer. He had seen and deplored brewers' advertisements with green hop-leaves as their sign and symbol; he had associated hops with drunkenness and sin. It astonished him to learn that they did no more than give the beer its bitter flavour, making it, in his opinion, even nastier than it would have been otherwise. He could now look kindly upon hops; he could feel quite proud of picking seven bushels of them in a day.

Carol, who was the only person who dared to tease George, put the hop-bine round his neck, another like a wreath of honour upon his shining brow. He looked very absurd, a grave and desiccated Bacchus, swaying from side to side on the golden green heap in the trailer, as the tractor bumped along the rough track through the Home Ground.

## 5

The bines which had draped George's withered frame were hung upon the wall with all the others, making an arbour of hops within the old oast-house; in the bright lights they glowed, green and golden, like a frieze round a Grecian vase. Dave had swept the hop-floor until you could slide across it; and then he had put away his tools with a valediction: Lie thee there thee buggering broom, thee sodding shovel lie thee there, thee frigging forks I sharsn't need thee for another twelvemonth thank the Lord. He had damped down the furnace and gone off to the Royal Victoria with his saved-up precious thirst, so long hoarded, at last to be recklessly squandered. "I'll maybe treat meself to a *rage* of beer." Now doubtless he was sleeping off eighteen pints or so in his cottage at the end of the lane.

The band, which Carol had hired from Ledbury, was just beginning to warm up. Jill Ferrers, with some of her pony club friends, was warmed up already; whenever the music stopped she root-tooted on a hunting horn. It made an excruciating noise in the confined space of the oast. The hunting girls and their boy-friends loudly hollered. The band leader, to keep them quiet, said: "Take your partners for the Paul Jones."

There was hardly room on the hop-floor for all the couples. Jill Ferrers and her gang, thrusters and devil-take-the-hindmost ones, were swept by a kind of centrifugal force to the outside of the circle, where they revolved rapidly and without much regard for whom they hacked on the shins. They let out animal yelps every few seconds. But in the middle of the room there was an area of quiet such as lies at the centre of a hurricane, and there Marianne danced with Tim, Carol with Charles, Poppet with Bill, content to shuffle along in a traffic jam and hold each other tight. Poppet, brown as a berry, looked less distraught and tormented. She clung to Bill and whispered: "Couth!" to Marianne as she went by her. Marianne glanced up at Tim and winked. "Well, I wonder . . ." Carol came close to them, and she looked the sweetest little *boule de suif* imaginable in her new taffeta dress.

"Sure it won't come off?" she giggled to Marianne over her shoulder.

"If it does it'll be Charles's fault, not mine!"

Contented in Tim's arms, pressing herself against him, for in such a crush it was safe and secret to do so, Marianne said:

"First time we've ever danced together."

"No." Tim laughed.

"No?"

"Three years ago—"

She had completely forgotten that time in the village hall.

"And then we went outside and you scratched my face. Like a cat," Tim said.

"Some French chap said: God made the cat so that man could have the illusion he was caressing a tiger. You take care!"

The band was cheerful, noisy and brash. They were giving full measure for the first round of the Paul Jones; later they would confound the cheats by playing just a bar or two and suddenly stopping. Marianne willed them to keep on playing. There was much comfort in being close to Tim; for she was still a little frightened when she thought about the discovery they had made this evening. Tim had come up to fetch her in his car. As he swung round in the farmyard at the Hope the headlights had picked out a glint of metal, something small and silvery shining at the bottom of a stack of baled hay. The lights had swept past it; but Tim had stopped and put the car into reverse. He had backed slowly until the glint was in the lights again. He had said:

"Hey, half a minute. That looks familiar."

So they had found the Lyle's Golden Syrup tin with the petrol and the candle: Black Barty had been busy on the night of the full moon! A hole had been scooped out under one of the hay-bales; the tin had been cunningly planted there. But the candle apparently had only burned down a little way before it had gone out. Perhaps there hadn't been enough air under the bale to keep it alight; perhaps some timely draught had snuffed it.

On the way to Sollarshill they had taken the tin to the police station and Croft had put it on a shelf beside his other exhibit, the tin they had found at Sollarshill; but, as he explained to them, there was no real evidence against Black

Barty, who hadn't been seen since he left the Royal Victoria at closing-time. He'd be back in the Forest by now; and Croft did not think he would be in a hurry to show himself near Sollarshill again.

Tim had said, as they came out of the police station:

"Now don't think about it any more."

But she was still thinking about it.

"What a lucky little wind that put out that candle!"

"Lucky, too, that you saw the light underneath the straw in our Dutch barn. Think how it would have burned," said Tim. "Samson would probably have been frizzled, then the big barn with the hop-pockets in it would have taken fire and *whoosh*—the whole crop gone."

"So it was just as well," said Marianne demurely "that we were doing what we did?" She turned up her eyes to him, the look he always called Cat-with-cream, and Tim laughed down at her and she was to him as the bark is to the tree as they danced together. It was hateful when the music stopped and she had to leave him. Out of the lucky dip of the Paul Jones she drew three hot-handed youths in succession who all made the same opening remark: Are you going to the meet to-morrow? Then they said: We came with Jill Ferrers.

The fourth time Marianne found herself without a partner, and she went and sat by Mrs. Sollars, who had "just looked in for half an hour." "I shan't stay," she said. "I want to get Father off to bed early." And that was the first time she had ever called him Father to Marianne.

"Oh dear," said Mrs. Sollars, looking across the room. "We've never had a gipsy here before; but what could Carol *do*?"

Ram was dancing with Sue. He had solved her problem at last by going to see old Manasseh and asking him to take her under his care. He had tried Wisdom first, but Wisdom had flatly refused, and Mami had fallen into a rage at the very idea: "That chai of Black Barty's! Too light-fingered for the likes of we!" Manasseh, however, had yielded to Ram's entreaty; he wintered down south, somewhere near Lyndhurst, so there would be no likelihood of an encounter with Black Barty. Sue would join him before he set off with his six caravans to-morrow morning. Ram had asked Carol if he might bring Sue to the dance.

"Possibly unchivalrous to leave her alone in our camp while we go off on last-night jollification?" he had said.

Now, as he danced with her, he was wearing white gloves, with which he held her delicately, a long way from him. ("Hottentots and diddy-kyes!" John Sollars had grunted when he saw them, and then had angrily strode out.) But even in her cheap red dress Sue looked much prettier, Marianne thought, than any of the hunting girls; and of course she danced by the light of nature, as all the gipsies did.

"He being a foreigner, and she being a sort of a foreigner," said Mrs. Sollars doubtfully, "I suppose it's all right in a way."

## 6

In the kiln before the hop-floor Carol had rigged up a bar where the little maid Polly was serving drinks. Tommy and George had been in the bar almost ever since the dance started, and Tommy was doing very well for himself because Polly poured out two drinks every time he asked for one, and Tommy promptly downed them both. George was still teetotal save for applejack, which was the subject of their earnest conversation.

"I'll tell you what, Tommy; I'll tell you what we could do," George was saying. "Your still was quite a good idea in a way, but I think I've had a better one. Couldn't we achieve the same result, more easily, by *refrigeration*?"

Tommy blinked at him in grave admiration.

"George," he said, "you're a brilliant fellow. I never

thought you had it in you. We could."

"Put in a refrigeration plant, freeze the water out of the cider as it were, remove the ice, and you get, surely, exactly the same stuff as the product of distillation? And excellent stuff it is," said George. "I think it has great commercial possibilities."

"After all," said Tommy, "the Tomkins fortunes were founded originally on a little still. When that first Tomkins, in Birmingham, set up his primitive plant to make peppermints—"

George laid his hand on Tommy's arm.

"You're right, Tommy. A family tradition, you might say. We'll go into this together."

"Of course it will need a bit of capital; and—er—I'm afraid, dear boy, that there's still your mortgage—" said Tommy doubtfully.

"I've been thinking," said George. "I've been thinking very hard. Things have presented themselves to me in a different light, somewhat, since I have been down here. For the moment, at any rate, I'm not going to worry you about the mortgage—"

Upstairs on the hop-floor Miss Ferrers cheerfully blew her hunting horn.

## 7

"That's just the excuse I've been waiting for," said Tim, scrambling down the wooden steps into the kiln, pulling Marianne behind him. They slipped quietly past George and Tommy and out into the yard. Others seemed to have had the same idea. Carol and Charles scuttled past them, then Poppet and Bill, then Ram and Sue. Miss Ferrers was emptying the room.

Marianne said:

"I think it's the most revolting noise—"

"You wait till you hear it to-morrow morning," said Tim. "At the covertside very faint and far off; and then the hounds come streaming out and you see the red coats against the yellow wood!"

They were going cubbing together to-morrow. Tim added:

"You'd better keep close to me, till we see how your pony behaves."

"W.a.f.," she laughed. "That's how you're taking me, isn't it? 'With all faults'!"

It would be the first time she had ridden her black pony; the first time she had gone hunting with Tim.

"Oh Tim," she said. "The fun of doing things together for the first time!"

"Sometimes better the second time," said Tim, pulling her to him. She gave him a punch in the ribs for that.

"I was being romantic," she said. "Look at our moon."

It was only the vestige of a moon, a mere cedilla in the sky.

"It's going," she said.

"It's done us proud, hasn't it?"

"It's jolly well done us proud."

They were kissing when John Sollars came suddenly round the corner of the oast. They didn't hear him coming and he didn't see them until he was nearly on top of them. He stood for a moment in his rooted attitude, gravely regarding them.

"Looking at calves?" he said at last, and stumped away. He had been counting the pockets in the barn: the last time he need count them. There were two hundred and sixty-seven. The hops were in. To-morrow he was going for his X-ray.

He hadn't thought about it until now. All the afternoon he had been taking cuttings from his geraniums. It was the only gardening job he did himself. In common with all farmers, he hated fiddling with gardens. But his father, like Dickens, had had a passion for geraniums; he had built a greenhouse specially for them and had always taken the cuttings in September. It had become a tradition that John should do the same autumnal task. The pleasant smell of the geraniums was still on his hands.

He thought: Wish they could take a cutting from me.

Then he glanced back and saw, by the light from the oast-house windows, Tim and his girl going hand in hand through the yard: Tim, that tall young limb, a cutting of a kind.

Another such before long, from the way those two were going about it!

So you went on, he thought, in a manner of speaking. Nature took her cuttings in her own way.

## 8

They listened to John's steps as he went towards the oast-house door: old steps but firm, a long stride still, wearily jaunty. They matched the mood of his sickness, half-sardonic, half-jovial. Tim was still puzzled by it. " 'Looking at calves'!" He laughed. "Well, we will." He took Marianne's hand and led her across the yard. There were whisperings and stirrings among the buildings and between the hayricks. "Those missioners!" said Tim. They heard Carol's giggle from the direction of Ye Olde Farme Shoppe and caught a glimpse of Sue's red dress in the little light which came from the oast-house windows. By this light they could just see Sally's calf when Tim pushed open the loose-box door. It came towards them, strong and upstanding now, and nuzzled Marianne's hand. "In two years' time," said Tim, "he'll be another Samson." The calf's white face in the darkness made Marianne think of the badgers in the wood, and of other things on the night of the full moon. She was aware of Tim's mischief as he put his arm round her, very much aware of her own. But they could hear the band playing in the oast

—a gallop now, a loud thumping of feet, all the pony club girls would be prancing up and down with their dresses slipping off their shoulders.

"*No,*" laughed Marianne, and pulled herself away from Tim as Miss Ferrers madly blew her hunting horn, emphasising the ineptitude of time and place. "No, you oaf; we must get back to your guests."

They ran across the yard together and then, opposite the oast, Tim said: "Just before we go in—show you something," and he opened the door of the great barn. She had never been in there before, and he switched on the light so that she could see the beams overhead. The barn had been built when the house had been built—the same hands, probably, that had hewn the house timbers out of oak trees from the Old Wood had raised into place those mighty kingposts and trusses under the roof of the barn, which ever since then had kept the weathers from the good crops grown at Sollarshill: wheat, barley, and hops.

This was the barn which would have burned, perhaps, if she hadn't seen the light of Black Barty's candle. The pockets stood all round the walls, row upon row, long white sacks awaiting collection by the brewers: two hundred and sixty-seven of them at twenty-seven pounds apiece.

"So it's over," said Marianne, as she looked with awe at all those pockets in the great barn.

"Never over," smiled Tim. "Ploughing to-morrow, when we come back from cubbing." Ploughing, fertilising, ridging up the little "hills" whence the hops sprang; hoeing with the special kind of hoe which was called a kerf; restringing, starting the little green shoots up the strings—up they'd go next June each one like Jack's beanstalk! And then, at the end of August, the gipsy caravans would come over the hills again; and so to another hop-picking and another harvest moon.

Never over. Leaning back against one of the hop-pockets, she pulled Tim to her for a kiss before they went back to the dance. The sack was rough against her shoulders, she could feel the hops tight and hard within it and smell the sweet smell of them. "Never over," Marianne repeated happily, and kissing Tim she hugged to herself an immeasurable contentment, that the pattern of their love would lie within this larger pattern, of the planting and the ploughing and the growing and the harvest, and the red Herefords and the green hops.